THE GLASS RAINBOW

The Glass Rainbow

A Cracked Slipper Novel, Book 3

Stephanie Alexander

This is a work of fiction. Names, characters, organizations, places, events and incidents are either the products of the author's imagination or are used fictitiously. Any resemblance to actual persons, living or dead, or actual events is purely coincidental.

Distributed by Bublish, Inc.

ISBN: 978-1-64704-090-1 (paperback)
ISBN: 978-1-64704-089-5 (eBook)

To my mother, Dianne Wicklein, and my grandmothers, and my great-grandmothers. To all the women who came before.

"So as through a glass, and darkly
The age long strife I see,
Where I fought in many guises,
Many names, but always me."

—General George Patton

"But remember that forgiveness too is a power.
To beg for it is a power, and to withhold or
bestow it is a power, perhaps the greatest."

—Margaret Atwood, *The Handmaid's Tale*

"Such a mad marriage never was before."

—William Shakespeare, *The Taming of the Shrew*

PART I

CHAPTER 1

A Long Road Ahead of You

After fourteen years, Eleanor Brice Desmarais knew the passageways of Eclatant Palace like she knew the patterns of her own thoughts. She took turns and stairs and ducked low-hanging tapestries without pausing; an unusually tall, unusually blonde woman, with unusually straight carriage. The servants were accustomed to the sight of Eleanor rushing about the castle. They bowed and asked for her blessing, for they'd long since overcome their fear of her mismatched eyes. Eleanor had twice vanquished the most feared magician in the history of the kingdom of Cartheigh. Her eyes— one robin's egg blue, one reddish-brown— could not possibly be as unlucky as everyone once thought.

Eleanor lifted the skirts of her ivory gown as she climbed the last staircase on the way to King Casper Desmarais's receiving room. White dress against white skin and the marble steps made her all but invisible until a flash of crimson besmirched the colorless tableau. A red parrot dropped from the chandelier onto her head, a jaunty kite let loose from a high wind. She tapped his scaly feet. "You'll ruin my coiffure, Chou."

"I've never liked you in braids, anyway." Chou Chou flapped about on her head. His wings were like a matched set of elegant feathered fans—the sort the older ladies carried to chapel on hot summer days.

"Thank you for the breeze. It *is* warm for LowAutumn."

"Don't bore me with talk of the weather. I want to know why His Majesty wants to see you."

"If you couldn't find out, no one can. We'll know soon enough."

Chou left Eleanor's head as they approached the Fire-iron door to the receiving room. She picked a stray red feather from her hair and shook out her skirts. Chou landed on a suit of armor. "I shall stand guard, my lady." He tucked his beak under his wing and promptly went to sleep.

Eleanor's nerves did a jig in her stomach as she waited before the door. Colors swirled under its silvery surface, barely perceptible, like a whispered riddle. She panicked whenever the king formally requested her presence. The same refrain rang through her head, an overused chorus in a bad opera.

He knows. He knows. He knows.

For over four years the secret had held, but she could not be sure of its safety. She never knew when, or how, King Casper would discover that Prince Gregory's wife, the mother of his grandchildren, had conducted a decade-long affair with his son's dearest friend.

The door opened and Orvid Jones, the Chief Magician, announced Eleanor's arrival. No camaraderie touched Orvid's brown eyes, nor did he show his buckteeth in the flash of a smile. He'd treated Eleanor with all the warmth of a snuffed candle since he learned the truth about her relationship with Dorian Finley, Duke of Brandling. She had long since given up trying to make amends.

Eleanor crossed the room and stopped before her father-in-law. Casper sat on his Fire-iron throne, a stout man with thick auburn hair that was finally going gray, like clouds giving in to sunset.

"Eleanor, good day," said Casper as she curtsied. "Gregory, offer your wife a glass of wine."

Eleanor turned to the refreshment table. She'd been so focused on the king, she'd not noticed her husband skulking in the corner. His lack of welcome did not surprise her. Husband and wife rarely spoke, except during public appearances. They didn't say much in the nursery or at meals. They were even silent on the frequent, unfortunate occasions when Gregory visited Eleanor's bed and attempted to plant a male heir in her belly.

"Eleanor doesn't drink wine before dinner. Do you, sweetheart?" Gregory took a seat in his own Fire-iron throne beside Casper. Both men crossed their ankles and rested their elbows on the armrests. They so resembled one another—aside from a few layers of fat, a mustache, and Casper's graying hair—that Eleanor might have been looking into a distorted mirror.

"Correct, Husband. I like a clear head when I'm managing the children's affairs."

"It is certainly wise to be alert to all affairs."

Thankfully, the innuendo floated over King Casper's head. "Speaking of the children," the king said, "I have some news. About Leticia."

"She's to be wed," said Gregory, before Eleanor opened her mouth.

At first, the comment didn't register. "Who's to be wed?"

"Leticia."

Eleanor shook her head. "She's twelve years old."

"The Duke of Brandling has had great success repairing relations with the Svelyans," said the king. "Not that I doubted he would."

"Dorian has always been a charmer, as we all know," said Gregory.

Oh, Gregory, how clever you think you are with your veiled insinuations. Under other circumstances, Eleanor may have thrown a reciprocal double entendre his way. Something so subtle as to be beyond his recognition, for safety's sake. Not enough to stoke the dragon's fire, but sufficient to soothe her own smoldering pride. In this critical moment, with both men's judgment and authority bearing down on her, she only had conversational space to fight for her daughter.

"He convinced King Peter Mangolin to consider my daughter as a bride for his son, Crown Prince Samuel. Peter has invited me to visit. Meet his son. Tour the kingdom. A gesture of friendship unthinkable five years ago. I'm heading north in four days."

"Gregory, you can't be serious. Leticia? Married to the Svelyan prince? Dorian loves Ticia, he would never—"

She stopped herself and shut her teeth around her opinion. In their unspoken agreement to avoid one another as much as a royal couple feasibly could, they eschewed the subject of Dorian above all others. Before today, Gregory hadn't so much as spoken his name to her in years. Sweat beaded on her forehead. For Dorian's sake, she must not goad Gregory with reminders of their former familiarity. Especially if the two men would soon be reunited.

"They honor Ticia with their consideration," said Gregory. "Samuel will someday be the second most powerful king in the known nations. She'd do well to be his wife."

Eleanor pictured Leticia, her sunshine child, trapped in a drafty Svelyan Castle. Locked in a gray mist, beyond the Dragon Mines. A hundred miles of jagged mountains between Ticia and her family, a barely passable field of battleaxes turned sharp side up. Married to a Svelyan lord she didn't know—and surrounded by a language she would not understand.

"She's *twelve*, Husband." Eleanor clung to the rational. "A child, not a wife."

"High time we settle on plans for her," said Gregory.

"Is it safe to travel to Svelya?" Eleanor asked. Casper always hesitated to send his only son and heir into danger.

"A battalion of the Unicorn Guard will escort Gregory," the king said, "and our finest magicians. Orvid Jones himself will accompany him. This is a mission of goodwill. Leticia's betrothal will help secure an alliance with our old enemies."

The room sank into silence. Both men watched Eleanor. They knew what was coming. She tried to hold her tongue, HighGod knew she did, but it slipped from her grasp like a slippery fish.

"Please, Your Majesty. Ticia is too young to be married. And sent away—to Svelya? She'll be so frightened—and we don't even know this Svelyan prince. What if he's cruel, or stupid, or a drunkard—" The Svelyan prince took shape in Eleanor's mind. A hulking blonde man with squinty eyes, bad breath, and heavy hands. "Please. Don't do this. Your own granddaughter—and the next heir—"

"Leticia is not my heir," said Gregory. "As of this moment, I have no heir."

The king laced his hands over his belly. "Leticia's importance to the crown lies in her marriage. As for an heir, you produced a son once. You can do it again—with prayer and effort."

Eleanor was too distraught to be mortified by the king's reference to carnality. "You can't. It's not right. She's *my* daughter!"

Eleanor's words tinkled off the Fire-iron chandelier over their heads. Casper rubbed his mustache and stood. Eleanor dropped a curtsy as he approached. She expected a reprimand, but he spoke softly, as if addressing a tired toddler. "Do you think I have no care for my own granddaughter?"

"I cannot imagine, sire, that if you did you would send her away."

Eleanor stared at the king's belt. The Fire-iron *D* embossed on the buckle rose and fell with his labored breathing.

"Go with Gregory," he said.

"Sire?"

"Go to Svelya. Meet with the prince. Report your estimation of him to me. I will take it into consideration in my final decision."

Eleanor rose. "Oh, Your Majesty, thank—"

"I'd not planned on her coming along," said Gregory as he stood.

"I've decided."

Gregory raked a hand through his hair. "Father, I don't want to take her."

"I won't be any trouble on the journey, Gregory," Eleanor said. "I promise."

"I'm sure Dorian will be pleased to see you both after so long," said Casper. "Now, you're dismissed. Go prepare. You have a long road ahead of you."

"Must you go?"

"Yes, darling," Eleanor said to Leticia. "Your father needs me."

"No, he doesn't." Ticia shook her head so adamantly that her auburn plaits slapped her cheeks. "He'll have Vigor and the rest of the unicorns and Orvid Jones. He'll see Uncle Dorian. We need you. Natalie and I."

"You must take care of Natalie for me. You're the older sister."

Natalie danced around Eleanor's skirts, grabbing for her mother's waist. Eleanor picked her up. "Heavens, love," she said as she kissed Natalie's silky hair. "You're getting so big. I shan't be able to pick you up much longer."

Natalie grinned and gently bopped Eleanor's nose. "Mama, you should stay," she said.

"I won't be gone long, sweetheart. I'll be back before you miss me." She set Natalie on the ground. She wrapped her skinny arms around Ticia's waist, and Ticia kissed the top of her head. For a precious moment, Eleanor marveled at her daughters' beauty. Ticia with her dark red hair and reddish-brown eyes, even features, and long, slim form. As for Natalie, from portraits, Eleanor knew her to be the spitting image of her aunt, the Princess Matilda, who had died in childbirth before Eleanor came to Eclatant. Matilda, a legendary beauty, had strawberry blonde hair, large greenish-hazel eyes, and a smile that lit up a dark room in the heart of MidWinter. Natalie even had a dusting of light freckles over her nose, just like her aunt. Like Ticia, she was tall for her age and slender.

Despite being quite familiar with the signs of human reproduction, Eleanor hadn't recognized them during the anxious chaos proceeding Dorian's expulsion from Eclatant. Low and behold, Natalie entered the world only seven months after he went north—a welcome blessing in those long months of acute mourning. She continued to surprise and delight Eleanor every day. At four years old, she could already read and write her name. She spent hours pouring over storybooks. In that vein, she reminded Eleanor of her poor son, Nathan, gone over five years now. Nathan, however, had a serious and somewhat reserved temperament, while Natalie charmed everyone. Like Ticia—and truth be told, like her father. Eleanor adored her children equally, but she sometimes thought little Natalie inherited the best of her parents.

"You're coming back tomorrow, Mama?" Natalie asked.

"Not tomorrow."

"The next day?"

"Not the next day, either." Eleanor sighed. Natalie always understood more than she should. Her mother would find no respite from guilt in the child's obliviousness. Eleanor offered her a stuffed unicorn. She cringed at the thought of how Natalie would grow during her absence, but not as much as she hated the idea of Ticia married to an unknown Svelyan.

As usual, Ticia would not be deterred. "I still don't understand why you have to go—"

"I told you. Poppa needs me." Eleanor felt no need to inform Ticia of her potential matrimonial fate.

"—and why you must take Chou Chou!" Tears filled Ticia's eyes.

"Darling, Chou and I have been together since I was Natalie's age. He'll never let me go without him."

The wooden nursery doors opened, and Gregory strode into the room. Ticia ran to him. She pelted him with questions about the journey, but he steered her in the direction of her easel. The opportunity to impress her father distracted her from her troubles.

"It's very good, sweetheart." Gregory ran a finger along Ticia's portrait of her unicorn, Cricket. "Try a darker gray around the muscles in Cricket's haunches. Think of the shadows."

Ticia's brow furrowed. She took up her charcoal pencil and a smudging rag. "Shadows..." she whispered and set about following her poppa's advice.

With Ticia occupied, Natalie dropped her toy unicorn and jumped into her father's arms. "And you, little one. Or"—he lifted Natalie above his head and she squealed in delight—"maybe not so little. Perhaps Pansy feeds you too many sweetmeats."

"She's perfectly healthy," said Eleanor.

Gregory laughed. "Of course, she is. She'll be as graceful as Ticia and my darling Matilda. Not like me as a child. So round! In those portraits in father's study I look as if you could roll me down the hall. Do you need help with your packing?"

Gregory's chatty mood and solicitousness unnerved her, in light of his usual abject distaste for company. Eleanor kept her own tone light and pleasant for the girls' sake, but she watched him out of the corner of her eye as she folded a blanket. "I'm nearly ready. Since we're going on unicornback, there's not much to be done."

"I've written to King Peter. He shall have his finest seamstress at your disposal when we arrive. Your new gowns will be the height of Svelyan fashion."

"Thank you for allowing me to accompany you."

Gregory set Natalie in front of her dollhouse, where she started a lively conversation with the figurines. He walked to Eleanor and took her hands. He spoke in a whispery voice, as smooth as a ream of the Svelyan silk he'd promised her, but his gripping fingers cut into hers like blunt sewing shears. "That was the king's decision, not mine. Just know if I catch wind of any impropriety, I'll cut off his manhood and serve it to the dragons on a Fire-iron platter."

With that, he left. Eleanor sat on the edge of Ticia's bed. She knew exactly who's manhood risked removal from his person. The sun slid behind a cloud, and Eleanor's shadow faded on the woven rug below her skirts. Her trembling fingers danced over the Fire-iron and diamond chain around her neck. She touched the dragon choker's center stone. Even if she raised the memory in her mind, the one that magically united the dragon choker with Dorian's ring, Rosemary's spell was not powerful enough to bridge the distance between them. She could not make his ring glow with comforting blue fire. He would not feel her heartfelt attempt to remind him she still loved him. Regardless, she thought of the broom closet anyway, as she often did. When the red stone warmed her chest, the room didn't seem so cold.

The day of Eleanor and Gregory's departure dawned gray and drizzly, as if HighGod were preparing them for the North Country weather. Eclatant's formal courtyard spread out before Eleanor, in all its imposing glorification of the Desmarais family and the Great Bond. A thousand purple and green banners flapping in the wet breeze gave the impression of so much polite applause, and the rose bushes clung stubbornly to their blossoms, as if dropping a petal would be sacrilege. Eleanor stood next to her unicorn, Teardrop, beside the larger than life statue of Caleb Desmarais. The first Desmarais king peered down at his descendants and their subjects from the back of his own stone unicorn, the great stallion, Eclatant. Both man and mount wore expressions of benevolent tolerance. Eternal patience with those to whom they'd handed their collective legacy three hundred years ago.

Eleanor tucked her hair into her cloak. She inhaled the scents of wet livestock and baking bread. Chou yawned in her ear. "Always so early with these northern voyages. The sun is barely awake. The chickens are peaceful in their coop."

"Look a long journey in the face, as the witches say." Eleanor kissed Teardrop's silky muzzle. The mare snuffled her neck. Her ears pricked, and her white lashes blinked over her liquid eyes like the wings of excited dragonflies. She shifted her mighty haunches, and Eleanor felt anticipation flowing beneath her ivory hide. "Not quite time to go, dearest. We're to have a formal send away."

"The air is so clean in the North," Teardrop said in her breezy voice. "I remember the taste. Like water from a deep spring. The smell of the dragons. Burning rocks."

Chou landed between Teardrop's ears and nibbled her forelock. "Do you remember so well the smell of Giant Buzzards, carried on a cold wind?"

"Hush, Chou," said Eleanor as she hauled herself into the saddle. "We'll not have you complaining."

Chou whistled. "Sarcasm is complaining at its highest form. A sign of intelligence."

Eleanor laughed and patted Teardrop's twitching neck. She had not been to the North Country in over thirteen years, and she'd never left Cartheigh in her thirty-two years of life. Despite agonizing over leaving her girls, she shared Teardrop's excitement. Her own eagerness, however, went beyond a long ride, clean air, and a herd of dragons.

Eleanor had not seen nor heard from Dorian since he quietly left Eclatant to serve as the king's ambassador to Svelya. She often wondered if she'd ever lay eyes on him again. The crushing grief over his absence had become part of her persona, as much as the birthmark in her left eye or her tendency to break into a sweat under duress. It sat, deep in her chest, through parties and chapel services. It did not abandon her during Ticia's lessons, on evenings when she rocked Natalie to sleep, or when she bustled about town on her charitable endeavors. Between his loss, and the deaths of Nathan and her oldest friend, Margaret Easton

Delano, sadness was Eleanor's constant companion. She pictured it as a black cat with pale green eyes, purring along with her own heartbeat.

"Fare thee well, my darling girl!"

Rosemary's voice rang across the cobblestones. The witch clipped toward Teardrop on feathery legs, with no hint of her one hundred years of life in her easy stride. Eleanor smiled at her teacher. "Abbottess, you didn't need to make the journey from Afar Creek to see us off."

"The Abbey will carry on for a few hours without me." Rosemary looked up at Eleanor with dancing dark eyes. "How long in coming, this journey."

Eleanor squeezed Rosemary's hand. The witch was, other than Chou Chou, her oldest companion. Rosemary had schooled Eleanor in secret through her years of imprisonment in her father's house. Eleanor clung to Rosemary's letters and lessons, slivers of hope under the harsh rule of her stepmother, Imogene Brice. Fourteen years ago, when Imogene refused to allow Eleanor to attend the Second Sunday Ball, Rosemary conjured Eleanor's romantic notions into existence with a lovely gown and a pair of glass slippers. When the dream fell apart, shattered by the twin realities of her dismal marriage and a passionate, forbidden love, Rosemary kept Eleanor and Dorian's secret for almost ten years. No one had shaped Eleanor's life like the Abbottess of Afar Creek Abbey.

Rosemary squeezed back. "Promise me you will take care." The witch glanced at Gregory, mounted on his white stallion, Vigor. "There will be many eyes upon you."

"I hear you well," said Eleanor. "The girls will have their regular tutors from the Abbey, of course, but perhaps you can find time to visit?"

"Of course. Leticia and I will write to you. Soon Natalie will be writing her own letters."

"Help Leticia with her penmanship. I fear the artist in her makes for sloppy correspondence. Don't let her play with the cracked slipper. She likes to show it to Natalie." Eleanor's heart hurt. "I will miss them so. Perhaps I should have woken them."

"No, let the children sleep. I will personally see to them this morning. Ah, here is the Godsman." Rosemary's brows lifted. "That one isn't much more than a child himself."

A young man in brown robes joined King Casper beside the statue of Caleb Desmarais. He looked to be less than twenty years old, slim and slight. Eleanor only took such measure of him because he so clashed with her memory of Marcus, the Godsman who'd turned traitor six years ago. She couldn't help but compare the young man's nervous piety to Marcus's hulking arrogance.

He wasn't always such, she thought. *He was a good man, until Ezra Oliver twisted him about. Marcus helped us as well as he could, in the end, and he lost his life for it.* Anger simmered between her ears. *Damn Oliver. Murdering, manipulative disgrace to magic.*

The king said a few words about the growing friendship between Cartheigh and Svelya. His secretary scribbled the speech on a piece of parchment. The next few days would find printing press copies of the king's good intent spread over the capital city of Maliana and beyond. Casper turned to the young Godsman. "I ask for the blessings of HighGod on my son, his wife, and their party."

The young man cleared his throat. The conviction in his voice belied his youth.

"HighGod, we ask you to protect His Highness, Crown Prince Gregory Desmarais, on the long road ahead. In him, you've entrusted the power of the Great Bond. The mystical gift to Cartheigh. The intertwining of unicorn, dragon, and the Desmarais family. As he travels North, he will venture into the heart of the Bond itself—the Dragon Mines. From whence flows all the wealth and peace you've bestowed upon this kingdom for three centuries. Like the Fire-iron the dragons create with their breath, like the numinous calm that exists in the touch of horn on scale, like the undying love between prince and king and these most noble steeds, all elements of the Great Bond are connected. We pray you will watch over Gregory, the keeper of this gift, and aid him in his quest to continue the work of Lord Brandling, far across the Scaled Mountains. May the friendship between Cartheigh and Svelya become a bond in itself, for the mutual benefit of both nations."

Eleanor watched Gregory throughout the Godsman's speech, and despite her bitterness toward him, she saw him as he appeared to everyone else in the courtyard. A powerful man of thirty-five with a ramrod back, a broad chest, and a chin like a sawed-off tree trunk. The light rain darkened his red hair to brown. It clung to his neck and only accentuated the strength in his shoulders. He held his head high throughout the young man's prayer. When the Godsman finished, he offered this, with a simple elegance: "You do me honor, and you honor the Bond. Might that I am worthy of HighGod's protection, and the privilege of my station."

Eleanor knew Gregory at his worst. His most drunken and childish, slovenly and vindictive. But even she couldn't deny a great king existed inside him somewhere.

CHAPTER 2

GREAT CHAINS SET IN MOTION

THE EXPEDITION PUSHED NORTHWARD for two days. Villages on the outskirts of Maliana gave way to country estates. As the land coarsened, the settlements became fewer and farther between until only a few secluded farmhouses dotted the greenish gray landscape. The Clarity River shrunk to a glorified creek. Hunched hills straightened into the beginnings of the Scaled Mountains. Eventually, signs of human habitation disappeared. Eleanor hoped for a sight of the wild unicorns that lived in the marshes south of the Mines, but they encountered only hawks and wild donkeys. Eleanor's fingers went numb in her riding gloves. The wind kept up a constant whistle in her ears and brought with it a progression of smells and sounds like a sensory map of the voyage: lowing cows, rank peat moss, and finally, the acrid smell of Fire-iron dust.

They passed through the tiny hamlet of Peaksend Village and crossed the road to Peaksend Castle, the northern stronghold of the Desmarais family. Eleanor had never been inside Peaksend. She eyed the granite fortress with morbid interest. Her mind's eye had created a picture of a matching Svelyan monolith skulking in mountains, awaiting her daughter.

Gregory called a halt at the entrance to the Dragon Mines. Chou emerged from Eleanor's hood. "Smashing! We're here. It looks the same. Probably has for three hundred years."

Eleanor stroked his head as the Dragon Mines churned before her. Miners pushed bockety handcarts loaded with hunks of meat and chunks of glistening raw Fire-iron. They shouted and cursed one another, but the working unicorns went about their business with their usual tail-swishing tranquility. They came and went from the seven dark holes in the mountainside. Some of the caves spewed sparks, some leaked smoke, and one accepted human and unicorn visitors in complacent quiet.

"Only one cave extracting?" Eleanor asked Gregory.

Gregory nodded. "Yields were less than expected this summer." He didn't elaborate, but Eleanor read his mood in his squinting eyes and the hand that raked his hair.

Eleanor and Teardrop followed Gregory and Vigor down the narrow path into the Mines. The Unicorn Guard trailed behind them, a wedding procession of white hides and silver horns. Eleanor's boots squelched in the mud when she dismounted, but she didn't care. She stretched her arms above her head, happy to have both feet on solid earth.

Matt Thromba, the mine boss, made his bow-legged way toward Eleanor and Gregory through the chaos. He bowed to Gregory and kissed Eleanor's hand. She hugged him, and he blushed under his three-pronged beard.

After chatty exchanges about the weather and the journey, Gregory went to business. "When will cave five be cool enough to begin extracting?"

"In three days, sire," said Thromba. "But the yield in cave six has been a fine one. Dragons went deep this summer, they did."

"Still, one cave isn't enough."

Orvid Jones joined the conversation. "Has the mood improved down below?"

"Some," said Thromba. "Not as keen as I'd like them to be, honestly. Only two litters this year. The bulls spatting, and the does on the cold side."

Gregory's hands went to his hair again. "What's the matter with them? I fear to say, it reminds me of Oliver's meddling."

Thromba shook his head. "Nothing so bad as that, sire. When Oliver snooped about it drove the beasts mad. You remember how we had to chain Blondie in the courtyard to keep him from killin' himself and maybe a few others? No. This is just a bit o' irritation, like they've all caught a cold or summat. I'm thinking it might be the groundwater."

"Ah, that makes sense," said Gregory. His hands returned to his pockets.

"What's wrong with the groundwater?" asked Eleanor.

"A river runs through the caves, so it does. Dragons don't drink much, but they do need a drop here and again. They wade in the river once a season. Tremor told me it's a right sight. The dragons burn so hot, you know, that the water level sinks below 'em. Poor creatures have to chase it with those long oul' jaws while it's evaporating right before their eyes."

"How awful," said Eleanor, but the thought of a herd of dragons wading in an evaporating river fascinated her.

"Ach, they manage, Your Highness. A good swig or two can hold a bull over for three months. But, you see, that swig must be clean. Fresh. Dragons can eat just about anything, but they're temperamental about their water. Every ten years or so, when the summer rains get too heavy in the mountains, some filth gets sent down the river. Filth from up north."

"What kind of filth?" asked Eleanor.

"Ach, Your Highness, you with your questions. It's not a proper topic." Thromba's face flamed again.

"Tell her, Matt," said Gregory. "She'll only dig it out of me, or Orvid, if not."

"If you say so, sire, but it's right unpleasant. You see, there's a small ogre camp about a hundred miles from here—"

"An ogre camp?" Eleanor's mind went to the myriad lessons she'd had in her youth on ogres and the Ogre Wars of five-hundred years ago. There were three camps. The two largest were in northern Svelya, and a smaller one was somewhere on the Carthean-Svelyan border. "Svelyan magicians manage the ogres, do they not?"

Thromba nodded. "They do, but even magicians can't control the rains. When they get so heavy…it washes the…Oh, HighGod, sire. I can't say it."

"It washes the ogre piss and shit into the groundwater. It goes sour," said Gregory. "Ogre offal is quite harsh. Fouler than Giant Buzzard droppings."

Eleanor blushed. "Oh, well. That does indeed make sense."

Thromba scrambled on. "We're hoping once the next watering comes around in fortnight or so, all will be well."

On that pleasant note, they broke up to allow the travelers time to sup and wash as best they could. Orvid joined the Unicorn Guards in the miner's tents. Eleanor and Gregory retired to the two-story wooden cabin that served as lodging for important guests. She climbed the stairs to the simple bedroom, but Gregory remained in the sitting room before the fire. He poured himself a tankard of ale and sat on a rough bench with his bow across his lap. He chewed on a hunk of dried beef.

The sun slipped behind the mountains as Eleanor changed into a cotton nightdress. She touched the pile of dragon robes spread across the bed: Fox, wolf, rabbit, bear. She recognized some of them from her last trip to the Mines with Gregory. Her heart hurt, for although she knew she loved Dorian even then, she'd enjoyed Gregory's company. She'd held out hope their marriage might somehow be salvaged.

The door creaked behind her, and she slid under the robes. Gregory blew out the candle. He didn't say anything as he pulled off his boots, but Eleanor heard his belt sliding through its calfskin loops. She clenched her teeth.

Gregory lifted her nightdress and rolled her onto her stomach. He pushed one of her legs aside and worked his way inside her. She wasn't ready or willing. Her body had no response. Nothing but friction between them, like sanding paper on a rough board. Eleanor buried her face in the fox-fur robe. It pulsed with a dragon robe's weird living warmth beneath her nose. She inhaled the scent of musty fur and waited for Gregory's latest attempt at impregnation to come to a merciful end.

He pulled away from her, his breathing loud in the uncomfortable silence. He'd not slept beside her in years, but on this night, he had nowhere else to go. The space between them was an overgrown garden of awkward resentment. A thorny hedgerow that poked Eleanor's back even as she squirmed to the edge of the bed. She curled on her side and shut down her mind. Within a few minutes, the exhaustion of the voyage and two night's fitful rest on the hard ground claimed her. She fell asleep.

A restless dragon's cry woke her sometime in the wee hours. She rolled onto her back.

Bad water. The thought swam through her fuzzy mind. It joined the remnants of a dream about a burning thirst and a receding river. An oily rainbow sheen covered the water, and somehow, the river itself burst into flames. *The dragons must not drink it!* she thought as she opened her eyes.

Gregory had left the bed. He slept upright, in a wooden rocker, with his chin resting on one elbow and his tankard in his lap.

Two days later, the travelers set out again, into the heart of the Scaled Mountains that separated Cartheigh from Svelya. At times the mountains blocked Eleanor's view, only to have the gaps between them open up to an endless line of sight. Rows of spiky granite stretched beyond her eyes' ability to find an end to it all. Eleanor alternated between claustrophobia when the mountain walls closed in and terror at the unfathomable emptiness when the cliffsides below them plunged into dark nothingness. The wind constantly got in her way. It surrounded her on all sides, as tenacious as a cloud of gnats. It blew into her nose and lifted her hair. It set her eyes to water. It so seared her nostrils that by the second day she no longer smelled anything. Just a wind scent—cold and damp but otherwise anonymous. It yammered at her in its monotonous, whistling voice, and she wished the path would widen out. The single file line provided little space for conversation but plenty of room for uncomfortable thoughts.

Anticipation still flavored most of her ruminations, but fear had crept into the recipe, like a pinch of pepper in a sweet soup. She couldn't keep her hands off the dragon choker.

It's been almost five years. What if something has changed? Perhaps he's found a lover. She bit her lip. *Does he know I'm coming? What shall I say when I see him?* She'd undoubtedly be limited to innocuous, milquetoast salutations. *Hello, Your Grace. How nice to see you. You're looking well.*

The fear grew through a hundred miles of mountain peaks—and three nights' sleep in a rough tent with Chou Chou snoring contentedly beside her head. On the morning of the fourth day, she whispered her doubts to Teardrop as she tightened the mare's girth.

"Unfortunately, no amount of contemplation will ease your mind. Only he can give you the answer you seek. You have no choice but to wait and see."

Eleanor kissed Teardrop's nose. As usual, the mare was gallingly rational. And exasperatingly correct.

Their party slogged through another long day and uncomfortable night. On the fifth morning, the steep drops disappeared, and the path morphed into a road encased between two rock walls. An ancient artist had carved intricate designs into the granite: Birds, wolves, mountain goats, and even the odd dragon. Skinny Svelyan letters spelled out messages no one in Eleanor's party, save possibly Orvid Jones, could decipher. A three-story wooden gate appeared as the sun rose above the travelers' heads. Armed sentries peered down at their foreign visitors, human and unicorn alike. The guards shook their lances and shouted instructions. The gate to Nestra opened with the grinding of great chains set in motion.

Eleanor caught her breath at the Svelyan capital's strange beauty. The city leapfrogged the Gammon River. Houses, shops, and chapels perched on a freshwater archipelago interconnected by stone bridges. The Gammon pooled in superficial calm in sheltered nooks between five wooded islands. Along the straightaways, rapids raged around jagged boulders as if the river might shake the rocks loose and hurl them at the city above. The citizens of Nestra, blond dots draped in dark furs, crisscrossed bridges and steered long canoes through the Gammon's calmer harbors. The stronghold of the Svelyan kings braced itself across the river on the city's north end. Instead of solid land, Gammonreil Palace rested on a Fire-iron bridge. The span's arches and buttresses reflected the churning currents. Beyond the castle, a waterfall cascaded over the nearest mountain in a never-ending liquid curtsy. The falls kept up a low, rumbling growl, like a captive lion bored in its cage.

"The ground hums below my feet," said Teardrop.

"HighGod's eyebrows," said Chou. "What a place."

Eleanor couldn't have said it better herself.

Gammonreil Palace had no courtyard. There was no space for one. The eastern bridge led directly to four sets of Fire-iron doors.

"Leftover from the days when Svelya controlled the Mines," whispered Chou.

Eleanor nodded. Teardrop stepped across the threshold into the largest hall Eleanor had ever seen. Even Eclatant's Great Hall didn't compete with this cavern, which could surely house half the dragons of the Mines, with room left over for a smallish ball. Six marble fireplaces encircled the room. Eleanor looked up, past the mounted heads of giant northern elk. Stone chimneys met a ceiling of iridescent glass windows. Prismatic light rained into the hall, like the many-hued spells of a hundred magicians.

"Is that roast pork I smell?" asked Chou.

"You don't eat meat." With a gurgle, Eleanor's stomach reminded her that she did not share her parrot's herbivorous tastes.

"But with pork comes rosemary bread and pear pudding." Chou sniffed and licked his beak.

"Don't count on it. Don't you remember Christopher Roffi's rabbit stew?"

The Svelyan courtiers whispered in their guttural language and pointed at the unicorns. Teardrop snorted at their rudeness. Lords and ladies in clusters of dark blues and greens quietly compared their impressions of the visitors amongst themselves. Eleanor's riding leggings would surely incite considerable chatter, as she doubted anyone in the hall had ever seen a woman wear pants. As for the local ladies, even the younger women showed little skin beyond their bare necks. Thick fur lined every bodice, as if they had sprouted winter coats to cloak their modesty. The men, heavily clad in their own furry garb, resembled the bested animals peering down from the fireplaces. Above the neck, however, all traces of ruggedness disappeared. Their eyes were icy snowflakes, frozen in their pale, elegant faces. Eleanor caught a dark head here and there, but for the most part, her white-blonde hair would finally be commonplace.

Bugle blasts—three short, one long— silenced the crowd. The caller announced Gregory, Eleanor, and their Chief Magician, Orvid Jones. They dismounted and approached the winding staircase at the end of the hall. The Unicorn Guard waited behind them at a respectful, watchful distance. Vigor's wide hoof slammed a protective warning against the marble floor, overriding the soft click of Eleanor's boot falls.

A small welcome party waited for them in the center of the hall. A short woman with chin-length white hair and delicate features unabashedly examined Eleanor. Her wide eyes gave her a look of perpetual surprise. When she moved, greenish light followed her. It hovered around her head like grassy fog. Her fur-trimmed gown resembled those of the other ladies, but Eleanor immediately surmised her to be a witch.

A young man, not yet twenty years old, stood beside her. He was tall, but his thick robe did not hide his slightness of frame. A mop of black hair framed his babyish but pleasing face.

"Prince Samuel?" whispered Chou.

"I hope so," whispered Eleanor. While the lad didn't have the look of a conquering hero, he had potential. He couldn't have been less like the husky, grizzled northern liege of her nightmares.

The third man wore a hood, but as he stepped forward to greet them, his height and ambling walk gave him away. Eleanor's pulse blasted against her temples, a trumpet fanfare of her fear and desire.

Dorian pushed the hood away from his face. She first noticed his beard—it accentuated the already strong angles of his face. Hints of gray dusted his thick dark hair. Unlike the Svelyans around him, he still wore it past his ears, as if he'd chosen that bit of cultural milieu to cleave him to his homeland.

"On behalf of King Peter Mangolin," Dorian said, "I welcome my prince, Gregory Desmarais, son of Casper and heir to the throne of Cartheigh, to Gammonreil. Praise HighGod for your safe journey."

"HighGod's blessings on you, old…friend," said Gregory. He put a stiff arm around Dorian's shoulder and stepped away.

"King Peter would have been here to greet you himself, but he is indisposed. He sends his Chief Sorceress, Agnes, and his son, Prince Samuel of Svelya, in his stead."

For a moment, the designation of Chief Sorceress distracted Eleanor from her inspection of Dorian. She touched Chou's scaly foot with one hand, communicating her surprise and interest with the brush of a finger in the lifelong language of their avian-human partnership. She hadn't realized Peter Mangolin put his highest magical faith in a woman. She'd never heard of such in any nation or read of it in any history book. From what she knew, Svelyans hewed close to traditional notions of masculine and feminine. Closer even than the average conservative Carthean. Chou chortled his mutual curiosity in reply.

Gregory stepped forward to greet the Svelyan prince and the witch, and Dorian turned to Orvid Jones. Hostile cream-colored light seeped from the magician's nose as they embraced, as if Orvid exhaled dirty frost. Apparently, he'd no more forgiven Dorian's disloyalty than he had Eleanor's.

Once he'd left Orvid's chilly embrace, Dorian turned to Eleanor. He gazed past her shoulder, as if he anticipated another visitor, then he bowed and took her hand. She'd hoped to touch his skin, but he wore leather gloves. "Your Highness," he said.

Eleanor felt Gregory's gaze, and Orvid's, crawling over her like a plague of locusts. "Lord Brandling," she said. "How nice to see you." She cringed inwardly, for the greeting sounded as lackluster as she'd predicted.

"And you," he said. "Welcome." He met her eyes as he straightened, ever so briefly, but she saw nothing in his gaze. She felt nothing. He was a bearded man in a heavy cloak, an elegant diplomat, a beautiful stranger.

CHAPTER 3

EVERYONE HERE HAS A SECRET

ELEANOR'S BEDROOM AT GAMMONREIL did not quite meet expectations after the fabulous Great Hall. It was half the size of her room at Eclatant, with dark stone walls that looked inclined to hold the damp. Two solid blue tapestries trimmed with brown fringe hung on either side of the room, like rugs in a painting with skewed dimensions. The tapestries lorded over a simple wooden desk, two chairs and a small table, a simple fireplace, and a low-slung wooden bench covered in furry cushions. Only the bed impressed. Carved from a chunk of solid granite, its four thick posters bore sculptures of battling angels and demons.

"I shall sleep with my head under my wing," said Chou. "Lest I wake to those fellows and think myself trapped in a nightmare."

Eleanor laughed. She didn't mind the coziness. The linens smelled clean, and the bearskin dragon robe across the bed certainly appealed to her. She walked to the small window. To her surprise, she discovered a dark wooden door, painted to match the pattern of the stone walls. She cautiously opened it and stepped out onto a spacious balcony. Chou landed on the Fire-iron bannister. The clean mountain wind ruffled his feathers as he whistled his appreciation for the view. The five jagged islands of Nestra spread out before them, and the grumpy river huffed and puffed around the Gammonreil Bridge four stories below. Eleanor shaded her eyes and squinted at the Scaled Mountains. They rose in an endless series of immobile stone waves, separating her from home.

"We have a southern view," Chou said, as if sensing her longing to see Eclatant far beyond the peaks.

Eleanor shivered, and travel exhaustion suddenly caught up with her. A Svelyan maid drew her bath and laid out a nightdress, and within an hour, she crawled into bed. She pushed her anxiety over Dorian's aloof greeting to the side.

He's being careful. Tomorrow he will smile at me, and I'll know all is well.

She closed her eyes on that happy thought. She woke to a brown velvet gown trimmed in white rabbit fur hanging from one of the bed posters, a plate of buttered toast, and a message from the Chief Sorceress. The magical lady in question appeared at Eleanor's door promptly at nine o'clock, as promised, just as Eleanor's Svelyan maid finished her hair. Eleanor joined the tiny witch at the wooden table with a cup of tea.

"How are you finding your space?" Agnes's high, wispy voice clashed with her harsh Svelyan accent, but at least Eleanor understood her. She felt a pang of nostalgia, as Agnes's idiosyncratic tweaking of Carthean grammar replicated her old friend Christopher Roffi's take on the language.

"Very nice," said Eleanor. "Although, the maid and I did have a time. Our language barrier is as steep and thick as the mountains between your country and mine. I think I frightened her, poor woman."

Agnes laughed, and her tiny nose crinkled. A pretty thing, she was. If she were not a witch, she'd have attracted many male admirers. "I'm sure she has been hearing of your story for years. Poor, pretty girl becomes a princess with the help of a magic spell. We are all knowing of the glass slippers in these days."

"Ah, well." It always surprised Eleanor when people spoke of her story with such reverence. Surely, she was not the first person of lean means to find herself unexpectedly elevated. Perhaps Rosemary's magical intervention made for a particularly interesting tale. "That happened a long time ago." She took Agnes's hand. "I'm so thrilled to meet you. A Chief *Sorceress.*"

Agnes colored, but Eleanor sensed her admiration pleased the witch. "My king honors me with his faith."

"Pardon, but I did not think Svelyans were so forward-thinking."

"As a group, we are far from it," said Agnes. "But the former Chief Magician was an unusual man. He formed a deep friendship with the Abbottess of C'adda. The Abbottess, bless her, was seeing some measure of talent in me. She asked him to take me on as his apprentice. So he did."

"And your talent blossomed under the nose of the king."

She nodded. "The old magician passed on five years ago, HighGod's blessings on him as well, and he recommended me to take his place."

"Amazing. King Peter agreed with his choice?"

"Surprisingly, yes. The king is a surprising man—in many ways." Agnes's delicate features darkened for a moment. "The lords were not so keen on my elevation. I fight for my position every day."

Eleanor shook her head. "Why are men so frightened of powerful women, magical or common?"

"What will they do with themselves if women no longer need rescuing?" This time Agnes squeezed Eleanor's hand. "I am so pleased to have you here, Your Highness. I am hearing you are a woman of learning and strong opinions. It can be lonely here at court. The lords might dislike me, but their wives and daughters—what is the word?—they *detes*t me."

"I have known many such women. I probably don't hide my contempt as well as I think I do. I'm afraid my persona has never leant itself to popularity at court."

"Then we shall be detested together." Agnes waved her hands, and two green birds shot from her fingers. They circled Eleanor's head and disappeared in a puff of verdant smoke.

Chou raised his head from under his wing. He stretched and left his perch for the table. "Have we some feathered company?" he said with a yawn.

"None so handsome as you, sir," said Agnes. "Nor so exquisitely plumaged."

Chou went all puffy at the compliment.

"Agnes," said Eleanor, sensing an opening. "Speaking of handsome, what can you tell me about Prince Samuel? He seems a likely lad."

Agnes abruptly retreated into formality, her face bland, and her hands folded on the table before her. "He is a blessed young man, our esteemed prince."

"Yes, but what is he like? You know he's to marry my daughter. Is he kind? How does he pass the time? Riding, or hunting, or maybe—"

"I must be going. Surely you'll have time to get to know His Highness yourself during your visit."

"Of course. I'm sorry—"

"I shall be seeing you at the dancing tonight." The witch smiled. "Promise me we will talk of literature and history? I am having a strong desire to drive the Lord High Chancellor mad with academia."

"Certainly!" Eleanor hadn't had such an appealing invitation in years.

Agnes took her leave, and Eleanor and Chou flopped in a comfortable heap on the huge bed.

"What a fascinating woman," said Eleanor. "I shall enjoy getting to know her better."

"Indeed," said Chou. "But for one so frank about her own tribulations, she certainly wasn't eager to discuss her prince."

"Perhaps they value the privacy of the royal family."

"Or perhaps Prince Samuel has some corpses in his cupboard."

"Chou, that's morbid." She rolled onto her back. "He's not even a grown man yet. How many secrets could he be hiding?"

"This is a palace, Eleanor. Everyone here has a secret, knows a secret, or is looking for a secret." Chou stretched his wings. "Which reminds me, we've been here an entire day. It's high time I take a turn about the castle and—"

"See what you can see."

He whistled and took off. Eleanor stared at the thick beams crisscrossing the ceiling above her. She pictured Samuel's pleasant face and the gentle way he'd kissed her hand. Of course, Agnes was simply showing respect, and Chou simply sought gossip to take back to Eclatant. She sat up and reached for the handwritten schedule beside her bed. She perused a list of the day's events. Surely some function would put her in the same place as Dorian. *Ah, an afternoon strike stick league.* It sounded terribly boring, but Dorian was a celebrated strike stick player. She could stomach an hour of pipe smoke, clacking balls, and whiskey drunk courtiers. To look upon that loving smile she so longed for, she'd tolerate almost anything.

Eleanor had never been overly concerned with fashion, but even she found her new Svelyan wardrobe to be a dull affair. The dress she donned for dinner replicated the one she'd worn during the day, with slight variations in color (dark-blue) and fur (red fox).

"Do I smell like a smoking lounge?" she asked Chou as she spritzed herself with peachberry perfume. She'd flittered around the strike stick hall for an hour, but Dorian hadn't shown. "What a waste of time."

"I get a whiff of pipeweed when I land on your hair," said Chou, "but since no one else sits on your head, your olfactory anonymity is secure. You'll smell as fresh and flowery as all the other ladies."

"I wish Anne Iris were here. She'd do something to liven up this dress." She winced as the silent Svelyan maid twisted her hair into a painfully tight knot at the base of her skull. "Or Pansy to fix my hair. I fear if this good lady pulls any harder, my eyes shall migrate to the sides of my head."

Chou waddled along the mantle in his version of a seductive sashay. "The princess entered the ballroom, resplendent in boring blue, like a furred river flounder."

Eleanor sprayed him with her perfume.

An hour later, Eleanor, her stretched scalp, and her peachy parrot joined the rest of King Peter Mangolin's court in the ballroom. She determined the ostentatiousness of the Great Hall to be purposeful, to make up for the lack of decoration in the rest of the palace. Like her bedroom, the ballroom had dark walls bedecked with bland tapestries and small fireplaces. Agnes added a bit of flair with lovely magical touches. The sorceress circled the edges of the ballroom, directing schools of enchanted silver fish. They swarmed the ceiling like pirouetting mirrors. She'd also enchanted the floor tiles. As the guests' boots and slippers skipped over them, they flashed in time to the dance steps. A trio of fiddlers plunked away in the corner, and the ever-present smell of roast meat hung in the air. A pleasant scene for an evening's socialization, but Eleanor's nerves returned with a vengeance as the servants passed wine and bits of cheese. She felt Dorian's absence just as keenly in this strange castle as she had within the familiar walls of Eclatant. Perhaps more so. Here, he might be purposefully avoiding her.

She longed to visit with Agnes, but with the witch otherwise occupied, she had little choice but to cling to Gregory. He introduced her to various Svelyan lords and ladies. Some of the men spoke Carthean, but the women merely nodded and smiled and looked her up and down with their frigid blue eyes. She tried to focus on the faces before her, but she still couldn't find Dorian. Her insubordinate eyes searched for him over fur-bedecked shoulders and around hands outstretched in greeting. An hour ticked past, and he did not appear. Finally, Gregory presented her with someone compelling enough to hold her attention.

"Prince Samuel," she said to the young man. "I'm so pleased to have a chance to speak with you."

He took her hand, gingerly at first, before he seemed to remember what he should to do. He gave it a firm squeeze and a kiss. She took measure of him at close proximity: his thin frame, thick black hair, and dark blue eyes. He had pale skin and a full mouth.

"I'm also pleased to speak with you, Your Highness. You are very lovely—as everyone is saying you would be." His cheeks flamed until his face matched his rosy lips.

"You flatter me, sire," she said. "I've borne three children and nursed them through long nights. I can see it in my face these days."

"Surely you adopted your children, madam, so lithe and lovely are you."

Eleanor's mouth hung open for a moment, and then Prince Samuel chuckled. He exhaled, as if relieved to have landed a successful first compliment. Eleanor relaxed herself. *This fellow does indeed have potential.*

"Remember, Eleanor, princes will say anything to win a smile from a lady."

Eleanor ignored Gregory's jab and focused on the boy before her. "How old are you, Samuel?"

"I'm nearly nineteen, Your Highness."

She tried to hide her surprise. With his slight frame and fey voice, she'd assumed him closer to sixteen. Still, better than the man of thirty-something she'd imagined on the journey.

Gregory excused himself to get a drink. Eleanor and Samuel chatted about the voyage and her lodgings for a time, before another young man, this one blond and strapping, called him away.

"He seems a pleasant sort, once he gets comfortable. Charming, in fact. His Carthean is excellent," said Eleanor when Chou landed on her shoulder. "It *is* odd that Agnes evaded discussing his character. I wonder why?"

"You can try to ask the lady herself," said Chou as Agnes eased through the crowd. Narrowed eyes and a few pointing fingers followed her. She grasped Eleanor's hand. Green smoke puffed between their fingers.

Eleanor complimented her on the magical entertainment, and Agnes professed admiration for Eleanor's earbobs before they turned to more intellectually stimulating topics. Eleanor mentioned the trouble with the dragons and her fascination with their watering habits. "Those poor creatures chasing water that forever evaporates before them. There's something tragic in it."

Agnes sighed, and Eleanor sensed the weight of her position in the green light behind her eyes. "It is sad, but life is hard. Why should dragons be immune to challenges?" She pointed across the room. "Uncouth it may be to speak of such before dinner, but you did mention the ogre camps. Those magicians in the corner? They're part of the Ogre Watch."

A cluster of magicians sat around a high table. They wore black robes trimmed in black fur. They kept to themselves, and no one seemed bothered by their seclusion or inclined to infringe upon it.

"I'm surprised to see such men among polite company," said Chou.

"It is true," said Agnes. "They rarely leave the camps. But a few are visiting once a season to give their report. Of course, they are an unsavory lot. No faulting of their own, for how can one be cultivating manners when surrounded by ogres through day and night?"

"They keep watch at all times, do they not?" asked Eleanor.

"It is quite a trying job. The—how are you saying it? The walls—the Restraints—must be maintained. A complex spell."

"That's why they are so well paid," said Chou. "All the kingdoms in the known nations tithe the Ogre camps."

Agnes tapped the little purse hanging from her waist. "The magicians of the Ogre Watch earn their coin, for sure."

"I should like to see an ogre," said Eleanor.

Chou rolled his eyes. "Of course you would. Just like you'd like to examine the mouth of an angry dragon, just to see if you'd be burned."

"Tsk, Your Highness," said Agnes. "I doubt very much you will see one, nor should you wish it! Few women are allowed to visit the camps."

"Women aren't allowed to visit the Dragon Mines either, but I've been there. Twice."

"Of course, that would be up to Prince Gregory. But thankfully, if he refuses, you will—as we like to say— eat your luck for supper and get no seconds. If you don't see one at the camps, you won't see one ever. HighGod willing, *no one* will ever be seeing an ogre outside of the camps. In this lifetime or your great-grandchildren's."

Two days later, Eleanor finally met the elusive King Peter Mangolin, the Mountain Lion of Svelya. She took an audience with him in his receiving room—a circular chamber on the palace's top floor. Many small windows created a pretty patchwork view of the river valley. The view of Peter himself, however, could not be described so kindly.

She had heard he'd been suffering from an illness—some manner of wasting disease. The old man who sat on the Fire-iron throne before her did not appear strong enough to stand, let alone lead a great nation. She guessed his age at somewhere in the realm of eighty years. He had not a hair on his head, although he did have copious white eyebrows. His blue eyes had faded to a nothing color. He rather reminded Eleanor of a male version of Hazelbeth, the Oracle of Afar Creek Abbey.

Like Hazelbeth, King Peter's voice did not match his decrepit frame. He spoke with all the rich intonation of a long-practicing Godsman at the pulpit. He had only a hint of his native accent.

The old man greeted her. His smile revealed two remaining front teeth, so he resembled an ancient, grinning rabbit. "Come closer, child. My ears are tender. All of you, closer." He waved to Dorian, Gregory, and Prince Samuel. They formed an attentive ring around him.

"Does your daughter fancy you, Your Highness?" asked the old king.

"I'm afraid Leticia takes after me in the face, Peter," said Gregory. "Although she's shaping up to have her mother's fine figure."

"She's beautiful," Eleanor said. Gregory's sexualization of the child mortified her.

Peter laughed. "I'm sure she is. Do you hear that, Samuel? A pretty flower. New blossom."

Eleanor blushed. The old king's salaciousness made her skin crawl, as if she were watching a rat drool over a piece of spoiled meat. The young prince had even less luck controlling his embarrassment. He shuffled his feet and mumbled something unintelligible.

"What color are the girl's eyes?" Peter squinted into Eleanor's face.

Eleanor blinked, in an old shield against such scrutiny. "Brown. Both of them."

"Good. One less reason for my High Council to oppose."

"Who would oppose my daughter?" After discussing Ticia like a fine brood mare, Gregory suddenly assumed the role of protective father.

"Some would prefer a Svelyan match for Prince Samuel," said Dorian. "Or possibly a Kellish princess."

"Samuel's own mother was a Talessee duchess." Peter scowled. "Hence his mop of black hair that he insists on keeping so girlishly long." The rabbit teeth reappeared. "Not that you Carthean gentleman look the least feminine. No accounting for custom, is there?"

While Eleanor tentatively liked Samuel, the conversation seemed to be heading in the direction of a signed treaty. "Let's not get ahead of ourselves, sirs. Leticia is but twelve, and we're here to discuss a possible match to benefit all parties."

"That's not the impression Lord Brandling gave me," said the king.

It *was* true. Dorian, of all people, was pushing a match between her daughter and the Svelyan prince.

"We must ensure everyone is agreeable," said Eleanor.

"I'm in no rush," said Samuel.

"Wise." Eleanor tried to catch Dorian's eye, but his darted between Gregory, Samuel, and King Peter. Damn his impassive face and refusal to look at her. "The pitfalls of rushing into marriage are many. Once the deed is done, it cannot be undone."

"Do you see some problem with my son? Something wrong with him?" asked Peter. "He's a fine young man. A strong stallion. Any woman in the world would be blessed to have him!"

"We're not speaking of a woman, sire, but a child," said Eleanor.

"Eleanor, watch yourself," said Gregory.

"It's fine, Father—I'm in no hurry—we can wait as long as—"

"Silence, boy," said the king, and Samuel's mouth snapped shut. "I'll set the time, and the date, and the lucky partner." Peter grinned at Eleanor, but it didn't touch his eyes. "Let us end this discussion now and think on it. All of us. Lord Brandling and Princess Eleanor are dismissed. I'll keep my son and Prince Gregory here with me for a time. We shall speak freely, as a king and kings to be."

Gregory ran a hand through his hair, but he grunted a goodbye. Eleanor heard a warning behind it.

He needn't have worried. Dorian followed Eleanor from King Peter's receiving room. As the door closed behind them, she rounded on him.

"How could you?" she asked. "Push a marriage match for Leticia, at her age? Send her away from me, from her sister? From Cricket and Eclatant and everything she knows?"

Dorian opened his mouth, but Eleanor cut him off.

"You, of all people, who knows the misery of those trapped in a loveless marriage! After everything we suffered!"

"HighGod above," he said. "Keep your voice down."

"Did you hear how that old pervert talked about her?"

He leaned toward her and spoke in a harsh whisper. "I've been writing to Casper and Gregory about this for over two years."

"What?" said Eleanor. "I've not heard one word about a marriage until two weeks ago!"

"Exactly. They won't consult you. Leticia's hand is a bargaining tool, nothing more. She'll have no say in whom she weds. Princesses—princesses of the blood, that is—never do. Gregory's sister Matilda married a Talessee duke twenty-five years her senior when she turned thirteen."

Eleanor paled. Matilda had died in childbirth only a few years later.

"Casper and Gregory will marry her to whom they choose, no matter what I or anyone else says. When I met Samuel I thought, here is a nice young man. Relatively close to her age. Better she be married to the son of an old pervert than the pervert himself. I'm trying to make the best of it."

Make the best of it, thought Eleanor. *That's what I've been doing for fourteen years.* She crossed her arms across her chest. "No," she said. "I won't allow it."

"*You* won't allow it?"

"I will *not allow* it."

Dorian turned in a circle, shaking his head. He chuckled or sniggered—she wasn't quite sure how to categorize it— the kind of condescending, exasperated laughter that turned Eleanor into a spooked cat, hackles raised and claws drawn.

She planted both fists on her hips. "Ticia will choose her own husband, when she's ready. Perhaps she'll be queen herself."

"Eleanor, you're not being realistic!" Dorian threw up his hands.

"I've never been realistic. Not about love." She stalked down the varnished staircase. Her skirts tangled in ungraceful clumps around her legs.

"Eleanor. Damnit. Eleanor!"

She nearly tripped twice, so she grabbed the layers of thick cloth and hoisted them almost to her knees. A passing chambermaid gasped at the sight of her scandalous woolen stockings. She didn't care. Her eyes burned.

He smiled at her, yes, but it hadn't been loving or reassuring, only patronizing. He said her name, but it wasn't a gentle expulsion of tenderness. Instead, he'd vented his frustration at her perceived unreasonableness. She'd felt a distinctly inimical inclination to punch him. In short, their first private conversation in almost five years was an unqualified disaster.

CHAPTER 4

QUICK, QUICK, SLOW

ELEANOR AND DORIAN AVOIDED each other for the next two weeks, as well they should, but not out of fear of Gregory's wrath. The argument played itself out in Eleanor's head again and again, but yet she still came to the same conclusion. Good intent or not, she could not accept the idea that Ticia should have no options but marriage to Prince Samuel, pleasant as he might seem. She was Gregory's heir, whether he longed for a son or not. Dorian accused Eleanor of being unrealistic, but what about Gregory and his father banking on Gregory and Eleanor having another son? Ticia couldn't very well be queen of Cartheigh while married to the Svelyan king.

She pondered that conundrum as she lay in her bed at night when sleep eluded her. King Casper had long expressed his position: No Desmarais queen had ruled in her own right. The Bond must be protected by a male heir in Caleb Desmarais's lineage. Gregory seemed inclined to agree with him, despite his own daughter's claim to the throne. Eleanor thought this made no sense. Ticia was as much Caleb's descendant as Nathan had been. Of course she carried the Bond within her. Eleanor had no opposition to having more children— she adored her two girls, and she would welcome the chance to mother another little boy. But only HighGod knew if she'd have any more children at all, much less a boy.

Sylvia has a boy, her seditious mind reminded her, as she stared at the sputtering fire in the fireplace one quiet evening. She had never wanted to believe her stepsister's youngest child, John-Caleb, was Gregory's son. But perhaps her husband and father-in-law were holding onto an illegitimate son as the ace up their silken sleeves.

But he's not acknowledged as a Desmarais. Although Gregory could acknowledge him. But what if he's not Gregory's son. Is that a greater risk to the Bond than a true female heir? Damn it. What are the rules, anyway? Does anyone really understand the Bond?

She longed to further explain her position to Dorian, and ask his opinion of these pressing succession questions, but as it had in the past, the precariousness of their association came between them. *If there remains any special association between us.* Another saturnine puzzle. Since the argument, her confusion had only grown. She knew less about his mysterious emotions today than she had when she arrived at Gammonreil. With no words said, and no safe mechanism for resolution, the conflict felt larger with time instead of smaller. Like a feared infection, it spread the more they avoided it.

As the days grew shorter, King Peter's health improved, and he showed himself at more social functions. To Eleanor's further discomfort, Dorian usually accompanied him.

"From what I hear," said Chou, the feathered scion of information gathering, "King Peter's mysterious ailment ebbs and flows. The malignant tide rises with severe headaches and vomiting—"

"Disgusting, Chou," said Eleanor.

"Then the fever dries up the river, so to speak, and he feels better for a while. Peter is quite taken with Dorian. Something about that man attracts royalty like hungry children to a freshly baked pie."

She didn't ask where or how her gossipy bird had learned the details of Peter's illness or of his affection for her erstwhile lover. As the silence between Eleanor and Dorian stretched on, and the dinner parties became intolerable, she wished the malignant tide would rise once more, thus requiring Dorian to sit by the old man's bedside again.

Her first month in Svelya came to close, and the court prepared for the Harvest Fest. Eleanor wondered if she'd ever been so lonely. She longed for the busy release of her charity work. During the years of Dorian's exile, she'd thrown herself into ministering to the poor with renewed fervor. Despite the demise of Queen Camille's School for Girls in Meggett Fringe, she traveled into the slum to teach casual reading classes to the peasants' children. She did the same in Solsea during the summers. She recruited the Godsmen of Humility Chapel to distribute leftover food from Eclatant's overzealous kitchens to the poor. She collected donations from the courtiers for injured or ill servants. She visited the witches' nurseries, where she cuddled babies and comforted exhausted new mothers. Nearly every day, she found some way to be of use to someone in need. It didn't resolve her pain, but it gave her something to think about other than the losses of Dorian and her son.

Here, in Nestra, she had no such outlets, nor did she have anyone besides the perpetually busy Agnes with whom she could spend time. She had Chou and Teardrop, but she missed Ticia and Natalie, and Rosemary and Anne Iris. She'd assumed close proximity to Dorian would ease her solitude, but she didn't know if he still cared for her, let alone how to settle the disagreement over Ticia's future.

Perhaps five years apart is simply too long. The morose thought followed her into King Peter's ballroom on a chilly Friday evening. Once again, Agnes's spellwork— dancing Harvest Fest fruits and vegetables— occupied most of the witch's attention. Eleanor found herself alone. She lingered beside a group of Svelyan women. She didn't understand a word they said. For all she knew, they were dissecting her wardrobe and criticizing her posture, but at least it eased the awkwardness of standing on her own.

Dorian hovered at the head of the ballroom, near King Peter's throne, beside Gregory. He sipped a glass of whiskey. Pretty blonde women came and went from his side. He danced with several of them. Eleanor panicked when it appeared he escorted the same woman around the floor twice, until she realized she couldn't differentiate one fair head from the next. *How plain I must look to him now,* she thought.

Chou landed on her shoulder. "The king asks for you."

She cautiously joined Gregory and Dorian at Peter's feet. The three Cartheans wore contrived, tightlipped quasi-smiles, a semicircle of deadpan poker players before a veteran card dealer.

"I haven't seen you dance, Your Highness," said the king. "I've heard you have quite the light foot."

"I do enjoy dancing, Your Majesty, but I'm afraid I don't know the steps." She pointed at the couples swirling around the floor. The fiddlers' tunes were pluckier than the smooth Carthean numbers she heard in her own palace's ballroom. The music was not quite a reel but required more bounce than a waltz. "I'll embarrass myself and my partner."

"Nonsense!" said Peter. "All must dance in my ballroom. I'll not tolerate wallflowers. Lord Brandling!"

Dorian dipped his head.

"You've spun many a lady around this ballroom. They've all left your arms in a swoon. Had to be carried off the floor." Peter guffawed at his own joke. "Can you not assist your own princess? Gregory, what say you?"

"Well. I— certainly. Why not?" Gregory's mouth twisted from a wishy-washy smile to a feigned grin. To Eleanor, who knew Gregory's natural, buoyant humor, the expression looked at best contrived, and at worst, physically painful.

Whether it be his poor eyesight or his alcohol intake, Peter didn't notice the tension between his guests. "Jolly good!" he said.

Gregory took Eleanor's elbow and squeezed it. She winced as he eased her toward Dorian.

"As you both wish, of course." Dorian held out one hand. His face was a lovely mask, shutting her out as he had for weeks. She forced the corners of her mouth to turn up and hoped this smile looked passably genuine.

Dorian led her onto the floor. Agnes dimmed the lights, and HighGod forbid, every eye in the ballroom went to Lord Brandling and his princess. He took her by the waist. His hand felt dry in hers for the first few steps until she started to sweat.

The music picked up again. A clippie, almost flippant tune. *Quick, quick, slow. Quick, quick, slow. Slow, slow, slow, repeat.* Eleanor was a fine dancer, and Dorian a fabulous partner, and they knew each other's rhythm. Their bodies were in time, even if their minds were not.

Dorian stared down at her as their proximity demanded. She felt as if he were looking through her eyes, down her throat, and into her heart. He blinked and ground his jaw, but he said nothing. Then the music stopped.

The crowd applauded, and Dorian dropped Eleanor's hand. He stepped away from her. She waved to King Peter, who raised a fist in salute. She turned and made for the nearest manservant. She wiped her neck with one of his silk napkins. "Perspiring," she said to no one in particular. "Ha. How embarrassing." She thanked HighGod for the warmth of a hundred bodies in the ballroom. The sweat of her exertions gave her reason to wipe the tears.

A few days later, Eleanor met Agnes outside Teardrop's stall in Gammonreil's brick and granite stable. Agnes had seen a herd of wild unicorns from a distance once, but otherwise, she had only seen romanticized depictions of the horned creatures in paintings and tapestries. Overcome with curiosity, she'd asked Eleanor for a personal introduction. The tiny witch stood beside the ivory mare. She emitted tendrils of inquisitive green mist, a fern in the shadow of a white birch tree.

Svelyan horses were much larger and heavier of bone than Carthean bloodstock but just as nosy. Chestnut, piebald, palomino; they peered over their stall doors. They watched Teardrop from under their shaggy forelocks and sniffed the timothy-scented air. They muttered in Svelyan, an equine chorus singing in a foreign language.

"What are they saying?" Eleanor asked.

Agnes cocked her head and listened. "Horn. Horn. Sharp, sharp, sharp."

Teardrop blew raspberries at the horses. "Everyone in this nation is so rudely forward."

Agnes squinted at the mare. "I see it. She speaks words, but there's more. Her eyes, and her ears—"

"If you understand me, please ask your friends to mind their manners." Teardrop circled the stall.

As if eager to prove herself, Agnes walked down the line of stalls and firmly told the horses to keep their noses and their comments to themselves. For the most part, they complied, but a particularly inquisitive bay mare continued spying on Teardrop through a crack in the wall.

Teardrop turned to her water bucket, and Agnes changed the subject to Eleanor's latest academic obsession.

"Are you finding the book helpful?" Agnes asked.

"You mean *Keeping the Beast at Bay*? Yes, very. The best book I've read on the ogre camps."

"You'll drain our library of ogre-related material before the Waning Fest."

"I'm running out of books in Carthean. Perhaps Rosemary can send me something new."

"It seems a strange topic for a princess. Why are you so fascinated?"

Eleanor couldn't tell Agnes the whole truth. The dragons' discontent had sparked her interest in ogres, but constant study also provided a distraction from the ever-present specter of the disastrous fight with Dorian. She gave her a middling answer. "Anything that affects the dragons affects a Carthean princess. Of course, I know the basic history— five hundred years ago, ogres came out of the far east, possibly from the Impassable Mountains beyond Kelland. They terrorized the known nations, all in an attempt to appease their god and fulfill some strange prophecy."

"All creatures do terrible things in the name of their gods," Agnes said.

"Who would guess such gruesome creatures even worship gods?"

"Gruesome creatures have gruesome deities," said Teardrop.

"It is strange to think of monsters creating mythology, rather than being part of it," said Agnes. "At first, the human kings assumed the ogres were unthinking beasts, like bears or giant buzzards. Or the laughing leopards that roam the plains of Talesse eating carrion. But it is true. Ogres have their own strange culture. Their god, Cra, demands murder and destruction. If they win his favor, they believe he'll deliver them to paradise."

"Pray tell," said Teardrop. "What constitutes an ogre's paradise?"

"I imagine a place where there are many slow, fat animals," said Agnes. "Ogres can survive on nothing but rocks and sticks. But they love a good hunk of meat, as long as they don't have to work too hard for it. In ancient times, they migrated from kingdom to kingdom, killing and destroying, in the hope that Cra would finally be satisfied. As is often the case with gods and prophecies—how to say it— Cra was not hurrying to keep his part of the bargain—no matter how much chaos his followers wrecked in his honor."

"My ancestors retreated into the marshes during the Ogre Wars," said Teardrop, "Boggy land would not support the ogres' bulk. We call it the Time of Hoof Rot. They nearly killed off the last of the dragons."

"Clearly, they're sentient," said Eleanor, "but not terribly intelligent, if they were lured into the camps."

"You know how they were trapped, don't you?" asked Agnes.

"My history lessons told of a scheme. One that made the ogres believe the camps were their promised land."

"Do you have your book?"

Eleanor nodded and removed *Keeping the Beasts at Bay* from her satchel. She handed it to Agnes, who flipped through it. "Ah, here," she said as she pointed at a section of text. "Read this."

Eleanor cleared her throat. *"In one of the most important acts of espionage in history, the chieftains of the five ogre tribes were convinced to enter the camps through manipulation of their dreams. A magical imposter posed as Cra himself and told the leaders to take their people into the purported promised lands, where they were quickly and permanently trapped behind the Restraints. The mastermind of this plan was—"* She smiled in delight. "Hazelbeth of Afar Creek Abbey!"

"That great lady posed as the ogre god," said Ages, "and protected millions of creatures. She probably saved dragons from extinction. All through manipulation of dreams."

"The Oracle still makes use of dreams. She's visited me in my sleep. Once, she even brought Chou Chou along!"

"She must have realized we'd never be able to truly defeat the ogres in armed battle. They're nearly impossible to kill. They are not fearing fire or poison. Their hides are like granite. They live for thousands of years. We can't even starve them out, since they will eat dirt itself and thrive. They can't swim, but otherwise, the only way to kill one is with a Fire-iron blade or a unicorn horn." She slashed at her own face and midsection. "In the underbelly or an open eye."

"There's a soft spot there," said Teardrop. "Our stories tell of a stallion called Moonhorn, who killed four ogres himself."

"At first, the kings of the known nations squabbled among themselves and tried to front their own armies, with little success. Once the kingdoms united, with their magical might and the assistance of the wild unicorns, the combined forces killed a few dozen ogres, but it wasn't enough. The invading force numbered close to a thousand beasts. All intent on destruction."

Eleanor shivered at the thought of a thousand ogres roaming the beautiful fields and forests and valleys of Cartheigh, killing and maiming and spewing filth into the lakes and rivers.

"And still the ogres are contained. It's a sort of miracle. What manner of magic can trap a thousand ogres for five hundred years?"

"I've seen the Restraints. They are difficult to explain." Agnes bit her lip. "While they are appearing to me as a sheet of water, you might see... a block of ice? I am not certain."

"The ogres cannot pass?"

"No one can pass. But they would melt, or fade away, if even an hour passed without a conjurer working the spell. There is always a magician in meditation before the Restraints. Two others stand watch beside him, should he fall asleep, lose his thoughts, or his heart stop beating. We all are owing our security to a handful of reclusive magicians in the middle of the mountains."

They lingered for a while, chatting about the magical theories behind the Restraints. Agnes tried to explain, and Eleanor listened, but as the witch waxed mystically esoteric, she found it beyond her. No matter her intellect and her desire, she only understood so much. Witches were witches, and she was not one of them.

"HighGod's whiskers, Chou," Eleanor said. "It's freezing, and only HighAutumn. How cold will it be in High*Winter*?" She wrapped a sheepskin dragon robe around her shoulders. It was a quiet Tuesday evening, and Eleanor and Chou were sharing a tin of chocolate-covered almonds by the fire in her bedroom.

"Hopefully, we will be home by then." Chou hopped into her lap and squirmed under the robe. His feet scratched her through her nightdress. "What's in the parcel?"

"What parcel?" asked Eleanor.

"The parcel on your desk. It arrived this afternoon while you took tea with Agnes."

Eleanor stood and dumped bird and robe onto the floor. The sheepskin muffled Chou's irritated squawk. Brown paper crinkled under her fingers as she picked up the parcel. She loosened the reams of twine wrapped around it. Chou lit on her hair and peered over her forehead. "What is it? Who is it from?"

Eleanor pulled a note from the first layer of brown paper. She recognized the hand. "Rosemary," she said. "Chou, it's rude to read over someone's shoulder—er, head."

"I'll save you the effort of repeating what she said."

Eleanor shrugged and read on.

Darling girl,

I do hope this finds you safe and comfortable in Nestra. Leticia and Natalie are healthy, although they miss you and their esteemed father. I've enclosed a note from Ticia, and even Natalie included a few words! She's so bright! Eleanor found the girls' note in the layers of paper. She kissed it and set it on the desk. *I send a gift for you from Hazelbeth—our beloved Oracle. When she heard you were to be separated from your children for an indeterminate amount of time, she conjured this spell so you might see them.*

Chou landed on the desk. He tugged at the package and spoke around a beak-ful of crinkling paper. "Wha-i-sit?"

Eleanor shooed him out of the way and opened the package. A cylindrical object rolled onto the desk. Its slivery color and smooth surface gave it away as Fire-iron. Some gentle hand had carved a pattern of leaves and hummingbirds along the thicker end. The glass lens on the tapered end blinked at her.

"A kaleidoscope." She lifted it to her eye. It was surprisingly light, like all Fire-iron creations. She peered into it and spun the far end, but she saw nothing but blackness. She returned to Rosemary's letter.

Inside the kaleidoscope is water from the Watching Pool itself, collected by Hazelbeth's own hand. The water is mixed with sand from the Pool's edge. You must turn the handle twice left and twice right, until the bird meets the leaf, to see its colors.

Eleanor ran her fingers over the smooth end until she found two rough spots: a tiny bird and an oak leaf. She spun the kaleidoscope twice left, and then twice right, until leaf and bird touched. She peered inside again.

The inner workings of the toy came to life in a bright rainbow of shifting water and multicolored grains of sand. She watched, fascinated, as the colors created geometric patterns that made her think of Harvestonian quilts. Chou nibbled at her ear. "My turn!" he said, like Natalie demanding time on her mother's lap.

She held up the kaleidoscope to his eyes. "Lovely!" he chirped as she read the rest of Rosemary's letter. *If you know the true spell, there is even more. Twice left, twice right, and then four times left again. The kaleidoscope will show you something you long to see. You cannot select the image, but if you think hard enough on it, you may have some influence. Take care of it, Eleanor, for it is a unique magical treasure, the likes of which I have never seen.*

HighGod willing, you will return to us soon. All my love,

Rosemary, Abbottess

Chou muttered in annoyance when Eleanor retracted the kaleidoscope. She spun it as instructed. She peered inside and gasped.

She was looking into her daughters' nursery, with every detail in bright relief. Pansy sat in the rocker with Natalie in her arms. Natalie turned the pages of a storybook. She pointed out pictures and words. The old rocker squeaked comfortably along with Pansy's ample, shifting weight. Ticia curled on her bed with her sketch pad. Candlelight lit all three beloved faces and the room's cheerful furnishings: The bright yellow sun on the purple and green rug, the girls' purple and gold patchwork quilts, and even the oil painting of Nathan across from Ticia's bed. Eleanor could almost smell Ticia's charcoal pencils.

She watched for the better part of an hour, with all the fascination of a theatergoer attending a beloved production, until the light dimmed. Slowly, shadows overtook her children's faces and the welcome familiarity of their bedroom. The kaleidoscope went dark.

She lowered it and rubbed her eyes.

"Did you give yourself a headache?" asked Chou. She told him of the fading. He waved his head from side to side. "So, the visions don't last forever."

"No, but what a gift. To see the girls— just as if I were standing beside them. I'll have to write Hazelbeth and thank her." She turned the kaleidoscope in her hands. "I hope it shows me the same scene tomorrow."

"Maybe you can learn to influence it. Are there other places you wish to see?"

Eleanor blushed, for she first thought to spy on Dorian. "I can't think of any—" Her eyes widened. "Chou!"

"Yes?"

"I've an idea!"

"Yes?"

"A brilliant idea!"

"For the love of all that is holy, Eleanor. You'll set me molting. Out with it."

"What if this kaleidoscope can show me Ezra Oliver?"

Chou's head feathers stood on end with excitement.

"Rosemary said it can show me things of meaning…and perhaps I can influence it…" Eleanor cleared her throat. "I must focus."

She turned the kaleidoscope again and thought of Ezra Oliver's face. The flat nose, receding chin, and watery brown eyes. She pictured his gray magic. Unfortunately, she also remembered disappearing dragons, pestilent plagues, and even exotic plant life. All her memories of him jostled around her head, full of superfluous information. When she looked into the kaleidoscope, it remained dark.

She set it on the table. "Nothing," she said to Chou.

"Ah, well. A first attempt—"

Eleanor's door swung open. Gregory stood in the threshold. He grasped the doorframe with one hand. "Parrot. Take your leave."

Chou cast a nervous glance at Eleanor. He whistled—an avian version of *yes, Your Highness.* He flew out the window in the direction of Teardrop and the stable.

"Hello, Gregory." Eleanor offered him a tentative smile.

"Don't lie to me."

"I merely said hello."

He crossed the room. "When did you do it? When did you find time?"

She backed away from his mottled face and the sour stench that flowed from him like whiskey cologne. "Time for what?"

"No one's seen you—but I'm sure the two of you found a way."

She shook her head in comprehension. "We haven't. I swear."

"I'll kill him. I fucking will." He covered his face with his hands. A chuffing sob tried to make its way out of his mouth, but he stifled it and muttered lamentations. "How could he? How could you? Will this knife ever leave my heart?"

For a moment, his sadness pulled at her. "Gregory—"

He took both her arms, as he had so many times before. Although it had been several years since he'd thus accosted her, Eleanor felt as if she had permanent indentations in her biceps. The shape of his thick fingers burned into her arms like a brand on an expensive cow. The wind of his boozy breath bore her sympathy away.

"We haven't even spoken." She twisted away from him, pushing in vain against his boulder-like biceps.

"Liar!"

Eleanor's mind raced. "All right, we *did* talk—"

"I knew it!" He shook her.

"I told him off! For pushing Ticia's hand on the Svelyan prince. He presumes to tell me what's best for her."

Gregory's grip loosened. "You're angry with him?"

"I was infuriated." A true statement.

"Well… as you know, I tend to agree with him—"

"It's for you to decide. Not Lord Brandling." That was a stretch. It wasn't Dorian *or* Gregory's place to decide for Ticia. In Eleanor's view, only Ticia should make that choice.

He let go of her and stumbled against the granite bed. He grabbed one of the four posters. His hand covered a gargoyle's neck, so the carving appeared to be screaming for mercy. "You're right. He is exceedingly arrogant. Always has been. Ah, damn. I'm going to bed." He spoke over his shoulder. "Not here. I won't subject you to my presence tonight. Nor me to yours."

"You may sleep where you choose."

"I know that. I always have. Maybe if I had stayed in the right bed a long time ago, I wouldn't have lost my best friend. Haughty prick that he is." He laughed. "Or my wife, either. Mouthy harpy that *she* is." Gregory kept sniggering as he stumbled toward the door. Eleanor let him go, but his words lingered after he left.

During the years between Nathan's death and Dorian's expulsion, the barely controlled hostility between them became unsustainable. The pressure of their grief, his growing suspicions, and her bitterness had exploded on the day Abram Finley confirmed Dorian and Eleanor's treachery. During the first year of Dorian's exile, her every interaction with Gregory marinated in his juicy, simmering anger. Slowly, they'd drifted apart, until the distance between them solidified into a hardened clay of his gruff resentment and her perpetual sadness. They left each other alone, except for the methodical efforts to produce an heir, and that was fine with her. Those interactions were certainly unpleasant, but she sensed Gregory didn't enjoy them either, and they both knew

Casper expected them to have another son. It was simply part of their collective role as the Crown Prince and his wife.

As she sat on the bed, she acknowledged that she'd been too consumed by her own sorrow to think much about how Gregory felt. Intoxication aside, this disjointed interaction marked their most open discussion of his feelings since the day he discovered the affair. She wasn't sure what to make of it. Still, if Gregory believed her angry with Dorian, it surely couldn't make things any worse.

Eleanor couldn't keep the kaleidoscope to herself. Such an interesting object demanded discussion, so two days later, in her bedroom, she handed it to Agnes.

"We call this a *mar'menon*," Agnes said. "It translates, roughly, to *glass rainbow*."

"That's lovely," said Eleanor. She gave the witch instructions, and Agnes peered inside. She sucked in her breath.

"What do you see?" asked Eleanor.

"My sister," said Agnes. "And her grandchildren."

At first the idea that Agnes had a sister with grandchildren took her aback, but then she remembered. "Oh—of course, you must be—"

"Sixty years old." Agnes touched her own preternaturally smooth cheek. "This spring."

"Do you miss her?"

Although Eleanor knew witches and magicians did not usually maintain relationships with their non-magical relatives after joining an Abbey or a Covey, she wondered how anyone, even a magical being, could forget his or her family. A loving family, anyway. Eleanor would happily have forgotten her stepmother and Sylvia, had she been called to the Abbey, but she couldn't imagine casting aside her love for her father. Although he died long ago, she still remembered him with poignant affection. If she'd been ripped from him as a child, she would have been crushed.

Agnes kept her eye on the image inside the toy. "I remember her fondly, but I cannot say I *miss* her. I saw her, once. She came to the palace to offer her respects when Peter named me Chief Sorceress. I greeted her as I would any other of my king's subjects."

"Yet I see some tenderness in how you watch her now."

Agnes lowered the kaleidoscope. "I sometimes wonder where life would have taken me had I not been called to magic. I'd be an old woman. Maybe a shoemaker's wife. My father was a cobbler. Finest boots in Nestra." She shrugged. Eleanor noticed her skin wasn't quite perfect, despite her youthfulness. Two deep lines were etched in her forehead—letters in the universal language of disquiet. "A much simpler life, with fewer troubles."

"But no opportunity to do great things."

Agnes snorted like a baby piglet. "Great things, yes. Hmmm. I suppose it's good to see her happy."

Maybe I'm imagining she cares, Eleanor thought. *Just because I can't understand it.*

Agnes was staring into the fireplace, so Eleanor touched her knee. "What do you make of the kaleidoscope?"

"It's a powerful thing. You say the Oracle herself conjured it?"

Chou joined the conversation from his perch on an unlit candelabra. "The Oracle has long held affection for my mistress."

"You are fortunate. I would be honored to meet such a powerful witch."

"She may be mastermind behind the ogre camps," said Eleanor, "but even the Oracle was never a Chief Sorceress."

"She is too special to serve a mortal king. She serves HighGod and magic itself."

"Speaking of powerful magicians!" Chou prodded Eleanor to elaborate with a shake of his tailfeathers.

Eleanor explained her idea about using the kaleidoscope to find Ezra Oliver. "The Oracle said I may be able to influence the visions..." She trailed off at Agnes's increasingly wrinkled brow.

"Do you think it's really necessary to find Ezra Oliver? In these days of friendship between our two countries, I don't see the need to focus on one magician. He's probably off in the desert somewhere or in the mountains, where he has plenty of space to conjure." She sipped her tea. "In our coveys, they say he always seeks more space for his magic."

Chou whistled. "HighGod forbid he find enough space to conjure whatever he can dream up. We must find him, eventually."

"It seems he is very good at hiding. It's been several years since anyone has seen him, correct?"

"Yes, but now I have a new means of looking." Eleanor tucked the kaleidoscope into a green and purple silk bag. She kept the cracked slipper in a similar sack, in her bedroom at Eclatant. Slipper, choker, ring, and now this kaleidoscope. She marveled at the gifts of Afar Creek Abbey.

"A glass rainbow," she said to Chou.

"I like it," he said. "It conjures up a pleasant image in my mind. Pardon the pun."

The parrot whistled in appreciation of his own wit. She stroked his head as Agnes said goodbye and took her leave. Eleanor hoped their comradery and mutual curiosity about the Oracle's gift had distracted the witch from whatever stressors deepened the lines between her eyes. As she stared into the fire, however, her mind returned to her estrangement from Dorian. She sighed. Always, some important matter required pensive rumination. Distractions were all well and good, but in Eleanor's experience, they never lasted long.

CHAPTER 5

AN ISLAND AMONG ISLANDS

ELEANOR WOKE BEFORE DAWN on the first day of LowWinter. She tossed and turned for a while before climbing out of bed. Chou snoozed contentedly on his perch, and the Svelyan maid had not yet begun her quiet morning creep around the chamber. Eleanor sat in a chair in the darkness with the kaleidoscope. She watched her children sleep until the reluctant winter sun finally rose over the mountains, like a hungover partygoer peeking out from below his bedsheets. She donned a simple gray housedress, threw a beaverskin dragon robe over her shoulders, and twisted her hair into a messy bun before stepping out onto the balcony. She shivered when the mountain air hit her exposed neck, and she put the kaleidoscope to her eye again. This time, it showed her a wild unicorn herd somewhere in the Great Marshes. Shiny white mares grazed while their gangly foals, invigorated by the chilly air, capered beside a fast-moving stream. She watched for a while, enjoying their playful freedom while her fingers stiffened from the cold. When the vision went dark, she blinked and rubbed her stinging eyes. She'd go blind or freeze if she kept this up, but she didn't have anything else to do so early in the morning. On a whim, she grabbed a handful of walnuts, took the time to run a brush through her morning bedhead, and stepped into the drafty hallway. She hardly looked the part of visiting royalty, with her lumpy fur robe and drab gray dress, but she doubted she'd run into anyone at this hour. Not in the library.

She clipped through Gammonreil's narrow passageways. Dim even at noon, they were positively dark at this wee hour. She lifted her skirts so as not to trip on a mop or a slick floor. The servants bowed and moved out of her path. She opened the library doors just as the first smells of baking bread crept from the kitchen.

As she expected, she found the library deserted. The librarian had not yet rung the opening bell, but no one would tell a princess she couldn't enter. She lit a candle and headed for the ogre books. She held her candle up to the hundreds of volumes lining the shelves. Her frustration grew as the light revealed book after book in Svelyan, but nothing she understood. She leaned toward the bookshelf, as if proximity might increase comprehension.

"I have a translation book."

She spun around and bumped her forehead against her candle. A blob of hot wax dropped onto her skin. She gasped and swiped at it.

"If you need one." Dorian handed her a handkerchief. "I'm sorry."

She scrubbed at the hardening wax. "It's fine. You surprised me."

"There's some there, in your hair." His fingers brushed her hairline and then darted away. They regarded each other in uncharacteristic silence. She took measure of him. His height. The burgundy Svelyan tunic. The still unfamiliar beard. She turned back to the books. The spot on her forehead already felt raw.

"You must have picked up the language by now," she said.

"Conversational, yes, but I miss nuances. Thankfully, the High Council all speak Carthean."

"We are an arrogant people. To expect everyone to speak our tongue."

"I agree. But Cartheans have never put much stock in teaching our children foreign languages."

"Rosemary taught the students at Queen Camille's."

"Rosemary has always been a march ahead of the battalions."

"Where are the translation books? I shall try them, for I'll not get much further as I am."

He led her down a passage between the stacks of books. The shelves loomed up around them like a forest. Wooden shelves. Paper foliage. Leather blossoms. Eleanor watched Dorian's shoulders. She pictured his bare back.

He stopped so suddenly she almost ran into him. He pointed out a few books on Svelyan-to-Carthean translations. She took two from the shelf and tucked them under her arm. "Thank you," she said.

"You're welcome." He touched her hair again. "The wax. It's still there."

"I'll take a bath."

"A bath."

"Yes." She bit her lip and then shut her mouth and swallowed, embarrassed.

"Do that again."

"What?"

"What you just did. With your mouth."

Her heartbeat sounded like a drum salute in her ears. "You do it," she said.

His mouth crept closer to hers. She watched until his face blurred and then closed her eyes. She felt the gentle pressure of his teeth on her lower lip, and then his tongue slid into her mouth.

She dropped the books and wrapped her arms around his neck. He brushed a few errant blonde strands away from her face and ran his fingers over her nose and her cheeks. She buried her hands in his hair, as she had so many times, and felt it curl around her fingers. The beard tickled her lips and chin, and then her neck, but she hardly minded a bit of scratching. Not when his hands were on her waist, where they belonged.

He pressed her against the shelves. She reached down to help him as he fumbled with his belt and her skirts. Once they'd cleared a path through the layers of silk, he slid into her. She bit his shoulder to keep from screaming. He braced one arm against the books, but the volumes slid out the other side with a crash. His arm disappeared to the shoulder. He wrapped it around Eleanor's head and pulled her closer. She buried her face in his chest.

She gripped his hair and tugged his face toward hers. "Look at me," she said.

She watched him finish. The color in his cheeks; his clenched teeth and wide pale eyes. His brow wrinkled, and he exhaled. He pulled away from her at the last second and slid his face onto her shoulder. He held her up, but she felt him trembling. She smelled his shaving tonic, like the beloved fragrance of a childhood garden.

"HighGod," he said.

He still loves me, even after years apart and a wholly unpleasant reunion, she thought. She felt tears of relief coming on as he set her on her feet again. Their argument suddenly felt ridiculous.

He glanced left and right down the passageway, and then through the spot left by the spilled books. He buttoned his leggings and adjusted his belt. She started babbling, intent on ensuring he knew exactly how *not angry* she was. "Dor—I'm so sorry I yelled at you about the betrothal. I was angry, but know you meant well—"

"Not now," he said. "You must leave."

"But I want to talk about—"

"Return to your room, right away."

Her brief elation was a swooning damsel, collapsing onto a fainting couch upholstered in insecurity. "Back to my room? After we just—I—when will I see you?"

"Eleanor." He gripped her hands between his. "Please. You're sorry, and I'm sorry. That's all the apologizing we have time for. You must *go*."

With his wild eyes and tense posture, he resembled a stag searching the surrounding woods for a hunting party. Eleanor herself had taken root in the worn wooden floor, unable to walk away from him even as he begged her to go. "Dorian, please. You're so cold."

He raked a hand over his face, as if trying to swipe the correct expression across it. "I don't mean to be. I'm sorry. I—"

Somewhere in the depths of the stacks, the librarian rang the opening bell.

"If you won't leave, darling, then I must." He gave her hand one last squeeze, and he disappeared.

Dorian needed air. Despite being one of the larger and more spacious enclaves of Gammonreil Palace, the library was suddenly closing in on him like a coffin. He felt as if he were about to be buried alive.

Alive for now, he thought. *But if someone saw us...*

He grabbed his cloak from the desk where he'd been studying before Eleanor's unexpected appearance. He said good morning and good day to the librarian, walked through the Great Hall, took a left, and clipped down a set of stairs toward one the castle's less conspicuous exits. As he approached, one of the guards opened the door. He shoved one arm into his cloak sleeve, and then the other. He stuffed his hands into a pair of gloves. It was warmer than usual for a Nestra LowWinter morning, but Dorian longed for the sunny early winter days in Maliana, when he often had to strip layers rather than add them. He thought of his manor house in Harper's Crossing, Laralee, and the warm spring breezes over Lake Brandling. His brother Abram had been managing the estate since Dorian's exile. Abram had gained that benefit by betraying Dorian's greatest secret to Gregory, but ironically, he'd been forced to retire from court to avoid reminding Gregory of his humiliation. After almost five years, Dorian no longer hated Abram. He missed anything that smacked of home, even his bitter, jealous, turncoat brother.

He strode across the Gammonreil Bridge onto the closest and largest island of the river archipelago, Devery. Many of Gammonreil's wealthier citizens lived in Devery Village, in elegant, several-story houses with spindly staircases and porch railings. Carthean courtiers would fancy the village homes on the small side, but in Nestra, dry land was hard to come by. Shops, tearooms, inns, and artists' galleries lined the village's main street. Merchants, servants, and messengers bustled past him as he strode across the cobblestones. He couldn't understand their low Svelyan accents, so the conversation around him blurred into a tangle of cannibalized consonants and vociferous vowels. The smell of horse manure clashed with the heavy herbal perfumes that floated out of the ladies' dress shops. He picked out nutmeg and cloves. Svelyan women didn't have ready access to floral scents, so in his experience, most of them smelled like baking bread.

Eleanor smelled like peachberries, as always, he thought. She must have brought her perfume from home.

He walked faster. He ignored the shopkeepers who took note of his elegant ermine fur cloak and his expensive Kellish cowhide boots and tried to lure him into their stores. He made his way toward a small public garden overlooking one of the Gammon's quieter coves. He visited often when he wanted to get away. Save for the occasional old couple sitting on the ancient Fire-iron bench, he usually had the garden to himself. Thankfully, he found it empty today. He leaned against the stone wall that prevented one from tumbling into the river. The wind died down, and he heard the water below him whispering chastisements.

"That should not happen again," said a voice from over his shoulder.

He spun around, terrified, as if the river had raised its voice to him. Chou Chou sat on stone flowerpot, partially hidden among some wilting chrysanthemums. "You scared me, old friend," Dorian said.

Chou flew across the garden and landed on the wall beside him.

"Not as much as Eleanor scared me when she told me about the library encounter."

Dorian leaned on his elbows. "We were terribly reckless."

"We both know she's not always the most cautious person when her emotions get the better of her. Once I reminded her of the danger, she remembered it, but she felt more relief than fear at first. She suspected you fell in love with another—or at least fell out of love with her."

Dorian snorted a laugh. Chou fluttered in place, and a few red feathers floated down into the grumbly water.

"I didn't mean to startle you," said Dorian. "But you can't be serious."

"It's been nearly five years." Chou lifted his wings in a shrug. "It's not a completely outlandish speculation."

Dorian exhaled. He thought back over the endless days and nights he spent in spasms of grief and loneliness, to say nothing of his crushing anxiety about Eleanor's safety. Her lack of faith frustrated him. Especially given the way she'd berated him over Ticia's betrothal.

"Don't be cross with her," said Chou, as if reading his mind. "You're both suffering. You suffer more discreetly than she does, but you and Eleanor have been through different battles in the same war."

The parrot's analogy struck home. "It's so hard, Chou. We can't talk about anything. At least in the old days we met every now and then. Hash out whatever needed hashing. This forced silence is a magnifying glass between the sun and a piece of dry paper."

"You wrote a letter once, to explain your love."

"I told her it would be the only love letter I ever wrote to her."

"If you write again, I will carry it to her."

"It's so dangerous, for all of us."

"One letter can't be much more dangerous than the emotions that erupted among the library shelves this morning. The two of you must cut the tension between you before you both strangle on it."

Dorian listened to the river, but he no longer heard admonishments.

The wind had returned. It whipped up lapping waves that sounded more like applause, cheering him on.

Bless Chou for helping us, he thought. His own avian companion would do the same, and even if the parrot and his raven, Frog, heartily disliked each other, they'd cooperate on this mission. "Meet Frog here at six o'clock this evening." He stroked Chou's red and blue head. "Where would any of us be without our feathered friends?"

"Dead, most likely," said Chou, and he took off for the palace.

Eleanor fumbled with Dorian's note. Chou sat on her desk beside her, next to the candle he insisted she light, to ensure she burned the letter as soon as she read it. The little flame cast squiggly shadows over Dorian's words.

> *Dear lady,*
>
> *I am not sure where to begin, after all this time. The years have blurred together into an endless funeral procession. I suppose I shall start with the most basic of emotions.*
>
> *Fear. Every day, I lived in fear for your life, knowing you were always within an arm's reach—or a sword's reach—of harm. I had no way to know if the next letter from home would bring me news of your demise. Notwithstanding your husband's wrath, there is always the looming shadow of our great enemy, Mr. Oliver. I fear I no longer know how to live without fear. I will let that awkward phrasing stand, as it seems to prove my point as to the ubiquity of my terrible apprehension.*
>
> *I have always held my cards close, and despite living what feels like a long life as I stare down forty years of it, I can*

count those I love and trust on my fingers. Here in Svelya, I have made many new acquaintances, but very few rise above that piddling level of association. I left everyone I care about in Cartheigh. You being foremost, but also my sister and her family, Senné, and even, though you may resent me for saying it, the very person who drew us further asunder. I hope you can forgive me for mourning the loss of that friendship, even if you do not understand the pain.

I have become an island among islands here in Svelya. I study, and I attend functions where I am needed in my capacity as ambassador. I do everything I can to further King Casper's interests. Sometimes I ride in the mountains or walk around the city. Long ago I said I would never lie to you, so I won't deny I've experienced some physical release with a few women here, but in truth, it only exacerbated my sadness and longing for you.

When I heard you were coming to Nestra, I thought my heart would fail me. Knowing I would see your face and hear your voice, but also knowing your proximity to me might further endanger you. At least when we were apart, I could not imperil you with my lack of self-control and my presence, reminding him of what passed between us.

I apologize if I seemed cold and distant, but fear for your safety drove it. Please be patient with me, for I will have to get used to loving a living, breathing person again, rather than a beautiful memory. I have to relearn to live with my uneasiness in front of me, rather than the abstract, morbid fantasies that have haunted me these years. Still, as I promised long ago, I will find a way to love you. I will find a way to touch you again, soon. I pray you believe me and my words ease your own worry.

Eleanor read the note once more, before wiping her eyes and holding it to the flame.

"Should I reply, Chou?"

"If you have a reply, I will carry it for you. If you and Dorian don't have some means to understand each other's perspective on all that has passed, and clarify your feelings for one another, the silence will be more dangerous than the potential for intercepting a letter."

"I hate that you must put yourself in peril so I can say what I need to say." She stroked his head for a moment, then sat up straighter and smiled. "Wait, Chou. There's another way. How silly we didn't think of it."

"What way is that?"

"You are a parrot, are you not?"

As usual, Dorian couldn't sleep. He sat in a rocking chair in his simple bedroom beside the fire with a book in his lap—a collection of Svelyan poetry, translated into Carthean. Like all such verses, the poems lost some of their beauty in translation. Still, Svelyan poets were stoically romantic, for their lovelorn lamentations were formed from mountain granite and rivers of melted snow. Their sentiments paired well with his mood.

His mind wandered as he watched the fire. He hoped Eleanor slept soundly, secure in his love, and (he chuckled to himself at the thought) perhaps less likely to snap his head off next time she disagreed with him. He tried to remember the last time he'd slept all night without waking, but in truth, that elusive night of peaceful repose could not be recalled. He thought of his childhood, curled up in his bedroom in Floodgate Manor after a long day of sailing on Lake Brandling, deer hunting, or a long ride in the forest. He remembered how he closed his eyes and his limbs stung sweetly from exhaustion. Flashes of the day's activities would rush around in his mind, chaotic and repetitive, like early good dreams. His father, Andrew Finley, was a constant in those memories. His siblings, Abram and Anne Clara, flitted in and out of them, but Mr. Finley dominated, with curly brown hair and laughing hazel eyes and height that, to Dorian, seemed to rival the pine trees surrounding the estate.

When he and Eleanor spoke of their childhoods, she always asked him about his mother. *Did she never join you? Not even on picnics?*

Dorian would shrug and try to avoid the topic, but over the years, Eleanor had dragged the sad story out of him. Other than Eleanor, only his late father, siblings, and Gregory knew the whole truth. Tabitha Finley was the daughter of a book binder. With her black hair and pale eyes, she was the most beautiful woman in the Lake District. She'd birthed her three children, and then she had put them aside like ill-fitting boots. She stayed in her room while her jovial husband played the roles of father and mother as best he could. She paid more attention to her lapdogs than she did to her two sons and her daughter. She passed on her looks to Dorian, as well as her own father's love of reading. She left him nothing else, good or bad. He saw her a few times a month, and she usually looked like she'd been crying. Sometimes he heard her softly sobbing when he passed her room. She finally expired from whatever sadness drove her in Dorian's twelfth year, not long before his father followed her to HighGod.

Of course, Eleanor pressed him for more. She couldn't fathom such coldness or neglect in any mother. She herself doted on her children's every move, and although she'd never known her own mother, she assumed Leticia Brice would have done the same for her. Sometimes Dorian believed she'd romanticized her late mother to the point that no one, not even Eleanor herself, could live up to the speculative Leticia's mothering skills. Still, she gave it a good go.

Dorian felt oddly defensive of Tabitha, even though he hadn't cried at her funeral and could not say he missed a woman he'd never really known. He only said his father told him she wasn't always that way—she'd been rather shy and had a streak of melancholy, but she laughed often and loved to share her books with him. She'd been a great dancer and a fine sailor in her own right. Andrew never came out and said so, but Dorian understood. Something about having children had stolen her light. Maybe he couldn't miss her because he felt guilty. He and Eleanor had probably bonded over the understanding that both of them had exacerbated their mothers' demises. Eleanor's birth had killed her mother outright, but really, Dorian and his siblings had done the same to Tabitha. Even if it took longer and allowed others to judge her harshly.

Eleanor had suggested Dorian's intense sense of responsibility for everyone around him and the country in general came from his unexamined sadness over his mother's life and death. While the idea appealed to his rationality, Dorian, for all his tendency to self-reflect, didn't like to think something so theoretical could drive such a huge part of his nature. It made him feel out of control.

Like I lost control in the library, he thought. Guilt over giving in to his urges wrestled with the lack of regret it had happened. He'd already rehashed every passionate moment a thousand times.

You only have the luxury because you didn't get caught, his ever-present fear reminded him, like a self-righteous Godsman lecturing a sinner.

He stood with the vague idea of getting a drink and turning his back on smug Fear and overbearing Guilt, those emotional court jesters. A tapping at the window overrode the crackle of the fire. He opened it, and Chou glided across the bedroom. "It took you long enough. If I'd stayed outside any longer, my wings would have frozen. I could have fallen to my death."

Dorian ran a hand over Chou's smooth back. "It's not that cold, and you don't feel icy to me.

"My natural habitat is the jungle—"

"Your natural habitat is a Fire-iron perch beside a basket of biscuits." Dorian tapped Chou's scaly foot. "No reply from Eleanor, I see. Well, I suppose it's safer."

"I have a reply."

"Where?"

Chou ran one wing over his head. "In here."

"Ah, do you mean you—"

"Shhh. Let me prepare." Chou squared up and closed one eye. The open yellow one glared at Dorian. "One light eye, one dark."

"Yes. Right. Carry on, Your Highness."

Chou whistled, and then Eleanor's somewhat husky, whispering voice slipped from his beak, complete with her clipped, well-to-do Maliana accent.

> *"Dear sir,*
>
> *When I received your letter, I first thought of how I longed for such from you every time I saw a courier enter the palace grounds. Of course, I knew it was not possible, but still, I held onto that dream for years, waiting for some nameless messenger to knock on my chamber door and bring me your words. As you said so eloquently, we have become fantasies to one another. Yet now, here we are, once again in the same space, and we must figure out how to exist within the framework HighGod has set around us.*
>
> *You apologized, and I must as well. I have been so caught up in missing you and longing for our reunion, I didn't think about how we have experienced the past few years so differently. I experienced loneliness, but I still had my other loved ones around me. I experienced fear for your safety, but I realize now that I took comfort in knowing you were*

thousands of miles away, out of his immediate reach. Yes, I had to manage his anger, but in all honesty, for the past few years, he and I came to a place of tolerance. We both have a job to do and a role to play, for the kingdom and the children, and we do as we must. It was not pleasant, but I wasn't trapped in a faraway land surrounded by strangers and wondering every second if you were in mortal peril. You, my love, have had a much harder go of it.

So now I feel silly. I so focused on you giving me some sign your feelings remained true, and I doubted you because you seemed so cautious, when really, you were wise to do so. I will not abuse Chou's poor bird brain—"

Chou interrupted himself. "Of course, I found this part offensive, but I did promise to recite word for word.

"—abuse his poor bird brain by stuffing it too full of my apologetic longing. Please do know I have no more doubts, and I will do my best to control my emotions for both our safety. But know also I do not regret what happened today in the slightest, for I have longed for it with all my soul all these long years."

Chou gasped, and his own voice returned again. "So thirsty."

Dorian took up the pitcher beside his bed and poured water into a clay cup. He stroked Chou's head as he slurped. "How do you remember all that?"

"My bird brain, you know," Chou said and belched. "Superior memory."

"Clearly. Thank you for the message." Dorian felt much lighter. He might actually be able to sleep now. How much simpler life would be, if only he and Eleanor could speak openly and frankly every day.

If we could speak so every day, we'd be living a different life.

He thanked Chou again and stood by the window as the parrot gracefully floated across the empty space between his room in the western wing of the palace and Eleanor's room in the southern tower. He stripped off his tunic and climbed into bed. For now, this was the life they were living, and if the temporary serenity of a resolved disagreement would grant him a relatively peaceful night's sleep, he'd take it.

CHAPTER 6

UNORTHODOX TASTES

FOR THE NEXT FIVE days, Eleanor and Dorian sent their love back and forth via her choker and his ring, but they didn't so much as lay eyes on one another. Eleanor came down with a cold, and given King Peter's relatively fragile state, he forbade anyone with the slightest hint of illness from partaking in court events. By the fifth day, she'd consumed several gallons of the grumpy castle healer's carrot-infused cold tonics and twice sat for an hour in a bathing room filled with steamy air, magically enhanced with mint and tea oil. Her voice still sounded as if she had a clothespin on her nose, and a cough tickled the back of her throat, but the old witch grudgingly allowed her to attend the evening's entertainment. She spent an hour with a pair of cooling poultices over her puffy, reddish nose before joining the courtiers in the ballroom. She'd no sooner curtsied to the king before Prince Samuel took her arm.

"I so enjoyed your dance with Lord Brandling," Samuel said. "You're both singularly talented dancers. You look as if you belong together."

"We've known one another a long time."

"You must start the dancing tonight."

She looked around the ballroom, trying to find Gregory. "Oh, Your Highness—I don't think that's a good idea—"

"I insist." Samuel steered her toward Dorian at the head of the ballroom. "The musicians have been practicing a Carthean waltz in preparation for the Waning Fest…the Snowbird…Do you know it?"

"It's one of my favorites," said Eleanor. She and Dorian could dance the Snowbird in blinders and earmuffs.

If Dorian was surprised when Samuel dropped Eleanor on his arm and the orchestra struck up the Snowbird, he didn't show it. As he led her to the dance floor, she finally found Gregory. He assumed watch on the edge of the crowd. Eleanor saw his foot tapping out of the corner of her eye. Probably *not* a response to the beat of the music.

She faced Dorian. "Evening, Your Highness," he said. His voice was as bland as the cold tonics she'd been downing over the past week, but he squeezed her waist.

"Good evening, Your Grace," she said in return.

"It has come to my attention that you're angry with me," he said.

She couldn't read his tone. It confused her, as she'd be befuddled if Chou Chou suddenly spoke only in Svelyan. "Pray, where did you hear that?"

"From Prince Gregory."

They separated and turned in slow time to the music. The fiddles ground out the familiar tune with just a hint of Svelyan up-tempo. Eleanor's skirt swung around her legs. She sashayed left, then right, and met Dorian in the center of the floor again. Their hands touched, and they spun in a slow circle.

"I did indeed inform him of our argument about the betrothal, not long after it happened." She stared past his shoulder at the courtiers. Gregory drifted past as they spun, another moon in their orbit.

"Very good," Dorian said.

She glanced up at him. "Was it?"

"I would like for you to continue to make sure he knows how very, very miffed you are with me, because I am an arrogant prick."

She suddenly understood. She bit the inside of her cheek and gave her chin a purposeful jut in his direction. "I see. Being that, in his estimation, I am a mouthy harpy, that should not be difficult."

They spun past Gregory again. He watched them, arms crossed, mouth twitching in a smile. Surely, he believed them arguing.

"Scowl at me, please," said Dorian.

She glared at him. She even rolled her eyes. He snorted, reminding her of Senné blowing away an irritating fly. Giggles built up in the back of her throat. She tried to swallow them, as she might endeavor to hold back pregnancy nausea. "You're insufferable, Lord Brandling," she said, enunciating each word.

"As are you, Your Highness." He fixed his mouth in a scowl, but his eyes twinkled. He spun her away from him and then pulled her closer as the dance required. "I have kept my promise. About touching."

He spun her away again, and she dropped a courtesy as the song ended. "Thank you. Now please remove yourself from my presence."

He gave her the slightest wink as he bowed. "As you wish, as always," he said.

Dorian left Eleanor with Gregory. He hoped their dance floor chat had further reassured her. When Gregory had asked him to discuss Ticia's union that morning, he assumed the prince had made a decision one way or the other. Instead, the entire nondescript conversation seemed intended to inform Dorian of Eleanor's anger. He made sure to note husband and wife's collective reference to Dorian's arrogance—and Gregory's bestowal upon him of a certain phallic pejorative. He left out his designation of Eleanor as a loquacious shrew, but perhaps even Gregory drew a line at saying such about his wife to anyone but the lady herself.

While part of him hated thinking about Eleanor discussing their argument with Gregory, he knew it would benefit both of them if

Gregory believed they were on the outs. He'd lived within their bizarre love triangle long enough to put aside his pride when necessary.

A shot of whiskey always sooths the injured ego, he thought. He looked for one of the servants who precariously maneuvered through the crowd with a wooden tray covered in small liquor glasses.

A gloved hand grabbed his forearm. "Did you discuss what needed discussing?" Above the black glove, a bright red woolen sleeve, trimmed with thick fur. Mink, perhaps, or maybe a rare black wolf. Only Samuel and his father wore the royal colors. At every event, they stood out like Chou Chou in a flock of starlings.

"Yes," Dorian said. He and Samuel spoke in Carthean, as they usually did, so Samuel could practice the language. "Thank you for providing the opportunity."

"You are saying nothing of it, Your Grace. If you need my assistance, you know you need only ask." Dorian was no fool, and he knew the prince had taken a shine to him, like most kings and princes he met. As a representative of his own country, Dorian had purposely cultivated their amicable relationship, but he genuinely liked Samuel. Dorian treated him kindly and patiently, and the boy had long since overcome his shyness.

"I'll help you, and the princess, when I can," Samuel continued. "After all, she is to be my mother-in-law. I must make alliances early."

"We shall see." Dorian scanned the crowd for a tolerable lady. It seemed imperative he pay attention to one female or another after his dance with Eleanor. Tall, blonde women abounded in the ballroom. "Who's that lady there? The one in the dark green?"

Samuel's own eyes were fixed on the beer barrels. "Aren't most of them wearing green?"

"The one with the feather in her hair. What's her name? Although there seems no point in talking to her. She's got eyes for you."

"Hmmm…what?" Samuel turned to Dorian. "Oh…I am doubting it, Your Grace. I am not one to attract the ladies. Not like yourself."

Dorian laughed. "You're the crown prince, and you're a fine specimen. Any lady here would take to you." He wagged a finger at Samuel. Crown prince or not, he felt close enough to the boy to speak his mind. "Get it out of your blood now, sire. You know Princess Leticia is like a daughter to me."

Once again Samuel sought the beer barrels. "That won't be a problem, I promise. Excuse me, will you?"

Samuel trotted across the ballroom. He brushed his floppy black hair out of his eyes as he went and tugged at his tunic. Dorian started toward the unnamed blonde woman, with the hope she'd emulate her countrywomen and speak not a lick of Carthean, hence negating the need to converse with her. For some reason he stopped and looked over his shoulder.

Samuel had met another young man beside the barrels. The same tall, strapping blond Dorian had seen him with on several occasions. Around here, one tall, strapping blond blended into the next, but this man stood out because of the dagger-shaped earrings he always wore. *Who is he?*

He decided he needed a beer instead of whiskey, but by the time he pushed through the crowd, Samuel and his friend had abandoned the kegs and were on their way out the door. Dorian followed them. He took two rights and then a left, but he came up short. "Damn," he muttered.

"You looking for someone?" A chambermaid peered at him from behind a cracked door. She had the requisite light hair, but her teeth were going gray, and she didn't stand much taller than Ticia. "Two someones, maybe?"

Dorian squinted at her and replied in Svelyan, "Maybe."

The maid retreated into the shadows. "They went to the sculptor room. That's where they go." The door snicked shut.

Dorian followed the chambermaid's suggestion and headed to Gammonreil's sculpture room. At the entrance, he ducked layers of stiff, musty-smelling draperies. Dorian received a tour of the sculpture room upon his arrival at Gammonreil, but he'd not returned since. It got little use beyond King Peter showing it off to those he needed to impress.

There were no lit candles, but the Fire-iron sculptures, relics of the days when Svelya controlled the Dragon Mines, had their own queer effervescence. Dorian could see five to ten paces ahead of himself, depending on his proximity to the nearest carved unicorn, knight, or Mangolin ancestor. He tiptoed on the marble floor and followed the sound of whimpering. Something like a hungry puppy.

A shadow moved on the floor. He gripped the snout of a Fire-iron wolf. The stone felt clammy under his hand, but his face went positively frigid as he peered around the statue.

Samuel reclined in the arms of a seated Fire-iron witch. His leggings were around his knees. He looked from the ceiling to his hand, which rested on the head of the tall blond man. He gripped the man's hair and moaned. The man pulled away from the prince's crotch and smiled up at him.

"Don't stop, please," Samuel said in Svelyan.

For once Dorian's composure left him. He stepped back, too quickly, and his elbow struck the Fire-iron wolf pup on the corner of the pedestal. Pain shot up his funny bone. "Damnit."

The blond man stood as if a puppetmaster had tugged a string attached to his head. Samuel yanked at his leggings. His eyes widened when they met Dorian's.

Dorian couldn't find any words. He needed time to think. He spun around, but as one must cease forward momentum when called upon to do so by royalty, he stopped at the sound of Samuel's voice.

"Lord Brandling," said the young man. "A word, if you please."

Dorian avoided looking Samuel in the face. The prince still sat on the Fire-iron witch's lap, giving the odd impression of a small boy in the embrace of a stone mother. The blond man stood beside him. Samuel dismissed the man, whom Dorian gathered was called Louis, in their language.

If the other young man felt embarrassment, he didn't show it. He even reached for Samuel's hand and squeezed it. He stopped short of a goodbye kiss, but his nonchalance alarmed Dorian, for surely the prince knew that no one—no one—could ever find out about this.

Samuel watched him go before returning his attention to Dorian. His face was blotchy red and white, as if he couldn't decide whether to be humiliated or afraid.

"So...you followed me here. That in itself is a crime. I was not giving you permission to enter my presence"

"My apologies, sire."

"Now you've seen...ah..."

Dorian's mind raced as they sunk into silence. He'd heard of men with such proclivities, of course. He had suspected it of certain individuals in the past and heard rumors. *Sir-So-and-So and the Earl of Such-and Such aren't really hunting comrades, they're more like sparring partners—swords drawn and so forth, hahaha*. He knew to avoid notorious establishments in the taverns and brothels of Pasture's End— those which were rumored to cater to unorthodox tastes. While the idea was generally distasteful to him, he didn't share the Godsmen's view that dallying with other men ranked alongside murder and treason amongst the sins most offensive to HighGod. There were so many other more onerous transgressions. Like sleeping with your best friend's wife for a decade.

He'd never discussed homosexuality with his Svelyan acquaintances. The topic hardly made for polite dinner conversation. He'd found Svelyans to be more conservative than Cartheans, however, in everything from tunics to taxation. He couldn't imagine the culture to be overly tolerant of buggery. Especially not in the man one day expected to lead the nation on the battlefield and produce an heir to the Mangolin throne.

"I've seen something, yes," said Dorian.

"What say you?"

"Your affairs are your own."

Samuel slumped in the witch's lap.

It had to be said. "But I cannot support your marriage to Princess Leticia."

Samuel sat up again. "What? Why?"

"Sire, if you are so inclined, I don't think your preferences will change."

"What does that have to do with marriage?"

"You can't possibly expect your future wife to tolerate—"

"I'm in no rush to get married, sir, but I shall have no choice in the end. Princess Leticia is as good a choice as any other. Princesses and queens have always looked aside at their husbands' dalliances."

Dorian thought of Eleanor. She'd never been able to look aside, and Ticia had inherited her mother's opinionated nature in spades. Besides, they'd have to contend with the shock to the girl's innocent sensibilities if she should ever come upon her husband engaged in…engaged in…

"Your Highness, with the greatest respect, I cannot support the match."

Samuel stood. "You must! It was your idea from the beginning. If you change your mind my father will suspect…and he already…" He trailed off, and Dorian understood. Samuel knew damn well that his affliction, if it could be so called, must never come to light. His father terrified him. He dreaded the old king's reaction should he discover his son's abnormality. Marriage would be his shield. Dorian pitied the boy, for although the Godsmen counseled prayer and study to cure such sickness of the mind, Dorian doubted anyone would choose such a pitted road if he could find an easier route.

"I won't tell him, Samuel."

"He might even kill me," the prince said in a ragged whisper. He wiped his eyes, and Dorian remembered how young he was. "But I'm sure he'll kill Louis." He covered his face with both hands. "I love him."

The idea was foreign to Dorian, but the pain and fear were not. "I said I won't tell. But I cannot support your marriage to Leticia. You must find another bride."

Samuel slumped in the witch's lap again. She looked down on him with a carved face full of compassion, as if she'd wrap her arms around him if only she could convince them to move. "Do you think I have any say in it? Who she is, or when it will happen? The little princess and I have more in common than you think. We're both at the whim of a king."

Chou brought news of Dorian's discovery to Eleanor following a particularly boring Sunday chapel. Naturally, the Godsman had conducted the service in Svelyan, and naturally, Eleanor hadn't understood a word. She spent the hour daydreaming and, she had to admit, watching the back of Prince Samuel's dark head and wondering what he and Ticia's children might look like. When Chou landed on her shoulder as she returned to her room, his whispers brought those fantasies to a crashing halt.

"You can't be serious, Chou."

"I am. As serious as one of those Svelyan Godsmen."

She looked over her shoulder. "The Svelyan crown prince?"

Chou lifted his wings in a birdie shrug. "It seems obvious now."

Eleanor thought of Samuel's soft voice. He held his hand over his mouth when he laughed. "I suppose he does hold his wine goblet in a way more reminiscent of—Oh, dragonshit. What a mess." She stopped at a Fire-iron bench in the Great Hall. She sat and looked up, as if admiring the multi-colored glass ceiling. She twisted her head from left to right, to ease the tension that had suddenly seized her shoulders.

Chou hopped from her shoulder to her lap. Against her chocolate gown, he resembled a tulip in freshly turned dirt. "It will be hard enough for Ticia to come here and marry a stranger, but if we add this dilemma?"

"No. It's not fair to her. It's not fair to him, either, really. We must tell Gregory."

"You can't. Dorian promised Samuel he'd keep the secret." Chou explained Samuel's precarious position.

"That's all well and good, but I must think of my daughter's happiness."

"Gregory and Dorian are different men. The former won't be so understanding."

Eleanor sighed. "You're right. Gregory isn't known for is tolerance of anything outside of his own definition of normal."

"Gregory and Samuel will be kings one day. They can be friends—or enemies—across the mountains."

"Relations between Cartheigh and Svelya are better than they've been in a thousand years—"

"Do you think that will continue if Gregory knows his fellow monarch is a little light in his leggings?"

"No. But still, I can't let him marry Ticia."

"Dorian knows it. He says to hold fast, and he'll try to convince Peter and Gregory to call it off."

"How?"

Chou shrugged. "If anyone can convince Gregory, Dorian can."

"Maybe in the old days. But not now."

"How quickly you lose faith in him."

Eleanor bristled. "I've never lost faith in him. Well…that is to say, I think—"

Chou's black tongue wagged at her like an accusatory finger. He opened his beak, and Eleanor's own voice chided her. *"What if his feelings have changed? What if he's taken a lover? What if it's been too long—"*

"Yes, Yes. I hear you."

"The man is a pillar of dependability. As steadfast as the Fire-iron walls of Eclatant. Constant and predictable, like the swinging tides—"

"Chou, your point is *made*." She smiled. "Although I'm sure Dorian would be annoyed at your description of him as predicable."

"He fancies himself brooding and mysterious, but to those of us who know him, he's actually rather boring."

"In the best way. Don't tell him you think he's boring, either."

Chou took off from her shoulder, and Eleanor returned to her room. She sat on her bed for a longish while. Amusement at Chou's bluntly accurate yet loving assessment of Dorian gave way to a dull sadness. She wondered why she didn't feel ecstatically happy, now that Dorian's love was a certainty once more.

Perhaps it's because I know nothing will change. It will always be this way. Every chance we have will be fleeting, and then the long, uncertain wait until next time will follow.

With her heart still heavy in her chest, she closed her eyes and lit the dragon choker.

CHAPTER 7

JUST THIS ONCE

TWO WEEKS LATER, ELEANOR heard Agnes planned to give Gregory a tour of the smallest ogre camp. She begged Agnes to find a reason for her to accompany them. Agnes convinced Gregory she required Eleanor's companionship by vaguely referencing monthly feminine woes, thus embarrassing the prince into acquiescing. When Eleanor thanked him for allowing her to come along, he grudgingly muttered something to the extent of, "I certainly didn't need to hear all that, but I acknowledge you have discerning eyes. Your observations will be of value."

Eleanor thanked him sincerely, and she and Teardrop made excited preparations. A battalion of Unicorn Guards from Eclatant and thirty-odd Svelyan cavalry chaperoned their trek over the mountains. The party left Nestra and headed southeast, toward the Carthean border. They were in the saddle before dawn and arrived at the camp before noon.

The ogre camp spread out over a high, flat plateau. Not a tree in sight. The rocks were smallish and flattish. Crude shelters made from sticks and mud dotted the plain, and gray smoke leaked in wisps from holes in the roofs. When they appeared on the horizon, the huts looked to be the size of a common farmer's cottage. As they approached, she realized they were too large for human habitation, like perverted dollhouses.

They trotted past the cluster of brick buildings that housed the magicians of the Ogre Watch. Gregory called the procession to a halt before a cluster of five Watchmen. Eleanor peered past their dour faces. She blessed Teardrop's height, for she wouldn't have missed this view for a cave's worth of Fire-iron.

An ogre stretched and spat on the dusty ground as it stepped from its rudimentary home. It had pinkish-gray skin, short legs, and wide bare feet. Its long face tapered at the top in a rounded point. Two sharp front teeth erupted from its square jaw. Those fangs crouched behind floppy black lips as if waiting for something to rend and tear. Its surprisingly large eyes were widely spaced, almond-shaped, and bright purple. Eleanor found them oddly pretty—particularly in comparison to the rest of the beast's face. It smelled, even from this distance, like vomit or sour milk.

Teardrop's muzzle wrinkled, and she jigged sideways as other ogres crept from their huts. The females had tufts of yellow hair hanging down their backs in scrubby braids and pendulous breasts. The juvenile ones shoved one another and yammered away at their parents in whining grunts. The creatures picked up smallish boulders and bit down on them, as if they were walnuts. Pebble-crumbs rained down into their laps. Two young ones got to arguing over a thick branch. They worried it between them like ugly puppies. Their mother—or the female beast Eleanor assumed was mothering them— stepped between them and roared down into their boxy faces. She grabbed the stick and thumped each of her children on the head. They threw rocks at her as they scurried away, but they bounced off the older ogre's hide like oil droplets in a hot skillet. To Eleanor's horror, a huge male squatted and relieved itself not three paces from the entrance to its hut. As the scent of steaming offal hit her nose, the sour milk smell suddenly seemed as sweet as cinnamon.

"Are you pleased you came?" asked Agnes.

"Pleased is probably not the right word," said Eleanor, with her hand over her nose, "but it's certainly interesting. I suppose I expected something like the Dragon Mines...but this...and those creatures..."

"Ogres, like dragons?"

"They *are* roughly the same size—"

"So are pearls and rabbit turds," said Agnes, and Eleanor laughed out loud.

Agnes pointed in the direction of the ogre huts. "Can you see the Restraints? I see them clear as pig blood in dry dirt. How do they appear to you?"

Eleanor squinted and tried to explain. "It's rather like the horizon on a hot day in Solsea. There's a shimmer..." She dismounted and followed Agnes down a rough path toward the Restraints. Puffs of dirt rose up around the witch's dragging hem. Floating debris blended with her magical mist, creating a little greenish dust storm.

As they approached the Restraints, the shifting air disoriented Eleanor. The ground itself seemed to bounce under her feet, and she focused on the back of Agnes's head. The swirl of green mist against the shimmering Restraint made her nauseous. She couldn't discern her distance from the magical barrier, until Agnes held out one white hand. The witch touched the quivering air, and green light dissipated from her palms. Her hand appeared detached, as if she'd plunged it into a fountain.

Eleanor reached out her own hand and then paused.

"Go ahead," said Agnes. "It won't hurt you."

Eleanor's palm met a cold, hard surface. It moved, as if a thin stream of water flowed over it. She placed the other hand against the Restraint and pushed.

Pins and needles shot up her arms. She'd had the same feeling many times as a child, after a jump from the hayloft and a hard landing on both feet. She yelped and jerked her hands away.

"I should have said it won't hurt you if you don't be trying to pass," said Agnes, "but that was only a warning. If you'd made a more purposeful attempt, you'd be on your back twenty paces behind us."

Eleanor rubbed her arms and inched closer to the Restraint. She squinted at it. Tentatively, she reached for the shimmering surface again. "Fascinating..."

One of the ogres, a female, finished her meal and stood. She swiped both hands over her mouth as she walked toward Eleanor and Agnes. A blob of grayish slobber struck the dusty ground. It congealed there, trembling, like a giant slug.

The ogre sped up as she approached. Eleanor instinctively took a few steps to her right, toward Teardrop. To her dismay, the ogre followed suit. She paid no attention to Agnes. She only had giant, angry, purple eyes for Eleanor. She squealed and rushed the Restraint.

Eleanor leapt back, but the ogre knew her own limits. She stormed before the magical wall, a particularly ugly boxer sizing up the competition. Eleanor felt the Restraint bending toward the ogre like a flexed bow. The beast screamed, but thankfully the Restraint muted the sound. She grabbed a rock, a crude pot, and a rotted animal carcass and threw them, like a disappointed theatergoer heckling a bad actress. The projectiles bounced off the Restraint and back into her face. She collapsed on her knees and clasped her hands over her head. She rocked to and fro and muttered in her guttural language.

Eleanor jumped when Teardrop's mane brushed her shoulder. "Is she praying?" the mare asked.

"What are you doing to the beast?" One of the Watchmen appeared from nowhere and took Eleanor's elbow. He tugged her away from the Restraint. Teardrop snorted a warning. He dropped Eleanor's arm, but he kept shooing her away from the angry ogre.

"Nothing!" said Eleanor. "I didn't do anything."

"Must be something," said the magician in the thickest Svelyan accent imaginable. His eyes widened. "That crown!"

Eleanor's hand went to the modest Fire-iron tiara on her head. Gregory insisted she wear some insignia of her rank whenever they made any kind of public appearance in Svelya. He himself had hung his grandfather's Fire-iron shield, engraved with an ornate D, on his saddle. Since she didn't have any elaborate weapons, she'd resorted to the smallest, simplest crown she had.

"You are—how do you say it? Provisioning it!" The enraged magician hopped along the path, as if his boots were on fire.

"You mean provoking?" Eleanor and Teardrop followed him. "I'm sorry, I didn't—"

Agnes interrupted with some words in Svelyan. The magician glared at her and spewed a few guttural sentences. He wasn't particularly tall, but he towered over the tiny witch. No matter. The green light swirling from her eyes made up for her diminutive stature.

"He says the ogres hate royalty," said Agnes. "Since they once fought the kings of the known nations and ended up trapped in this place."

"That makes me feel a bit better," said Eleanor as the Watchmen pointed at her, and the ogre, and rambled on in Svelyan. "For a moment, I felt like she wanted to slaughter me, personally."

"He says the ogress would find you a very worthy sacrifice to Cra. She'd be particularly happy to remove your head from your shoulders with that crown upon it."

"When you put it that way, I suppose it is personal." Eleanor removed the tiara and slid it into her rucksack.

"Stay away from the wall," said the magician. "For the sake of HighGod, keep that *miskar* out of sight." He pulled his cloak around his face and returned to the Restraint. Eleanor and Agnes's explorations had left dark spots on the wall. The spots disappeared as the magician chanted, and the Restraint became shimmering air again.

Eleanor walked backwards and watched him work. The ogre sat back on her knees but had gone eerily silent. She pointed at Eleanor with one long finger, and then drew an *X* across her own chest.

As Eleanor swung into the saddle, a jumping rope song flashed through her mind.

How I miss my love when we're apart

I'll count the hops with a cross-my-heart…

The ogre's gesture had nothing to do with love and everything to do with dismemberment. Eleanor shivered. In less than an hour, she had seen quite enough of ogres. No wonder they worshipped their own bizarre god. If there was a HighGod-forsaken species in the world, it lived behind those Restraints.

Eleanor and Teardrop retreated to the Watchmen's village. The circular settlement of eight brick houses surrounded a two-story stone library and a squat brick and stone kitchen. Eleanor sat at a long wooden table beside the well. A magician offered her a cup of tea. She took it with trembling hands and inhaled the odd reddish steam. She sipped. The tea tasted of mint, with a hint of cranberry. A soothing combination.

"You seem unnerved." Teardrop snuffed at Eleanor's tea.

"It's not every day one is threatened by an ogre. I assume *miskar* means *tiara*. Or something comparable. That ogress on her knees reminded me of a Godsman at penance. Agnes is right. Ogres may be dirty, but they're not stupid."

Eleanor surveyed the desolate land around her. Even a hundred paces from the nearest Restraint, the air smelled sour with ogre piss, as if an army of territorial tomcats had sprayed the magicians' village. "I don't see how these Watchmen seek out this life—steady pay or not."

She finished her tea, and a boring hour of unchanging scenery crept by. She and Teardrop made small talk, but finally, they settled into comfortable silence. The mare dozed on her feet. Her tail swished methodically, like a sweeping broom on a marble floor. Eleanor rested her head on her forearms. She covered her nose, but the acrid air penetrated the smell of her leather gloves. She hoped Gregory and Agnes would not be too long in their inspection.

She reached into her saddlebag and removed Hazelbeth's kaleidoscope. She thought to look in on her girls, but the kaleidoscope had other ideas.

At first, she didn't recognize the room that took shape in the swirling colors. A tall four poster bed, rich purple and green bed curtains, and a gold carpet embroidered with orange flames. She tilted the kaleidoscope and recognized a Fire-iron throne beside the window. Her father-in-law's thrones were all decorated with emeralds, diamonds, and amethysts. This must be King Casper's bedroom.

She blushed, for it was highly improper to spy on one's sovereign, but curiosity won out over deference. Servants came and went from the bed. They whispered between themselves. She turned the handle, and the view focused on a roundish lump in the bed.

Eleanor gasped. King Casper lay on his back with is hands folded across his chest. His face was pale. His graying hair splattered across his forehead.

HighGod, he's dead, she thought, until she detected the weak rise and fall of his chest. He shifted under the covers, and Eleanor made out a faint moan. A pageboy rushed to the bedside with a cup. Two of the lad's fellows lifted the king to a half-sitting position, and the first boy held the cup to his lips. He swallowed and coughed. Water and spit sprayed all over his helpers. A powerful healer Eleanor recognized from Afar Creek gently shooed the boys out of the way. The witch lay a cloth on Casper's forehead. Another healer touched her shoulder, and the women exchanged a few quiet words Eleanor would have given her pinky finger to hear.

Not dead, but surely very ill. The witches continued their consultation. Gregory must not know, for she'd heard nothing about it. Just as she was about to mount up and find him, his little retinue trotted into the village.

"Ah, Eleanor," he said as Vigor approached. "There you are. I heard about some mess with an ogre. What happened?"

"Never mind that…look!" She stood on tiptoe beside Vigor and handed him the kaleidoscope.

He looked as if she'd offered him a set of toy soldiers or a stuffed dragon. "I don't have time for amusements. We need to return to Gammonreil before dark."

"It's not a toy. Hazelbeth made it for me." He crossed his arms over his chest, but she continued. "It can show us things. Things we can't normally see!" She didn't want to inform the surrounding Svelyan delegation that King Casper might be on his deathbed.

Gregory sighed and took the scope. Eleanor rested a hand on Vigor's silky hide as he squinted into it. "Lovely. Desmarais purple. Desmarais green. It has good taste in colors."

She snatched it from him with a scowl. She peered into the scope, but the image of Casper's bedroom had faded to a montage of royal colors. She turned the scope in the correct direction, but this time it went straight to her children's nursery. For the first time, that view disappointed her.

She asked Gregory to dismount. Once he was on his feet, she tugged him away from the rest of their party. "I saw your father in the kaleidoscope. He's very ill."

"Impossible. We'd have heard something."

"I'm telling you, Gregory. Casper is very sick. The witches were there—"

"Maybe he just has a headache or a bellyache. You know how fat he's gotten lately."

"I thought him dead until he moved!"

Gregory laughed, but his hands went to his hair. "No Desmarais king has ever died in his bed before age seventy. You can kill us on the battlefield, but not in the prime of life—"

"Your father is sixty-seven—"

"Enough. I'm sure he's fine. A party arrives from Eclatant tomorrow—"

"You didn't tell me we were expecting anyone from home!"

"—and I'm sure they will be able to give us a positive report on all fronts. Now let me finish my business. I want to get back to the palace. I'll need to bathe overnight in a tub of mint leaves to rid this stench from my skin. I'm parched. Where's my flask?"

She watched his retreating back as he called for water. His avoidance of her question and sudden interest in personal hygiene, hinted at the identity of one of the impending Carthean visitors. A person she had absolutely no desire to see.

In comparison to Sylvia Easton Fleetwood, Duchess of Harveston, the angry female ogre seemed like wonderful company.

Eleanor watched her stepsister gracefully maneuver between clusters of Svelyan courtiers, a seasoned diplomatic in petticoats. Sylvia charmed the natives, even if she couldn't speak their language. They nodded their approval and waited patiently for her to grace them with a smile. She wore a modest black Svelyan gown trimmed with white rabbit fur. It was demure enough to be unthreatening to the ladies, yet still gorgeous enough to incite admiration from the men. Her dark hair and eyes, hint of alabaster cleavage, and narrow waist needed little ornamentation. If anything, she looked lovelier in Svelyan modesty than she'd ever been in more risqué Carthean fashions. A familiar concoction of emotions spun in Eleanor's stomach—a poorly mixed potion of irritation, suspicion, and begrudging admiration. Sylvia hung on Gregory's arm, and for his part, he looked perfectly happy to show her off, like a zookeeper revealing the last of a particularly rare species.

Eleanor had wild animals on her mind on this MidWinter evening. It was the beginning of the weeklong Waning Fest. Given their nation's relatively frigid climate, she'd curiously looked forward the Svelyan take on the beloved winter holiday. They did not disappoint. She knew the Waning Fest included a circus, but she never imagined the spectacle awaiting her.

She stood inside the *Tante Carell d'Jun*, the Tent of Beasts and Balance. It was a massive circular room, built directly into the rocky western side of Devery Island. The tenting, made of the thickest silk Eleanor had ever seen, hung between the rock formations in rich layers of red, black, and silver toile. The ceiling met in a pinnacle that towered over her head like the spire of a great chapel.

Six rings spread across the tent. They contained all manner of exotic entertainment, from conjuring magicians to stumbling funnymen to trained animal acts featuring beasts Eleanor had read about in her studies of foreign fauna. Swings hung from the ceiling, and acrobats dangled over the courtiers' heads like spinning human chandeliers. The tent hummed with conflicting musical accompaniment, lowing and screeching animals, and the *ooohs* of the crowd. It smelled of fried sweetbread and spilt beer, animal shit, and flower petals. Eleanor wandered between the rings with Chou on her shoulder and a wine goblet in her hand. The wine quickly made its way from her mouth to her bloodstream, then diffused its buzzing jolliness into her head.

"What in the name of a dragon's hot backside is that?" Chou flapped his wings in the direction of the fourth tent, where several blue gray beasts were entertaining an enthusiastic crowd.

"Elfantas?" Eleanor asked, in reference to the tusked creatures. Their Talessee trainer shouted at them in his lyrical native language. The largest elfanta blasted air through its three-pronged trunk in a jaunty, harmonious tune that reminded Eleanor of a bugle chorus. A pair of white rabbits the size of hunting hounds leapt onto the elfanta's head and turned backflips in time with its song.

"No," said Chou. "Past the elfantas."

"Let us see, shall we?"

Eleanor and Chou maneuvered toward the farthest ring. It was rather hidden in the shadows but still drew a substantial crowd. She noticed Gregory and Sylvia on the far side, but the performance before her quickly subsumed her attention.

"It seems the Svelyans are not as conservative as we thought," said Chou.

A man and a woman, naked but painted solid gold from head to toe, met in the middle of the ring. Some unseen magician cast a soft glow on them, and their bodies shimmered like fallen stars. Both were tightly muscled and indescribably lithe—two perfect sculptures carved out of decorated human flesh. The woman wore her short hair slicked against her head, and their eyes stood out against their golden faces. They faced each other. Their hands touched, and the crowd went silent.

They fell against each other and twisted apart. The man caught the woman's hand and pulled her to his chest. His back bent at an impossible angle, and she clung to him as his hands met the sandy floor behind them. She lay on top of him, so they formed a monochromatic rainbow.

There was no music, and no ambient sound to drown out the hullaballoo behind her, but Eleanor could almost hear the contortionist's breathing. *They're making love*, she thought.

The performance continued. The woman moved on top of the man, her breasts heaving and sliding over his chiseled torso. Eleanor's wine goblet kept coming to her lips, until she realized she'd been sipping at an empty glass. She exhaled, and between holding her breath and the wine, her head spun.

The man lifted the woman from behind. His hands cupped her breasts, and her legs locked around his haunches. He fell on his knees and seemed to take her from behind. His hands slid from her hips to her shoulders, and he spun her around. She wrapped her arms around his neck, and each one's face disappeared into the other's shoulder. They went still, and the lights blinked out. The audience heaved a collective sigh of pent up anticipation. The magicians slowly raised the lights. The dancers had disappeared.

Chou sputtered in Eleanor's ear. "HighGod, how very...ahem... it seems Gregory and the duchess were inspired to make it an early evening."

Eleanor briefly glanced in the direction of the spot recently occupied by her husband and his mistress, until another more interesting person found his way into her field of vision.

Dorian stood beside the ring. He'd removed his thick Svelyan fur cloak, revealing a simple cream-colored tunic, not unlike the one he'd worn the night Eleanor met him fourteen years ago. He'd pushed up the sleeves. Eleanor thought of his bare forearms, laced with prominent veins, and his long fingers. They stared at each other across the empty ring. She took a step in his direction.

"Eleanor—don't." Chou's voice took on a panicked twitter. "Not here. You must take care—"

"Hush, Chou." She blinked, her head swimming with wine and not a little bit of lust. "Fly off now, will you?"

"Oh, damn." He nipped at her ear but did as she asked.

Eleanor followed the edge of the ring, and Dorian did the same. They circled one another, like water flowing inevitably down a drain. She spun off, without any real sense of where she was going. She watched him over her shoulder. His green eyes followed her through the swirling crowds. Past the dangling legs of the acrobats. Around the runaway enchantments of the magicians: dancing bubbles, spinning firecrackers, cascades of Waning snow. As the hour grew late, the revelers grew drunker, but Dorian looked as unflappable as ever. He followed Eleanor and took sips from a Fire-iron flask.

She paused at the tent's edge, before a row of tiered wooden benches anchored in a rock wall. Guests dotted the seating, row after row of brown and gray and black robes. Red curtains hung from both ends of the structure. Eleanor stood on one end, Dorian twenty paces away on the other.

She pulled back the curtain and peered into the semi-darkness below the benches. Flickering light streamed through the gaps between the seating and the observing courtiers' legs, adding further swirl to Eleanor's spinning head. The far curtain opened, and Dorian stepped into the pulsating darkness.

The came together like the golden dancers in the circus ring. Eleanor reclined on a spare bench and pulled Dorian down with her. He ran his hands over her cheeks and down her nose, and she turned her face into his open palm. The music from beyond the walls of benches faded into the background. Eleanor recognized no danger in that moment. If someone screamed her name, she would not have noticed. She heard nothing but the brush of Dorian's hands on her skin and his quick breathing.

She kept her eyes open when he kissed her, so to commit the look on his face to memory. Streaks of light crossed his chin and his nose and left his eyes in darkness, but she knew he was watching her reaction to his hands. He always did.

He hoisted her skirts, and they fell on either side of the bench, like a spray of springtime phlox dressed in brown winter velvet. His hands were gentle on her hips and then between her legs. He whispered in her ear as he stroked her. "I wish we had more time…but…"

"Shhh…I'm ready." She reached down and unbuckled his belt.

He slid into her with the ease of a well-carved key into the correct lock. She groaned against his chest and tugged at his tunic, wishing for all the world the layers of fabric between them would disappear. She wanted to be as naked and free as the golden dancers. He braced his arms against her ears on the wooden bench. His mouth against hers tasted of whiskey, but it didn't bother her. There was a sweet headiness to the whole thing. His whiskey, her wine.

He moved quickly inside her, and she arched her hips toward him. The bench scratched her bare shoulders, but her petticoats saved her tailbone. She wrapped her legs around him, pinning him to her, and with his weight, herself to the bench. She took hold of his hair in one hand and a gripped his half-dropped leggings in the other. She bit his lip and ground her hips into his.

He started to pull away from her, as he always did, but she held on. "No—don't. Just this one time." She pulled his face toward her chest and clenched at him with her legs.

He drove into her, once, twice...and cried out. For a moment, his eyes appeared in the striped light, and Eleanor climaxed with him. He collapsed onto her chest. She clung to him, refusing to let go.

Dorian lay on top of her, kissing her neck and saying her name, and Eleanor didn't think of anything else. She didn't think of a baby. It was just this once.

Svelyan culture sometimes flummoxed Eleanor. Modest clothes and naked dancers didn't seem to mesh, nor did their dichotomous dining habits. Dinners at Gammonreil were more formal than any she'd suffered through at Eclatant, with precise manners, meticulously arranged seating charts, and the most miniscule of polite small talk. The other meals, however, were a sort of culinary free for all. The court took breakfast and lunch at long tables in an oblong dining room. Lords and ladies came and went from the tables at their leisure, with no apparent care for who sat with who or who ate what with which fork. Servants bustled about, dropping off platters of food and pitchers of juice and ale, and the courtiers served themselves from silver ladles. Eleanor wished she spoke Svelyan, as to join in the laughter and debate. She once watched a magician throw a cherry at an old man's forehead during a spirited argument, perhaps about politics or religion. The cherry rebounded into the man's bowl and exploded, dousing him with onion soup.

The morning after her circus rendezvous with Dorian, Eleanor came upon Sylvia in the raucous dining room. The duchess looked remarkably bright eyed, while Eleanor herself had risen early because her pounding head prevented her from sleeping until noon. Within seconds of waking, the previous evening's liaison came back to her. Anxiety made her head hurt worse. She felt as if ogres were running through her brain in cement boots, screaming warnings and bashing their fists on the inside of her skull. Part of her wanted to hide in bed all day, but the braver side of her nature sought the reassurance of the breakfast hall. If no one treated her with any kind of suspicion, surely that must mean she and Dorian were safe.

She'd avoided the mirror as she left her bedroom, but she knew the wine had puffed her face. She bit the inside of her cheek at Sylvia's glowing friskiness. The duchess merrily plastered butter on her toast, as if she'd just awoken from twelve hours of sober sleep in a ten-layer feather bed fanned by angels.

One of the servants waved Eleanor in Sylvia's direction. It must have made sense for the two women, who shared a common language, to sit together. He didn't know they also shared a lifetime of ill-will and competition.

"Good morning, Sister," Sylvia said with a smile as Eleanor slid into the chair beside her.

"And to you."

"Did you sleep well? I tossed and turned all night!"

Eleanor briefly contemplated Gregory's abrupt lovemaking. "All night? That is saying something." She accepted a napkin and a glass of pear juice from the grinning servant. She swallowed juice in three gulps and set the goblet on the table. The pounding in her head got louder with the sudden cold. The servant set a heaping plate of turkey eggs mixed with mushrooms and bacon before her. The greasy smell turned her stomach. "Can you pass the toast?"

Sylvia obliged and then scooped up a hefty serving of eggs. The gooey concoction landed on her plate with a splat. "Perhaps it's not ladylike, but I've such an appetite today! Physical exertion, you know. But the witches do say it's healthy." Sylvia waved her egg-laden fork. Bits of yellow goo flew across the table, only to be swiped up by a passing servant before they had a chance to congeal.

Eleanor looked around the dining room. While she and Sylvia—as the visiting prince's wife and mistress, respectively—attracted some attention, she saw nothing more than polite curiosity on the faces of the breakfasting courtiers. No one pointed at her. She didn't detect the shape of Lord Brandling's name on anyone's lips or catch it in any of the jovial conversation around her. Eleanor relaxed some and took the reins of the conversation. "How fares King Casper?"

"Fine. Fat and grouchy, as always."

Eleanor frowned. "He's not ill? Or indisposed?"

"No. He sent me off with a wave, a kiss, and his compliments to John-Caleb. I can't believe he's soon to be five. Such a strong boy. Very sturdy, and such thick hair." Sylvia always went out of her way to find a physical resemblance between her suspected royal bastard and the Desmarais family, for, to her chagrin, John-Caleb was her own spitting image. "His shoulders are *very* broad, you know."

"You're certain the king is well?"

"Yes. Why should I say he was if he wasn't?"

Eleanor thoughtfully chewed her toast. The kaleidoscope couldn't have lied, but it had been four days since her visit to the Ogre camp. Shouldn't they have heard something by now? If Sylvia had come from Eclatant…

Gregory slid into the chair across from Eleanor and Sylvia. "Good morning, ladies," he said, as if it were perfectly normal to sup with one's wife and one's mistress. "You're both looking lovely."

Sylvia beamed at him. "You're looking well-used, sire."

Gregory laughed. "I'm feeling thus. How nice to see the two of you sharing a table." His jovial good humor further assuaged Eleanor's nerves. Surely if he had any suspicions about last night he wouldn't be sitting here giggling away amidst the cereal and sausages.

"Our seating arrangement is a courtesy to the servants, not a choice." Eleanor decided to retire to her chamber with her headache and her dignity. She stood to leave.

Sylvia leaned across the table. "I'm sure you wanted to see John-Caleb—"

"Ah...probably not the best place for children," said Gregory. "A diplomatic visit—"

"—but I thought it too cold for him up here. We can't be risking his health. I left him in Harveston with my mother."

Eleanor stopped. "You've been to Harveston?"

"Yes."

"You didn't come directly from Eclatant?"

Sylvia's jaw jutted, so she resembled an irritable lapdog. "I left Eclatant two weeks ago."

"So you wouldn't know if the king has been—"

At that moment, Dorian stormed into the dining room. A flurry of high-ranking Svelyan courtiers followed him, including Agnes. The servants scrambled to get out of Dorian's way. They precariously balanced plates of food and pitchers like jugglers trying to manage too many balls. Dorian made a straight line for Gregory and fell to his knees.

"Your Highness. We've received word from Eclatant. Your father, King Casper, has gone on to HighGod."

CHAPTER 8

A HUNDRED MILES FROM NOWHERE

ELEANOR SAT ON TEARDROP'S back on the Gammonreil Bridge. Her eyes stung, but she didn't know whether to blame it on the river wind, exhaustion, or grief. She'd not slept in the twenty-four hours since the messenger brought new of Casper's death, and she'd spent several of those sleepless hours crying. She'd had a strange relationship with her father-in-law, but there had always been a quiet respect between them. He'd supported her when Gregory had not, and on one memorable occasion, he told her of his faith in her ability to guide the prince when he became king. Now the hour was upon them all, and Eleanor already longed for the comfort of Casper's gruff, steady leadership. She could almost feel Carthean disquiet floating across the mountains and settling over Gregory's traveling party like mist over warm water. Chou Chou curled in the pocket of Eleanor's cloak. She stroked his head. "Stay still. We'll ride hard, and you might fall out."

He responded by clenching his talons around her fingers and nibbling on her palm.

Samuel and Agnes stood with Dorian and Gregory on the ground beside Teardrop. King Peter sat in an invalid's wheeled chair. "You know the route?" King Peter said in a low voice.

Gregory nodded. They would not take the direct route to Cartheigh. Peter had suggested a more roundabout way through the mountains to the Dragon Mines. Longer, but fewer travelers. Gregory's passage would be less noticeable.

Gregory clasped hands with King Peter, then Samuel, and finally, he kissed Agnes's cheek. Eleanor's eyes burned again as she said goodbye to Agnes. "Thank you. You've been a great friend to me these last months."

Agnes squeezed Eleanor's hands between her own. To Eleanor's surprise, a few greenish tears tracked down her face. The witch nodded without speaking and pressed her lips together. Eleanor was further touched that such a powerful woman would so feel her absence.

Gregory climbed onto Vigor's broad back and shouted to the Unicorn Guard. Gregory had allowed Dorian the privilege of unicorn-back. His mount, a white unicorn stallion, was beautiful and powerful, but he could not possibly reassure him like Senné, his old friend and companion. *How Dorian must pine for Senné!* she thought. If Gregory ever reclaimed Teardrop, she'd feel the same way.

Gregory addressed the crowd. "Thank you for your hospitality. Cartheigh will always remember the good will of our Svelyan neighbors. I leave you with a heavy heart, but one that is warmed by the fire of your friendship."

The crowd called out blessings in Svelyan and fractured Carthean. The Unicorn Guard filled in the spaces around Gregory and Vigor, and Eleanor and Teardrop, like a shining mass of melted snow. She glanced over her shoulder at Dorian, who had casually taken up the position on her left flank. She touched the spot on her neck where the dragon choker hid under a wolfskin dragon robe. She felt the necklace there, a nodule in an expanse of warm fur. Dorian nodded, a barely perceptible gesture that comforted her more than the raised lances of the soldiers around her. The procession started toward the gates of Nestra.

"We're going home," said Eleanor to Teardrop.

"We are. Home to a different world."

"It's still Eclatant."

"A new king. A new Eclatant. They are one in the same."

Dorian watched the fire and, as Eleanor had imagined, he missed Senné. His mount was a fine one, but he longed for Senné's quiet, rational counsel. Unicorns drifted around the edge of the campsite. The flames glanced off their slivery hides and threw orange and yellow reflections into Dorian's face. He always felt safest when Senné stood guard with him. It was like having a bit of nighttime on your side.

He glanced at Eleanor and Gregory's tent, but for once the thought of them side-by-side under a heap of dragon robes didn't distract him from his other worries. He looked up at the mountains surrounding the campsite and listened to the unicorns and the mutters of the few soldiers who had yet to fall asleep. He shivered despite the heavy dragon robe draped over his shoulders. Without the fire, each breath would be like inhaling cold granite.

Dorian had always known this day would come. While he loved the old king and would never wish him harm, he had looked forward to Gregory assuming the throne. Now, given the country's shaky allegiances, and Ezra Oliver's continued elusiveness, he wished King Casper had lived another twenty years. Casper had been a stabilizer, and a great one for gathering men of talent and opinion around him. Gregory took few opinions but his own, and until almost five years ago, Dorian's. He wanted to help the prince, and Casper had expected it of him, but he wasn't sure how to do so when he and Gregory barely spoke.

A tent flap rustled behind him. Dorian turned, hoping it would be Eleanor, but the prince emerged with a bearskin dragon robe draped around his shoulders. He shuffled to the edge of the firelight and took a piss into the darkness. He started back to the tent, before apparently changing his mind and approaching the fire.

"Are you tired? I'm awake. I can watch." Gregory ran his fingers through his hair. It stayed up even when he lowered his hands.

"I'm fine. It's not safe for you to watch."

"We're a hundred miles from nowhere. No one out here but a few lost giant buzzards."

"Get some sleep, Your Highness."

Gregory sat down instead. "You're grinding your teeth. What's wrong?"

Dorian's mouth twitched at Gregory's observation. The prince knew him well. He pulled a parchment map from his saddlebag and unrolled it. "I just wonder about our route. If we go this way"—he traced a northern pass—"no one will know where we are."

"Why should that matter? Only King Peter and his son and the witch know our plan."

"You're the king—"

"Not until the coronation."

"—and it just seems wise to take every precaution."

Gregory studied the map and then shook his head. "It will add at least a day to the journey."

"Two."

"I need to get back. As soon as possible."

"But our current route takes us through the Northern Swamps. They're even more treacherous than the Great Marshlands around the Dragon Mines. There's one path. Single file. If we're attacked, we'll have no cover."

"Who would attack us? It's like the end of the earth out there. No one knows we're taking a route other than the one that brought us here."

"Greg—"

"We're staying the course. It's too long as it is."

"I—"

"No. Everything has changed, Dorian. The crown is the only thing that matters. I must get to Eclatant." He exhaled, and Dorian saw his breath in the firelight. "You of all people should understand that."

"Of course, I understand it." Dorian rarely lost his temper, but he felt its warmth in his face, as if someone had stoked the fire. "It won't matter how long the route is, if you don't even make it to Eclatant!"

Gregory didn't respond for a long moment. "Do you suppose to tell your king where he shall go?"

Dorian pressed his fingers into his eyes. "Of course not, Your Highness."

"Good. Because I'll tell you where you can go. You can go fuck yourself." He stood, and with the thick robes draped around his chest and his wild hair, he looked like an exasperated lion. He started to return to his tent but stopped and squinted into the darkness. "The unicorns."

Dorian joined the prince on his feet. Several unicorns were indeed whinnying, although they didn't sound particularly alarmed. Just curious. Dorian drew his sword at the sound of clopping hooves.

A heavy gray warhorse appeared in the firelight. Its rider slid to the ground and landed nimbly on both feet. Even with a heavy black robe across his shoulders and draping his face, Dorian recognized the lithe form.

Prince Samuel pushed back the fur hood. Dorian grimaced. Samuel had black eye, a lacerated upper lip, and a gash across his left cheek. "Might I join you, sirs? It's been a cold ride."

The soldiers carried bags of medicinal herbs and bandages, and as the lone woman in the party, the task fell to Eleanor to repair Samuel's damaged face. Although she had little knowledge of healing arts, she had a mother's touch and sympathy, and Samuel relaxed under her gentle fingers.

His story came out. His father's valet had caught Samuel in an indelicate position with Louis, his burly blond lover. Louis managed to get away, and Samuel bore the brunt of King Peter's rage. "I think it wounded his pride more than anything," Samuel said to Eleanor as she dabbed his swollen forehead. "The humiliation of owning up to his son's perversion. At least Louis escaped. Although I am having no idea where he is, nor any way to find him." For the first time since she'd begun her ministrations, a few tears tracked down Samuel's cheeks.

"Try not to cry, dear," she said. "It will sting. I'm sure you'll find him." She felt for Samuel. He would have more trouble than the average heartbroken young man when he started looking for like-minded fish in the sea.

Dorian gave Gregory a vague explanation for the prince's presence—something about a family disagreement. Gregory was too distracted to ask for more information, but he balked at taking Samuel with them. Eventually, he acknowledged he'd taken unintentional custody of the heir to the Svelyan throne. It wouldn't do to send a fellow crown prince traipsing across the mountains without protection. He decided Samuel would accompany them to Eclatant, and then he would return to his father. Samuel paled at this declaration but relaxed when Dorian squeezed his shoulder.

On the third day of the journey, they reached the Northern Swamps, a vast expanse of boggy, flat land at the edge of the foothills. Scrubby bushes dotted the landscape, like abandoned piles of dirty clothes. A raised dirt path meandered through interconnected pools of stagnant water. The rancid smell of rotten vegetation hung over the travelers' heads. Only the screeches of a few circling hawks and the unicorns' hoofbeats broke the still silence.

Chou peaked from Eleanor's pocket. She figured he'd have something to say about the terrain, but for once, he conveyed his opinion with his silent retreat back into her robe. Teardrop fell in line behind Vigor, in the center of the line of thirty unicorns, near as many martial magicians mounted on horses, and Samuel's gray charger. The first of the Unicorn Guard stepped onto the path. The stallion's hooves dislodged a few pebbles, and they landed in the pool below in a series of *ker-plunks* that rousted an algae-covered turtle. It hissed at them and then disappeared into the dark water.

"It will take all afternoon to cross the swamps," Gregory called over his shoulder. "We'll eat as we ride. Get comfortable."

Eleanor daydreamed as the sun rose higher. She thought, as she always did when given long stretches of time to just that, of her son, Nathan. He'd be nine this year and training his own unicorn. One of Vigor's sons, of course. She squinted at Gregory in front of her and tried to shrink him down to nine-year-old size. The wind lifted his auburn hair, just a hair darker than Nathan's had been in life. The old grief, so familiar that she no longer remembered life without it, stood up in her throat and stretched.

Teardrop's ears had been turning in attentive semi-circles. They suddenly pricked and framed Gregory's broad back between them. "What's that sound?"

Eleanor held her breath and listened. A *blip, blip, blip*...much like the drip of a light summer rain, but the sky above them remained a brilliant winter blue. She looked down at Teardrop's feet.

The swamp around them came to life. Tiny fish bounced along the water's murky surface. Their silvery sides flashed in the bright sunlight, reminding Eleanor of Agnes's dancing fish display during her first party at Gammonreil. Another turtle made its plodding way up the bank onto the path. Assorted snakes and frogs slithered and hopped around and past it, with little care for a hundred deadly, smacking unicorn hooves. Chou emerged again. "They're on the move. Why?"

Gregory called the procession to a halt and dismounted. He kicked a passing lizard. "What the dragonshit is this?" he muttered. "Dorian!"

Dorian's unicorn edged his way past the others, nearly sending several younger, lighter stallions into the brink with the agitated fishes.

A fat swamp rat ran between Vigor's legs. Dorian's brow furrowed. "I don't like this. Greg, mount up."

The sound of sloshing water, much louder than any aquatic disturbance caused by the frantic minnows and frustrated frogs, jerked Eleanor's attention back to the swamp. The water gurgled, and two white eyes appeared in the black water.

It was a catfish. A bristly leviathan. It loomed out of the water, roughly the size of a bull and propelled by its tail. Black scales on its back faded to sickish gray on its flat belly. Its mouth was a gaping cavern framed by eight spiky whispers, each one the length of Eleanor's arm. It grunted out a HighGod-forsaken noise that started as a low moan and ended in a bark. It smelled of long submerged dirt.

Eleanor screamed. Chou burst from her pocket like a sprung arrow. He squawked in terror and shot toward the sky.

Dorian grabbed Gregory's shoulder. "Mount up!" he yelled. The water churned around them as more catfish, each one as huge and smelly and malevolent as the last, rose out of the water.

Gregory stumbled against Vigor. He stared at the giant fish in front of him, as if confronted by a warped reflection of himself. The fish's fins flapped like stubby wings, and it bark-mooed into his face.

Gregory leapt onto Vigor's back and drew his sword. He slashed at the fish, and a hunk of its lip landed in the roiling water below it. It barked again and hurled itself at Vigor's legs. The stallion hadn't expected it and was nearly tossed into the water on the other side of the path. The strip of land between the two lines of fish suddenly seemed absurdly narrow. Eleanor could have walked across it in a few paces. They had nowhere to go but forward.

The fish's powerful tail swatted and whacked at Vigor's dancing legs. It roiled and flailed and landed in the water on the other side of the path.

Dorian swatted Vigor's rump. "Ride on! Take Eleanor and ride on!"

More huge fish hurled themselves at the unicorns and horses in a barrage of muscular cannonballs. The martials shot fireballs at them, and the Unicorn Guard slashed at them with swords and knives, but their scaly hides were thick. The cramped space put the unicorns at a disadvantage, for their long horns were ineffective weapons against several tons of writhing fish meat under their own feet. They did more damage with their sharp hooves.

Gregory hung from Vigor's back by one leg. He reached out over the water, trying to strike the fish before they tripped Vigor. The soldiers around him shot arrows at the beasts.

"Dammit, Gregory!" Dorian pulled an arrow from his own quiver and fired, striking one of the beasts in the eye. It rolled onto its back as Dorian aimed again. "You must get to Eclatant! Remember the *crown*, man!"

That word broke through Gregory's battle lust. He gave Vigor his head, and once they maneuvered past the rest of the frantic Guard, the stallion took off headlong down the narrow path. Teardrop followed, her breath coming in frantic rasps. Several fish followed them like dolphins after a fishing boat. They jumped over shallows and rocks with surprising grace. Vigor and Teardrop leapt them when they flung themselves across the path. Each fish was a fence in a hunt where they'd become the foxes.

The creatures couldn't possibly keep up with the unicorns' breakneck pace. Eleanor felt sure they'd escape until two fish flopped into Vigor's path. He leapt the first monstrosity but didn't have space to clear the next one. His forelegs clipped the second fish, and he stumbled. Gregory flew over his head and rolled on his shoulder. Teardrop reared, narrowly missing Vigor, and Eleanor clung to her neck. Vigor tried to regain his footing, but a third catfish struck him squarely on his right side. Both unicorn and fish landed in the bog.

"Vigor!" Gregory slid down the shallow bank, his sword drawn.

Teardrop tossed her head. "Should we go on? I don't know. I don't know!"

Another catfish landed with a jelly-like thump between Teardrop and Gregory. Its tail was a shockingly effective method of propulsion. It squirmed toward Teardrop. A gaping mouth gnashed around repetitive, droning barks.

Chou dropped from the sky and landed on the fish's head. In one quick slash of his black beak, he ripped its eye from the socket. With the persistence of an unusually quick slug to a vat of beer, the fish kept coming. Chou flitted from one side of its flat head to the other, slashing away in a vain attempt to distract it. Teardrop lowered her horn, and Eleanor felt frantically at her pockets for a weapon. She raged at her lack of a sword, but Gregory had never seen fit to allow her to defend herself.

She shoved her hand into her saddle bag and emerged with the sharpest item she had on hand: a hoof pick. She gripped the pick by its polished wooden handle, cocked her arm, and threw it.

Eleanor had never wielded a hoof pick in any endeavor aside from equine husbandry, but by some miracle, the two Fire-iron prongs found their mark. They buried themselves in the catfish's head, between its remaining eye and the empty socket. The fish thrashed and flipped over on its back. It went still, but for the death twitches of its tail.

Chou landed between Eleanor's shoulder blades. Gregory stood knee-deep in the dark water. He screamed his unicorn's name and hacked away at the giant catfish, but he couldn't reach far enough to do much damage other than a few deep cuts and a severed fin. Three fish swarmed Vigor and pushed him farther into the murky water. The stallion's head appeared and disappeared as he fought for breath.

"HighGod. HighGod. HighGod," said Chou.

"Teardrop," said Eleanor, "we have to help him."

Teardrop whinnied and took a few steps to the edge of the path, but Vigor resurfaced. His brown eyes rolled back to the whites. Murky water dripped from his impenetrable hide in dark streams, and against the water, his coat looked whiter than ever. His lips curled away from his teeth. He screamed a high, shrill stallion's call. It was a command.

"He wants us to go on. Take Gregory," said Teardrop.

"No! We can't leave him," Eleanor said.

"It's what he wants. He will sacrifice himself."

As crucial seconds passed, it became clear they couldn't help Vigor. Soon Gregory would fall into the water, or one of the fish would drag him in. Vigor screamed again and bit one of his attackers. Blackish blood ran down his muzzle. The fish surged over him, and his head disappeared.

"Gregory! We must go!" Eleanor said.

Gregory shook his head. Teardrop eased to the edge of the path. "Remember the crown, Your Highness."

"Fuck the crown!" Gregory cried. "I've left my men—I won't leave my stallion!"

Vigor's head appeared again. He drew a rasping breath that tore at Eleanor's heart. Mighty as unicorns were, like all other land-dwelling beings, they needed air. His weakening voice rang out again. This time, he used his old friend's name. "Gregory—please!"

Gregory lowered his sword. His free hand went to his hair as he backed up the bank. He slashed at the belly of the fish Eleanor had killed. Putrid guts spilled onto the path. Chou moaned, and Eleanor put a hand over her nose. Gregory sheathed his sword and took Eleanor's hand. He swung onto Teardrop's back. Teardrop leapt the split fish and raced for the end of the path, now visible a few miles in the distance. Gregory sobbed against Eleanor's shoulder as the sound of Vigor's final battle faded behind them.

Dorian returned, on his own, late that night. The scene of the battle stretched along several miles, a narrow trail of compressed carnage. Dorian's unicorn nickered under his breath as he picked his way through bodies and discarded weapons, spilt saddle bags, and the odd lost boot. Dorian pulled his robe up over his nose to block the stench of catfish meat and guts gone putrid in a few short hours on dry land.

They'd lost fourteen horses, ten soldiers, and five magicians. Those casualties in themselves were difficult to swallow, but the additional death of four unicorns, including Vigor, put the losses at catastrophic. Dorian had been in the Carthean army for twenty years, and he'd never witnessed a unicorn death. During the heat of battle, he'd wished for Senné's sharp hooves and cool head, but now he thanked HighGod for the stallion's absence. He didn't know how Gregory could stand losing Vigor.

The bodies of the fallen floated in the water around him. He had trouble identifying the men or the horses, but the unicorns stood out in stark white relief. No movement in their graceful limbs. Only the gentle wag of white manes and tails against the wet darkness. There would be no recovering the bodies. Once the wounded were able to travel, they had to move on with far less protection. Dorian wanted Gregory back at Eclatant as soon as possible. The addition of Samuel didn't ease his mind, either. The thought that he might have overseen the deaths of two potential kings did not escape him.

He dismounted and picked up a Fire-iron sword. He poked at a dead fish, laid out across the path like a perverted Fest party supper. The attack made no sense to him. He'd never heard of catfish going on the aggressive. Dorian made it his job to be informed about all aspects of any journey, from provisions to pathways to potential unfriendly wildlife. None of the books he'd read about creatures of the North Country had hinted that schools of catfish might stage a complicated, organized ambush.

No, they're fish, for the love of the Bond. Stupid creatures who live only to suck sludge from river bottoms. "Dammit," he whispered.

Dorian thought of only one option. Magic must be involved. But who could conjure a spell to control such beasts? Who would want to attack them? Either question on its own had several conceivable answers. Taken as a rhetorical duo, however, Dorian came up with only one man.

After a brief overnight stop at the Dragon Mines to offload the wounded and replace the lost members of the Unicorn Guard, both two-legged and four-legged, Gregory's protective escort continued south. Dorian insisted on a breakneck pace and little rest. Eleanor caught him quite literally looking over his shoulder, as if he expected Ezra Oliver to appear at any moment. Eleanor shared his trepidation. Although she longed to find Oliver and bring him to justice, she hoped to come upon him of her own fruition. He'd once again sprung upon the Desmarais family, a jack-in-the-box that everyone knew would explode eventually.

She had little doubt her magical nemesis had coordinated the piscine attack, despite the lack of proof. Like Dorian, she knew of no one else with the willpower and the capability. Orvid Jones validated their position. "Those fish have no brainpower of their own," he said. "A magician the likes of Oliver could control them like living swords."

The thought brought her no comfort. Every creature, from biting gnats to the odd stray sheep, suddenly posed a threat. "Stupid animals abound in the north," said Chou as he bounced along on Teardrop's head. His voice vibrated with her staccato trot. "We'll be set upon by crickets and rabbits."

The Great Marshes tapered off around them. Rolling hills and meadows dotted with short pine trees and patches of flowering heather replaced the bog-lands. The sun was barely above their heads, and Eleanor's rear end throbbed against the saddle. At least the temperature rose as they moved south. She couldn't see her breath, even at this early hour. She clung to the hope of an unseasonably warm day.

Teardrop stopped without warning as Eleanor removed her thick gloves. Chou shot down the mare's forehead and came to a rest with both wings wrapped around her silvery horn.

"I smell..." The mare lifted her muzzle, and Chou slid back in Eleanor's direction. Eleanor reached toward Chou with both hands and was nearly unseated herself when Teardrop veered off the road. Her hooves left deep grooves in the stodgy earth.

"Eleanor, where are you going?" Dorian reined in ahead of her. She wondered if he'd asked Orvid to conjure him an extra pair of eyes in the back of his head.

"I don't know! Teardrop, we should stay with the Guard."

Teardrop plowed on toward a stand of tall heather. Her head disappeared into the greenish brownish bush.

Chou hopped down Teardrop's neck. "Oh! A baby!"

"A baby, out here?" Eleanor dismounted, with Dorian's shout of disapproval ringing in her ears. Curiosity and mothering instincts overpowered her. She eased Teardrop's head aside and peered through the brush.

She gasped. A baby indeed, but not a human baby. A tiny unicorn looked up at her with exhausted brown eyes.

Gregory's hand appeared on Eleanor's shoulder. "A wild one."

She straightened and shaded her eyes. "Where's the mother? The foal can't be more than a few days old."

"Hours," said Teardrop from the other side of the bush. "The mother is here."

Eleanor's leather riding boots squeaked as she walked around the heather. She covered her mouth with her hands.

With her white hide and blood-drenched flanks, the mother unicorn stood out like a bone-deep wound against the winter mud. Teardrop nosed her cheek, but she didn't move.

"She's gone," said Teardrop. "Time enough to clean her baby, and then the wounds of birth must have overcome her."

"How horrible." Eleanor knew the dangers of unicorn pregnancies and deliveries. The tiny horns could prove deadly to the mother, if not correctly attended. "Why was she alone?"

"Perhaps the foal came early, or perhaps she had a personal reason."

"For facing this by herself?"

"Stallions are very territorial, even more so out here in the marshes. If a stallion suspects one of his mares has strayed, perhaps he would kill the foal."

"How awful," said Eleanor, all the while thinking that men and stallions where not so different. She returned to the baby in the bush. His head rested head on his spindly legs. "Poor orphan. You must be hungry. Gregory, help me. He'll be heavy."

Gregory crossed his arms over his chest. "Yes, he will be. Better to leave him there, protected in the bushes. Perhaps the herd will come along and smell him, as Teardrop did. Have pity."

"We can't leave him."

"What else do you intend to do with him?"

"Why, take him with us, of course. Back to the Paladine."

Gregory laughed. "Eleanor, that foal weighs as much as a half-year heifer. You can't just scoop him up and tuck him in your saddle bag like Chou Chou."

"Teardrop can carry him."

"We're keeping a leg-breaking pace as it is."

"I don't mind, sire," said Teardrop.

"It won't work. He'll die of hunger."

"I'll make gruel for him, from my bread. It might tide him over," said Eleanor. "We'll be at Eclatant by tomorrow morning."

Gregory glanced at Teardrop, who had returned her head to the bush, and then he pulled Eleanor aside. He lowered his voice. "It's not just the inconvenience. This unicorn isn't like ours. He's wild. He's not a part of the Bond."

She scowled. "He's a baby, Gregory." The more she pictured the orphaned foal starving to death in the darkness, the more determined she became. "Bond or no Bond, he's a unicorn with a soul and a heartbeat. I'm not leaving him here."

"He won't do well in the Paladine!"

"How do you know? Has there been a wild unicorn in the Paladine?"

"No, but they're different. Any time humans try to interact with the wild herds, they spurn our efforts. They look down on Bonded unicorns. They value their freedom above all else."

"We can take care of him and then set him free. Show the wild unicorns our good intent."

"He'll slow us down and then die anyway."

"I'm bringing him. You can either help me or leave me here."

Thirty minutes later, Eleanor's rear end recommenced bouncing in the saddle, but now the baby unicorn lay across her lap. Dorian had secured the colt's legs beneath Teardrop's belly, and Eleanor wrapped one arm around the little animal's silky neck. She whispered to him, but he didn't make a sound. He just glanced up and her now and then with tired eyes. She hoped a little bit of the gruel she'd spooned into his open mouth had found a way to his belly.

"A mare will nurse him in the Paladine," she said to Chou. "Not much farther now."

His muffled voice came from her pocket. "Yes, of course." He didn't sound wholly convinced the colt would make it that long.

"Hold on, little one." She watched Gregory's profile from his mount beside her. It was strange to see him astride any unicorn but Vigor. His features had settled into an unyielding scowl. She stroked the baby's nose. "We'll be home soon. What shall we find when we get there?"

No one answered her question. Not Teardrop or Chou. Not Dorian, nor her husband, the imminent king. They would simply have to wait and find out.

PART II

CHAPTER 9

KINGS NEVER REST

THERE HAD NOT BEEN a coronation at Eclatant in thirty years. As a rule, the Desmarais never wasted an opportunity for ostentatious displays of wealth and power, but family tradition did not hold with extravagant ceremonies to introduce the new regime. King Casper's elaborate state funeral lasted two days. Conversely, Gregory's coronation ceremony took place in the king's receiving room and lasted less than an hour. No more than twenty important magicians and High Council members attended. Eleanor hardly saw Gregory or Dorian for most HighWinter. Both were ensconced in the High Council Chamber. She herself had been the highest-ranking female member of the family for over a decade, so as the queen consort, little changed for her but the size of her headwear. The crown, a heavy Fire-iron concoction of amethysts, diamonds, and emeralds, gave her a headache. She felt like one of the Mendaen women she'd seen in paintings, balancing a bushel of barley on her head without touching it.

As her first official queenly engagement, Orvid Jones suggested Eleanor host a luncheon for the noblest ladies in the land. She wrote the invitations by hand and closed them with her wax seal (HRH EBD, inside an ornate letter Q in the form of a dragon's tail). She sent them to Harveston and Harper's Crossing—and to Sage and Point-of-Rocks and the few year-round members of the Solsea aristocracy. The women came in a flood of silk and lace and high-heeled slippers. Eleanor personally welcomed each one as she arrived. The servants greeted each lady with a meal reminiscent of her hometown. Thick nut bread for the Harvestonians. Venison and cheese for the Harper's Crossing ladies. Wine and apples for those from Sage. Dried fish with heavy ale for the Solseans. A little bit of everything for the Point-of-Rocks nobility, who were accustomed to purchasing all manner of exotic produce at their city's famous bazaar. Eleanor's dear friends, Anne Iris and Eliza, coordinated the special meals. Eleanor blessed them for their social know-how. Somehow, those graces still evaded her after all these years.

A heavy rain fell throughout the luncheon. The rattle of raindrops against the ballroom's towering windows forced the ladies to chat in unbecomingly loud voices. Servants rushed between the chattering clusters with trays of grapes, sliced apples, and long-stemmed glasses of gold dust, a popular mix of pear juice and sparkling white wine. The more gold dust the ladies consumed, the louder the conversation became. In the hope of lowering the overall shrillness in the room, Anne Iris asked the flutists to play tunes in low octaves.

After a quick trip to the blessed silence of the water closet, Eleanor joined Anne Iris and Eliza beside the chocolate fountain. She caught Anne Iris mid-cattiness. "Did you see Sophia Porter's hair? I think my grandmother was partial to that style."

"Anne Iris, really, can we not talk about something of substance?" Eleanor asked. "The Duchess of Harveston's shoes, perhaps."

Eliza laughed in her quiet way, then cleared her throat. "She'd certainly showing them off. Although, I do wonder if she's flashing her shoes or her enviably slim ankles."

Eleanor found Sylvia amidst a group of admirers, as always. The ladies looked too enthralled to be focused on Sylvia's footwear, style maven that she might be. Sylvia's arms flailed, her eyes widened, and her hands clenched before her chest.

"I imagine she's telling everyone the *Tale of Sylvia and the Horribly Trying Journey*," said Eleanor.

Anne Iris sighed and touched her own full bosom, grown ampler with time and a happy marriage. She batted her eyelashes. "It was *so dangerous.* A week in a carriage, crawling across well-traveled roads under escort of Unicorn Guard."

"And uncomfortable," said Eliza. "I had only five servants and a martial magician to attend me."

"Ladies, who might you be discussing?"

To Eleanor's surprise, Imogene Easton Brice squeezed between Eliza and Anne Iris, a bee between two unreceptive blossoms.

"Mrs. Brice," said Eliza, who always chose politeness. "You're looking lovely."

She was indeed. Eleanor's stepmother had certainly maintained her good looks. Dark hair with only a few strands of silver, flashing black eyes, and a tiny waist. She'd taken to wearing higher necklines, so perhaps her cleavage was showing some wear, but the rest of her was annoyingly well preserved.

"Good evening, Mother Imogene." Eleanor had never been able to think of her stepmother by any other name. Anne Iris had no need to be civil to Imogene and had no aversion to being rude, so she didn't say a word. Instead, she sipped her fourth cup of gold dust and glared.

The four women settled into silence. Eleanor searched for something benignly pleasant to discuss, although in truth, she saw no real need for incivility. For years, she'd rarely interacted with her stepmother, and then only in stiff politeness when social gatherings forced them together. The last time they'd had a row of any sort had been on the heels of Ezra Oliver's first disappearance, after Eleanor was nearly sent to the gallows for treason. She believed Imogene had been part of that first plot to take her down, but she'd never found proof. She'd finally stood up to the woman, and although her late stepsister Margaret had sworn Imogene would never get over Eleanor stealing Sylvia's hypothetical crown, Eleanor had sensed her stepmother recognized the change in her. She was no fool, and she realized a grown, increasingly seasoned princess should not be trifled with in the same manner she'd manipulated a frightened orphan. On at least one occasion, Eleanor had even overheard her warning Sylvia of the danger of rubbing her dalliances with Gregory in Eleanor's face.

Surely, Sylvia's position and her own great fortune had negated her mother's need to scheme. Although the duchess was not a princess, Imogene's wrangling had landed her a fabulously rich husband and bought them both the security she'd long sought. She'd retired into privileged, matronly dignity, mooning about over her four grandsons. The late Duke of Harveston had spawned three of them, and the oldest held claim to that title. Of course, one could not forget little John-Caleb, celebrated possible royal bastard.

Imogene interrupted the awkward quiet. "I would ask you to speak kindly of Sylvia," she said to Eleanor. "With my sweet Margaret gone, she's the only sister you have left."

Anne Iris guffawed. Her face had gone blotchy from sparkling wine. "Sister, indeed."

Imogene ignored her. "Truly, Eleanor. I would say the same to her, if I heard her speaking ill of you."

Anne Iris's chest swelled until her breasts resembled two jellyfish jiggling on the surface of a tossing sea. "The queen can speak ill of anyone she wishes. Especially your floosy of a daughter."

Eleanor put a hand on her arm. "Peace, Anne Iris." She examined Imogene's face, and her posture, for some insidious innuendo in her message of mollification. She saw nothing but a mysterious benevolence. Imogene's goodwill intimidated her more than any predictable ire. Fear made her defensive. "I cannot promise I will speak no ill of your daughter. You can't promise she'll speak no ill of me." She braced herself for Imogene to cut with her next remark.

"It's true that I cannot control either of you young ladies. Still, I hope the two of you learn to compliment one another, just as you have always *complemented* one another." She curtsied and eased past them. She joined the crowd of worshippers around her daughter.

"What in HighGod's name did that mean?" asked Anne Iris. "You and Sylvia have never complimented each other in your lives."

"Not sincerely," said Eliza.

"I believe she meant that she hopes we'll learn to praise one another," said Eleanor, "since we've always been... counterparts?"

Anne Iris rolled her eyes. "Counterparts in Gregory's bed."

Eliza laughed into her hand. Gold dust sloshed over the edge of her cup and dribbled down her arm. "Anne Iris. Quick. I'm a mess."

Anne Iris complained while she dabbed at Eliza's elbow with her handkerchief. "A few drips of wine does not a mess make..."

Eleanor lost the substance of their chatter, and she watched Imogene quietly stand sentry over Sylvia's dramatic rendering of her voyage. As if sensing Eleanor's eyes upon her— the eyes she'd regularly denounced as an evil sign— Imogene looked back at her. She tipped her head and raised her glass of gold dust.

Old memories rose, unbidden and unwelcome, of Imogene's black stare following Eleanor in the dim light of the Brice House. Eleanor would be bent over some task—scrubbing the wooden floors in the hall perhaps— and she'd feel that opaque gaze upon her from the sitting room or down the staircase. Always, darkness peering out of the darkness. Shadow from shadow.

She put a hand on her stomach. It flipped inside her, like an empty water flask tied to the side of a bouncy pony. She suddenly felt lightheaded, and a little bit queasy.

"Eleanor, are you well?" asked Eliza.

"Yes. I haven't eaten, that's all, and two glasses of gold dust..."

Yellow lights swam in front of Eleanor's eyes. She grabbed Eliza's arm.

"Goodness," said Anne Iris. She steered Eleanor to the nearest chair.

Eleanor sat and rested her forehead on her hand. Imogene's appearance had spooked her, and she'd been so busy that she hadn't eaten since breakfast, but still, she'd never considered herself a swooner. Since many ladies at court fainted regularly, Anne Iris always insisted on having a healing witch at every party she hosted. Within moments, an old woman appeared at Eleanor's side with a glass of cold water.

"There now," said the old woman, as Eleanor obediently took a sip. "You look famished, Your Highness. Might I offer you something?" She fished around in her bag and held out an apple and a hunk of hard cheese. Eleanor took the apple. The smell of the cheese overwhelmed her— like sour milk. She fought the urge to push it away from her face.

"Thank you." She took a bite, and to her relief, the apple tasted fine, indeed. "I did need a little something."

The old witch smiled and patted Eleanor's shoulder. "Yes, you did, dearie. Next time don't wait so long. Not wise for one in your condition."

Eleanor swallowed, too soon. Her snack got stuck in her throat. She coughed, and to her disgust, a bit of apple lodged itself in the back of her nose. Her eyes watered. "My condition?"

"That little one can't be waiting so long."

"What little one?"

The witch laughed, as if Eleanor had just asked her to turn the apple into a worm and make it dance a jig. "How silly! The little one in your belly, of course."

Eleanor set the apple on the table. Her urge to vomit suddenly had nothing to do with nausea—or Imogene. She put a hand on her stomach and remembered the Svelyan circus. The dim tent, and Dorian staring down at her as he made love to her.

Just this once.

The next day, Imogene returned to Harveston to spoil her grandsons. Eleanor had new worries, so ruminations on Imogene's odd behavior barely tipped the scales of her burdens. She would not see her stepmother again for two years. By that time, her strange solicitude made sense, and everything had changed.

Dorian and Gregory leaned against the paddock gate and watched the wild unicorn colt frisking with his adopted sister. The colt harried the older filly from one end of the paddock to the other, his tiny hooves flashing in the LowSpring sunlight. The filly hid behind her mother's wide belly and squealed her annoyance. The mare—and older, patient, one-horned matriarch—moved between the two and gave the colt a stern nip. He squealed and capered through a bale of strewn straw. The mare exhaled a breezy laugh, and within seconds, the filly joined him.

"They're getting along all right," said Dorian. The fence creaked under his weight.

"As well as any siblings," Gregory said. "Young Dasha lives up to his name."

Dorian grunted agreement. Eleanor had bestowed the Svelyan word for *wild* on the colt, and it fit. "The mare seems taken with him. Wild or not."

The colt nosed at the mare's milk bag, and she nibbled at the fuzzy hairs on the end of his tasseled tail.

"Does he speak yet?" asked Dorian.

"Not that we can decipher. But the Paladins have hope we'll be able to communicate with him eventually. Maybe never with the clarity we get with the Bonded unicorns but something. At least he hasn't died," said Gregory, with grudging admiration. "Tough little fellow."

Dorian watched Gregory out of the corner of his eye. Since their return to Eclatant, he and Gregory had reached a tentative peace. Gregory's new responsibilities sat on his shoulders like a herd of trumpeting elfantas. No matter how he felt about Dorian personally these days, Gregory needed all the cool heads he could find.

"It's rather funny, isn't it," Gregory said. "How this mare just took the colt in. No questions asked. Just like Eleanor picked him up off the ground. Mothers are all the same."

"Most mothers, anyway."

Gregory turned around and leaned on the fence. "Sorry. Didn't mean to bring up unpleasant memories."

Gregory knew almost as much about Dorian's mother as Eleanor did.

"My mother couldn't be a mother. Perhaps that's why I appreciate it so much in those who can. Like your mother."

"She was a jewel." Gregory smiled. "Remember how we used to say any child who had my mother and your father—"

"Would have been the happiest child alive. I remember."

"Now all our parents are dead. We're grown orphans, left to fend for ourselves, and in my case, rule a country. It's funny how I've spent my whole life preparing for this, yet somehow it felt like it would never actually happen."

"I'm here to help you, Greg. In whatever way I can."

Gregory crossed his arms over his chest and changed the subject. "What news from the Mines?"

"The water should have cleared by now, but Thromba says the dragons are still not quite right. Fire-iron yields are up in some caves but down in others. He's quarantined a few big bulls who wouldn't stop fighting. One flattened a nest of eggs, and the mother went berserk. Ripped the bloke's foot right off."

Gregory turned around and tugged at a loose board on the fence. It creaked and then cracked off in his bare hand. Dasha tossed his head and regarded Gregory with curious, unafraid eyes. "Do you think we can trust the Svelyans? After the Catfish Fight, I wonder. We never really knew if Peter Mangolin was behind the Roffi incident with Caleb's Horn. HighGod, it seems so long ago. Trivial in these days."

Dorian took a moment. "I cannot say for sure whether King Peter orchestrated the Horn debacle, although it seems likely. Given our repaired relations in the past few years, and the amount of time I spent with him, I do believe his *current* motives are honest."

"How can you be sure?"

"I suppose I can't. But think, in the end, every king wants to protect his crown, his wealth, and his legacy. Just because Peter reached the conclusion that attacking the Desmarais would be the best path to security twelve years ago, it doesn't mean he still feels the same way. Times change, and kings are eminently changeable. Besides, we had Samuel in our ranks. I don't think Peter would have risked his heir being eaten by a swamp monster—even if they are in the midst of a family spat."

"True. Samuel swears Peter had nothing to do with this new attack. Crown prince or not, he has no love for the man right now. I think he'd tell us if he knew anything."

"Perhaps we should visit the Mines. Access the situation. We can take Samuel with us that far and then have the Guard escort him home."

Gregory mulled this over. "I'd like to go, but I'm needed here. You go. Take Samuel and Orvid Jones. The sooner the better."

"I'll begin packing now, if it pleases Your Majesty."

Gregory finally met Dorian's eye. He didn't look angry, but the hurt remained. "It does please me. HighGod speed, Your Grace."

Eleanor had a headache. For two hours she'd been staring into the kaleidoscope, willing it to show her the whereabouts of Ezra Oliver. No luck thus far. She'd seen Gregory and Dorian in the Paladine, watching the wild colt gallivanting with his adopted mother and sister. The fragile truce between the two men heartened her—for the sake of the crown, and for the sake of Dorian's safety. With Dorian once more in close proximity to Gregory's wrath, Eleanor understood how he felt during his exile. She prayed to HighGod her husband and her lover would find a way to coexist peacefully.

The kaleidoscope also showed her the children at their lessons in the library, and interestingly, Agnes at her desk at Gammonreil. No matter how she pictured Oliver, however, he didn't appear.

"Perhaps you're trying too hard," said Chou from his perch on the unlit candelabra on her writing desk.

"How can I try too hard?"

"Why do you think we count sheep when we can't sleep? It distracts us from what we want most, and then it happens."

"No. I just need to concentrate." She screwed her eyes shut, thought of Oliver's gray magic, and peered into the kaleidoscope again. "Damn! Still Agnes." She glared at her friend, bent over a letter of some sort, unaware of Eleanor's frustrated spying.

"I think you're avoiding other stressful topics."

She rested one hand on her midsection. So far only Chou knew about her condition. A week after the ladies' luncheon, she knew the old witch was right. She'd done this several times, and always the symptoms were the same: sour stomach, coppery taste in her mouth, and an aversion to milk and cheese.

"You have to tell him," said Chou.

"But I can't be sure it's his."

At that moment, Eleanor's maid, Pansy, announced the very person under discussion. Dorian entered the chamber in his traveling clothes. Eleanor rose and smoothed her skirts. Chou landed on Dorian's shoulder and affectionately nibbled his ear. Eleanor and Dorian exchanged polite greetings.

"You're off on a trip?" she asked.

He nodded. "To the Dragon Mines. You're the queen consort. I came for your blessing."

"You have it, of course." Eleanor wrung her hands, but she smiled. "A long visit?"

"Several months. But Gregory is allowing me to take Senné."

"That's wonderful!"

He smiled back. "We're looking forward to a long journey together, the old black devil and I. I wanted to ask you, before I left, if you've had any luck seeing Oliver…in your…" He pointed at the kaleidoscope. She shook her head, and they both fell silent. There was nothing to say that could be said.

"Safe travels," said Eleanor.

"Thank you. I'll see you in the spring."

"Dorian—wait."

He paused, his hand on the doorknob. Her news, her fear, and her warped excitement sashayed around her mouth. In the end, she wouldn't send him off to the Dragon Mines with such a burden. Not when she didn't know if the pregnancy would stick.

"Nothing," she said. "Do take care."

"And you. Always."

Six weeks later, Dorian felt as useless as ever he'd been in his thirty-eight years of life. So far, he'd reached no conclusion about the dragons' odd behavior. Matt Thromba continued to insist it was simply taking longer than usual for the river to run clean. In the meantime, the dragons were behaving like moody teenagers forced to sit though chapel. Petulant and lethargic. Fire-iron production was down. Not a bad as the dip a few years ago when Oliver spooked in and out of the caves, but not the robust yield Gregory would want in his first year at the helm of the Mines. Dorian assigned three unicorns to keep watch in each cave through all hours of the day and night. He spent hours combing the hills around the Mines and came up with nothing unusual. The same damp landscape, floating giant buzzards, and wind laced with Fire-iron dust. He wanted to believe Matt about the water, but it had been months since the summer rains, and a particularly dry winter. No reason the offending ogre offal wasn't sitting in disgusting heaps in the ogre camps, just as it did for most of the year.

In addition to presiding over a herd of irascible dragons, Dorian had to contend with Prince Samuel. He had thought Gregory the most bull-headed prince alive, but Samuel challenged him for that bag of loot. Each evening, once the dragons were reasonably calm, Dorian spent hours with Samuel, pleading with the young man to go home. Samuel wanted none of it. The mines fascinated him, so he said.

"He's more afraid of his father than he is of a herd of cantankerous dragons," Dorian said to Senné.

"The dragons have done him no harm. Not so in regards to his father."

"At least he's agreed he won't push for the match with Ticia. If only Gregory would agree with him."

"You could tell Gregory that Samuel only has carnal relations with men."

Dorian tugged at Senné's forehead. "Must you always be so blunt?"

Senné seemed to shrug with his eyes, as if to say, *it is what it is.*

"No," Dorian said. "I promised Samuel I'd keep his secret. The most I can tell Gregory is that Samuel himself isn't keen on the match. But it doesn't matter, anyway. If Gregory and Peter demand it, it will happen."

Finally, Dorian sent a note to Gammonreil stating that if King Peter wanted his heir apparent to come home, he would have to convince the boy himself.

A letter arrived a week later, in which King Peter professed his deep sadness at his son's absence and his hope that fences could be mended, or at least propped up. He even promised to allow Louis to return to court. Peter's platitudes were probably a load of ogre offal in their own right, but the possibility of seeing Louis lit a fire in Samuel's lamp. Thus Samuel summed up their compromise with a sage observation.

"I suppose a buggering heir is better than no heir at all," he said.

On a cool MidSpring morning, Dorian and Samuel made their way into the Scaled Mountains under escort of Unicorn Guard. A few surprisingly peaceful hours went by, in which Dorian admired the grandeur of the mountains around him and wracked his brain for a reason for the dragon's malaise. Some illness that they'd been unable to detect? Some new magical interference?

"We're met," said Senné. Dorian called a halt. He shaded his eyes and peered up at the ridge above them.

Fifty soldiers on horseback surrounded a hooded rider on a chestnut charger. "Father?" Samuel asked.

Dorian shook his head. "It can't be." King Peter, in his perpetually weakened state, would not be able to make the trek himself.

The rider removed her hood. Agnes's short blonde hair floated around her head, and she blinked against the wind. She clucked to her mount, and the Svelyan contingent picked its way down a steep path. Agnes met Dorian and Samuel in a relatively flat spot of patchy grass. Her guardians trailed behind her back up the ridge.

"Good day, Your Highness. Your Grace. King Peter sends his eternal thanks to His Majesty King Gregory for keeping Samuel safe during this time of family disagreement."

"It's been our pleasure to host him."

Samuel had gone quiet, his face aflame, as if every soldier in Agnes's escort knew his secret. "Let's carry on, Agnes," the prince said. He turned to Dorian. "I'll keep talking with my father about plans for uniting our two kingdoms."

Dorian nodded. He understood Samuel's unspoken follow up to that last statement: *or undoing those plans.*

Agnes shifted in her saddle. "I would speak to Lord Brandling alone for a moment."

She dismounted, and Dorian followed her to the edge of a steep embankment. "A long fall," the sorceress said.

"Those at the highest heights always have the farthest to fall—and the fewest friends willing to catch them."

Agnes crossed her arms over her chest. A mockingbird chased a hawk across the gray sky. Dorian admired the smaller bird's gumption.

"Svelya is a friend to Cartheigh," Agnes said. "King Peter asked me to reiterate that to you. He is in your debt. Your... what is the word? Discretion, that's it. Your discretion about Samuel...the king is an old man. He fears for his legacy and the state of the kingdom should he soon meet HighGod."

"Samuel is a fine prince. Just as no man should be defined by his wife, Samuel shouldn't be defined by his lover."

"Should a woman be defined by her husband?"

"I believe each person must exist separately. Or risk living half a life."

"King Peter would choose half a life for Samuel, over this path. Still, he knows you could have told King Gregory. How long would it be before he told the Kells and the Talessees. Who would respect the Svelyan crown then?"

Her words sounded unfair, but Dorian knew them to be true. "Do you know if Peter still favors the marriage with Princess Leticia?"

"I believe he does. He will insist on Samuel marrying to produce an heir. He won't care if Samuel pictures Louis in his mind while he attends to his husbandly duties. Ticia is as fine a wife as any."

"Who else knew of our path through the Northern Marshes?"

Agnes watched the hawk and the mockingbird. She pointed one hand in their direction, and the hawk glowed green. It shot toward the clouds, then flew off toward the mountain walls with a screech. The mockingbird made a few confused circles, searching for its lost enemy, before disappearing in the other direction.

"Only the king, the prince, and myself knew your path. No one else at Gammonreil. The fish attack must have been some form of enchantment."

"You've heard of our longstanding feud with Ezra Oliver. Orvid Jones thinks he could conjure that kind of spell."

"From what I've heard of him, I'm sure he is capable. But didn't he vanish years ago?"

"Yes. But he's a vicious dog. You put him out of your house when he bites you. He might wander some, but he always returns to the place where he once got a square meal."

"I see. It sounds like you're wise to keep vigilant." She slipped her white hands into black leather gloves. "King Peter respects Gregory, but he admires you. You can count on his friendship."

Dorian thanked her, and they both returned to their mounts. Dorian worried Samuel's boot. "Take care, Your Highness."

"I will, Your Grace.

Dorian thought about advising him to be wary and watch his heart, but in the end, it was too awkward. He slapped the haunch of Samuel's gray charger. The horse fell in line behind Agnes's chestnut, and the entire procession made its slow way up the ridge. Samuel and Agnes waved before disappearing in a flutter of red and black flags and clinking armor.

Dorian called to his own troops and reined Senné back down the mountains, in the direction of the Mines. Over the next quiet hour, Senné's rolling gate rocked him into quiet contemplation. Agnes was right about the Svelyans' indebtedness to him, and hence to Cartheigh, for keeping Samuel's secret. She seemed honest in her desire to prove her nation's loyalty. Dorian looked forward to sharing that good news with Gregory.

"HighGod." Senné tossed his head. "What's that stench?"

Dorian sniffed a few times before he caught the scent that had already reached Senné's sensitive muzzle. A sour, rotten smell. Like long spoiled meat. He grimaced. "Giant Buzzards? They nest further south."

The scent reached the Unicorn Guard behind them. It inspired whickers and mumbles of disgust. Senné shook his head again. "It's coming from below us."

Dorian blanched as Senné leaned over the edge of the path. The cliff slid away from them with a steepness that even a unicorn could not have managed. Dorian felt as if he were sitting on a pirate's plank above a sea of jagged boulders.

"I don't see anything dead." Dorian scanned the rocks for a decomposing animal, perhaps a deer. Senné leaned farther over the edge, and Dorian slid back in the saddle. A few pebbles came loose from the edge and tinkled down the mountain. They hit the boulders below.

A boulder shifted, although outside of an earthquake, a rock of that size should stay still.

"That's no boulder," Dorian said out loud, shocked.

Wide purple eyes blinked up at him. A dark mouth opened in a monstrous yawn and sent another wave of rotting stench into his face.

The ogre stood and stretched its gangly arms. It regarded them with greedy eyes and took hold of one of the larger boulders farther up the cliff.

"HighGod," Dorian said. "It's going to climb up here."

"No, the rocks won't hold." Senné snorted his relief as the ogre skidded down to its rocky bed. Dirt and small boulders rained down into its face. It blinked and wiped its eyes. It tried again, but it sneezed before it got in a second toehold. It slid down again on its knees. Greenish snot hung in grotesque ribbons from its nose. It shook like a dog after a swim. Snot smacked against the cliffside with in stomach-turning splats.

Dorian's men and unicorns muttered and whinnied in alarmed disbelief behind him. Swords were drawn from scabbards in smooth strokes. Dorian held up his hand, and they fell silent. The ogre made one more halfhearted scramble up the cliffside. It seemed to decide they weren't worth the risk of falling or the annoyance of more pebbles in its eyes. It leapt down the cliff in a few bounces, sending boulders crashing into the dry ravine below. Within seconds, it disappeared around a bend in the old river.

A few relatively uneventful weeks passed in the North Country, with no answers about the dragon's malaise, or the bizarre appearance of a runaway ogre. Dorian sent word to Eclatant via unicorn runner. Gregory's return correspondence was appropriately alarmed and surprisingly cordial. *Get word to the Svelyans,* he wrote. *If anyone can make some sense of this, you can. Take care. Gregory.* Dorian appreciated his king's confidence, and he sent another runner to Svelya to inform Gammonreil, but his inability to do anything else frustrated him.

One dreary evening, Dorian sat in a wooden chair in front of the two-story cabin that served as sleeping quarters for important Mine guests. He'd draped his saddle across a wooden rack for a well-needed cleaning. He'd already polished the leather and moved on to the Fire-iron bits: the buckles, clasps, and stirrups. His back ached from two hours bent over the rack, and his eyes were slightly crossed. Senné snuffled at the nape of his neck.

"There's a bit of grass in the girth."

Dorian swatted at him. "Would you like to do it? You're the one who wears it."

"If I had thumbs, so I would."

Dorian laughed and tugged at the stallion's forelock. Senné reciprocated by nibbling Dorian's beard. He'd decided to keep the facial hair he'd slowly accumulated over several years in Svelya, and the stallion was still getting used to it. Otherwise, it was jolly old times again. Now that they were reunited, Dorian wondered how he'd managed without him.

Senné snorted. "Bad weather approaching."

Dorian looked to check the skies and found Orvid Jones's perpetually unfriendly face. "Afternoon, Orvid," he said.

"A letter for Your Grace. From Nestra."

"Thank you. How are you feeling? Thromba mentioned you were ill in the stomach."

Orvid blushed. "I'm fine now."

"I'm glad to hear it." Dorian would never stop trying to win back

Orvid's favor. Their High Council positions demanded they spend considerable time together, but it was more than that. He simply liked the man and respected his opinion.

He opened the letter to Samuel's fine hand.

Your Grace,

I hope this letter finds you well and the dragons improved. My father's illness is flaring again, and he sends his apologies for not taking up a quill himself. I will do my best to convey our collective sentiments. We received your letter about the ogre you saw in the Scaled Mountains with great trepidation. My father requested a census of the ogre camps and a security review. The report from the Ogre Watch gives cause for alarm. Four ogres are unaccounted for, all from the southern camp Prince Gregory visited last year. A female and three males. The Ogre Watch is flummoxed by the situation, as are the rest of our magical scholars, for there has been no obvious break in security. You will receive a full report from my father's High Council, but I wanted to personally express both my frustration at this turn of events and my country's dedication to our mutual national friendship and to solving this conundrum.

With warm regards,
HRH Samuel Mangolin

Dorian waited for Senné to finish reading over his shoulder before he handed the letter to Orvid. Orvid reached the end and looked up. "I assume we're thinking the same thing?"

"Oliver," said Dorian. "He can transfer living beings from one place to another. He did it with dragons. Why not ogres?"

"I find it difficult to believe he could get in and out of the ogre camps without any of the Watch noticing. The ogres aren't hidden in caves, like the dragons were."

"He got in and out of the Mines. He simply appears where he wants to be. He doesn't have to cross the Restraints. He avoids them." Dorian rubbed his eyes. His hands smelled like saddle soap. "So, let's say Oliver plans to pull ogres from the camps. To what ends?"

"An attack, obviously," said Orvid.

"But how can he control a pack of ogres?"

"The ogres were manipulated once before," said Senné. "Who knows what they'll do if they think it will give them a chance to appease their god."

"Horns and fire," said Dorian, suddenly overwhelmed. "In a few months, we'll be facing the Ogre Wars all over again."

Creamy light leaked from Orvid's ears like spilled thoughts. "We can't wait for Peter's High Council to produce a full ogre accounting. I'll write to the Talessee and Kellish kings. This is a potential disaster for all nations." He shuffled off. His black cloak flapped around his knees like the broken wings of a downed crow.

Dorian stood and flexed his back. He wiggled his fingers, his mind already on a letter to Gregory, and another to Samuel and Peter at Gammonreil.

"There are others who should be alerted." Senné raised his muzzle and sniffed the wind coming from the south. "My brothers and sisters in the Great Marshes."

Dorian ran a hand down Senné's ebony neck. "Of course. Unicorns suffered through the Ogre Wars as well. They'll need to be prepared." Carriage wheels spun in Dorian's mind, kicking up ideas like sprays of pebbles. "Perhaps they'd want our help."

Senné whistled a laugh. "I'd not count on it. They prefer to fight their own battles."

"But we fought alongside one another five hundred years ago. Strength is in numbers! You go, Sen. Find out if they'll meet with us.

Tell them Gregory himself will come. Let them know we can help each other."

"I'd like to visit them," said Senné. "There are other black unicorns in the wild. I've even heard tell of spotted—any route, I'll make the journey, to spread the warning. But I don't think they'll be keen."

Dorian untied a messy braid in Senné's mane. The hair, even tangled, was like silk between his fingers, reminding him of Eleanor's petticoats. He shook out the fine strands. "I know one thing. I can't send you off to the wild unicorns looking like I've had my hands on you."

At Eclatant, the Awakening Fest came and went, and still Dorian remained at the Mines. To Eleanor's alternating elation and horror, her pregnancy continued without complication. She kept it firmly to herself, although she knew Pansy suspected something. They'd lived in the same space for too long. Sometimes Eleanor caught the maid watching her with a look of motherly concern that brought tears to Eleanor's eyes. She prayed hourly for word of Dorian's eminent return. She wished she'd told him about the pregnancy before he left, for now it seemed vital that he be aware of it. She'd have to tell Gregory something eventually, but an irrational need for Dorian to tell her everything would somehow be all right kept the news firmly behind her lips, a rare jewel in a locked case.

Finally, on a warm HighSpring morning, Gregory visited her in the nursery with a letter. Ticia was drawing as usual, and Natalie and Eleanor were having tea, along with biscuits and grapes. Natalie kept up a steady stream of chatter. "Mama, have some tea. Tishy, here's your tea. Poppa, tea for you, too. Chewy, tea."

Chou nibbled the edge of a discarded biscuit. "Natalie, *Shoo-shoo*. Chewy is embarrassing."

Natalie grinned at the bird. "I call you that 'cause you're always eating."

Chou squawked in mock outrage and spat his biscuit into the child's lap. Eleanor left them to their silliness and joined Gregory by the window. "Lord Brandling writes." He handed her a letter. "Read it."

She unfolded the letter and blinked back tears at the sight of Dorian's small, neat writing.

> *Your Majesty,*
>
> *I hope this letter finds you and your family well. Most everything is as it has been here in the North. The dragons are ornery. There are renegade ogres on the loose. Fire-iron production is low to fair. This letter, however, isn't meant to expound on what you already know. There is one interesting new development, should you endeavor to give it your consideration.*
>
> *Senné recently visited the wild unicorns on a mission of warning about the escaped ogres. At my request, he asked if we could count on the assistance of the wild herds, should the ogre threat become imminent. He took our own good will and desire for mutual safety. I told him we'd send someone to the herds on a diplomatic mission, perhaps your own Majesty, as I believe an alliance with them would be of great benefit to our cause. If I may remind you of some obscure history that may have slipped your mind over the years since your school days—*
>
> Eleanor bit her lip to hide a smile. Gregory cared little for formal schooling. Any obscure history he retained resulted from lessons subtly facilitated by Dorian, Eleanor, or Orvid Jones. They were not the vague memories of a rambunctious boy who counted the minutes until the magicians released him from class. The prince's vanity

and his prickly temper, however, required his counselors to use a gentle hand when they spanked him with the proverbial paddle for his youthful academic mediocrity. *Well played, my love,* she thought, before reading on.

—the wild unicorns were invaluable during the Ogre Wars. Nearly half of the documented ogre slayings involved unicorns piercing the creatures' bellies with their horns. Of course, those were the days before the Desmarais came to power. Now, praise High God and your family, we have our horned comrades under the Bond. Still, the more sharp horns we have, the better chance we stand to slay them. In addition, the renegade ogres are hiding in the North Country, where the wild unicorns know every tree and rock and bog. They can be our eyes, ears, horns, and hooves in places we'd never think to watch and search.

The lead stallion, who is called Terin, is a proud creature. He, like many of his fellows, distains the influence of man. He welcomed Senné but said he wouldn't align his herds with our armies. Senné pressed Terin to simply meet with us.

To Senné's surprise, Terin agreed, under one condition.

He said he'd only meet with the queen.

Apparently, word of Her Highness's goodness has reached the ears of the wild herds. They've learned, through passing contact with Bonded unicorns around the Mines, of her concern and care for Dasha, the orphaned unicorn foal. Terin is impressed with what he's heard, and he is curious. Senné warned him the chances of Eleanor being allowed to journey north on her own were slim, but he insisted. The queen or no one, he said.

So, out of love of my country and your own self, I ask you to allow the queen to travel North to the Mines. We will escort her as far as the edge of the wild unicorns' territory, and Terin will meet her and take her into his protection. I realize the unorthodox nature of this request, but I pray you will consider it.

Your servant,
Dorian Finley, Duke of Brandling

Eleanor finished reading and looked up at Gregory. She expected a snide comment, or perhaps a slap to her face, but Gregory simply gazed past her out the window. She'd noticed little changes in him since the crown unexpectedly landed on his head, years before he thought it would. Of note, he spent more time thinking and less time talking. Or at the very least, he did more of the former before the engaging in latter, so she waited for him to speak.

"The common folk," he said. "Now the wild unicorns. You attract unusual admirers."

"Thank you," she said.

"Do you wish to go?" As he turned to her, the morning sun struck the side of his face. There, in his sideburns, she noticed the sparkle of a few gray hairs amidst russet. There were dark circles under his eyes. She remembered the old magician's proverb, *princes must sleep heavy in their youth, for kings never rest.*

"I wish to be of service. However the crown needs me."

He kissed her forehead. "Then go. Bring me good news—and an alliance."

CHAPTER 10

A New Alliance

Eleanor dismounted in the Mine yard. She stretched her arms over her head, and then her hands went protectively to her stomach. She'd managed the two-day voyage north, but she planned on lying down as soon as possible.

She inhaled the smell of burning wood and Fire-iron dust and rubbed her chapped ears. HighSpring or not, northern afternoons were still cool. The miners bustled around her, offering water and dried beef and apples. Their mix of accents surrounded her like harmonies in a raucous song, from Maliana gutter speak to Lake District drawl to the nasally twang of the Harvestonians.

"Your Highness!" Matt Thromba draped a sheepskin dragon robe over Eleanor's shoulders. "Warm yourself."

She laughed. "Matt, you'll weigh me down. I'll not be able to climb the stairs."

"Aye, but you shan't be cold. Lord Brandling is down below. He asked me to see you to your quarters."

"Thank you. I'll be along in a moment." Eleanor turned to Teardrop. The mare glared at her. Chou perched between Teardrop's ears with a mutually accusatory expression on his face, and Eleanor felt like a student with two unsatisfied teachers.

"Tell him soon," said Teardrop.

"Tell him. Tell him," said Chou, sounding very parrotlike indeed.

They'd not let up on their litany since the departure from Eclatant. Both unicorn and bird insisted she tell Dorian about the pregnancy the moment she laid eyes on him.

"I will tell him. But I must find a good time."

"You'll be telling that man," whispered Teardrop, "you may be pregnant with his child, but you can't be sure, because the other possible father is his former best friend and king."

Chou's head waved on his pliable neck. He whistled. "There will never be a good time to deliver that news."

Eleanor joined Matt Thromba in the guest cabin. She ran her fingers over the simple wooden furniture. The place always smelled musty, and the wind kept up a constant whistle in the eaves. The walls were thin. They didn't muffle the sounds of the camp: bangs, whinnies, and the occasional roar of a dragon. Still, she once again found the cabin to be cozy in its rustic simplicity.

"I put fresh robes on the bed upstairs," said Thromba, "and there's milk in the larder. Lord Brandling will be staying with me in my cabin while you're here."

"Of course, tell him thank you for allowing me to oust him." She pointed at a cot in the corner of the small sitting room. "But who—"

"Orvid Jones will sleep there. Just to make sure you're safe through the night."

"Oh, certainly." Eleanor turned away to hide her blush. It didn't take a genius intellect to surmise Orvid knew his presence would keep Dorian and Eleanor from heeding any late-night urges.

The door opened with a squeal, and Dorian stepped into the room. He rubbed his boots on the woven mat. He was luminous, but it wasn't just the thin layer of silver Fire-iron dust that covered his tunic. His pale cheeks were flushed, and his eyes sparkled. Eleanor grinned back at him. It had been two months since they'd seen each other.

"Your Highness," he said and bowed.

"Your Grace." She glanced at Thromba as he rubbed a cloth along the little dining table and hummed. "Matt, I'll take care of that. Surely you have other work that needs your attention."

Matt's brow wrinkled. "I suppose so, Your Highness. There's those sheep what need culling."

"Don't let me keep you."

"I should get to it before dark." He left the cabin, muttering under his breath about fleece and mutton. Dorian closed the door behind him.

"I fear that was too obvious," Eleanor said.

"If anyone is clueless about that sort of intrigue, it's Matt Thromba. He's spent the last twenty-five years surrounded by miners and dragons. Maybe a yearly whore."

They regarded each other across the planked floor. Both were painfully aware of the open windows and thin walls. "I'll carry your bag upstairs," said Dorian.

"Wait," she said. He paused with her small satchel in his hand. She pointed to a chair by the fire. "I must tell you something, but I have to keep my voice down."

She peered out each window and checked behind the door before joining him. In a halting, whispering voice she told him of the pregnancy. Emotions ricocheted across his face as she spoke. Elation, terror, somber acceptance.

"I'm sorry I didn't tell you before you left," she said, "but you know my history. I didn't want you to lose sleep for nothing, if it ended on its own."

"I understand." He leaned back in his chair, his teeth grinding like the mortar and pestle of an overzealous baker. "I don't know what to say or how to feel."

"I've felt the same. Part of me hoped the pregnancy would fail and save us all the worry."

"Did you really?"

"It was a very small part. I want this child, Dor. I just fear for him… or her."

"How certain are you that it's mine?"

She blushed. They'd always had an unspoken rule to avoid discussing her simultaneous carnal relations with both men. "I can't be certain. Not at all. He'd just been with Sylvia, but he still… in the tent on the journey home from Nestra—"

"Enough." Dorian waved his hands, as if to ward off the image. "I see what you're saying. Honestly, between you, me, him, and Sylvia, the proximity of one to the other turns my stomach." He pressed his fingers against his temples. "Oh, HighGod, Eleanor. If it looks like me, he'll kill it. For sure. Kill you."

"He didn't kill either of us before."

"This is different! You're supposed to provide him an heir, and you have my bastard? If it's a boy…" He stood. "You have to run away. Get away from him."

She watched his frenzied progress across the floor. He thrust his hands into his pockets.

"You know I can't do that. I can't leave the girls, and there's nowhere to go. We've discussed this a thousand times."

He sat again. "I know. I do. But in all these years of dread, I've rarely been this frightened."

"I've thought of nothing else for the past two months. I've prayed on it. There's nothing to be done but face it. I'll get down on my knees and beg for his mercy. At least for the child. Or maybe it will come out as red-headed as all my others, and we'll have driven ourselves mad for nothing."

"What about this trip—you, going to the wild unicorns in this condition? I can't believe he let you come."

"He doesn't know yet. If I can help him by making a new alliance, perhaps he'll be more lenient."

Dorian stared into the fire. "Perhaps." He took Eleanor's hand and squeezed it before quickly letting go. "How often I've wished for this. Our child. My son or daughter. HighGod giveth, and the king can taketh away."

Two days later, Eleanor started her short journey south, through the Great Marshes, to the wild unicorn's territory. Teardrop followed Senné, and five more Unicorn Guards took up the rear. Eleanor watched Dorian's back. He'd been somber but tender. She wanted nothing more than to wrap her arms around him and stroke his hair.

They traveled all day and stopped only to eat. The land flattened out, and they skirted the wettest part of the marshes. Only short, sparse trees grew in the boggy ground. Their branches reminded Eleanor of clutching, grasping arms reaching out from quicksand. "The unicorns stay on the fringes of the marsh, for the most part!" Dorian shouted to her over his shoulder. "The grazing is better. But they can navigate the bogs. They can find solid ground where a man would see a sink hole."

As the sun sunk below the low hills in the western sky behind them, Eleanor picked out a group of unicorns about a half-mile in the distance. The whiteness of their hides blended with the monochromatic landscape, so they seemed to materialize out of thin air. As they approached, their party revealed itself as five mares and a stallion.

Eleanor had never seen such a stallion. He was taller even than the late Vigor. His mane reached his knees, and a fringe of white beard hung from his muzzle. He called his party to a halt. He tested the air with his long muzzle as they waited for Eleanor and her escort.

Senné stopped, and Eleanor sensed uncharacteristic nervousness on the black stallion's part. Dorian rested a steadying hand on his neck. Senné cleared his throat with a snort. "Greetings, Terin. This is

Teardrop." He introduced the other unicorns in the Guard. "The man on my back is Dorian Finley, the Duke of Brandling, of the far eastern lake lands."

"Greetings, Senné the Black," said Terin. He stared at the visitors from under his thick forelock. "Greetings to the rest of the Bonded." Eleanor detected a bit of distain in Terin's voice and the set of his ears. "And to the man, but it's the woman we're interested in."

Senné backed up until he was even with Teardrop. "This is Eleanor Brice Desmarais, Queen of Cartheigh."

Terin approached Teardrop. Eleanor felt the mare stiffen under the saddle. Terin's muzzle snuffled from Eleanor's toes, up her legs, and down her arms. She leaned back to avoid his horn. He blew into her belly several times and glanced up at her. She blushed when he met her gaze, for he somehow recognized the pregnancy. His nostrils, amazingly clean and shiny despite never having been touched by a soft brush, nuzzled her neck and whiffled in her ear. She fought a nervous giggle.

"So, you are Queen Eleanor. Welcome. You and the mare follow me. Good day to the rest of you."

"Terin—we shall erect a shelter for Her Highness—if it's not too much trouble—" Senné's usually wise and detached voice took on a distinct babble.

Terin's ears waved. "Yes. A fine idea. You come. And the man. The rest of you wait."

Dorian took a bundle from one of the guards. It contained a pile of poles and canvas. Senné and Teardrop followed Terin and the mares toward a stand of trees.

"We often shelter here, during rough weather," said Terin. "The trees block the wind. The predators know it's our place. They stay away."

"How reassuring," said Chou from Eleanor's pocket. She hushed him, for she didn't want Terin to demand he return to the Mines with Dorian. She doubted the stallion would appreciate a mouthy bird disturbing his mystical tranquility. She wanted Chou to stay with her, for comfort, but also because Dorian had rightly insisted. Should she be in any danger, Chou could be back at the Mines, as the parrot flies, in two hours.

Dorian dismounted and assembled her tent. Senné and Teardrop shifted and swished their tails. Senné's ears waved constantly, and Teardrop dug a hole in the boggy dirt with one restless hoof. The wild unicorns watched in intent silence. Teardrop and Senné were chatter-bugs compared to this taciturn lot.

Dorian finished fiddling with the tent and straightened. Eleanor peered inside. It was small but cozy enough, with a raised bed covered in dragon robes, a small pile of books she'd brought from Eclatant, extra riding leggings, plenty of candles, and paper for writing. Three canvas bags held dried meat and fruit, cheese, and tea. Dorian left a pot and a flint.

"You can build fires out here. All those dragon robes will have you sweating, no matter how cold it gets at night." Worry etched squiggly lines across his forehead. "You'll be just fine. Of course, you will."

"Are you trying to convince me or yourself?" She rested a hand on his arm. "Don't fret, Your Grace. It's much nicer than the hayloft I lived in at my father's house. I fear the bears less than I feared Mother Imogene in those days."

He didn't return her smile or her levity. "If anything goes amiss, send Chou Chou to tell me. Don't set off on your own."

"Yes, sir," she said and saluted him.

Dorian turned and strode toward Terin. The stallion's ears pricked in surprise at his rapid advance. He reminded Eleanor of Gregory or his late father. Those who were treated with constant deference never quite knew how to react to anything else.

"I am entrusting the jewel of our nation to you. Our most precious queen." Dorian held out his hand, and Terin tossed his head. He watched Dorian from one dark eye, and then he lowered his face to Dorian's own. Dorian gently laid his gloved fingers on the stallion's muzzle. "Take care of her. She is invaluable."

"You have my word, Lord Brandling," said Terin.

"We will see you in ten days." Dorian swung onto Senné's back. He didn't look at Eleanor, and she was glad. If he'd met her eyes, she surely would have wept.

Once Dorian disappeared, Eleanor turned to her horned hosts. Teardrop shuffled closer, and she put a hand on the mare's withers. She radiated protective warmth through Eleanor's leather gloves. The quiet stretched on, with nothing but the unicorn's swishing tails and the odd buzzing fly to break the silence.

Chou Chou's blue head poked from Eleanor's pocket. He glanced around the somber crowd and then climbed up Eleanor's cloak. He stretched his wings as he dragged himself along by this beak and talons and hopped onto Eleanor's head. "Here we are, all together! What shall we do now?"

The six wild unicorns pricked their ears. Terin stretched his long neck in Chou's direction. "I smelled a bird," he said, "but I've never seen one such as you. Are you a cardinal? Or a red raven?"

"Chou Chou is more closely related to the turkey family," said Eleanor.

Teardrop whinnied a laugh, and Chou spat at her. The mare on Terin's left spooked and bumped into her compatriot behind her.

"Peace," said Terin. "Peace, mares and peculiar birds." Eleanor detected a hint of amusement in the flare of his nostrils. He nosed the spooky mare. "This is Penla. The leader of my mares. She usually has a very cool head."

Penla narrowed her eyes at her stallion, and in that small gesture, Eleanor recognized the mare's authority. She had an unusually dark silver horn. Eleanor made a note of it, for unicorns looked eerily similar until one got to know their individual mannerisms.

"Greetings, Your Highness, and Teardrop," Penla said.

Teardrop dropped her head in deference. Penla reached her muzzle toward Chou. "And to you...friend bird...it is *Chew-Chew*?"

"*Shooo Shooo*," said Chou, his black tongue hanging out. "Natalie and these unicorns are determined to change my moniker."

"Chou to his friends and admirers," said Eleanor.

"Of which there are many, surprisingly," Teardrop added.

Chou went puffy with pleasure. "How kind. How very kind."

"Please let me know if you need of anything," said Penla. "We realize this is not the sort of shelter to which you are accustomed."

"It will do just fine," said Eleanor.

"I see you've brought your own food, but we can show you where to find other nourishment. Roots, berries."

"Berries, lovely," said Chou.

Eleanor pinched his beak in an old hushing gesture. "Thank you. We shall be ever so grateful."

"You must be tired," said Terin, with an undisguised eye on Eleanor's mid-section. "You should rest. But I'd ask after the foal you found in the marshes. How does he fare?"

"He's thriving with his surrogate mother. Gregory—my husband, the king—feared he wouldn't survive."

Terin pawed at the ground. "His blood is strong. He'll survive. Penla, have two mares stand guard over the queen."

"I'll stand guard," said Teardrop, defensively.

"Certainly. But I'd have some of my own stand with you. Your lives are in my hands. Excuse me. I have mares and foals east of the Last Thicket that need looking after."

Terin left at a loping canter. His long tail waved a dignified goodbye. Penla nosed Eleanor toward the tent. "Rest, Your Highness."

Teardrop snorted, and for a moment, Eleanor was a schoolgirl with a new friend and a jealous old one. Chou Chou broke the tension by landing on Penla's head. The mare jumped sideways, and Chou flapped around her ears. "Peace, lady mare! You'll pitch me into the bog!"

Penla stood still with her front legs splayed and her eyes crossed in an attempt to see the bird on her head. Eleanor stroked her nose. "You'll get used to him. He's really quite amusing."

Chou hung upside down from her horn. His beak cracked into a beguiling grin. "Just give me a chance, Mistress Penla. I'll soon have you rolling in the peat in hysterics."

"Doubtful," said Penla, but Eleanor sensed a unicorn's version of a smile in her expression. Chou had that effect on nearly everyone, eventually. He was a feathered goodwill ambassador crossed with a court jester.

We need all the goodwill we can muster in this endeavor, she thought. *If HighGod decides to use a charming bird to build alliances, so be it.*

The days fell into a quiet rhythm. Before Eleanor knew it, six days had passed in the unicorns' company. She rose early each morning and climbed onto Teardrop's bare back. Her ornate saddle and bridle seemed ridiculous in the middle of a marsh. Besides, Eleanor and Teardrop had never had a need of rein or stirrup to communicate. Teardrop's warm hide penetrated Eleanor's calfskin riding leggings, like a hot stone in a cold bed, easing the creeping ache in her slowly expanding hips. Chou flitted around their heads like an Awakening ribbon as they followed Penla and the other mares on their casual grazing tours.

Eleanor had never had so much free time. Not in her childhood days under Mother Imogene's iron thumb, nor since she'd taken on the hectic duties of princess. The unicorns did not plan their wandering. Their keen noses led them to the best marsh grass. They didn't speak much, and so Eleanor and Teardrop, and even Chou Chou, mimicked their silent serenity. It was a relief after the hubbub of court life. She became accustomed to the peaty smell and the chattering of the swamp squirrels. The marshlands folded around her like an earthen cradle.

Terin appeared several times a day, only to disappear to look after his other mares. Roughly fifteen mares made up Terin's herd—a large group by the standards of the wild—and they spread out to ensure everyone found enough forage. Other stallions kept only a few mares, and some were content to pair off in couples. Some young stallions lived in small groups, and some older stallions lived alone. They had few social conventions, but one held fast. A mare chose her stallion, and once she did, she must remain true to him. When Eleanor asked after the custom, Penla seemed surprised.

"It's just you seem so…"—Eleanor struggled to find the right word—"…free, or unhindered. Why should it matter so much?"

"The mares carry and feed the young. Stallions protect them. It's a sacred duty. Why should a stallion risk himself and his children in the protection of another's foal?"

"What happens if a foal is born"—Eleanor started to say out-of-wedlock, but that didn't seem quite right—"with the wrong father?"

"We turn the mare away from the herd. She can go to the father of her child or find her own way."

Eleanor scowled. "That seems unjust. Where is the father's punishment?"

"I agree, but it's our custom. Are things fair between male and female in your traditions?"

Eleanor couldn't argue with her there.

Dorian sent his raven, Frog, to check on Eleanor every other day. She always sent him back to the Dragon Mines with sincere messages detailing her most robust health. She didn't exaggerate. The peace did her and the baby good, and this pregnancy progressed with fewer aches and pains than any other. Aside from the twinges in her hips, she felt quite healthy. She ate when hungry, slept when tired, and spared her growing belly any containment by corset or stays. The simple cot in her tent provided more support for the growing child than feather pillows had for Ticia, Nathan, or Natalie.

One morning at the beginning of her fifth month of pregnancy, the mares accompanied Eleanor and Teardrop to the small stream where Eleanor filled her water flask. She had asked Dorian if she might stay another week, as she still wasn't sure what Terin wanted of her, and he'd yet to say anything about an alliance. Dorian agreed, but his letters revealed his escalating concern. *If Terin does not make a decision soon, you must return. For the sake of ALL the travelers.*

She knew who he meant by *ALL*. The baby in her belly had already taken shape in their minds. A child to be protected.

The HighSpring sun baked the back of Eleanor's neck, and she shivered. If she were at Eclatant, perhaps they'd be packing for Solsea, although Gregory had hinted that he might spend his first summer as king in Maliana. A wise choice, but Eleanor missed Trill Castle. The first truly warm days always made her crave salty air and sand beneath her bare feet.

She shaded her eyes with one hand. This terrain couldn't be less like the dry Solsea cliffs. The heat and a belly full of fresh blackberries made her drowsy. The mares nibbled at clover growing in clumps beside the creek. She scooted onto Teardrop's haunches and rested her head on the mare's withers. She wiggled until her belly settled comfortably into the curve of Teardrop's back. The other unicorns fanned out around her. Terin appeared, a silent white shadow.

"Does Terin ever eat?" whispered Eleanor.

"All beings must eat," Teardrop replied.

"Except ogres, apparently."

"Eating dirt and rocks is still eating."

"I think they're fortunate," said Chou. "Far less starvation when one can make a nice stew from some pebbles thrown in a mud puddle."

"He never lowers his head to graze," said Eleanor. "He just watches all the time."

"He has much responsibility."

"It must be tiring. Feeling so responsible for everyone." Eleanor thought of Gregory and the weight he now carried. Thousands of lives depending on his choices. She felt a pang of sympathy.

"Having so many mares would be tiring." Teardrop lifted her head and waved her ears, a unicorn's version of wagging eyebrows. "I'm sure they exhaust him in more ways than one."

Eleanor's laughter skipped across the marsh grass. Penla's head jerked in Teardrop's direction. Upon realization that her visitors were merely gabbing away unnecessarily, she resumed her demure grazing.

"Teardrop, how scandalous of you," Eleanor whispered. A few sniggering giggles escaped her as she pictured proud, noble Terin hiding behind a thicket from another randy mare. "I must talk to him. Soon."

"Shall I approach?" asked Teardrop.

Just as she said it, Terin turned and silently disappeared into the nearest thicket.

"Damn. Next time I see him, we need to push the matter. Before Dorian turns up and whisks us to the safety, comfort, and the luxury of the Dragon Mines." Eleanor closed her eyes against the bright sunlight.

She rested her cheek against the silky pillow of Teardrop's mane and adjusted her belly. Her fingers wound through the soft hair. She stroked it the way a child would finger a favorite blanket. She closed her eyes and drifted off, lulled by the sound of ripping grass and the gentle movement of Teardrop's shoulders as the mare sought out the most tender shoots.

A rumbling voice woke her as the sun began reached its peak. "Your Highness. I'd speak with you, if I may?"

Eleanor sat up and yawned. She stretched her arms over her head. "Of course." She slid to the ground, happy that Terin had instigated a conversation himself, rather than her trying to corner him as he came and went like an early spring breeze. She followed him to the edge of the creek. Her boots squished and squeaked in the mud below her.

Terin got the point with the usual forthrightness of his kind. "I've never had any fondness for your Great Bond, as you call it."

Eleanor scraped her heel in the mud. "I understand why."

"It always seemed like servitude to me."

She nodded.

"Teardrop does not seem your servant."

"She's not. She's one of my dearest friends."

The stallion raised his muzzle and inhaled in a series of long breaths. Always, always watchful. "What commonality do you find in one another?"

"We don't have much commonality at all. If anything, it's our differences that bring us together." Eleanor thought of Teardrop's blunt honesty and detached world view. "She tells me the truth. She makes me see things in a way I couldn't without her. Maybe I do the same for her."

"And your husband? I heard he let his favorite unicorn die. Left him in the swamp, to be eaten by monsters." Terin's ears flattened against his head.

"That's not true. Gregory loved Vigor with all his heart. He wouldn't leave Vigor's side. Vigor begged him to go."

"Why would he do that?"

"If you saw your own death coming, imminent and unstoppable, wouldn't you want to save the ones you love?"

Terin finally lowered his head to snatch a mouthful of grass, but he was upright within a few seconds. He sniffed as he chewed thoughtfully.

"I believe he also asked Gregory to leave him for the sake of the Bond," said Eleanor. "It meant that much to Vigor, too. The Bond is his life's work, his pledge. Gregory is the embodiment of it."

"How so?"

"It is believed the Bond passes through the male line of the

Desmarais family. If Gregory were to die without an heir, there is a fear the Bond would die with him."

Terin turned to Eleanor with curious dark eyes. "Perhaps you carry the heir in your belly now."

"We'll know when the child arrives." *Dorian's child*, said the voice in her head. She returned to the original subject. "Like you, Gregory has much responsibility. He must look to the safety of his people—and the unicorns and dragons. Sometimes he must make hard choices. Vigor knew it."

"I sympathize with him." Terin butted Eleanor gently with his nose. "Tell me about the young one. The colt you saved."

"His name is Dasha. He's thriving. Bright and strong."

"I knew his mother. She was one of my mares."

"Really? Then why was she—" Suddenly, Penla's story of cast-out mares, those who stray from the herd stallion, made sense.

"She was very young. A wanderer. She was bound to encounter some young stallion on his own."

"And you sent her away? To give birth alone in the marshes?" Eleanor couldn't hide her disappointment. She'd thought Terin too noble for such behavior.

"I let her stay on with the herd, even though I knew the foal wasn't mine. The responsible stallion disappeared—"

"Men and stallions have something else in common."

"But once her time came, she couldn't remain. It's enough to care for my own offspring. To protect them and their mothers. I cannot be responsible for the children of other stallions. It grieved me, but it is our way."

"It's a horrible way. You knew she might die."

"Some don't."

Eleanor crossed her arms over her chest and seethed as she pictured the young mare alone in the marshes, bleeding to death with her baby at her side.

"Hard choices," said Terin.

Eleanor didn't respond.

"When Dasha is old enough, will he be part of the Bond?"

"It will be his choice," said Eleanor. "He can stay or return north to his own kind. Although I cannot imagine he'd get a warm welcome anywhere."

"He'll be welcome here. In my herd. Until he's old enough to truly be on his own. All stallions leave their home herds at some point. They must make their way in the world."

"Yet *another* commonality between men and stallions. Always, you think you must prove your worth. Still, thank you. I'll keep that in mind as he grows."

"You are an interesting creature. I can tell you spend much of your time thinking. Are all humans like you? Is your husband?"

She had to answer truthfully. "Some of us think more than others. Perhaps I think too much."

"That seems impossible."

"Gregory does not think the same way I do. But he will do anything to protect us— humans, unicorns, dragons— from the ogres. If you join with us, you and your herds will be under his protection, too."

"Or perhaps he will be under mine."

"Perhaps."

"You can tell your husband he will have the loyalty of the herds. I'll see to it that the other stallions agree. If the time comes, we shall be allies."

Relief seeped through Eleanor, like the first warm dunk into a hot bath. Which—if she were being honest with herself— sounded very nice. She rested a hand on Terin's neck. "Let us hope the time doesn't come."

CHAPTER 11

KEEP THINGS SIMPLE

ELEANOR RETURNED TO ECLATANT at the beginning of LowSummer, but Dorian remained in the North Country at Gregory's request. He saw no reason to argue, given Gregory's civility. His gnawing worry about Eleanor and the baby followed him day and night, but he recognized the benefit of distance. If he were close to her, he might give himself away with his feverish concern. He relied on visitors from Eclatant to keep him updated on her health, and he found relief with each positive report. She'd finally told Gregory about the pregnancy. The palace was a twitter with excitement over a new member of the royal family. Every person in Maliana with any knowledge of babies, pregnancy, and female persons in general would fuss over Eleanor every hour of every day.

"The princess is in fine form," said Orvid Jones over a breakfast of toast and dried ham one morning. "His Majesty is hoping for a son, of course."

"Of course," said Dorian. "As is all of Cartheigh."

My son. The refrain rang though Dorian's head multiple times a day. *My daughter. Our child.* He both dreaded and prayed for the child to be his.

"His Highness will be visiting the Mines himself next week." To Dorian's relief, Orvid seemed to be softening to him, too. Orvid's loyalty would always be to the crown, but Lord Brandling and the Chief Magician had a shared interest in keeping Gregory on a steady path.

Dorian swallowed his pear juice. "Is it safe for him to journey north?"

"General Claiborne has four garrisons stationed outside Peaksend, not to mention the Unicorn Guard who will accompany the king. That reminds me, Lord Smithwick and his family have left for Solsea. The fortress is virtually empty, should the king decide to stay there."

"Good old Brian. Duke of the North Country. I'm sure he'll be ready for some summer festivities after an extended stint in his damp northern realm."

"He visited Maliana for the Awakening, of course, so he's only been back a few months. Although, being that he's a family man, you can't blame him for wanting his children to experience some sunshine."

The idea of Brian as a benign patriarch irked Dorian, given Brian's past as a fervent womanizer and Dorian's own life of perpetual solitude. "I suppose. But I've not seen hide nor horn of him since I've been here."

"If you're here as Gregory's eyes, there's no reason for him to visit at the Mines."

My presence is reason enough for him to actively avoid the Mines, Dorian thought. Brian was Gregory's cousin on his mother's side, and a scion of one of the most powerful families in Cartheigh. He and Gregory had been playmates since they could crawl. Dorian's appearance at court when all three men were teenagers permanently displaced Brian as Gregory's sword hand man. The rivalry between them was as deep as the lake in front of Dorian's childhood home, and as thick as the Fire-iron walls that surrounded Brian's family estate just outside Maliana. Years ago, Brian resented Dorian being handed a title before him. Now Dorian felt jealous of his domestic bliss. HighGod had quite a sense of humor.

Gregory arrived with a small retinue six days later. He chose to travel light and under cover of darkness. Circles of exhaustion hung under his eyelids like used teabags. He dismounted in the Mine yard at dawn on a Tuesday. He patted the neck of his new unicorn, a gorgeous young stallion called Monument. Monument trailed behind him as he walked toward Dorian and Orvid.

Gregory spoke in the gentle voice he always used with unicorns but rarely used with anyone else. "It's all right, lad. Take a load off. You've worked hard, and you deserve it."

"Call upon me if you need me."

"You do the same, if you need me." Gregory exchanged greetings with Dorian and Orvid. They chatted briefly about the journey.

"The cabin is yours," said Dorian.

"We can bunk up. Have them set up an extra bed in the downstairs common room. No need for you to huddle in a tent with a smelly sergeant."

Orvid raised his eyebrows and glanced at Dorian in obvious surprise at his king's solicitude.

"Thank you," said Dorian. "I've been reading at night, and the light is better from the fireplace."

Gregory cleared his throat and swept a hand through his hair. "What have you been reading? Something useful, I hope."

"I believe so. I'm reacquainting myself with the habits of—"

"Ogre! Ogre!" The frantic voice finished Dorian's thought for him.

Three yelling farmers on fat ponies careened into the Mine yard. Matt Thromba elbowed his way around a few of his workers and a pile of raw meat. His three-pronged beard flopped over his shoulders. "You lot! What do ya think you're after? Barging in—where's the guard?"

The first farmer slid to the ground. His ruddy face looked about to explode with pounding adrenaline. "The unicorns at the gate let us pass, sir, they did—"

"Bloody hell! You've not got authorization!"

Gregory put a hand on Thromba's shoulder. "Let the man speak, Matt."

The farmer blanched when he recognized Gregory by the crown on his head. Dorian feared he might faint from exertion and shock.

"Your Majesty, HighGod above." He and his two fat fellows fell to their knees.

"Stand, sirs. Thank you for your blessings, but pray, how can we help you?"

"An ogre, Your Majesty. I own a farm…a little place…ten miles south. We're the last homestead before the Mines."

"I know your farm. I've passed it many times."

"This morning, I heard a ruckus in the barn. Cows squealing like caught rabbits—" The farmer put a fist to his mouth and tears leaked from his buggy blue eyes. "Looked out me window—and it was right there in my paddock!"

"Dragon's teeth," Dorian said. "Where is your family?"

"We ran, sir. Took the ponies and ran. These two are my young brothers. My wife and children are with my father at our closest neighbor's farm, but I fear for them. We watched from afar. I believe the ogre is gone, but what if it moves on to the next home place?" He dropped to his knees again.

Gregory put a hand on the man's shoulder. "We will investigate. If there's anything left, we'll salvage what we can." He pointed to Dorian and Orvid. "You two mount up. Bring twenty of the Guard. Matt, we need more security at the Mine Gate."

Thromba and his miners rushed to do Gregory's bidding. Dorian whistled for Senné, and Orvid called for his own mount. The king drew his sword. "Monument won't be getting that much-deserved rest."

The ogre had indeed done its damage and left. Dorian surveyed the devastation from Senné's back. The beast had destroyed the cozy thatch-roofed farmhouse. It either stepped on the roof or dropped something roughly the size of an ox cart through it. Half the thick stone chimney lay in rubble beside the front door. The demolished roof alone was a catastrophe. North Country farmers were hardy, but given the near constant rain, a sound roof was a necessity.

Dorian peered through one of the windows at the roof obliterating projectile. It was a Fire-iron plow, probably passed down through the famer's family for generations. The Fire-iron's mystical strength ensured the valuable device itself survived the ogre's wrath, but it sliced the kitchen table clean in half. Tipped over chairs and shattered clay cups and bowls lay across the knobby wooden floor, along with a spilled pot of congealing stew.

He turned to the farmyard. The ogre had overturned bins of dried root vegetables and stomped them into the wet ground with its huge, flat feet. The family's personal effects moldered in putrid mud: furry robes and blankets, books, a few candles, and a pair of homespun pants. Only a few signs of livestock remained, including a discarded cow's leg, scattered wool, and chicken feathers.

The family's poor sheepdog lay in a furry black and white puddle beside the stone barn. The ogre must have flung the dog against the rocks when the animal tried to defend its home and family. A lone chicken crept gingerly through the wreckage, clucking softly. The sound made Dorian think of his kindly childhood nanny examining his messy nursery. *Tsk-tsk. What have we here?*

"It spared the barn, at least," said Gregory.

He'd no sooner said it than the barn door fell off its hinges, crushing a wheelbarrow and a tool bench.

"Horns and fire, what a mess," said Dorian. "Thank HighGod the family escaped in time. It's a miracle no one died."

"They'll have a hard time surviving the winter," said Orvid. "All their livestock gone."

Gregory walked to edge of the ogre's footprint. "Didn't even spare the damn turnips and carrots. Don't these things eat rocks and dirt?"

"They can *survive* on rocks and dirt," said Dorian. "They'll eat almost anything, if given the chance."

"Remember, with ogres, it's not just about appetite," said Orvid. "This destruction is an offering to Cra. An attempt to convince him they're worthy of his promised land."

Dorian believed in HighGod. The world and all the creatures in it had to come about somehow. An all-powerful creator made sense, but he disdained the complicated mythologies of other cultures. How did the ogres purport to know what their god wanted? Didn't his very omniscience mean they would never understand? It struck him as terribly arrogant. This family had paid the price for the beasts' self-righteous superstitions.

"They haven't done much appeasing of him in the past five hundred years, have they?" Gregory asked.

"Which will make them all the more dangerous now," said Orvid. "To make up for lost time."

Gregory covered his nose. "God, the stench." Noxious steam rose from the mud.

"Step back, Your Majesty," said Orvid. "That ground is teaming with disease. The longer it festers, the worse it gets."

Gregory stepped away from the footprint. The sludgy stew percolating inside it belched out a foul-smelling bubble. Dorian returned to Senné. His ears were pinned to his head. Most observers, those only familiar with horses, would take the stallion's stance as simply aggressive. Dorian knew better. Senné's flattened ears showed his distaste for the whole sorry situation.

"I believe we're not the only ones who are curious about what happened here," Senné said, nostrils quivering.

Monument raised his own great head and inhaled deeply. He coughed and his pink tongue flashed around shiny white teeth. He shook out his mane. "Others are coming."

Gregory put a hand on his sword, but Dorian followed Monument's line of sight. He made out movement across the marsh. More white, approaching fast.

"The wild ones," Dorian said. *They've come, as Eleanor said they would.*

Terin led four other unicorns into the barnyard—all powerful, mature stallions. It was surprising, as grown, dominant stallions rarely interacted unless necessary.

Senné nickered a greeting. Terin returned it with a snort and a flick of his tail before cautiously exploring the carnage with his companions. They mirrored Senné and Monument's disgust with their flattened ears and hacking coughs. One stallion spooked when the survivalist chicken darted from behind a hay bale and ran through his legs, squawking. The Bonded unicorns watched their wild cousins curiously, as men might watch foreign visitors in their own country.

When Terin seemed satisfied that he'd sniffed all the foulness he needed to sniff, he and his fellows approached Gregory. The king stood beside Monument, who trembled with excitement.

"Greetings, King Gregory," said Terin. "It seems our interests are already aligning."

"We're glad to see you and your friends."

"We don't often come together like this. But unusual times call for unusual friendships. Among unicorns, and among unicorns and humans."

One of the other stallions spoke up. "King, did any of you see the ogre?"

"The meaning of this stallion's name is Whisper," said Terin. "So named because he never does."

Dorian bit his lip to keep from smiling. Even among unicorns, male specimens never missed an opportunity to spar with one another.

Whisper bared his teeth and arched his neck. He appeared younger than Terin, but he was nearly as large, with particularly long legs. "I see no need to hold my tongue or wait to be called upon," he said.

"We didn't see the creature," said Gregory. "We only have the report of the farmers and the evidence before our eyes."

"Now it's gone," said Terin. "Where?"

"It must be hiding in the mountains somewhere," said Orvid. "Perhaps several of them have set up some kind of camp."

Terin peered at Gregory from beneath his long lashes. "What would you have done, Your Majesty, if you'd seen it?"

Gregory shrugged. "I didn't come to try and stop it, truth be told. Not this time. More to observe it."

"I agree. I'm not so arrogant as to risk the safety of my herd, and my companions' herds, on a battle with an unknown entity."

"Perhaps if my men and unicorns had joined you, we may have had a chance to kill it."

Monument joined the conversation, tentative at first. "How many would we need to kill an ogre, Your Majesty?"

Gregory demurred to Orvid, who replied, "It's not a matter of numbers. More of strategy. To allow for a man, or a unicorn, to get close enough to strike its belly with sword or horn.

"I understand." Monument looked resigned, as if he'd already accepted that he'd probably meet an early end while trying to slice open an ogre.

"There must be other ways to kill them," said Dorian. "I think we should put it to study, Your Majesty. In the Coveys, the Abbeys, and the library at Eclatant."

"That is wise," said Terin, "Upon consideration, one of our own should go with these men and their unicorn friends, so we know what they know. Whisper, I'm bestowing this honor on you."

Whisper's ears pricked in surprise. "Me?"

"Your loquaciousness might finally prove useful. You can be our voice."

"What of my mares?"

"I shall look after them."

"If you think it will help our herds, Terin, then I will go," said Whisper, but his tail flicked irritably.

"Thank you. I do believe your presence will bring great value." Terin own tail swished slowly back and forth, as steady and unaffected as a clock pendulum.

Dorian's years of reading subtle unicorn language served him well. Terin felt pleased with himself. He'd reiterated his superiority, placed a liaison of sorts at the palace to ensure the wild unicorns' interests were represented, and perhaps he'd even add a mare or two to his own herd in Whisper's absence. In many ways, Terin managed his own court, way out here in the hinterlands. Not so different from Eclatant.

The rest of the wild unicorns bid them farewell, and Whisper grudgingly fell into step beside Senné. He paced along without speaking. Senné also seemed lost in his thoughts, so Dorian allowed his own speculations to take over.

Orvid and his magicians would rise to the challenge of updating the known world on all forms of potential ogre eradication. He assumed Rosemary and the witches of Afar Creek Abbey would contribute their own knowledge. But in the end, he would count on one un-enchanted person to produce the most innovative and novel ideas. She had no magic of her own, only a brilliant mind and a dogged will.

Four months later, with Dorian still trapped in the North Country and Gregory on his way home from a meeting with the Talessee king, Eleanor lay in her bed with a tiny boy child in her arms. Piles of books and manuscripts lay around the bed, like leather-bound icebergs floating on pale blue sea of woven rugs. She'd passed the last few days before the child's birth on witch-ordered bedrest, so she'd used the time to do some frenetic ogre research, but now, she felt too tired to do anything but stare at her son's face.

Maids bustled in and out. They removed dirty linens and empty pitchers. They relit vanilla candles that had burned too low. In the two days since her newest child's birth, Pansy refused to let the light go out. Even at night, gentle candlelight tickled the walls, and the sweet, comforting vanilla scent did the same to her nose. It was MidAutumn and still warm in Maliana. Eleanor longed for the Solsea breeze, but she'd agreed with Gregory's decision to remain at Eclatant for his first summer as king. Even in an ordinary year, she wouldn't have been allowed to travel close to the birth. Desmarais children must enter the world via Eclatant, in close proximity to the watchful eyes of Afar Creek's babycatchers. Given the totality of the circumstances, it was inevitable. The royal family had stayed home and sweated with the rest of the capital.

She wiped a bead of perspiration from the end of her nose and gazed down at her son. Her living, healthy, fat little boy. She'd spent the last two days in spasms of gratitude for his safe arrival.

The babycatcher had grinned as she placed the shrieking child into his mother's arms. "All I can say, Your Highness, is I've never seen such a robust baby. In form, or in lung capacity."

Truly, while her three surviving children had all been healthy at birth, he was quite a specimen. The largest of the four, by far. She had yet to name him, as Gregory would have the final say in the next Desmarais king's name. She thought he might choose Casper. Perhaps Nathan again, as their late son would have been the third Desmarais king to bear the name. She hoped he'd avoid Caleb. Sylvia had already usurped that holy Desmarais moniker for her as yet officially fatherless son. Any route, there was no need to get her heart set on something when Gregory would have every right to change it.

The baby yawned, and she stared at his miniature features, trying to determine who he resembled. The child's face and coloring gave her neither the relief of obvious Desmarais parentage, nor the terror of recognizable Finley descent. Frankly, he didn't look much like her others. Ticia, Nathan, and Natalie had all distinctly resembled Gregory, first and foremost because each came into the world with a head of reddish hair. This baby was as bald as a strike stick ball. The little peach fuzz he had appeared to be white blond. No shock of black hair to give him away as a Finley. His eyes were the milky gray, common to many newborn babes. While Ticia's eyes had always been dark, both Nathan and Natalie's had changed in their first year of life, to light blue and green, respectively.

I'll torture myself trying to find resemblances between him and Dorian. Or him and Gregory. Or him and myself! What a ridiculous mess!

Chou landed on the bed beside her. While they couldn't speak outwardly about the child's pedigree, they politely tiptoed around it. They whispered as if their speculations might wake the baby.

"He's very blond," said Chou.

"Do you recall how I looked as a babe, Chou? There are no portraits of me from those days."

"By the time I left the nest and came to you, you were already walking about in bloomers and chattering away. I recall your hair was short—about to your chin. Not like your girls, toddling around tripping over their own braids."

"We can ask Rosemary. She'll remember."

Chou gently ran his beak over the baby's head. He looked up at Eleanor from one round yellow eye. "Show me your ears," he said.

"Why?" Eleanor asked, but she reached up with one hand and tucked her hair behind the appendages in question.

Chou hopped onto her shoulder. "Your earlobes," he said, as he nipped one. Eleanor squirmed. She giggled, and the baby whimpered. She kissed his smooth cheek.

"They're shockingly bare at the moment. I didn't have time to accessorize before giving birth."

"No, silly. They're not attached."

"I beg to differ, Chou. Last time I checked, they were." She tugged one to prove her point.

He rolled his eyes. "Look at the baby's earlobes. They connect right to his head. Yours, they hang down."

"So what?"

"Most people have earlobes like yours. The kind that hang down. The baby's are attached."

She raised her eyebrows. "Why do you know this?"

"Anne Iris once explained it to me. She has shockingly small earlobes. She only wears pearls because they're light, and she prefers studs over dangly earbobs."

Eleanor laughed. "I suppose you're right. I've never thought about it." She fingered the baby's tiny ears. "This little one's earlobes could be telling."

"What do you know of Gregory's earlobes?"

Eleanor thought, hard. Gregory's ears were small and stuck close to his head, but she remembered nothing about his earlobes. She focused on Dorian— his ears endearingly stuck out a bit, but for the life of her, she couldn't picture his earlobes, either. Even if she'd nibbled them many times, she could not call to mind their exact shape.

"I can't remember. No one's earlobes are coming to mind. They don't attract as much attention as a well-muscled arm or an obvious bulge in the leggings." She laughed harder. How ridiculous, that she'd be sitting here, obsessing over the earlobes of two different men.

Chou joined her snickering. "Try to imagine Gregory wearing Queen Ambrosia's sapphires. That might help."

Eleanor guffawed at the image of Gregory, preening about in his late great-grandmother's gaudy Fire-iron earrings. Her flaccid stomach muscles and tender ill-used nether regions yowled at her, and not in mirth. "Ouch, Chou. I can't laugh. My insides aren't ready yet."

The baby opened his eyes and stared up at her. "I think your earlobes are perfect, little man," she said. "But I will certainly examine the king's aural appendages when he arrives home."

Pansy knocked on the door and peeked around the corner. "Your

Highness, are you awake? Princess Natalie is begging to visit her little brother."

"Certainly. Where is Tish?"

"She went down to the stables to tell Teardrop and Cricket all about our wee man. But Natalie has been sitting outside the door since breakfast!" Pansy opened the door, and Natalie crept into the room. She quietly climbed up on her mother's bed in her sweet white linen dress with its green and purple ribbons. She tucked her bare feet under the covers.

She reached out with one hand and ran her fingers over the baby's head. "He's so small," she whispered.

"You were even smaller," said Eleanor. She kissed Natalie's fingers. They were tipped with bright color. Each miniature nail a shiny red. "Natty! Did Ticia paint your fingernails? You know Poppa would not approve."

She didn't say so, but only well-to-do prostitutes like Pandra Tate painted their fingernails. Shocking that Natalie had found someone to do it for her. Even Ticia, with her subtle adolescent thumbing of the rules and love of color, would probably not be so bold as to gussy up her little sister like a Pasture's End trollop.

"No." Natalie offered no other explanation, but she held out her skinny arms. Eleanor couldn't resist the wondering look on her face.

"You may hold him, but then it's straight to Pansy to remove that red."

"I dream in this color, Mother." Natalie wrapped her arms around her brother. "It makes me feel warm."

Eleanor's brow wrinkled at her daughter's odd statement. "Watch his head." She adjusted the baby in Natalie's lap.

Natalie kissed him and crooned into his face. He could not focus properly yet, so he stared up at her with slightly crossed eyes.

"Do you like this color too, baby?" She wiggled her fingers in front of the baby's face. Eleanor blinked. For a moment, Natalie's red fingernails went fuzzy, as if the color were drifting away from her hands and dissipating into the air.

I need something to eat or a drink of water, Eleanor thought. The bright red streaming from Natalie's fingers only got darker. *Is she bleeding?* "Natalie, love—"

Eleanor reached for the baby as Natalie hugged him.

Red light enveloped her two children, so dark and thick, for a moment Eleanor could not see them. Chou whistled and fluttered to the top of one of the bed posters. Eleanor cried out. She reached blindly into the mist as it swirled toward the ceiling. It slowly changed from red to magenta to pink. She grabbed Natalie's arm.

Natalie smiled at her. "Don't worry. I'm keeping him warm."

Eleanor was afraid to take the baby from Natalie. She looked up at Chou in a panic. Pansy ran into the room. "Is everything in order, Your Highness?"

Eleanor nodded, but she felt as if she might throw up. There was only one explanation for the red light. She certainly didn't want Pansy, or anyone else, to know about it.

"We're fine, thank you. I'm just a nervous new mama, for the fourth time."

"Ah, well, every new child is a wonder, and this one has been long in coming." The maid hummed to herself as she peeked over Natalie's shoulder. "What a good big sister you are!"

"Thank you, Pansy." Natalie tapped the baby's nose.

Chou landed on Eleanor's head. "Her nails," he said.

The red splashes on Natalie's nails had disappeared. They were clean and pinkish again.

Eleanor needed answers, but she didn't want to scare her daughter. "Natalie, where does the red light come from?"

"I suppose from inside me. Rosemary has her own light. It's white." She looked up at Eleanor. "Rosemary is a witch, but I've not seen normal people like me have their own light. Do you have any light, Mother?"

Eleanor shook her head. Her heart constricted in her chest. “No, sweetheart. I have no such light.”

Chou whispered in her ear. “Eleanor, you know what this means. It means Natalie is *not* normal.”

She nodded. Natalie, her brilliant, charming, beautiful daughter, was a witch.

To Eleanor, the shocking revelation meant only one thing. Witches lived among their own, as did magicians. In abbeys and coveys.

She would lose another child. Several unknown babies lost to the mysteries of miscarriage. Nathan to a terrible, unstoppable disease. Now Natalie, lost to magic.

Eleanor wasted no time. She called Rosemary to Eclatant. The next morning, in Eleanor’s Chamber, Rosemary spoke to Natalie about her warm red light, and to Rosemary’s surprise, Natalie conjured a bright red cloud of magical energy with no guidance or assistance. Once the light dissipated, Rosemary gently advised Natalie to keep it to herself for now, and she sent the child to the nursery with Pansy. Eleanor had just finished nursing the baby, so for the first time since his birth, Eleanor asked Pansy to take him for an hour or so.

“Bring him back if he fusses,” said Eleanor.

“We’ll be fine, Your Highness,” said Pansy. “Little man, with his two sisters watching out for him.”

“Natalie,” Eleanor called out. “Remember what Rosemary told you. Let’s keep things simple… for now. Especially when Little Brother is around. Yes?”

“Yes, Mother,” said Natalie. Eleanor hoped the child’s concern for her small sibling would make her extra careful about heeding Rosemary’s advice. Eleanor wasn’t particularly concerned Natalie would hurt her brother or anyone else. She was a tender, gentle little person who loved just about everyone. She simply didn’t want to raise any suspicions.

Eleanor and Rosemary regarded each other in tense silence until the sound of Pansy and the children faded behind the thick oak door of Eleanor's chamber. Chou perched on the back of the sofa behind Rosemary's head.

"How long has this been going on?" asked Rosemary.

"I honestly don't know. I hadn't seen any signs before yesterday and then suddenly, *poof*." She waved her hands in front of her face, miming an explosion.

"It's usually that way. Children don't come out of the womb conjuring."

"I don't understand. There are no magical folk in my family. I've never heard or read of any in the Desmarais family."

"Our power doesn't necessarily run in families. It's a blessing that strikes like lightning. I'm the only magical person in my own family. Of course, there are some new witches or magicians who can say, *oh, my uncle conjured at First Covey, or my cousin is a sorceress of Afar Creek,* but for most of us, it's unpredictable."

"Isn't she young to be displaying magical power? She's just turned five."

"On the young side, but not out of the question. I was nearly six. I heard Mr. Oliver showed his power early. He had just turned four when the Covey claimed him."

"Orvid Jones told me he hid his magic, because he didn't want to leave his family."

"It's very rare to be able to exhibit that much control with no training. Orvid is an unusually powerful magician. But even he eventually had to answer the call of his abilities. At age nine, was it?"

"Eight," said Eleanor. "So Natalie might have a few years—"

"I would advise against it. It's dangerous for young witches and magicians to try to contain their power. Dangerous for the youngster, and dangerous for those around him or her. Some have gone mad. Or accidentally blown up their own homes."

"HighGod," said Eleanor. Perhaps Natalie *could* unwittingly hurt someone.

"Can you make an exception?" asked Chou. "After all, Natalie is a Desmarais princess. She has a claim to the throne. Must she leave Eclatant?"

Eleanor grasped blindly at Chou's suggestion. "You're right! The royal family, of course, it's different. She can stay here. You can tutor her here!"

Rosemary took Eleanor's hand. "No, Eleanor, my love. You know in your heart, that's not possible. If Natalie is a witch, she must come to the Abbey. Be with her own kind. Learn to manage her magic—and to let it blossom."

Eleanor stood. Despite the lingering pain from the birth, she paced behind the sofa while Chou stalked across the cushions. The two of them about-faced and crossed paths like soldiers walking off demerits. "Rosemary, I just *can't* let her go. I can't. She's too young."

"She doesn't have to leave tomorrow, but you cannot put it off too long."

"Gregory won't allow it!"

"It doesn't matter what Gregory wants, for once. Thousands of years of tradition command it. The Oracle will sense her power, if she hasn't already. She identifies all magical children, male and female, all over Cartheigh. Even First Covey comes to her to confirm who should be collected."

Eleanor's back hurt. Her breasts hurt. Her pelvis ached, as did everything in between it. *How can it be, that my body should work so hard to spark so much life, yet life always takes my children from me?*

"Gregory wants to send my first baby— my Leticia—to HighGod knows where, to be someone's wife. Nathan—sweet Nathan—dead and gone. I've had three miscarriages. Now the Abbey is going to take Natalie? My darling, brilliant Natalie?"

"She is brilliant. Just like her mother. Do you remember, how when you were small, I wanted you to have magic?"

"You wanted to take me to the Abbey to live, to save me from Imogene. But the Oracle wouldn't allow it because I'm not a witch."

"It's true. I wanted to get you away from Imogene. But I also wanted to take you to the

Abbey so you might reap the benefits of our life. Surrounded by women who dedicate their lives to gaining knowledge, cultivating power, and sharing it with others. *Helping* others."

"But I still learned. From you. From your hidden teaching all those years."

"True. That is what the Oracle saw for you. It served you well. Served Cartheigh well. But have you ever wondered what it would be like to be able to dedicate yourself wholly to the wonders of your mind? Exist in a sphere where there are no distractions? No one telling you that you can't speak up, or that a woman is somehow less?"

"But what about love? Family? She'll never have children. Or a husband."

"We both know marriage isn't necessarily a source of love—and look at the pain your true love has brought you."

Eleanor refused to acknowledge Rosemary's logic about her personal romantic life. Gregory might have made her miserable over the years, but he'd given her Leticia and Natalie and Nathan. Perhaps this new baby. Or perhaps Dorian had blessed her with her little son, as he had blessed her with years of love and dedication, despite the pain of it all. "I wouldn't change any of it. Natalie won't even be allowed to spend time with her sister and brother."

"We have our own ways of loving, Eleanor. We love all people the same. We also have the gift of magic. You can't understand the comfort and peace of magical power."

"You told me yourself the witches' life doesn't come easy for you. That you wished for your own child."

"I did, at times. But as you would not trade the results of your romantic endeavors, I would not trade my magic for anything in this world. You have to understand, magic changes you, once you experience it. I did miss my family. I would have loved to have a child of my own. But in my younger days, I simply wanted it all."

"I have a family, and I have my love of learning. I have responsibilities, and I make a difference in this world. It's not a perfect life, but it lets me experience all facets of existence."

"Except magic, which you cannot comprehend."

Eleanor's jaw jutted. "I do not want my children holed up, away from the people who love them the most."

"I cannot expect you to understand. It's different for you. When a commoner has a magical child, most are in awe. Ready to send their child to the Abbey or Covey as an honor. Even as a way to give the child a better life. You see Natalie's life here as an honor—and a blessed one." She turned to the parrot. "Chou—can you help me explain?"

"Rosemary, you know I always look at both sides of the coin. The faces tell different versions of equally interesting stories. But I can't play the two-headed jester in this situation. I agree with Eleanor. I cannot bear the thought of little Natty ripped away from us."

Rosemary stood. "I can tell we won't get much farther today. I will keep this quiet, for now. But you must tell Gregory when he returns. Natalie won't be able to hide it herself much longer anyway."

"What if it goes away?" Eleanor said. "Her magical power. Remember Marcus? His did."

"Eleanor, that is exceedingly rare." Rosemary had never spoken to her so matter-of-factly, and in truth, so condescendingly. "There is no point in ruminating on it. Natalie is a powerful sorceress in the making. Stop looking for ways to make her power go away. It's selfish of you. She will only hate you for it in the end."

Rosemary gathered her belongings and left without another word.

Eleanor stood beside the fireplace. Chou lit on the mantle. "I've never been at odds with Rosemary, Chou."

"You know she's probably right. As much as we hate to admit it. Perhaps it's a blessing. Natalie will never have to marry an old Svelyan prince. Or a young homosexual one."

Eleanor rubbed her eyes. "She's my baby. That's all I know. And Rosemary is going to take her away from me."

Over the next three days, Eleanor kept all three children close to her. Leticia and Natalie were content to dote over the baby. Tish drew several portraits of him, and Natalie could be counted on to hold him for an hour or so, while Eleanor caught up on her correspondence and read reports from the kitchen about supplies for the upcoming Harvest Fest. Soon, visiting courtiers would descend upon them, all in spasms of excitement over the new prince. Gregory would have to balance the urge to show off his heir with fear for his safety. Eleanor planned to station healing witches at the palace doors. She'd instruct them to turn away anyone who sniffled, sneezed, or exhibited the slightest sign of a rash.

To her relief, Sylvia had apparently decided to remain in Harveston. John-Caleb's claim to the throne looked more and more remote, bastard or not. Sylvia had no reason to celebrate the birth of Gregory's legitimate male heir.

Natalie did her best to contain her magic, but when she relaxed, Eleanor noted a faint pinkish cloud floating around her and her little brother. She didn't have the heart to criticize her beyond gentle reminders to *keep things quiet*. As for the baby, he seemed perfectly content in Natalie's arms. If anything, he slept more soundly when she sprung a magical leak.

On the afternoon of the fourth day, with Gregory's return imminent, Eleanor dressed in one of his favorite olive green and gold autumn gowns. Pansy styled her hair in the long, looping swirls he liked, complete with golden ribbons. Ticia wore white satin, and Natalie chose a red velvet gown that was more appropriate for winter, but Eleanor didn't argue with her. She was understandably developing a fondness for red, and Eleanor hoped her bright dress would make any evidence of magic seem a mere reflection of the silk. Two hours after lunch, blasting trumpets announced Gregory's arrival. The girls went into spasms of excitement. Eleanor left the baby with Pansy and took her older children to the Great Hall to greet their father. He scooped them both into his arms and covered them with kisses.

"Poppa!" Leticia squealed. "I'm too old for that."

"You'll never be too old for me to pick you up, Tish, or too tall. Although, you may be taller than me someday!" He tickled Natalie under her chin. "My little angel. My Natalie Matilda."

"Hello, Poppa. I trust you had a safe journey."

Gregory laughed. "Such a little lady! I did indeed." He turned to Eleanor. She lowered her eyes at his tender expression. "Here is my dear wife."

"Husband." Eleanor couldn't look him in the eye. She wasn't sure why. Guilt? Fear? Both?

"You're looking well. I have heard tell of the good news, of my handsome son's arrival. HighGod be praised. We have the heir we've sought for so long."

"I look forward to you meeting him."

"It is my first priority," said Gregory. "I cannot tell you how much joy this brings me. Especially when we've had so much loss of late." He kissed her hand and then kissed both of her cheeks. She sensed nothing devious or passive aggressive in his voice, but given the circumstances and their long history, she couldn't relax.

"A quick bath, and then I'll see my boy. Ho, Melfin!" he shouted to his old valet, who stood at the foot of the staircase awaiting his orders. "Draw my bath!"

Eleanor asked Pansy to take the girls to the nursery. She rushed to her chamber. She blew past the two guards outside the door. Two nannies stood watch over the baby's cradle, along with Chou Chou.

"Is he awake?" She dismissed the nannies and bent over the cradle. The baby slept peacefully. She gingerly lifted him, clutched him to her chest, and stroked his head. She sat on the bed and rested him on her lap. He was so perfect, and so frustratingly unlike either Gregory or Dorian. Fat cheeks, snub nose, big grayish eyes, pink lips, and no hair. He was simply a beautiful baby, not unlike her girls' porcelain dolls.

"It's good that he's so nondescript, isn't it, Chou?"

The parrot crouched beside her on the coverlet. He nodded. "Even if he grows to look like Dorian, if Gregory falls in love with him, perhaps he'll be blind to it."

"We can only hope." She examined the baby's fingers, and then his chin, and then his earlobes, again. After what seemed like an eternity, Pansy announced Gregory.

Chou flittered into the rafters as Gregory tiptoed toward the bed and sat gently beside Eleanor. As if sensing a visitor, the child blinked and yawned. As all new babes are wont to do, he stared at the ceiling above him.

Gregory didn't say anything, and as the silence stretched on, Eleanor wondered if he heard her heart beating against her rib cage. She finally stole a glance at him out of the corner of her eye.

Tears tracked down his face. He reached for the baby, and she handed him over. *Dear HighGod, are those happy tears? Please let them be happy tears.*

"He's bigger even than Nathan," Gregory said, and Eleanor's panic subsided. Happy tears, but bittersweet. The mention of Nathan called up her own personal agony.

"He is," she managed to croak out. "And just as strong."

"Stronger, even. Nathan will always be my first-born boy." He held the baby close to his chest. "I will go to my grave missing him. His death is the greatest regret of my life, and I have many regrets."

"Oh, Gregory—"

"Hush now, my wife. His little brother will see his grown years. If it takes every breath in my body to see him live to take the crown, so be it. Thank you for bringing him into this world."

"What is his name to be?"

"Cyrus. He will be Cyrus the First. He shall have his own name, and his own legacy."

Gregory gingerly put an arm around Eleanor's shoulder. She let herself feel what she needed to feel. For now, at least, it didn't matter who had fathered him. She and Gregory had both longed for him, and here he was. For the first time in years, they shared a beautiful moment—one that would stay with her forever. The memory of a child lost, and the infinite potential of a new child born. Little Cyrus, the boy king.

CHAPTER 12

How the World Works

Four months passed, and Cyrus grew into a fat, happy baby who chuckled endlessly and never stopped moving. Unlike her other children, he was not a good sleeper. He nursed ravenously—several times a night. In exhausted desperation, she called for a wet nurse for the first time in her nearly fourteen years as a parent. Every five days or so, she turned Cyrus over to a buxom blonde woman who had nursed many of Maliana's little aristocrats. She went to bed immediately after supper, with Pansy and Chou standing guard at her door. The maid and the parrot wouldn't let anyone disturb her. Not Gregory or the girls. She always fell into a deep sleep and woke up in the same position as morning light crept into her room. Sometimes she drooled on her pillow. Not very fitting for a queen consort, but she didn't care. The sleep got her through another five days, until she needed to catch up again.

As for Natalie, Eleanor asked Rosemary to give her private lessons in the deepest corners of Eclatant's library. Even Eleanor hadn't perused many of those stacks, as they contained books in Old Talessee. She only knew a few words of modern Talessee, much less the five-hundred-year-old version. Eleanor promised Rosemary she would tell Gregory as soon as Orvid Jones and Dorian returned. She didn't have any real reason for delaying, but Rosemary grudgingly agreed, and the two women loved one another too much to continue fighting. In the meantime, Rosemary provided Natalie with some magical release and lessons on how to control her power.

"She lit a step ladder on fire," Rosemary told Eleanor one HighWinter afternoon.

"HighGod." Eleanor sighed. "You know I hate to be wrong, but she may indeed harm someone."

"I taught her an extinguishing spell. Or, I should say, I showed it to her. She watched me perform it once." Rosemary snapped her fingers. "Like that, she performed it herself."

The days wore on, and Eleanor vacillated between contentment and despair. Her new little boy enthralled her, and he still remained safely anonymous in appearance, but she dreaded the thought of Natalie leaving her. Whenever she imagined it, she burst into tears. Once at the breakfast table, and once in chapel. She blamed it on exhaustion and post-pregnancy tender sensibilities, but she took to having a bit of a cry about it each morning, on her own in her bathing room, to get it out of her system.

In LowSpring, at a birthday dinner for Raoul Delano, Gregory announced the imminent return of the Duke of Brandling and the Chief Magician. Eleanor wanted to jump from her chair and do a happy jig, but she clapped politely with everyone else. To her relief, Gregory didn't even look at her to gauge her reaction to his news. Perhaps he was finally moving past the old hurt and anger.

"Don't get ahead of yourself," said Chou, when she mentioned her optimism. "Let's re-examine his happy mood once Dorian is here. Along with whatever unpleasant news he brings from the North."

She adjusted Cyrus's head as he happily nursed. His little feet bounced, as if he couldn't wait to start running on them. "It's been oddly calm, hasn't it? Nothing more about ogres. The dragons are still in a collective foul mood, but Fire-iron production is creeping back up."

"Again, don't get ahead of yourself. Oliver always goes quiet for a while after first raising his head. I think he goes back to planning. He always plucks every feather from the chicken before cooking it."

She laughed. "Chou, how morbid. Aren't there a few chickens in your family?"

"A fighting rooster or two, perhaps. Cousins on my father's side." He crowed, and Cyrus jumped in her arms.

Chou looked down at him. "A king must have nerves of steel, little prince."

Cyrus bopped the parrot on his pretty blue head. Chou toppled off the arm of the rocking chair.

"Dear Chou, are you hurt?" asked Eleanor.

"No. I consider it an honor to be the young prince's first sparring partner."

The baby fell asleep in Eleanor's arms a few minutes later. She tiptoed over to the bed. She lay him on the coverlet and snuggled in beside him herself. "We have nothing on the agenda but waiting for Dorian and Orvid to return," she said. "I think a nap is in order."

"I shall keep watch, Your Highness," said Chou.

"Thank you, Sir Parrot." She curled next to her little son, who snored soft baby snores. She fell into a deep sleep, the kind of intense daytime sleep that leads to unsettling dreams. Her sleeping mind placed her on a black road with yellow stripes, and she suddenly felt certain someone was watching her. Bright white lights rushed toward her. She turned to run but she couldn't move fast enough. She cried out for Dorian as the grumbling lights bore down on her.

He body jerked. She woke out of fear she'd jostled the baby. For a moment, she wondered if she were still dreaming. Dorian sat in a chair beside the bed.

"Am I awake?" she whispered.

"You are. We arrived before dawn this morning. Only Gregory and a few other members of the High Council know we've returned."

She sat up, still groggy. "I'm sorry. I must look horrid. How did you get in here?"

"I asked Gregory for permission to see the prince, and he granted it."

"Did he? That was... kind of him." She wanted to add *and surprising*, but it didn't need to be said.

"I told Pansy I have a message to deliver. I suppose I do." He dropped his voice to a whisper and smiled. "I can't say it out loud, but you know my sentiments."

"I share them. As for this little one, he doesn't know you yet, but he will love you." Eleanor lifted the baby into her lap, and he curled instinctively toward her breast. "As all my children do."

Dorian's gaze darted from the baby's bald head to his fuzzy green socks. She read anxiety in every line of his face. She turned the child toward him. Cyrus grunted and opened his eyes. Dorian leaned in. For a moment, Cyrus stared in confusion into Dorian's unfamiliar visage. Then he grinned. A fat blob of baby drool plopped onto his white cotton shirt and slid down to his short pants. He kicked his legs, squealed, and reached for Dorian.

"HighGod," Dorian said, again in a whisper. "He's the most beautiful child I've ever seen."

She spoke haltingly around her own fears. "He—he doesn't really resemble the girls, does he?"

Dorian glanced over his shoulder. "He simply looks like a lovely, plump cherub."

They stared at each other for a moment, as there were no safe words to be said, and then Dorian laughed. "My prince!" he said. "Might I hold him?"

Eleanor handed the baby over. Dorian cooed into his face. Cyrus continued grinning away, as he always did. He pulled his chubby legs toward his belly and sucked on Dorian's finger. He slobbered all over Dorian's ring, which glowed a happy blue, just a few shades lighter than the dark hue he and Eleanor used to call to one another.

"Truly, Eleanor, for once HighGod is making things easier for us. This is the most happily anonymous child ever born."

"Rosemary said he rather resembles me, for I was a little baldy. But she also said I was always spindly."

"From what I remember my father telling me, my hair was always dark. But I was very, ahem, hearty."

She tried to keep her voice neutral. "You were a big child?"

"According to family lore. Father dubbed me his little lake whale."

"Gregory, too, was a rather portly baby. The portraits tell us that much. But not particularly long of leg, from anything I've heard."

As if to prove a point, Cyrus flopped both legs across Dorian's lap. In few more months, his feet might just about touch the floor. No doubt, he was unusually large in all respects.

"He'll have the queen's height, and the king's breadth." Dorian wiped at a tear. It tracked a squiggly line in the road dust clinging to his cheeks.

"His father's breadth."

"Perhaps. Eleanor, this child is the greatest gift you could give the kingdom. The greatest gift you've ever given me, as his most loyal subject."

She reached out and squeezed his hand, because she needed to touch him in this moment. His hair had grown out some, and when he leaned down to kiss Cyrus's forehead, the baby grabbed a handful of dark strands.

"Ouch!" Dorian leaned back, but Cyrus didn't let go. As Eleanor reached over to untangle the baby's fat fingers from her lover's hair, she remembered something. She pushed Dorian's hair behind his ear.

She finally got the longed-for glance at his earlobes. A good thing Carthean men didn't wear earrings, as he'd never have room for them. Unlike Gregory, who, she had recently observed, had normally floppy earlobes. The kind that would most likely become droopy appendages in his old age. Not so Dorian's. They were tiny, connected from his ear to his jawline. Just like his son's.

"This is quite possibly the strangest meeting I've ever attended." Although Gregory whispered, his voice was still jarring.

"It may very well may be one of the most important," Eleanor whispered back.

"When will it actually start?"

"When the Oracle decides to speak." She allowed her mind to drift back to pleasant blankness.

Eleanor and Gregory sat in the Oracle's cavern, in a little semi-circle beside Rosemary, Orvid Jones, and Dorian. Eleanor and Rosemary were accustomed to these audiences with Hazelbeth, the mystical and timeless magical seer of Afar Creek Abbey. They both sat quietly, inhaling the lavender-scented air and listening to the *bloop-blip-bloop* of the waters of the Watching Pool against its miniature sandy shoreline. Eleanor's body swayed, almost of its own accord, as if the Oracle's power had wrapped around her in a comforting hug and sought to rock her to sleep. Leave it to Gregory to disturb her peace.

"But why are we—"

"Husband. Patience, please."

Perhaps Gregory felt too intimidated by their surroundings to be annoyed by her hushing. He fidgeted and tugged at one unconnected earlobe. She'd developed quite a fascination with her husband's ears, ever since she clarified that her son had not inherited them. She imagined Gregory wanted to fiddle with his hair, as he always did when he felt agitated, but his earlobes were subtler.

Dorian and Orvid fared better than their sovereign. Dorian stared into the pool. He blinked slowly now and then, thus reassuring Eleanor he was alive. Orvid's creamy magic seeped from his body and swirled around him like a liquid blanket. His eyes were closed, and he whispered to himself. Eleanor wondered if he and the Oracle were already communicating in some way.

"What an unusual gathering this is." The Oracle's strong voice cut through whatever trance she'd place on Eleanor. She suddenly felt wide awake, as if Hazelbeth had sharpened all her senses with a magical knife.

"My husband just said the same, Wise One," said Eleanor.

Hazelbeth's deep set, watery blue eyes fixed on Gregory. "I hope all of his observations are as astute. Tell me, Your Majesty, do you consider yourself a watcher, in your own right?"

Gregory tucked his hands under his thighs. Eleanor sensed the follicles of his thick red hair screaming at him for a good anxiety releasing tousle. "I try... uh, Wise One. I try to observe everything around me and make my decision based on complete understanding."

"Hmmm," said the Oracle. "That is good. But tell me, do you believe any one man can really have complete understanding?"

"In my younger days, I did. Lately, I've realized that any truly wise man seeks the counsel of many others. Those whose own wisdom he trusts and admires."

"That is why we are here today," said Rosemary. "King Gregory knew he needed your insight."

"Honestly, Eleanor suggested we come. Dorian and Orvid encouraged it. I cannot take credit for their advice." Gregory peered into the darkness around him. "I am not always one to look for hidden answers. I prefer my information like my Fire-iron. Sparkling before me and impenetrable."

Hazelbeth let out a squeaking laugh.

Gregory smiled himself. "I felt a bit strange coming here, but now that I am here, I can feel the power in this place. I apologize if I seemed disrespectful. I am only anxious to hear *your* counsel."

"You have surprised me, Your Majesty, with your honesty. Pleasantly so."

Eleanor and Dorian exchanged glances across the pool. Sure as if they'd spoken, they transmitted their own pleasure at Gregory's transparency and humility. Eleanor continued to observe such welcome changes in her husband. It surely had something to do with the loss of his father and Vigor, or the weight of his kingship, or the long-awaited birth of his heir. Perhaps all of it.

Rosemary spoke again. "Wise One, the Svelyans now count a dozen gone ogres missing. There have been attacks on remote homesteads in Cartheigh and Svelya. People have died."

"These are alarming developments," said the Oracle.

"Will the ogres attack farther south?" asked Gregory. "Will they—"

"Your Majesty, remember, I do not see the future clearly. It is not a story I can see from start to finish. It is not like the moving pictures of the Other Worlds."

Eleanor heard the emphasis in her voice, as if *The Other Worlds* was the title of a famous novel or a great battle. Something abstract, but with a definitive identity. She started to ask for clarification, but the Oracle continued on her own trajectory, as she usually did.

"I do feel magical involvement."

"I knew it!" said Orvid. "Ezra Oliver!"

"He moved dragons across the country with a spell. There's no reason he couldn't do the same with ogres."

"Do you think he's after the dragons again somehow?" asked Gregory. "Mistress Hazelbeth, dragons are fragile creatures. There are so few left in the world. It is our duty to protect them, not just extract the Fire-iron. But if I'm being practical, we also need a strong Fire-iron draw this year. If we're to outfit the largest army we've ever raised, in armor and weaponry, we'll need fresh iron—malleable iron."

"It is not for me to direct you in the husbandry of the creatures HighGod has given unto your care. If we assume Oliver is involved, he has no love for the Bond. Surely, he will shed no tears over the dragons' discomfort. But, how does the saying go? There are larger fish in his pot that must be prepared for eating."

"Uh, yes," said Eleanor. "The saying is something like that."

Dorian stepped in, and in his diplomatic way, he steered the conversation back to the their most pressing concern. "Do you have a sense of Oliver's plan for the ogres?"

"It is hard to know. Oliver's thoughts crawl about like centipedes. One idea is chopped off, and another sprouts a hundred legs. He does nothing quickly or rashly."

"Has the Pool told you anything about what he's doing?" Eleanor asked. Many years ago, Hazelbeth had shared a vision of Oliver with Eleanor. She'd been able to see it by drinking water from the Pool. Oliver had long since learned to hide himself from such enchanted spying, but Hazelbeth and the Pool were also ever-evolving.

The old witch shook her head and confirmed Eleanor's suspicions. "He's far too wily these days. The Pool gives nothing more than vague hints as to his plans or his whereabouts."

Dorian pressed his line of questioning and added a bit of tactful flattery. "What of the ogres themselves? You were the one who visited them, in their dreams, five hundred years ago. You convinced them to enter the camps. No one outside the Ogre Watch has more direct experience with them than you do."

"That was a clever little plan."

"That *little plan* saved the world."

"It saved *our* part of *this* world. Other places, and the Other Worlds, have their own battles."

Eleanor once again heard a subtle emphasis that made her think of a philosophical thesis. "Hazelbeth, you've mentioned Other Worlds twice now."

"You noticed. Well done."

"Other Worlds— whatever that means—must be relevant to our conundrums. You rarely speak of insignificant matters."

"And *you* rarely miss matters of significance." Hazelbeth dragged one spidery finger across the air before her, as if drawing an invisible timeline through eternity. "I have watched for eons. My awareness had grown as slowly as a mountain rising up from a flat plain. In the past century, I began to understand that ours is not the only reality. Other realms exist all around us. We sometimes get glimpses of them, but we cannot touch them with our bodies."

"I don't think we follow," said Orvid.

"I don't wholly follow myself when it comes to this topic."

"You haven't spoken to me of *other worlds*, Wise One." Rosemary sounded mildly miffed, as if the Oracle had left her out of some particularly juicy gossip.

"I have, here and there. You didn't recognize it. You must remember, for me, a century of contemplation is a passing fancy for you. I try not to speak of phenomenon I don't fully understand, lest I ignite a conflagration of magical speculation. But I will try to explain, because my heart tells me there is relevance." She pointed from one visitor to the next. "Each of you dream every night."

"I don't dream," said the king.

"You do. You just don't remember. Some people do, and some don't."

"I always remember," said Eleanor. "They fade as the day goes on, but when I wake, they are always there. Some have stayed with me since childhood. When I was very small, I dreamt of a giant rabbit. It had huge blue eyes..." She realized everyone was waiting for her to stop talking, so Hazelbeth could make her point. No dreams were as interesting in recital as they were in the dreamer's head. "Ah, anyway. I remember my dreams."

"Then you know, sometimes in dreams, nonsensical things happen. Somehow, they are wholly logical and acceptable in the dream. There may be people and places in your mind you've never seen before. Strange circumstances. Yet in your dreaming mind, you question nothing. This is how we touch the edges of other worlds."

"We travel to other worlds while we sleep?" asked Orvid.

"No. We simply hover in the space between them. Hence, in that moment, the rules and conventions of both make sense."

"But what *are* these other worlds?" asked Rosemary.

Hazelbeth took a moment to collect her thoughts, and Eleanor understood that for all the Oracle's ageless wisdom, she was truly a novice student of this topic. "I feel some worlds are vastly different from our own, but others might merely seem like warped versions of our existence, but with different histories and evolutions and rules."

Rosemary's brown furrowed. "What do you mean, rules? Like laws?"

"Not laws that come from the minds of men and women. The rules of nature. For example, in some worlds, there is no magic."

The visitors sat in flummoxed silence. Finally, Dorian spoke. "No witches or magicians? But how is that possible? How would anyone defend themselves or heal the sick? Who teaches and keeps the stores of knowledge? Without magic, there would be no unicorns. No fairies. Dragons would never have existed. You yourself, Wise One, would not exist."

"It is difficult for us to imagine, but I believe they find other ways to solve their problems. I sense power, but not magical. Potions, but no spellwork. I sense metal, but not Fire-iron."

Gregory suddenly spoke up. "I do remember one dream, from years ago. I sat inside a metal bird, flying through the air. There must have been a hundred other people around me, all in chairs. I looked out a round window at the clouds. Then I tried to stand up, but there was a girth across my stomach. A woman in a soldier's uniform told me to sit down. I felt trapped and struggled. I wanted to stand up and jump out, even though I knew I'd fall to my death."

The Oracle nodded. "Metal birds flying through the air, holding a hundred people. Impossible, we would say. But in the world with no magic, who knows what kind of strange contraptions they resort to inventing? A lack of magic would surely force the human mind to find other means of expressing its genius."

"If we find their world strange," said Eleanor, "then it must be the same to them, when they get a glimpse of ours. That is, assuming such things are reciprocal?"

"They are," said the Oracle. "Someone who can make easy sense of a metal bird carriage might have a dream about a dragon or a sorcerer's spell, and upon waking, they would find it wholly nonsensical." The old witch turned to Eleanor. "Do you remember me saying to you, many years ago, that I sensed you from the other side of the Pool?"

Eleanor nodded. The day after her wedding, when she met with the Oracle as she and Gregory left for their honeymoon. The Oracle explained how she had asked Rosemary to leave Eleanor with Imogene as a child, and told Eleanor she had high hopes for her future as a member of the Desmarais family. "You said, *I can sense you, from the other side of the Pool, but I cannot see you*. You said what has meaning and consequence becomes soft and harmless."

"That's the best way I could describe it then, but it makes more sense now. What I was trying to express, is that I believe there is… seepage. Between our world and others. Your story is an example. The story of the glass slipper princess. The peoples of other worlds know your story."

"That's impossible," said Eleanor. "How?"

"Perhaps their own dreams revealed it. I only know they all tell some version of it. But the story is warped and reduced. The space between worlds we glimpse in our dreams—shall we call it the In Between— is soft. Malleable, like the fresh Fire-iron you need for your armies." She conjured a ball of blue light between her hands. As she spoke, it turned black and shriveled, like a quickly wilting flower. "There is some rot in that softness of the In Between." The blue ball of light, so bright and pure upon its creation, sat on Hazelbeth's palm. A dark, dead blossom.

"Their version of Eleanor is in many ways the opposite of the woman who sits before us. You are not strong or independent. You're not a voice for change or justice."

Eleanor glanced at Gregory, to see how he reacted to the Oracle's words, but he listened in silence as Hazelbeth continued.

"On the contrary, these people use your story to subjugate their own women. They poured sugar water into the formula of your life. They made you meek and docile, to teach their daughters to be silent and compliant and patient, in the hope of a reward."

"Some in our world have followed suit," said Gregory. "Remember the Talessee storyteller at Raoul and Margaret's wedding?"

"How could I forget," said Eleanor. The Talessee yarn spinner had made a spectacle of Eleanor's path to the crown. He delivered a similar message of simpering submission and the ultimate prize: salvation by marriage to powerful man.

"I am telling you now of the other worlds, and how we touch them in our dreams through the In Between, and about the seepage between them, because I sense a connection to Mr. Oliver's activities."

Eleanor nodded, and her mind spun. Sparking ideas connected to one another, like the lit fuses of Waxing Fest fireworks. "When Oliver disappeared for several years, after the Roffi affair—

"You mean when you sent him into magical oblivion through a puddle of water from the Watching Pool," Rosemary said.

"Well, yes. That." Eleanor always became embarrassed when someone forthrightly stated her accomplishments back to her. "Even Hazelbeth had no idea where he'd gone and thought him dead. Yet he returned, with all kind of new theories and abilities." Her voice quickened as she put pieces together. "In this very cavern, during the Battle of Afar Creek over five years ago, he talked about how he'd wandered in pain. Between this world and the next. Stuck between the two!"

Dorian nodded. "He said he'd seen things we couldn't comprehend. Perhaps—like metal birds flying through the air!"

"When he made his way back here, he figured out how to move creatures, from one place to another," said Orvid. "What if Oliver used the In Between space to move the dragons, and now he's doing the same with the ogres?"

Hazelbeth nodded. "That would explain many things."

"But it doesn't explain what he plans to do with the beasts," said Dorian.

"That's true," said the Oracle. "But I sense that knowing *how* he does it may have some bearing on *why* he's doing it."

"HighGod," said Eleanor. "By sending him into the Pool, I unwittingly gave him the tools to terrorize us."

"You didn't' plan to send him into the Pool, and no one knew where he would go," said Hazelbeth.

"Hazelbeth," said Dorian. "Could you go to the ogres again, in their dreams? Perhaps you can glean some sense of what Oliver has planned for them."

"Or find out who is helping him," said Orvid.

"I can try. But I will only see what their dreaming minds allow me to see. As you would expect, dream conversations with ogres are rather unpredictable. It's not like eavesdropping on them during their waking hours." She turned to Eleanor. "I think you, Your Highness, may have a better means of eavesdropping on Mr. Oliver himself."

"The glass rainbow," said Eleanor. "If I can control it. I've tried to see him, but I can't find him."

"Keep trying, child," said the Oracle. "The kaleidoscope may disguise information in layers of visions like paint on a canvas."

"I hope not. I'm no artist. That's Gregory."

Gregory squirmed, uncomfortable.

"Do you paint, sire?" the Oracle asked.

"In my youth I did. When I had the time."

"Well, artists see things in a particular light, shall we say. Another pleasant surprise from the king."

"I don't want to be too surprising, Wise One," Gregory said. "My father was rather predictable, and he ruled for thirty years."

"Tsk, that was your father's time. This is yours," the Oracle said. She gifted them with another of her rare, oddly pleasant, gap-toothed smiles. "Unusual times call for a novel ruler."

Eleanor watched Natalie caper around the edge of the Paladine's largest training ring. Dasha, the wild colt, frisked along the other side of the fence. Natalie lifted her leg, and Dasha imitated her. She blew raspberries at him, and he neighed and snorted in her face. She collapsed, laughing, against the fencepost. Happy red sparkles, like hot little stars, danced around her head. Dasha spooked and inhaled a few. Natalie peered up and him and laughed harder at the shocked look on his face. "Does it tingle?" she asked.

Dasha's ears pricked, and then he sneezed. "It feels like hay is trapped in my nose."

"Natalie," Eleanor called. "Remember, keep quiet."

It had become their catchphrase for keeping Natalie's power a secret. So far, she hadn't asked many questions.

"Yes, Mother." The red light vanished. Natalie poked her face through the fence, and Dasha rested his muzzle against her forehead.

Those two have a connection, Eleanor thought. As a Desmarais princess, Natalie would someday have her own unicorn. Eleanor wanted her to be able to take advantage of the love, friendship, and wisdom that came with having a special horned companion, even if she lived at Afar Creek. She wondered if she was witnessing the beginning of Natalie's choice.

Perhaps it makes sense. They're both a little different from the usual participants in the Bond. Magical girl, wild colt.

She turned her attention to a more conventional pairing in the center of the ring. Cricket cantered across the sawdust floor. She popped over fences no horse could leap. Ticia sat on Cricket's back, graceful yet ramrod-straight. Her auburn hair braids bounced with each leap. She and Cricket had been together for years. Like Eleanor and Teardrop, they moved as one creature. They were so close, sometimes Eleanor wondered if they even shared thoughts.

Natalie called out to her, "Tish! How do you stay on there?"

Ticia reined in, and the unicorn turned toward the child. Cricket's long shadow stretched out in an extension of her slim black legs and engulfed Natalie. Nat showed no fear of the darkness. She wrapped her arms around Cricket's foreleg. She barely reached the mare's knee.

"Lots of practice." Ticia patted Cricket's neck. "And a wonderful partner, whom I trust." Like Gregory, Ticia shed some her silly, light-hearted personality when she spoke of the Bond. Her father had transferred his veneration to her as surely as he'd given her freckles.

Eleanor felt a blast of warm air on her shoulder. She turned to see Whisper, the visiting wild stallion. It was unexpected, as since his arrival, he spent his time with the Bonded unicorns and avoided unnecessary human interaction.

"Why do the girl and the black mare jump over these fences?" he asked.

"No real reason. Other than they both enjoy it, and it makes Ticia a stronger rider. If Cricket had to bear her away from danger, she'd have to stay in the saddle."

"As you did, when you fled from the stinking fish attack."

Eleanor shivered as she remembered the pure panic she felt when Teardrop leapt each flopping, blubbery fish. "That was not the first time Teardrop saved me. Once, she bore me away from an angry doe dragon."

"Only after you came to my defense," said Teardrop, as she joined them on the outskirts

of the ring. The mare butted Eleanor's thigh with her muzzle.

"The colt, Dasha," said Whisper. "I have not yet spoken with him. His adoptive mother has not wanted me to visit him."

Teardrop gazed mildly at Whisper. "Most mothers try to protect their children from unpleasant, unnecessary encounters."

Whisper snorted. "Clearly, she does not want him to be reminded of where he came from. Of his true family."

"His true family abandoned him."

"I don't make the rules. His mother broke them. That doesn't mean he's not one of us."

"Let's ask him what he thinks of his natural family. And of us, the Bonded. Only he can tell us his mind."

Teardrop approached Dasha's paddock. She spoke quietly to the brood mare who nursed him alongside her own filly. The mare laid her ears back along her head and blew a blast of harsh air in Whisper's direction, but when the Paladin opened the gate, she nudged Dasha in Eleanor's direction. He trotted into the ring. He stopped to nibble on Natalie's dress. "Lovely Dash," she whispered as she stroked his nose.

"Sparkly Nat," he replied.

He lowered his head, and she whispered in his ear, no doubt promising him more sparkles in the near future. He whickered a laugh and trotted across the ring toward Eleanor.

Eleanor introduced the colt to the stallion. Dasha's wide eyes flicked over Whisper's powerful, twitching haunches.

"Do you trip over it?" he asked.

Whisper stretched his long neck toward the colt and sniffed him. "What?"

"Your mane, sir." The silky hair in question hung past Whisper's knees.

"You don't need to call me sir. That's a man thing." Whisper snuffled along the colt's neck and down each leg. "You're a strong, solid little creature. Not too soft. Yet."

Eleanor felt Teardrop tense up beside her. She lay a comforting hand against her withers. Teardrop's tail flicked irritably behind her. It knocked a few buzzing flies out of the air as sure as if she'd shot them with arrows.

"Do you like it here, small one?" asked Whisper.

"Yes. I don't remember any other place. I remember Her Highness, the queen. She held onto me while we bounced along in the rain. Then I was here, with my mother. My mother's name is Meadow."

"That is not your mother. Your mother's name was Nannel."

Eleanor watched the colt for some sign of recognition. She saw none, just polite interest.

"I have heard Meadow did not carry me in her belly. Another mare did. You say she was called Nannel?"

Whisper nodded.

"It's a fine name. I'm grateful to her for giving me life, but she died, and Meadow raised me. She's my true mother. She is teaching me how to survive, and how to think. How to know what is right and what is wrong."

"What else is she teaching you?"

"She helped me learn to speak. It was hard, at first. Perhaps because I was born in the wild. My ears had to get used to the tongues of humans—and the voices of unicorns who spend their lives speaking with humans. But I can speak now. Just like I can speak to you. Although, you do sound rather funny. You look funny, too."

Teardrop whinnied an appreciative giggle. Before Whisper retorted, Eleanor said, "I'm sure Dasha simply means your speech is different, in both words and mannerisms. Since so much of the speech of your kind is said through action."

"Paradoxically, it is more difficult to understand a unicorn who talks too much," said Teardrop, with a passively condescending swish of her tail.

"Who says I talk too much?" Whisper shifted his formidable weight. His haunches rolled like boulders loosening before a rockslide.

"Only Terin, your own lead stallion."

"I have my own herd. I have no *lead stallion*."

"That's what you tell yourself."

"I'll show you a lead stallion. I could rip out your throat with my horn before you even realized I was there."

Eleanor gasped. "Whisper! That kind of talk is not—"

"I dare you to try it," said Teardrop. "I'll sleep with my eyes open every night, waiting for you."

"Now, now." Eleanor stretched her arms between the two huge creatures, as if she might actually have some chance of breaking up a fight between them. "Let's keep the discussion between Whisper and Dasha, shall we?"

"Dasha," Whisper said, "you are a wild unicorn. You are not like these unicorns here. You are not part of their Bond. When the time comes, I will take you home to the marshes."

Dasha's ears pricked. "Why would I want to go there?"

Clearly, Whisper had not expected that response. "Well—it's our homeland. The place where our ancestors have always lived. It's far from the world of man—and most other large creatures. It's usually peaceful and safe. Nothing but bright green grass, clean water, birds, squirrels, rabbits..."

"He's neglecting to mention the constant rain," whispered Teardrop. Eleanor hushed her once again.

"That sounds pleasant enough. But would I leave Meadow, and my sister, Quicken? And Teardrop?" His eyes widened. "Would I have to say goodbye to Princess Natalie?"

"Yes. You would."

"I can't imagine leaving my family— for I think they are my family—and I would never want to leave my princess. She is so special to me. I think we are meant to be friends, forever."

There is was. Dasha, a wild unicorn, rejecting a secluded life in the Great Marshes and accepting the Bond.

Whisper tossed his head. Eleanor read embarrassment in the pinkish color of his muzzle. "You are young. Of course your feelings may change as you mature and—"

"No. I'm sorry, sir. I don't think they will. I believe my mind is clear on this topic. Mother taught me I must listen to my own mind, for it is connected to my heart. If properly heard, neither will fail me."

With an exasperated snort, Whisper abruptly backed up. He kicked over a bucket in the process. Water sloshed across the cobblestone path that led from the training ring into the Paladine. His hooves smacked against the wet stones as he fairly stomped away, in a pique.

"Is he angry with me, Your Highness? I spoke true, as I've been taught."

"Perhaps he is, Dasha, but Meadow taught you well. While all beings should speak the truth, unicorns *always* do." She dismissed the colt, who returned to Natalie. The two of them stood beside one another like a toy soldier and her wooden steed, watching Cricket and Ticia take the fences.

"That was a disaster," Eleanor said to Teardrop. "Hopefully Dasha's preferences won't alienate Terin and the rest of the wild unicorns."

"Why would they care? Unless Terin is afraid all his stallions and mares will suddenly abandon the marshes and race for the Paladine, ready to take up the Bond." Teardrop shook out her mane. "That won't happen. Dasha is unusually young, and he has no memory of life in the wild. I've never heard of a wild unicorn changing course. Maybe Dasha is special in some way. He loves Natalie. She's special, too."

"You know, too? About Natalie."

"I've seen it for weeks. As have Cricket and Senné. You cannot hide magic from us that easily."

Eleanor didn't want to think about Natalie's magic, so she addressed the tension between Teardrop and the visiting wild stallion. "Try to be civil to Whisper."

Teardrop showed her opinion by blowing raspberries in the direction

Whisper had taken, but she said, "If he is civil to me, I shall return the sentiment."

Eleanor couldn't expect much more of her. Teardrop loved the Bond, so naturally Whisper's derision of it offended her. As unicorns went, Whisper was unusually emotional. Eleanor wondered if Terin sent him to Eclatant partially to be rid of his strident opinions for a while. One did not need to be an Oracle to predict friction between Whisper and the Desmarais unicorns, but what if the chasm between the Bonded unicorns and the wild ones was too great? Would they be able to work together at all, should the time come?

She wished she could talk to Dorian. She wondered how many hours of useless ruminating she had wasted over the years, when a simple conversation with her best friend and lover would have given her the immediate relief of an understanding ear and his composed, rational intellect. She hadn't even had the opportunity to speak to him about the conundrum of Natalie's magical power. She hoped he wouldn't be angry with her when the news finally came to light. For now, it seemed imperative that it be kept between Eleanor and Rosemary, like a pinky-swear secret between two schoolgirls.

I don't want to think about any of this anymore. Not Natalie's magic, and not bickering unicorns. Especially if I can't talk to Dorian about any of it. I need a simple topic. She called to her daughters and asked them what they'd like for supper.

That evening, after tucking the girls into bed, Eleanor called for the wet nurse. She was tired, but this time, she didn't want to go right to sleep. Instead, once the nurse retrieved little Cyrus, she sat on the blue silk couch in her bedroom, with a scratchy wool blanket draped across her legs and a bowl of cherries in her lap. She simply needed space to think clearly. She even asked Chou to stay with Ticia and Natalie.

While her feathery conscience often helped her see every passage of a mental maze, tonight she needed to direct her focus.

In the few days since their visit to the Oracle's cavern, Eleanor's attempts to see Ezra Oliver in the scope had failed. She felt as if she were staring into the high noon sky, trying to make sense of something between her and the sun. The brightness skewed the edges of the vision, and the harder she stared, the more distorted it became.

She sat on the couch for a while, chewing on cherries and spitting the seeds into a small porcelain bowl. She thought about magic, and the frustration of trying to understand something indecipherable, yet *beyond* a different language. Something more akin to a foreign way of breathing or an alien heartbeat. Her body could never accommodate it, no matter how much she studied. Still, she'd learned many things over the years. She ran through a list of different magical theories and histories she'd studied, searching for something relevant to her current conundrum. Blood paths—the mechanism by which Oliver had first stolen Caleb's Horn. Once deemed almost impossible to perform; now, quaint and outdated in light of Oliver's other achievements. Banshees. Tonal magic. Fairies. Potions for curing plagues. Magical residue. Magical intent.

She spit a last cherry pit into her bowl and set it on the small table beside her. *Magical intent.* She had learned from the writings of Oliver himself that the conjurer's intent had some bearing on his or her magical performance. Orvid Jones had used the theory to perfect the capture of tonal magic and magical residue, ultimately leading them to discover Oliver in hiding at Brother Lawrence's School.

What is Oliver's intent these days? she wondered. She didn't know the specifics of his plan, but she did know something of his persona. Hazelbeth said the meaning of the visions in the kaleidoscope might be hidden in layers, like a painting. Oliver's work of art was not a self-portrait or a precise *Still Life with Monsters.* Even the ogres would be mere figures on the landscape, trapped within the ornate frame of his scheme. How would he title his masterpiece?

Power? Maybe. But that's too simple.

Curiosity? No. Not quite. But something of the two.

Eleanor walked to her writing desk. She opened one of the small drawers and removed the green velvet bag. The kaleidoscope slid from the pouch to her palm.

No matter what she thought of Oliver's moral compass, or lack thereof, she could not deny his intellectual genius.

She took several long, deep breaths. She focused on Oliver—not the evil, pompous, cruel magician she knew so well, but on his ravenously curious, constantly seeking mind, and his insatiable drive to be the greatest, the most accomplished, and the most feared. Therefore, the most respected.

Achievement. Success. Triumph. Adulation.

She closed her right eye. Her blue eye. She peered into the blackness of the kaleidoscope through her dark eye. Suddenly, the kaleidoscope came to life.

She was instantly reminded of the vision from years ago, when Hazelbeth revealed Oliver's finagling via a cup of enchanted water from the Watching Pool. On that long-gone day, she looked through Oliver's eyes and witnessed him steal Caleb's Horn by forming the first successful Blood Path known to magic. This time, however, she was looking *at* Oliver, not *through* him. She saw a familiar slight man with a flat nose and a weak chin. His hairline had further receded into a semicircular driveway around his oddly pointy head. He sat at a wooden desk in his dark gray robes, in a nondescript room with one small, un-paned window set high in the wall above his head. She made out a few twinkling stars in the night sky. Something about the dark, heavy space made her think of the farm cottages she'd visited between Maliana and the

Dragon Mines. A cauldron hung from an iron rack over a roaring fire in a stone hearth. The fire provided decent light, but Oliver had set up several candles on his desk, as if he'd created a shrine to himself. His flattened square hat, the one that always reminded Eleanor of a lumpy meat pie, hung on the back of his chair. Two books sat on his desk, and one lay open on his lap. He was writing.

Instinctively, Eleanor stood with the kaleidoscope still pressed to her eye and stepped forward. To her delight, the vision shifted, and took her closer to Oliver. When she stood three paces from him the picture went blurry. In a panic, she gently spun the scope, and it focused again. She noted the title of the two books on his left: *The Natural Life of the Common Ogre*, and *Ancient Gods of Cartheigh*. She focused the kaleidoscope on the letter, and Oliver's swoopy writing. To her annoyance, the edge of the letter had slid under a stack of parchment and ledgers, hiding the salutation. She started reading where she could.

... clear you despise me, and I cannot blame you. You wanted to do something noble, but my control over you has only reiterated what you know deep in your heart—that you're a criminal of the highest order. Not that I am judging you for your deviancy, as I have been where you are. In the end, who is to say what is good and what is bad? Still, if the rules of man say you've sinned—and in your case they most surely and egregiously do—then you must face the consequences. So little in our lives is allowed to tread upon a middle ground, even though, as I've been trying to explain, the middle ground is perhaps the most important.

Oliver's arm slid across the page, blocking Eleanor's view.

.... I hear your pleas for me to let you be. You say you've done enough already, but there is always more to be done. Unfortunately, I will be the one to decide when our relationship ends. The only thing you have left to decide is under what circumstances will it continue. As it has been, with coercion? Or will you consider my offer? In the end, you could do more good than...

He shifted again, resting his elbow on the paper and his head on his fist. He paused, as if searching for the proper turn of phrase, like the world's ugliest suitor composing a romantic missive. He scribbled a few more lines, eyes scrunched and tongue poking from the side of his thin mouth.

....that middle ground. I can show you how to find it. How to purposely find it—not the haphazard nightly wanderings of common beings. You will see things that even a lifetime of magical study cannot explain. So, think on it. You will be part of this whether you like it or not. But, if you are as smart as I believe you are, you'll see it does not have to be a terrible arrangement, but a...

He paused and licked the end of his feathered quill. Eleanor's skin crawled in disgust. Unfortunately, once he found inspiration, he huddled closer to his desk. His flat nose fairly brushed the parchment. He smiled to himself as he resumed writing. He pulled the paper closer, revealing a scrawling salutation at the top.

Eager to see the name of his correspondent, she tried to move the vision again. She took a step to her right, but she ran into her desk back in her own room. She cried out in pain as the sharp corner drove into her thigh.

To her horror, Oliver sat up straight, as if he'd heard something. He looked over his shoulder. For a terrible moment, Eleanor thought he could see her, but his eyes swept past. Still, he must have sense something, because he folded the letter and stood. He narrowed his eyes and began chanting. The vision went blurry.

Eleanor tried to regain focus. She wiggled the scope and shimmied to her right. She made it three steps before she hit something obstinately unyielding.

"Ouch! Mother!"

Eleanor dropped the kaleidoscope. Ticia stood beside her, hopping on one foot and rubbing her bare toes, upon which Eleanor had clearly stepped in her hard-soled shoes. "Tish, I'm sorry, darling. Are you all right?" She grabbed the kaleidoscope as it rolled across the floor. *HighGod, I hope it's not broken!*

She picked it up and shook it gently, and to her relief, she didn't hear any tinkling broken glass. When she looked inside it, however, the vision of Oliver had vanished. She turned it this way and that, but it stayed dark

"You stepped on my toe!" said Ticia.

Eleanor felt mildly annoyed, in that guilt-inducing way of motherhood, where on one hand she felt sorry for her daughter's sore toe, but on the other hand, she'd *told* Ticia she needed some time alone this evening. Yet here she was, silently hovering and quite literally getting underfoot. Now the vision of Oliver had disappeared. Who knew when she'd see him again, especially if he'd sensed her interference and would know to hide from her. She might have lost her one chance to spy on him, but at least she could report back to the Oracle that she was right. There was some connection between Oliver, the ogres, and *haphazard nightly wanderings*, which she could only assume meant dreams.

"I'm sorry," she said. "Next time let me know when you're standing next to me, and I won't step on you."

"Perhaps *you* should open your eyes when you're jumping around the room."

Eleanor momentarily forgot Ezra Oliver in light of her daughter's disrespectful tone. "First, I was not jumping. Second, it's not up to you to tell me how or when to jump about in my own bedroom."

Ticia sat at the desk. "I'm sorry," she said, although she didn't sound very remorseful. Chou had warned Eleanor to be prepared for Ticia to lose much of her charm as she entered young womanhood—at least that which she directed at her mother. "What were you doing, anyway? Is that Natalie's toy?"

"No," said Eleanor. "It's not really a toy. It's a magical instrument." She sat in the chair across from her oldest child. Ticia had recently started experimenting with hairstyles, rather than defaulting to the two thick braids she'd worn for years. Her hair cascaded down her back in loose reddish waves, like a fox fur cape. The shorter pieces around her face were held back with a green ribbon that matched her dark green nightdress. When they slipped loose, she blew them away from her nose. Her reddish-brown eyes crossed a bit, and her nose wrinkled. She was a lovely girl, fiercely healthy and strong from hours in the saddle, who looked as if she belonged in the forest.

"Did Natalie make it magical?"

"No, the Oracle gave it to—" Eleanor rested her elbows on the desk. "What do you mean?"

"I mean did Natalie use her magic to enchant that kaleidoscope?"

So the secret was out. "You know?"

Ticia started to roll her eyes, then seemed to think better of it. Instead, she cleared her throat. "Yes, it's rather obvious. All the red light. Things moving around. A few nights ago, I woke up, and she was floating two feet above her bed, fast asleep. She talks in her sleep, too. Spells Rosemary taught her."

"Did she keep you up? Perhaps it's time you had your own chamber. I can speak to your father about it."

"Mother, why are you trying to keep Natalie's magic a secret?"

Eleanor decided to be honest. Ticia was going on fourteen and old enough to understand. Besides, in this rare case, the honest answer and the simplest answer were the same. "Because she's my baby, and I don't want to send her to the Abbey."

"Would that be so bad?"

"You want her to leave us?"

"No. Not if I'm being selfish. But for her sake, I think she should. As soon as she can. I envy her."

"Since when have you wanted to be a witch? There's not a lot of painting and drawing happening at the Abbey."

"No—but sort of yes. I mean not about magic, but it is about painting. If Natalie goes to the Abbey, she'll get to do what she loves, all the time. She won't be stuck here, at Eclatant. A slave to our family, like the rest of us."

Ticia's harsh language shocked Eleanor, but she sensed she needed to react in a way that made her say more, not less. "How are you and Natalie slaves to our family, Ticia?"

Ticia took a deep breath, and words spilled from her mouth like maid dumping a full chamber pot. "If Natalie is at the Abbey, she won't have to worry about the crown, being an heir, or producing one for someone else. I wish I would be called to paint and never have to hear anyone else whispering about how I may be queen if one of my brothers doesn't live long enough to be king."

"Where did you hear—"

"I've been hearing it my whole life. For one, when you paint, people think you aren't listening to them, but I've learned to listen for the right words. I know what everyone expected of me—after Nathan died and before Cyrus was born. I also know what would be expected of me if Cyrus doesn't live. Now, I not only fear for my little brothers for their own sweet sakes, I fear for myself."

"You have no wish to be queen?" Eleanor asked.

"No—never. Mother, I want to paint. I'd like to marry a kind man and live in Harper's Crossing… or Solsea. A clean, happy place. Away from Maliana with all its dirt and sickness and mobs of hungry, angry people."

"Away from Eclatant?"

"I love Eclatant, of course. I'll always want to spend time here with you and Poppa. I love the Fests and parties and tournaments. But even at Eclatant, my *home*, some people only like me because I'm a princess and maybe the future queen.

"I see." All these years, since Nathan's death, Eleanor had imagined her great fight for Ticia's claim to the throne, should she not have another male child. Yet here was her daughter telling her she wanted no part of it. "I understand you feel trapped. I've felt all the things you're feeling, here at Eclatant. But I also know what it's like to be cold and hungry, like those people who live outside the walls of this palace. I've visited with the dirtiest, and angriest, among them. I understand *why* they are frustrated. We sit up here, in our warm castle in our finery with full bellies—"

"I *know* that. But for the grace of HighGod, I might have been one of those people. But I need country air and sunshine and a paintbrush in my hand. I'll always do my best to help the less fortunate. I'm your daughter, aren't I?"

"You are."

"There are poor people in Harper's Crossing and Solsea. The grape pickers of old Sage Town. Can I not do good for them?"

Ticia had never shared Eleanor's love of learning or her passionate crusades. She'd always been a child of strong will but simple joys. Artwork, pretty dresses, celebrations. Unicorns and puppies and babies. These were the things Ticia loved the most. For the first time, Eleanor looked at her daughter as though through a kaleidoscope, but not an enchanted one. She zeroed in on the raw truth right in front of her. Leticia, miserable at the thought of ever ruling this kingdom. Jealous of her magical little sister for unwittingly finding a way out of being a princess.

Ticia reached across the table and took her hand. "At the Awakening, during the Children's Ball, I danced with Patrick-Michael."

"Patrick-Michael Harper?" Eliza's oldest son. "He's nearly fifteen now, isn't he? This will be his last season of Children's Balls."

"Yes. We danced together, and he told me he's always admired me. He's so handsome and kind and tall—"

Eleanor sensed where she was going. "Ticia, you're too young to be thinking about—"

"Who I might like to marry?" Ticia's jaw jutted, like Gregory's did whenever he wanted to make a point. "Do you think I don't know you and Poppa are already planning my marriage?"

Eleanor swallowed. "Who told you?"

"Mother! I'm *thirteen* years old! I'm not a little girl! I know how the world works." Ticia stood and stormed across the floor. "I'm a Desmarais princess. I have to marry a prince. I've heard it's to be Prince Samuel."

"It's not been decided—"

"I won't do it! I will *not* move to Svelya and freeze to death and marry some man I don't know! I *hate* being a princess!"

Eleanor stood herself. How hilarious! She herself spent her childhood dreaming of princes and castles. Every little girl in Cartheigh would give anything to switch places with Ticia, yet here she stood, ranting as if being a princess were the curse of her very existence.

"You may very well hate being a princess right now, but that is what you are. Just as the peasant girls in Meggett Fringe are what they are. We must try to improve the lot we are given and help others do the same."

"Your school didn't help those peasant girls. Poppa says it failed!"

"It didn't turn out as I'd hoped, but at least I'm trying to change things! You'd choose to hide away behind the walls of some country estate and throw parties and draw pictures! You'd do nothing with the good fortune HighGod has given you!"

Ticia looked as if Eleanor had slapped her in the face. "That's not fair! I told you, I want to do good. But *I am not you*, Mother!" Mother and daughter stared at one another. Tears slipped down Ticia's face, and she swiped at them. Her embroidered sleeve scratched her face.

Eleanor closed the gap between them. "Ticia. I'm trying to understand, and I'm on your side about marriage. I want you to wait and choose your own husband. But—you don't want to be queen? Not ever?"

Ticia shook her head.

"Clearly, I want Cyrus to live a long life and rule as the greatest king Cartheigh has ever known. But I always thought that if, HighGod forbid, the time came, *you'd* want to be queen."

"I can think of nothing that would make me more miserable. Except being sent to Svelya." Ticia's breaths came in short gasps. "Please, don't let Poppa send me there."

Eleanor pulled Ticia into her arms. She stroked her hair as she sobbed. "I will do everything in my power to allow you to choose your husband. I swear it." She looked into her daughter's bloodshot eyes. "But I will not *break* a promise, so I cannot *make* a promise."

"Poppa always listens to you in the end. Patrick-Michael is from a good family—"

"No more about him for now. You're too young to marry a stranger, but you're also too young to choose a husband. I want you to choose as a woman, not as a girl. Do you understand?"

"You were young when you chose Poppa—"

"Ticia—"

"But I know you would have chosen differently, if you'd waited. I know who you would have chosen."

Eleanor tried to think of a response but found none. It was too shocking, and too dangerous, to have this conversation with Ticia.

"It's all right." Ticia rested her head on Eleanor's shoulder again. "I love Poppa, but I love *him*, too. I see why you would have chosen him. I guess it would be good to wait a while. Meet other young men."

Eleanor bit her lip. "I want you to make the right choice and be happy."

"I will, if I can make the choice."

"We will do everything we can to make sure you have the chance."

"Now do you see why I envy Natalie? Have you asked her if she'd choose the Abbey over Eclatant?"

"Daughter, Natalie is five. When you're a parent, you'll know that while we give our little ones some choices, usually we limit them to the color of a dress or which bedtime story we'll read."

"Well, I *have* spoken with her. She told me she loves her red light, and she's sad you told her can't use it. But beyond that, the other day..."

Ticia pulled away from Eleanor and walked to the desk. She sat with a thunk of her bottom and a swoosh of her skirts that belied her tender years; the flop of one weighed down by the challenges of life. "I came into the nursery, and we argued. She was playing with my pearl comb earlier that day, and I couldn't find it. She's only five, but these days, she seems so much *older*. I was cross with her. I saw her fingernails. They were red again. I said, *I'm telling Mother!* And just like that, she shoved me across the nursery. I landed on my bed, but I hit my head on the posts. Can you feel it?"

Eleanor touched Ticia's hair, and she felt a hard knot on the back of her skull. Ticia winced and rubbed it. "As soon as she did it, she started crying. Begging me to forgive her and looking all over the nursery for that silly comb. Poor Natty. I felt terrible for speaking harshly to her. She is still little, even if, at times, she seems more grown up than me."

"She hurt you. Without meaning to do so."

"Yes. Please don't be angry with her—"

"No, of course not."

"— I think she's having more trouble keeping it to herself."

"Now it's not just about her happiness. It's about all our safety."

"But it's very much about her happiness, too, Mother. You know that as well as I."

"Her calling," Eleanor said. She rubbed Ticia's head.

Ticia leaned into her hands. "I do think we all have one."

"Sometimes more than one." Eleanor had lived her life by her callings—to learning, social change, leadership, family, love. In the end, a mother's true job was to help her children find their callings. Even if they were not the ones the mother would have chosen.

CHAPTER 13

A HERO AND A FOOL

OVER THE NEXT SEVERAL days, Eleanor spent as much time with Natalie as possible. Once she was honest with herself, she saw what Ticia did. Natalie did seem older, as if she'd woken up one morning and realized the world beyond the bright confines of the nursery was not warm and cheerful. She wasn't eating very much. She laughed when she tickled her little brother, and she skipped to the Paladine when they visited Dasha, but otherwise, she was subdued. On the few occasions Eleanor and Natalie were alone in the nursery, she asked if she could *please let it out*, and as soon as the red light seeped from her pores or her breath or wherever it came from, she reanimated, and talked until Eleanor's ears went red from the strain of listening to so much chatter. One quiet afternoon—while Ticia painted in the garden below the window, Cyrus napped in his cradle, and Chou snoozed on his perch—Eleanor sat with Natalie on the nursery rug. She chattered as she poured misty, blood red tea into her china tea set.

"Here, Mother," she said. Eleanor's teacup floated toward her, and she took it out of midair.

"Natty," she said, trying to keep her voice light and neutral. "When are you happiest?"

The child didn't pause to think. "When I play with Dasha, or when

Rosemary teaches me new ways to use my red light." She bit her lip, as if sensing Eleanor's heart constricting. "And when *we* play together. Or when I hold baby brother."

"It's all right, Daughter," said Eleanor. "There are many reasons to be happy, and those are all important ones."

A week later, Eleanor met Gregory in his receiving room just after lunch with her hair in a tight chignon. She'd learned to pull it back when she wanted to be taken seriously by a man. She thought of the last time she met King Casper here, going on two years ago, before the trip to Svelya. Now Gregory sat on his father's throne. The smaller one sat empty, waiting for Cyrus to be old enough to sit beside the king and learn his duties.

The king, thought Eleanor. *Not his true father. But his father in name and lineage. As long as Gregory never learns the truth.*

A question arose in her mind. One that had started nagging her as she nursed her son in through dark, quiet nights but had recently braved the sun to harass her during daylight hours. So frequently did it harangue her, she'd come to think of it not as *a question*, but *The Question*—an impressive moniker given the number of conundrums with which she wrestled on a daily basis.

What of the Bond? the damnable Question asked. *If Cyrus was not a true Desmarais, can he lead it?*

The Question raised the same valid concerns she'd ruminated on in Svelya, about John-Caleb— whether the Bond depended on a ruler having Desmarais blood. It irked her that she'd unintentionally recreated Sylvia's son's tenuous situation, albeit one strengthened by legitimate parentage. Cyrus was a Desmarais, born of the marriage between the king and his true wife. He must be known as Gregory's son for his very own safety. But Eleanor feared that by keeping her child safe, she might risk the stability of the nation and the lives of millions of her countrymen.

She glanced at Dorian, seated in a Fire-Iron chair beside the raised dais. He made it a point to continue scribbling on the parchment on his lap. She wished they could talk about their child, his safety, and his future as king.

Gregory waved her closer. Exhaustion deepened every line on his face. "Eleanor. To what do we owe the pleasure? We could have spoken at dinner."

"It's a matter of crown business, Your Majesty. But also about our children. I thought a private audience, here—"

"Is Cyrus ill?"

Dorian's hand stopped moving.

"No," she said. "He's so healthy the witches feel useless when they visit each week."

His quill resumed its *skritch-scratch* on the parchment. He crossed one leg over the other, and one booted foot bounced.

"Excellent," said Gregory. "Is this about Ticia's marriage to Samuel?"

"No, Husband. I'd like to speak with you about that, but—"

"It can't be tampered with right now. Not when we need the Svelyans more than ever. The arrangement must stand."

Through herculean force of will, Eleanor stopped herself from arguing that point. Ticia's plight remained at least somewhat speculative. Natalie's was as real as the bump on the back of her sister's head.

"I hope we can speak about the betrothal soon, but this is about Natalie." Before Gregory asked after Natalie's health or suggested a husband for her, Eleanor told him everything. From the first sign of Natalie's magic on the day she met her little brother to Rosemary's clandestine lessons and the bookshelf she set on fire to her current melancholy and inadvertent assault on Leticia.

For once, Gregory didn't interrupt. At some point, Dorian uncrossed his legs and set his quill and parchment on the marble floor beside him.

Eleanor finished her monologue with this: "I'm sorry I haven't told you sooner, but I wanted to be sure. As much as it breaks my heart, she must go to Rosemary."

After a long silence, Gregory said, "No. She's a princess of the blood. She will stay at Eclatant."

"Gregory, I will miss her too but—"

"This is not about missing her, although HighGod knows I will. I cannot set this precedent."

"What precedent?"

"Dorian." Gregory shifted in the throne and faced his old friend and advisor. "You've read just about every history book in my library. Has any member of the Desmarais family ever been called to magic?"

"Not to my knowledge, Your Majesty."

"That's what I thought."

"Natalie is the first," said Eleanor, "but that doesn't change—"

"What if Cyrus showed signs of magic?"

"If I may, Your Majesty," said Dorian. "That's highly unlikely."

"Rosemary told me magic rarely runs in families, and as Dorian just said, there's no history of it in the Desmarais family anyway."

"But we've never intermingled with your family," said Gregory. "Smithwicks, Harpers, Porters, Fleetwoods, the Talessee and Kellish royal families— but never a Brice."

"I have no knowledge of anyone magic in my family."

"How far back does your family tree go?"

"Not as far as you'd like, I'm sure, but—"

"You may not be magical, but you certainly have an affinity for the witches. Surely, this ability of Natalie's came from you."

"It came from nowhere," she said as her exasperation grew. "It came from luck or misfortune, depending on how you see it. It came from HighGod."

"If Natalie is sent to the Abbey, what's to say the Covey wouldn't try to claim Cyrus? Until we're sure he has no magic, Natalie isn't going anywhere."

"I see you point, Your Majesty," Dorian said, "but a few magical children don't show their abilities until they are as old as ten. By that time, Natalie may very well have gone mad—or killed herself or someone else."

"We'll keep close watch on her, so everyone is safe. Have Rosemary keep teaching her here at Eclatant."

"Gregory, it's breaking my heart to do this, but I see now we must. Natalie cannot stay here. Not for her sake or anyone else's. What if she hurts Cyrus accidentally?"

"True. Keep her away from him for now, and from Ticia."

"You'll keep her from magic and from her siblings?" Despite her efforts to douse the flames, Eleanor's temper flared. "You don't care about her at all!"

"Of course I do!" Gregory rounded on her. "Don't insult me! But I waited years for a male heir, only to lose him to the Burning, and then I waited years for another. I'll not lose this one to the Covey."

"Even if Cyrus *were* to be a magician, and you tried to keep him here, since when has a magician ever been king?"

"I'm finished with this conversation."

Eleanor was a bottle of sparkling wine. Gregory had shaken her, and predictably, she blew. "Dorian, for the love of the Bond, tell him he *must* let her go!"

Gregory's eyes narrowed, but before he unloaded on Eleanor, Dorian stood. "Your Highness, this is His Majesty's decision, not mine."

Eleanor almost clapped her hand over the lower half of her own face. She'd blatantly asked Dorian to disobey Gregory. If Dorian had done anything but roundly silenced her, Gregory might have sent both of them to the dungeon as penance. "You're right." She fell into a curtsy. "Forgive me."

"Go. Natalie needs her own rooms. You can select a proper spot."

"Yes, Your Majesty." Eleanor straightened, folded her hands before her waist, and walked toward the door. She cursed herself for ruining any chance of further conversation about Natalie's magic any time soon. Now she had turned the topic into an argument.

"Who's next?" Gregory's voice over her shoulder was almost a bark. She couldn't catch Dorian's subdued reply. She hated hearing him placate Gregory, and this time it was her fault he had to do so. In that moment, she made a pact with herself. She'd somehow gotten away with running off at the mouth all these years. Many times, she'd relied on King Casper's unlikely fondness to get her out of such gaffes. But Casper was gone, and Gregory wouldn't have the same fatherly tolerance for her outbursts. She was the queen consort now, not just a princess. She had her three children and Dorian to think of these days. She had to learn to clear the path in front of her goals by prudently supervising the mob, rather than setting loose the dogs.

Rosemary met Eleanor at the Paladine several days later with the inevitable news that the Oracle had sensed Natalie's power. She expected Hazelbeth to call Natalie soon. Teardrop stood between the witch and the queen, and Chou Chou sat on Eleanor's shoulder. The four of them watched fondly as Natalie and Dasha chased each other in a grass enclosure behind Meadow's stall. At a year old, he was recently weaned, and growing like the tall marsh grass that covered his homeland in unruly bunches. He towered over Natalie and would have broken the child's foot if he stepped on her shiny paddock boots. His hooves never came within inches of her skipping feet, and nor did his sharp, slowly lengthening horn. Across from Eleanor and Rosemary, Whisper also watched them.

"Whisper is returning north when Gregory and Dorian leave in the morning," said Eleanor.

"He'll tell Terin about the supposed slavery of his fellows."

"I can't understand how he could honestly see the Bond as slavery, after observing it for himself," said Chou. He flitted from Eleanor's shoulder to Rosemary's head. "He's seen nothing but love, cooperation, and mutual assistance."

Rosemary lifted one arm, and Chou stepped lightly onto her hand. Her thumb rubbed his red belly. "Some people—and unicorns— only see what they want to see, no matter how hard you try to show them your side. But unicorns are brutally honest. Hopefully, he'll report the truth, even if it's not what he predicted it will be."

"Will you discuss Natalie's calling with Gregory before he leaves?" asked Chou.

"I'll have to see what kind of mood he's in this evening. I'm afraid if I push, he'll just dig in."

"Dorian will convince him to see reason."

"Horns and fire, here he comes," said Teardrop.

"Gregory?" Eleanor looked over her shoulder.

"No. Someone even more stubborn and narrow-minded."

Whisper joined their circle. "I'm going home," he said. He looked at Teardrop when he spoke, but Eleanor knew he meant for the rest of them to hear him.

"Yes," said Teardrop. "We know you're leaving."

The exchange felt uncomfortable to Eleanor, even knowing that unicorns often spoke in monosyllables if there was no need to elaborate. Chou couldn't tolerate awkwardness, so as usual, he resorted to entertainment. He swung around Teardrop's horn, a feathery lasso about to be tossed. "Master Whisper, don't go!" He came to a stop and perched between Teardrop's ears like a jaunty red bonnet. "I still haven't managed to make you laugh. You'll ruin my streak of cheering up the terminally dour."

Whisper ignored him. "I'm going to ask the colt to go with me."

Teardrop's snort and rumbling neigh said all she needed to say. *Give it your best try and see where it gets you.*

Eleanor opened the gate, and Whisper entered the enclosure. Dasha's adoptive mother, Meadow, appeared in the open half door to her stall. She whickered a warning and struck her water bucket with one hoof. Eleanor and Teardrop followed Whisper. "The child," Teardrop said. Eleanor nodded, intent on retrieving Natalie. Whisper would not be so careful about where his hooves landed. Natalie scooted behind Dasha, out of her mother's reach.

"Come now, Natty," Eleanor said. "Whisper would like to speak with Dasha."

Natalie's eyes narrowed. "He wants to take Dasha away. Mother, don't let him."

"That is up to Dasha to decide."

Dasha looked small and spindly in comparison to the great stallion who bore down on him, but he squared up and faced Whisper like a strong sentry. "I know what you mean to ask, sir. My answer is still no. I'll stay here. With my family. Human and unicorn."

Whisper neighed, high and quivering. Chou's annoyed voice floated across the grass. "Now he laughs!"

Beside her, Teardrop breathed in shallow, threatening bursts. Eleanor had never felt this kind of tension between unicorns. "Natalie, come to me now," she said.

Natalie stood beside Dasha with one hand on his foreleg. She barely reached the top of his knee. *HighGod, she's so small.*

"Dasha," said Whisper. "If you choose this life, you'll not be welcomed back among us. You'll be an outsider."

"If Meadow has told me correctly, I would be an outside anyway. No mother. An unknown father. What herd would welcome me?"

"Terin told the queen you could join his herd."

"You know as well as I… he does not really want me there. Here, I am wanted."

"Notice he didn't say you'd be able to join *his* herd, Dasha," said Teardrop. "He only wants you to come with him to prove the Bond is unjust and wrong."

"In the wild," said Whisper, with a sneer, "Mares aren't always so free with their opinions."

"In the wild, they're left to die in the bushes, and their children with them."

"Stop, now," said Eleanor. "Dasha has made his choice, Whisper. Unless you plan to force him, you must let it go."

"I don't think you want to force him," said Teardrop. She flexed her neck. Meadow called out in a shrill whinny from her stall. "His mother and I will defend him."

Whisper laughed again. "I don't fear a sniveling bonded servant and an old brood mare."

Teardrop bared her teeth at him. Dasha's eyes widened. He nudged Natalie with his muzzle. "Natty, go to the queen."

"Are they fighting, Dash?" Natalie asked. "They shouldn't fight with each other."

"I've fought in more battles than you, stallion," said Teardrop. "What were you doing while I faced down dragons and came away clean? Oh, yes. Hiding in the swamp."

Whisper lunged at Teardrop. She dodged him and swung her head. Horn struck horn like clashing sabers. Eleanor sidestepped around them. Dasha grabbed the back of the Natalie's dress and dragged her out of harm's way. She struggled in his grip.

"Let me go, Dash! Let me *go, now!*"

Dasha dropped Natalie's dress as if it were too hot to touch. She landed on her feet, held out both hands, and blasted red light at the sparring unicorns. Both froze, as if made of cold Fire-iron. Teardrop half-rearing, and Whisper with his neck stretched long and low, as if going for her legs. Their sides heaved as they sucked air in and out, but otherwise, only their rolling eyes were mobile.

"Stop fighting!" Natalie cried. "Stop it right now. It's not *nice!*"

She stumbled backward and grabbed the sides of her head. Her spell held for another few seconds, before both Teardrop and Whisper crumpled in heaps of shuddering white. Natalie's red magic raced back toward her, and Eleanor lunged for her.

Rosemary had told Eleanor, years ago. *No magic is as dangerous as one's own turned against her.* That bit of information allowed her to defeat Ezra Oliver the first time.

Natalie's eyes flew open. She deflected the red light with her right hand. It ricocheted off a watering trough, then punched a hole in the stable wall and exited out the other side of the building. Meadow whinnied from inside her stall, and Dasha ran to his mother's aid. Natalie's terrified eyes followed the bouncing ball of red fire. She pulled at the magic, as if reeling in a fishing line. It swirled toward the sky. Natalie held her hands aloft, palms toward the sun, shoulders hunched for impact. Eleanor screamed her name as the red light fell.

It hit Natalie's hands and blinked out. She looked at her fingers, stumbled backward, and collapsed.

Teardrop and Whisper seemed none the worse for wear within a few minutes. They meekly left the enclosure, each mortified by his or her own behavior—and probably equally embarrassed to have been bested by a five-year-old girl. Natalie woke up as Dasha fretted over her, but she didn't seem to remember much of what had happened, nor could she explain it. She complained of a headache and exhaustion, so Eleanor carried her to her new room, down the hall from the old nursery. Rosemary and Chou trailed behind her. Ticia peeked out of her own new bedroom across the hall when she heard Eleanor fidgeting with Natalie's door.

"Chou," Eleanor said. "Go to Ticia and reassure her. Explain to her what happened and ask her to be quiet about it."

He whistled an affirmative and fluttered across the hall. Eleanor lay Natalie on her bed and loosened her boots. She rolled over in her bed and fell asleep before Eleanor set the boots on the floor. She sat on the edge of Natalie's bed, and Rosemary dragged a rocking chair across the room to join her. Eleanor brushed Natalie's hair away from her face. "You said Hazelbeth will call her soon," she said. "What happens then?"

"Usually we assign two witches to go to the child's home. To meet the little and explain what will happen to the family. That won't be necessary in this case, as you're already very familiar with the Abbey."

"Would you collect Natalie yourself?"

"That's a reasonable request. Perhaps Gregory will listen to me if I come for a formal collection. We've known each other a long time, after all."

"No disrespect, Abbottess, but I don't think he'll listen to anyone. Except Dorian, if we're lucky." Eleanor exhaled a long breath she felt like she'd been holding since she left Gregory's receiving room. "Yesterday, I made a vow to learn to hold my tongue in front of my husband. For many reasons, big and small, I probably should have been exiled or executed by now. The way I've spoken to him and the things I've done."

"You're right, sadly. Most kings would not suffer such."

"Casper tolerated me."

"He respected you. I think your talents reminded him of what his son lacked."

"Perhaps. But he also knew he could deny me in the end. He always had that prerogative. Now, its Gregory's. They're different men.

"You've said you believe Gregory is changing."

"I do. I think it started when he found out about Dorian and I. He never told his father, and despite his patience for me and fondness for Dorian, Casper never would have tolerated that indiscretion."

"It must have been humbling for Gregory to realize his own turbulent emotions are not the only deep feelings in the universe."

Eleanor smiled, for Rosemary clearly understood her husband as well as anyone could. "He's been further humbled by his responsibilities. I see it every day. In turn, it's softened him to me, and to Dorian. Still, I walk a fine line." She stroked Natalie's still little foot through the blanket. "But just because I'm going to watch my mouth, it doesn't mean I'm any less inclined to have my way."

Rosemary laughed. "That's the Eleanor I know."

"In the past, I've succeeded at reining myself in sporadically. I even managed it for approximately half an hour yesterday, but it wasn't enough. Sometimes I feel like I've spent my whole life screaming to be heard, but there are instances in which simply doing might be more effective than talking."

"I think I see which way you're driving the carriage."

"Natalie must go with you. Dorian will try to change Gregory's mind. But in the meantime, she can't stay here. The incident at the Paladine made that clear. I have to do what's best for her and have faith that Gregory's love for her will help him see the light." She chuckled. "It is bright red, after all."

Eleanor took Natalie's hand. The child didn't stir as her mother adjusted the covers around her shoulders. Her eyes were tightly shut, her lips pressed together in a thin line. The same way newborn babies slept when they were trying to block out the unfamiliar chaos of the world.

"After Gregory leaves tomorrow, I will bring Natalie to the Abbey myself."

Gregory eschewed the grand departure ceremonies of his father. The next day, he and Dorian quietly left for the North Country with thirty of the Unicorn Guard and thirty martial magicians trailing in their wake. Eleanor fought back tears when Gregory and Dorian came to the Great Hall to say goodbye to the children. She felt the wind of Dorian's departure blowing through her heart like the first hint of an incoming blizzard, but missing him wasn't the only source of her sorrow. She stood between Ticia and Natalie with Cyrus in her arms as Gregory hugged his daughters and ran a hand over Cy's peach fuzz-covered head. Natalie was his child, too. He thought he'd return from his trip and find her working on her letters in her bedroom or running about the Paladine. At least she'd save him from the emotional torture she would soon inflict on herself. By the time he returned, the deed would be done. She alone must face leaving Natalie at the Abbey.

After the midday meal, Eleanor and Natalie took a carriage across town, down the Hundred Heralds Street and across Smithwick Square, then farther along the Outcountry Road to Afar Creek Abbey. Natalie rested her chin on the open window. She hummed to herself and commented on the funny people who waved as their carriage passed. The carriage rolled through Afar Creek's front gate, into the courtyard. Witches bustled about, carrying books, baskets of plants and mushrooms, and fresh linens for the sickrooms. It smelled of sheep's wool and boiling herbs. Three girls, not much older than Natalie, climbed to the top of a stack of hay bales and jumped into the pile of loose hay below them. Each time one of them landed, a puff of colorful magical light rose from the hay. Blue, brown, yellow. The girls laughed and climbed over each other to get back to the top of the stack.

The squeaky carriage wheels and the shouting of Eleanor's guards drowned out the children's giggling. Eleanor lifted her skirts with one hand and took the arm of the nearest guard with the other. She stepped to the dusty ground. She turned around, and Natalie jumped into her arms. "Goodness, love," Eleanor said. "Warn me first! You're much heavier than your little brother."

"This is where Rosemary lives? Why are we here?" Natalie peered around. "Where are all the boys?"

Eleanor laughed at her daughter's powerful observation. "No boys live here, Natty. This is Afar Creek Abbey. Only witches live here."

Rosemary joined them, and Natalie embraced her teacher. Eleanor remembered hugging Rosemary at Natalie's age. How much she'd looked forward to the witch's visits to her father's quiet house before he died. How she'd longed to be able to embrace her during the dark days after her father passed away, when her stepmother ruled as the terrible usurper of the family throne. She'd had to survive on the affection that infused Rosemary's letters, as if she'd written the words in a beloved perfume. If she had to send Natalie to anyone, thank HighGod it was Rosemary.

They toured the Abbey, from the kitchens to the library, the conjuring rooms to the dormitories to the chapel. They talked to witches young and old. In one of the classrooms, Natalie clapped joyfully as she watched girls not much older than herself arrange themselves to form a rainbow of colors with their own magic. As they lined up, each girl conjured some enchantment in the color of her power. Blue birds. Yellow fish. Pink flowers, white kittens, and green leaves. Rosemary noticed the wistful look on Natalie's face, and she invited her to try to conjure her own enchantment. With a few waves of Natalie's hand, red hearts, red roses, and red parrots swirled around the children's heads. A few of the parrots shouted out greetings in voices that sounded eerily like Chou Chou. The witch who taught the class nodded, clearly impressed by Natalie's efforts.

By the time they returned to the courtyard, Natalie was beaming. Red light followed her every movement, so she looked as if she were trapped in a scarlet tornado of her own making. "Mother," she said, breathlessly. "This is the *most wonderful* place!"

Rosemary nodded, and Eleanor bit her lip. She knelt down in front of Natalie. "It is, darling. It is a special place, just for witches. Women who can perform magic."

"Is that what I'm doing?" She looked at her hands, covered in magical mittens of red light, as if she'd never seen them before. "Magic?"

Eleanor nodded.

"If witches do magic, and I do magic. Does that mean—" Her eyes widened. She grinned. "I'm a *witch.*"

Her voice held no fear, only relieved wonder. Eleanor bit her lip to keep from crying. "You are, my dearest girl."

Rosemary leaned toward Natalie with her hands on her knees. "I think you will be a very powerful witch, too."

"What's powerful?"

"It means you will be a very good witch, who can make lots of magic. All kinds of magic."

Natalie jumped in place. "Yes! I would like that. Shall I come here for my lessons?"

Eleanor smiled, determined to make the experience positive for her daughter. "Do you remember the rooms with all the beds? Girls who are witches live here, Natty. At the Abbey."

Natalie looked crestfallen. "You mean away from their mothers and fathers and sisters and brothers? And their unicorns?"

"Other little girls don't have unicorns, darling. But yes, away from their families."

Natalie observed the goings on in the courtyard for a few moments. "Home is not far away, Mother. You can come here and visit me."

Eleanor nodded, unable to speak.

"So can Poppa, and Tish, and little brother. But what about Dasha? He must visit me too. Or I will visit him." She scratched her head. "Or maybe Dash can come live here with me."

Eleanor was taken aback. The child cared more about leaving her unicorn friend than her family. "I don't know about that. Rosemary?"

The witch shrugged. "There is no precedent for such. Non-magical *humans* can't live here at the Abbey. I don't believe there's ever been a request for another kind of creature to live here. A mystical one, at that. We'd have to consult the Oracle."

"And Gregory," said Eleanor as she straightened. "He'll be losing a princess. I don't think he'll want to lose a unicorn—even a wild one. Besides, Desmarais children usually don't get their own unicorn until they are older. Seven, maybe eight years old."

"It seems we have time to work on that." Rosemary took Natalie's hand and walked with her to the steps of the chapel. Eleanor followed them. They sat on the marble stairs, the wiry old witch and the tiny girl. "Natalie, you are a magical being. As a witch, you will live here with us. Learn our ways. You won't be a fancy princess anymore. You'll have chores and wear simple dresses, like the other girls. But you will make magic every day. You will learn things your whole life through that you can't even imagine just now."

Natalie looked up at Eleanor. One tear slid down her face. She reminded Eleanor of her late son, Nathan, in her increasingly uncanny maturity. "I will miss you and the rest of our family. But Meadow told Dasha he must listen to his heart. I think my heart is telling me I should live here."

Eleanor sat down and wrapped her arms around Natalie. Red light leaked from the child's body, like Eleanor's own heart, melting. "You must do as your heart tells you, my darling." She swiped at her own eyes and looked into Natalie's tearstained face. "Eclatant is not far. I visit Rosemary in the Abbey. Witches come to Eclatant all the time. We will see each other often."

Rosemary reached around and squeezed Eleanor's arm. "You will see each other, but we must not give false expectations. The Abbey has its ways."

"No, we mustn't," said Eleanor. "But there has never been a member of the Desmarais family at the Abbey. The Desmarais have their ways as well."

The sharp spires of Peaksend Castle slashed the setting sun like knives piercing a bright red apple. Dorian stood beside Terin, who, thanks to Orvid's spell, distinctly resembled Senné. Terin rubbed his newly darkened muzzle against unfamiliarly black legs. He shook, rather like a giant black dog climbing out of a washtub. "It tickles," he said.

"The tingling should go away in an hour or so. I'm sorry, but it's the only way to help you avoid being seen at night."

"I've been seen every night of my life."

"You're not traveling to the Dragon Mines with the King of Cartheigh every night."

Gregory had invited his allies, including Terin, to meet in the North and discuss the ogre crisis. He'd hoped to meet with Prince Samuel, as the ailing King Peter could not make the journey, but with fifteen escaped ogres roaming the Scaled Mountains, Svelya declined to risk its crown prince. Peter sent Agnes in Samuel's stead.

Truthfully, Dorian was glad Peter sent Agnes instead of the young, inexperienced Samuel. He hadn't seen the witch since he returned Samuel to her custody, but a few minutes of conversation reminded him why Peter put his faith in her. They'd had a productive discussion, with each delegation reporting on the state of their forces. Gregory had sent messages to the kings of Talesse and Kelland, but both nations sent riders to politely decline participation. Unsurprising, as Cartheigh and Svelya always had larger armies and stronger will to fight, as if centuries of squabbling over the Dragon Mines had pumped bellicosity into the national bloodstream. The Kells and Talessees wouldn't join the battle until an ogre upended the Talessee king's breakfast table or took up residence in Kelland's royal stables.

Brian Smithwick, Gregory's cousin and old friend, served as their gracious host. He was still a handsome fellow, but with his sizable belly and thinning hair, the ladies at court wouldn't be tripping over their skirts to dance with him anymore. He had married a blandly pretty member of the Harper family and fathered three blandly adorable children. Given their subtle twenty-year feud, Dorian expected hostility from him, but he was uncharacteristically pleasant. While in residence at Peaksend, he seemed content to coddle his family and boss around his servants. He kept a lackadaisical, symbolic eye on the northern army but left the military maneuvering to several battle-hardened generals. He greeted Dorian with casual friendliness, and Gregory with the deference due his sovereign, and he made sure they were fed, warm, and comfortable.

How we've all grown up, Dorian thought. *Even old Smithy.*

The Mines were ten miles north, closer to the mountains and hence to the renegade ogres. Dorian and Orvid wanted Gregory to stay at Peaksend, but he would not be deterred. With multiple ogres defecating near the water source, the dragons remained discontented. Gregory insisted on visiting his mystical charges.

Orvid pleaded with the king. "The witches from Afar Creek are having some success cleaning the water. I'm sure the dragons will improve soon."

"I'm going," said Gregory. His tousled hair stood up from his head in auburn spikes and swirls, as if his own body insisted that he always wear a crown.

"At least go at night," Agnes said. "Everything we are knowing of ogres indicates they're only active during daylight. Great lazy hulks, they are."

"I suppose that would be safer," said Dorian, although he wasn't thrilled at the prospect of traipsing through the dark with his king. Ogres were not the only dangers.

Orvid grasped at her suggestion. "That is your best option, if one must choose. Ogres sleep like the long dead."

"That settles it," said Gregory, and so it did.

Now here they stood, in the courtyard as the sun set, waiting to escort Gregory to the Dragon Mines under cover of darkness. Orvid's spellwork had blackened over thirty members of the Unicorn Guard in magical nighttime camouflage. Only Senné remained in his natural state, as he was already a bit of animated darkness. The men wore dark cloaks over their Fire-iron armor. Terin had volunteered to go along, even when Dorian told him he'd be subject to a magical disguise. When asked why, he simply said, "I feel I should go," and Dorian didn't question him further. As for Whisper, he declined to join their nighttime escapades. He silently watched Terin morph from white to charcoal gray to obsidian. He didn't say anything for once, but Dorian detected disdain in the set of his ears.

Once darkness fell, the Unicorn Guard and a party of mounted martial magicians escorted Gregory through Peaksend's gates. Dorian and Senné stuck close to Gregory and Monument, and night closed in around them. They lit no torches, instead relying on the unicorn's keen senses to get them where they needed to go. They planned to hug the curves of the Clarity River. This far north, the river was wild and rocky. The sound of the river's rapids would drown out the hoofbeats of their mounts.

Gregory whispered to Dorian. "I know you don't approve of me coming out here."

"It's your decision, Your Majesty."

"Enough with the *Your Majesty* for now."

"All right. It's your decision, Gregory." Dorian could just make out Gregory's profile in the darkness. "Just like it's your decision whether Natalie goes to the Abbey."

Gregory sighed. "Is it really, though? There are some laws of nature and magic that are beyond the wills of kings. I acknowledge that Natalie must go. It's more a matter of when. If only I knew for certain that Cyrus has no magical ability."

Dorian took measure of his answer before he replied. "You're afraid magical ability runs in Eleanor's family, but didn't Oliver do considerable digging under her family tree, so to say, before she came to Eclatant?"

"Yes. The Brice family made their fortune in dragon robes in the last hundred years or so. Her mother's family, the Mallocks, were wine merchants, originally from Sage. Settled in Maliana around the same time. Both her parents spent time at court. Both were only children whose own parents died relatively young. When Leticia Mallock Brice died, Cyril inherited the remains of her family's fortune, and then when he died, Eleanor's stepmother inherited the Brice Estate and the last of the money. Her father was a poor businessman, so it wasn't much."

Dorian already knew most of this, but he grunted an affirmative, as if he'd never heard any of it from Eleanor herself.

"She has no living relatives," said Gregory. "No aunts or uncles or cousins on either side that we ever found. Her mother's family is difficult to trace beyond her grandfather's arrival in Sage as a young man."

"You're saying you have no way of knowing what kind of latent magical talents she may be harboring in her family line."

"You think I'm being overly cautious, but I've waited so long for my heir."

"The child will more likely die of a disease than be called to magic. Yet will you hide him away from the world?"

"No. Of course not. He must be in the world if he's to effectively rule a nation."

"True. If perchance he were a magician, he'd have to learn to live in the world as one, correct? Because if he did have magical powers, he'd have to rule with them."

A pause in the darkness. Dorian wished he could see Gregory's expression.

"There you go again with your old tricks."

Dorian kept his reply mild, but if he were a wolf, his fur would be standing on end. "What tricks, Greg?"

"Making me see the light without holding the torch too close to my face," Gregory said, and chuckled.

Dorian's hypothetical hackles smoothed themselves. "I give the best counsel I can, whether about magical princes or suspect nighttime trips to the Dragon Mines."

"I understand why you and Orvid advised me against coming out here. But I feel called to the dragons. I can't explain it, really. I've always loved the Bond, HighGod knows I have, but since my coronation, I *feel* it. As if my bones were made of Fire-iron. They ache for damp northern air. It gets worse every day. I will get no respite until I see the dragons."

"Did your father ever tell you he felt this way?"

"No. But during my childhood, he never went more than a few months without heading north. Matilda and I learned to avoid him when he went too long between visits. He was more fearsome, and when your father is a great king, he's intimidating on a good day. But when he returned from the Mines, he always brought us gifts from Smithwick Square, hugged Matilda, and picked me up and tossed me in the air."

"Seeing the dragons relieved his angst."

"It makes sense to me now. When he got too old to go himself, and started sending me, I think he got some relief through my presence. But he never laughed the way he did when he went himself."

"Can I do anything to ease your pain?"

"No, but thank you. My brain is heavy inside my skull. I think my mind will clear when I ride this great creature into the lair of his scaled friends." He patted Monument's neck, and the unicorn nickered his acknowledgment.

"For whatever reasons, I believe my father kept it to himself. Or perhaps he told Ezra Oliver, in the old days."

"As long as you don't want to move the entire court up here, I won't try to stop you in the future. I'm glad you told me."

Gregory rested on hand on the Fire-iron shield hanging from a hook on his saddle. "I'm glad you were here to hear me tell it."

The royal escort smelled them before they saw them. The stench came out of nowhere, unexplainable, like a sudden downpour of skunk spray. Dorian recognized it immediately; it was the same stench he'd inhaled on the mountain pass after he bid farewell to Prince Samuel. Senné sneezed, and Dorian instinctively clapped his hand over his nose.

He heard a few thudding footfalls over the rushing slap of water against rock, and then the muffled scream of a martial magician.

"Lights!" shouted Orvid Jones.

The light of two dozen conjured fireballs floated above the magicians, illuminating the flat meadow, a thicket of dense bushes, and the steep banks of the Clarity River. Clashing magical colors blended together into stripes of yellow white. The fallen magician lay in the stodgy ground, his neck clearly broken. His fellows looked around wildly and whispered among themselves. The fireballs hovered in tingling, crackling anticipation of their defense. The Unicorn Guard swung into a circle around Gregory and Monument. Spears were drawn. Necks flexed and horns stood at attention.

"Greg, hold fast," said Dorian. Senné shifted below him like a sturdy boat on a choppy lake.

Gregory gripped his sword, ready to contribute to his own defense. The source of the thudding footfalls remained just out of reach of the magician's light. Dorian prayed for a particularly large, stinky bear, but his gut (and his nose) told him only one creature stepped so heavy and smelled so rank. With a loud grunt, the ogre stepped into the light. Its purple eyes twinkled, grotesquely pretty in its disaster of a face.

It strode toward the cluster of martial magicians. Fireballs bounced off its hide, but at least their light seemed to confuse it. It covered its eyes with one apelike arm and lashed out with the other. It struck two martials from their mounts. The horses spooked and took off for the safety of the barns at Peaksend. The ogre stepped on one of the downed magicians. He screamed and went silent.

As he stared at the dead magician, Dorian made a decision. The man's bugging eyes and concave chest made it easy. "Greg!" he yelled. "We have to run for it. Ogres aren't fast, thank HighGod."

"I won't lead it to the Mines!"

"Back the way we came then!"

To Dorian's horror, a smaller ogre emerged from the darkness. One purple eye darted around the battle scene. A gaping socket, crusted over by a flattened tarp-like eyelid, marred the other side of its face. It strode toward the Unicorn Guard, its fists balled at its sides.

At Dorian's command, the protective circle around Gregory opened like a cracked nut to provide him an escape route. Fireballs flew past them in a staccato barrage of colors. They hit the ogre's hide and exploded. It swatted them, as if they were annoying, multicolored flies. Once it tripped and fell on one knee, but within seconds, it was on its feet again. Its fists were swinging hammers. Blackened unicorns dodged and weaved as the Guard peppered it with spears and arrows. With each projectile and stabbing horn, the warriors aimed for the groin or the beast's one remaining eye. Terin stood out from the others, for he had no rider. He harried the ogre. He stabbed its leg, its foot, its shoulder. The larger ogre, seemingly tired of killing martial magicians, turned its attention on the shadowy unicorns. It swiped one of the Guards from his mount, but unlike the horses, who listened when instinct demanded flight, the unicorn returned to the battle.

Dorian and Senné hung back with Gregory and Monument. Dorian's mind raced. *What if there are more of them?* Suddenly, their decision to travel at night seemed colossally stupid.

Senné and Monument needed light before racing headlong into the pitch-black, potentially ogre-infested night. He shouted for Orvid. The magician yanked his horse's rein, and the brave steed galloped toward Dorian through a haze of whizzing fireballs. Once he was within arm's reach, Dorian grabbed the magician by the elbow and tugged. His horse bumped into Senné, and Dorian lugged Orvid up behind him. Orvid wrapped his arms around Dorian's waist.

Senné parried left, and Monument followed him. They had to make a beeline through the two sparring ogres to avoid the thicket and the river. Monument whinnied as Gregory reined him in. "Wait, Dor," said Gregory. "It has a blind side. It's vulnerable." He pointed at the one-eyed ogre. "The unicorns are too close to see it."

"We need to get you away from here."

"One of us can charge it before it kills anyone else!"

"No, damnit! You're the king. You make the commands. But I refuse to let you—"

"All right. All right! Let's go."

Senné and Monument raced for the narrow clearing. The spinning magical spheres gave off oaky smoke, and Dorian's lungs screamed for real air. He heard Monument close behind, the cacophony of eight hooves like pounding hail on a tin roof, until Orvid shouted the king's name.

The hail slackened by half.

Dorian looked over his shoulder. Gregory's dark cloak lay in the churned-up dirt behind Senné. Gregory and Monument raced toward the one-eyed ogre. As Gregory had predicted, it didn't notice them coming in hard and fast from its blind side. Gregory raised his sword. The swirling fireballs set his Fire-iron armor ablaze with sparkling colors, as if he were encased in an impenetrable prism.

For a brief second, Dorian saw Gregory as he had been years ago, on the jousting field, sitting on Vigor's back. A powerfully built young man, full of his own youthful promise and the pride of his birthright. How he'd handily felled his opponents!

The vision blinked out as the ogre shifted in Gregory's direction. This version of Gregory was no sixteen-year-old playing at battle. This was a grown man, on a relatively inexperienced mount. Not the king in waiting, but the true ruler. He hurtled toward potential death.

"Senné!" Dorian yelled. "Orvid!"

The former spun toward the ogre, while the latter conjured five creamy white fireballs, bolts of captured lightning.

Gregory leaned against Monument's neck. The ogre pivoted toward him. Its single eye widened in surprise as Monument bore down. Gregory had time for one brutal slice of his sword.

He made the most of it. His Fire-iron blade cut through the ogre's belly as a wagon wheel might grind through rocky mud. The effort yanked the sword from Gregory's grip, and black blood gushed from the wound like rotten sludge from an overflowing peat bog. The ogre shrieked. It grabbed at its shattered midsection and swung wildly at the king.

Its fist caught Gregory's outstretched arm and shoulder, knocking him from Monument's back. His foot stayed in the stirrup, and his right leg twisted at a grotesque angle before it slipped free. He hit the ground flat on his stomach and gasped for air. He struggled to push himself to his knees. His leg wouldn't support his weight, and he fell facedown into the mud again.

The ogre grabbed his right foot with one hand and tugged him backward, then shifted its grip to his leg. Gregory screamed as the creature dug its thick fingers, tipped with torn, spiky nails, into his thigh. He rolled onto his back, yanked a dagger from his belt, and plunged it into the relatively thin webbing between the ogre's fingers. The ogre dropped him and squealed again. It stuck its hand in its mouth like a grotesque baby.

Monument skidded to a stop. He backed up and stood over the king, his sides heaving. Dorian leapt from Senné's back as Orvid peppered the ogre with fireballs, blinding it.

Dorian grabbed Gregory around the waist. Gregory's right leg flopped uselessly under him. He finally got a grip on Dorian's arm and balanced himself on his left leg. Dorian half dragged him toward Monument, only thinking that he had to get Gregory in the saddle.

The Ogre stumbled, but it kept swinging. Its lower body had turned from brownish gray to black, as if it were wearing pants woven from its own blood. It doubled over, one fist in the bloody mud, one clutching its belly. Its chin nearly brushed the ground as it gasped. Hot, foul smelling breath blasted across the clearing. An ebony whirlwind appeared in the shadow of its one violet iris. Terin pierced its eye with his horn.

The ogre fell against its compatriot. The larger monster reeled as one-eye's blood and eye fluid splashed its face. It grunted and grabbed one eye's arm. The injured beast fell to its knees. They exchanged frazzled grunts as fireballs and spears continued to pepper them. The big ogre lifted the smaller one's chin and must have decided they'd had enough. It dragged its friend into the shallow river, out of reach of the magician's light. It screamed all the way, as if enraged at them for defending themselves against the unprovoked ambush.

Gregory hung on Dorian. Dorian tapped his cheek, and Gregory looked up at him through gritted teeth, his eyes fiercely aware through the pain. Dorian wanted to punch him, but this was not the time to chastise his king. He had just saved them all, and now Dorian must get him to safety.

Monument knelt, his nostrils trembling like the wings of an agitated hornet. Dorian struggled to get Gregory upright. The king bit his fist when Dorian touched his injured leg. His foot dangled below his contorted knee like a fish hook on a twisted line. Several deep gashes lacerated his thigh.

Gregory gripped Monument's mane. "Did I kill it? Tell them to flee. All of them. They don't need to stay here for me."

"Greg, stop talking."

"I'm sorry, Dor. I couldn't let them die. Not like Vigor and the others, murdered by those damn fish—"

"You're a hero and a fool, and I need to get you in the saddle."

"It cut me with its nails. Ogres are pestilent."

"We'll worry about that later. They may return. Can you ride?"

"I have to ride."

"We must return to the fortress. Please, don't argue with me."

Gregory nodded, his face deathly pale.

"Orvid, ride with him," Dorian said. "Use magic to hold him up if you must. Dorian stood in front of Monument. He'd feared the young stallion would buckle under the pressure, but other than his flittering nostrils, he held his ground. Vigor couldn't have been more composed.

Dorian mounted and surveyed the destruction. He counted at least fifteen downed men and many horses. Three unicorns, dead. "Return to Peaksend!" he shouted. "Split into groups. Spread out."

Hopefully little groups of galloping unicorns and mounted magicians would look the same to ogres. If the creatures had targeted Gregory, they'd be less likely to find him.

"I'll come with you." Terin appeared soundlessly beside Senné. "I can fight freely if need be."

Dorian nodded. "Thank you for—"

"There is no time for thanks." Terin raced for Peaksend. Senné and Monument didn't wait for Dorian's cue. They knew a leader when they saw one and followed him.

The torches burning atop the craggy fortress walls were little bits of sunrise, assuring Dorian they would see another day. Gregory stubbornly clung to consciousness and Monument's mane with the same tenacity. *Surely, he can't be terribly injured if he can keep his eyes open and stay erect.*

Orvid's magical effervescence revealed their faces. The sentries called out from their perches atop the walls. "It's the king!"

The rallying cry reverberated down the line like a catchy tune. The Fire-iron gates opened, and Dorian and Gregory's little party tumbled into the courtyard. Within moments, Brian appeared in the castle doorway.

He ran down the few stone stairs into the courtyard in a pair of house shoes and baggy leggings. His belly peeked out from below his white cotton undershirt. "I couldn't sleep. I kept thinking the nighttime excursion was a terrible idea."

"We all realized that a bit too late." Dorian dismounted and reached for Gregory, who held out his arms like a child reaching for his father.

He groaned as Dorian eased him onto his uninjured leg. His face was a starched sheet. Dorian braced against him. "Greg, can you—"

Gregory vomited, a watery projectile that splattered onto the cobblestones and over their boots. His eyes rolled back in his head, and he slumped against Dorian. "Damnit. Brian!"

Brian grabbed Gregory by his left arm and jammed his shoulder up under the king's armpit. Gregory hung between his two oldest friends, his head hanging and a shock of auburn hair cascading into his eyes. It was not unlike the night before his wedding, piss drunk after a visit to Pandra Tate's brothel. This time, however, he was a hero, not an embarrassment.

Dorian and Brian dragged Gregory into the fortress. Gregory's right leg dangled uselessly. Dorian assumed his knee bore the brunt of the injury, but his leg bent at an impossible angle. Too far up to be a knee injury. He feared what they would find when they removed his armor.

They placed him on the closest available bed, in one of the smallish bedrooms reserved for visiting generals.

"Get Mistress Agnes," Orvid said to a chambermaid. "She's the best healer for miles."

Brian took Orvid's arm. "Do you think that's wise? She's the one who suggested traveling at night."

Dorian's stomach dropped. Under any other circumstances, the fact that Brian Smithwick made such a logical deduction before he did might have annoyed Dorian.

Orvid looked to Dorian for his opinion.

Dorian squeezed Brian's shoulder. "I see your point, Brian. I do. But until we can get him to another witch, she's all we have. We'll have to put some faith in her judgment." He found himself trying to deny Brian's insinuations. "She might have made a mistake in suggesting we travel in the dark, but we all agreed with her."

"But what if it wasn't a mistake?" Orvid asked. "What if we did exactly what she wanted us to do?"

A maid placed a cool cloth on Gregory's forehead as Agnes burst into the room with a wooden box under one arm. Her face paled as she took in the gory scene. *Is that surprise to see Gregory injured? Or surprise to see him alive at all?*

Dorian and Orvid stationed themselves at the end of the bed like hulking bookends. Brian stood by the door, ringing his hands. Agnes set her box on the bedside table and asked for more water and towels. She fished through the box for painkilling herbs. She stood beside the unconscious king with her eyes roving over his burly form. "Light more candles, please. We have to remove his armor first. Then cut through his leggings."

Gregory didn't move while Agnes gingerly removed his Fire-iron armor. As she revealed his wounds, Dorian felt sick, although he'd seen his share of gruesome injuries during his army days and stints at the Mines. White femur bone peeked through a tear in his leather leggings. Agnes made careful cuts along the seams, and Orvid Jones covered his eyes with one hand.

"You may leave, Mr. Jones. And you, Lord Brandling. There's no reason for you to watch this."

"He's my king," Dorian said. "That's reason enough." Orvid had raised suspicions about her judgment and her motives, and Dorian would not leave Gregory alone with her.

Orvid cleared his throat and wiggled his shoulders, as if preparing for a swan dive off a high cliff. "As it is for me."

"As you wish," she said. "I must set the leg. Better to do it now, while he's unconscious."

Later, Dorian couldn't recall all the details of Agnes's setting of Gregory's broken leg. He remembered little things, like the squelch of her fingers against his meaty, blood-covered thigh. The way he jerked in his sleep, as if he'd dreamed of tripping over a tree root. Agnes's grunt of effort as she pushed the leg into place. The coppery smell of blood, of course, but not just any blood.

The king's blood. My best friend's blood.

"I will try to stitch the wound closed, but it's not a clean cut." Agnes reached into her box and held up a spool of thin flax thread.

"No," said Dorian. "It should be unicorn hair."

Agnes set the thread on the bed beside Gregory. She straightened out of a hunch for the first time in hours and rolled her head from side to side. "Why?" she asked.

"It will help with the healing," said Orvid. He and Dorian exchanged glances over Agnes's head. Dorian had never met a witch with any kind of healing skill who wasn't aware of the restorative properties of unicorn hair. The Paladins swept it up from the stables and sent it to abbeys far and wide—even those outside of Cartheigh. He'd seen a witch in Svelya use unicorn hair to stitch King Peter's hand when he cut his finger trying to slice into a piece of beef.

"Oh, then certainly. Is anyone having some?"

"My wife keeps it in the dispensary. The witches from Boggydown, the little abbey just southeast of the village, gave us a stock of basic healing supplies. I've patched up my little ones myself, while we waited on the witch to arrive. I'll fetch it."

He returned with the spool of unicorn hair. Agnes held the shimmery strands aloft. She shut one eye, and her tongue poked out as she tried to insert it into the eye of her stitching needle. Dorian fidgeted. He felt as if it were all taking too long. He almost asked Brian to help her, since he clearly had some experience treating injuries himself. Finally, the iridescent hair slipped into place. Agnes set about her human needlepoint. She closed the flesh where possible.

After she set and stitched the leg, she applied a compress coated in a healing paste. She bound the entire limb with strips of soft cloth and tied it to a sturdy sawn-off tree limb to prevent movement. She washed her hands, mopped sweat from her face, and slumped into a chair beside the fire while the maids tidied up her supplies and wiped the king's bloody face.

How strange he looked, lying there in his bloodstained undershirt, his bare arms limp at his sides. One leg was still incased in the remains of his black leather leggings. The other swaddled in white bandages. Dorian took the chair beside Agnes. He started sweating. It was too hot to sit this close to the fire.

"We need to get him back to Maliana," said Dorian. "He needs the witches of Afar Creek. No offense to you, Agnes."

"None taken. My primary work is in sorcery. There will be many with more skill than I at Afar Creek."

Dorian tried to read her body language, but she communicated nothing but exhaustion. Understandable given she's just put a man's leg back together.

"I will advise you, though," she said. "He should not travel anytime soon."

"But if he stays here, the wound might fester."

She rubbed her eyes.

"Your Grace, we must indeed be careful," said Orvid. "The journey may be too much for him in this state."

Dorian pulled his chair toward Gregory's bed. The heat made him short tempered, but he immediately felt better without the fire baking the left side of his face. *Do I have a blindside, like that ogre?* The king didn't move, except for the gently rise and fall of his chest and the occasional twitch of his eyelids. Orvid knelt beside Dorian.

"You know him," said Dorian. "Losing his leg would kill him. He needs to see the healers of Afar Creek as soon as possible."

Orvid put a hand on Dorian's shoulder. "We will decide in the morning."

Dorian nodded. The weight of the decision sat on his shoulders like a sack of wet grain. He'd never longed for the sunrise so much, and dreaded it.

Dorian, Orvid, and Brian took turns sitting beside Gregory that night. Brian's watch took them just past the dawn. When Dorian returned to the sickroom, he found Brian hunched over Gregory, holding his hand.

"I can tell more about a fever from the hands than the forehead," Brian said. "With the children, I always take their hands."

Dorian leaned over Brian's shoulder. "What are the king's hands telling you?"

"Feel for yourself, Your Grace."

Dorian took one of Gregory's thick hands in his own. It was bizarre to see one rough, manly hand cradled gently in another. Knuckles, veins, calluses from gripping swords.

Gregory's hands were not yet hot, but they were very dry. And very warm.

"Brian, I have to tell you. I'm impressed with your nursing skills."

Brian looked up at him with one eyebrow cocked. For a moment, Dorian saw a flash of their old rivalry. "You have to insult me, don't you? Even here, before our king's potential deathbed."

"On the contrary, old fellow, I'm being sincere. Look at you. Of all of us, you're the one who became the true family man. Surrounded day and night by his adoring wife and children. The picture of domestic bliss."

"Gregory has a wife and children." Brian chuckled. "But we all know he's lacking in the domestic bliss arena. Raoul should have been the family man, if HighGod hadn't taken his wife and left him to raise that little girl alone."

"A tragedy."

"One among many over the years, since the raucous nights of our misspent youth."

"I envy you in your peace, Your Grace."

"I wish the same for you." Brian lay a fresh wet cloth on Gregory's forehead. "I wish he could hear us. He'd laugh. Tell us to stop whining and man up."

"We're like two drunk grandmothers, reminiscing at a wedding." Dorian adjusted the wet cloth before it slid off Gregory's forehead. "Have you told Orvid about the fever?"

"He just left. He went to pack. He believes you should leave for Eclatant right away."

"What of Agnes?"

"I can remove the leg." A soft voice floated over Dorian's shoulder.

He turned around. The diminutive witch looked at him with her big round eyes. In the twinkling orange firelight, her elfish features were foxlike.

"Have you ever removed a leg?"

"No."

"You plan to have your first go at it on the king?"

"I'm only trying to help."

Dorian crossed the room. Agnes blinked and took a step back. The fox usually stared down at rabbits, not up at dragons.

"I don't think you're qualified to offer such assistance. Besides, we are nowhere *close* to removing his leg. Not until Afar Creek sees him." He called over his shoulder to Brian. "Stay with him. I'm going to speak with Orvid."

He strode out of the sickroom. His mind hummed, as if his brain were on fire, not Gregory's. He found Orvid in his own bedroom, his bag half packed with robes and books.

"You think we should leave," said Dorian.

"Do you still think that's the best course?" Orvid tossed a shaving brush into his satchel. "HighGod. Don't change your mind on me now, when I've just made up my own."

"I haven't changed my mind. His fever isn't terrible now, but it may get worse. We should go." He paced the room. Such an important decision. "But... what about the witches of Boggydown. Or wait—what about the witches who are cleaning water at the Mines?"

"Boggydown is a glorified livestock hospital. The witches cleaning the river are sorceresses."

"But Agnes is a sorceress."

"She's also the first Chief Sorceress in the known nations. She'll have more skills at almost any form of witchery than any common witch. Just as I have more magicians' skills than all of most of my fellows, except the ones who have spent a lifetime honing a particular skill. No. Gregory needs the dedicated healers of Afar Creek. They're the best in the world."

"Why didn't Agnes know about unicorn hair?" asked Dorian. "Even I knew that. I don't like it, Orvid. It pains me that Brian Smithwick had to bring it to my attention, but now I can't put it out of my head."

"Nor can I. She's either treacherous, or far less intelligent than we thought. In my experience, given her stature in Kind Peter's court, the former is more likely. Still, she needs to come with us."

"She may be plotting some evil, and we take her with us?"

"She's the only healer we have. Once we get past Navigation Ford, we're in safer, more populous country. I'll keep a close eye on her." Orvid cast a fireball of creamy light. He rubbed his fingers together, and it crackled and popped as it elongated into a small shaft of lightning. "If Gregory gets abruptly worse, we'll need her. If she is a traitor, I'm sure she'll suddenly remember her loyalty with my proverbial sword against her neck."

"She won't be a fading flower. You just said she's the first Chief Sorceress in history."

With a snap of Orvid's finger, the lightning bolt swung in midair and shot across the room. Dorian stumbled against the wall, his hand instinctively going for the knife he always kept strapped to his boot. The lightning bolt stopped less than a hand's length from his nose. He held the knife in front of his face, flat side out. If Orvid had meant business, he might have gotten lucky and repelled his magic back at him. Or maybe not.

"I am the Chief Magician of Cartheigh. Trained by the most powerful magician who ever lived." The lightning bolt split. The two shards of magic hummed in the air beside Dorian's ears. He felt as if he were in a hive, and the bees were almost annoyed enough at him to sting.

Orvid winked, and the lightning disappeared. "I'm no timid tulip myself. As Mistress Agnes will learn, should she need a lesson."

CHAPTER 14

SPOUSAL DIPLOMACY

ELEANOR SAT BESIDE GREGORY'S bed. Five goose down pillows propped him up. He wore a simple silk shirt and a pair of soft cotton leggings. His manservant, Melfin, had cut off the right leg of the pants, so it ended in a jagged line above the layers of cotton bandages that still encased his broken leg. His feet were always cold, so he wore heavy wool socks. Ticia had knitted him a new pair as soon as he came home. On his left foot, a green sock with purple stripes; on his right foot, purple with green stripes. A cup of cold tea sat on the nightstand, alongside a few uneaten bites of the turkey eggs and bacon.

He'd been home for nearly three months. Dorian and Orvid had returned to Eclatant with Gregory lying in the back of a carriage pulled by unicorns. Eleanor couldn't find words to describe the terror she'd felt when she saw Gregory laid out like a slab of leftover beef. His lank red hair, plastered to his pale forehead, brought up paralyzing memories of her vigil at Nathan's deathbed. The next few days were a blurry procession of witches coming and going and meetings with the High Council. She sequestered Cyrus in his room, as if an ogre were sitting before the palace gate, waiting to swallow the last Desmarais male. Things had calmed down some now that Gregory's demise seemed unlikely—or at least not imminent.

While the witches thought the broken bone was healing, the lacerations on his thigh still festered. As feared, the wounds pulsed with a vicious pestilence that even the most powerful healers had yet to defeat. Whatever foulness lived in beasts had transferred itself from the one-eyed ogres ragged claws into the king's leg. The infection had taken up residence, feeding merrily on the king's muscly haunches and thriving on his dogged will to live. He had good days when the witches hoped they were making progress, but then the pain and putrid swelling would return for no surmisable reason. She pictured the malignant spirit in Gregory's leg as a slimy toad. It went into hibernation for a while and then woke, ravenous, and gorged on his flesh.

She fretted over his physical health, but the injury to his pride equally concerned her. To a woman, or even another man, it might seem like vanity. If faced with a similar predicament, Eleanor herself would think, *at least I am alive*. But the Gregory she'd known for over fifteen years defined himself by his physical prowess. He was never the smartest person in the room, but he was the strongest and the fastest. The best rider. The most talented swordsman. Only Dorian outshone him, and Dorian himself acknowledged that whatever physical superiority he had, Gregory made up for in bravery and brashness. She didn't know how Gregory's soul would cope if he lost use of his leg. When the witches made the dire suggestion that they consider removing the leg altogether, Eleanor retreated into the rationale that he wasn't strong enough to survive the surgery. In truth, Gregory had proved to have the strength of a grizzly bear. She believed his heart would keep beating if they removed his leg, but when he woke after surgery, it would break and kill him all the same.

On this pleasant HighSpring morning, she tried to brighten her thoughts and his mood by handing him the kaleidoscope. He looked up at her with tired, pained brown eyes, a lame hound who suddenly realized he was too old to keep up with the pack. "Is this your special kaleidoscope?" he asked her, his voice scratchy from lack of use. "The one that showed you Oliver?"

"Yes. Look into it. It will show you something you long to see."

"Myself with a new leg?"

"No, silly. Something real."

He shrugged and scrunched one eye shut. She gave him instructions for revealing the scope's magic. She held her breath as he spun it. Dorian had told her of Gregory's aching need to visit with the dragons. She prayed that whatever gods of magic controlled the kaleidoscope would be merciful and show him the Mines. She hoped a glimpse of the great scaled beasts working alongside the unicorns would bring him joy and strengthen him.

His open eye widened, and he smiled at her. She knew she'd gotten her wish.

"I can't believe it!" he said. "It's as if I'm there. It's a transfer!"

She listened as he chattered about the time-honored process of transferring the dragons from one cave to another, thus ensuring the constant production of Fire-iron in a rotation synced with what the earth below could handle. He mentioned Matt Thromba, and Tremor, the unofficial leader of the unicorns of the Mines. He fondly pointed out Blondie, a bull dragon with an unusual crest of light-yellow scales on the back of his neck. He scrutinized the beasts themselves, given their questionable health of late. "None seem glaringly ill. Good dark green color. No ragged wing tips. No weepy eyes." He shifted in his bed. "Thromba's letters said they're having luck clearing the water."

"I'm glad the witches have been able to help."

He twisted the scope. "Wait—it's fading."

"It only lasts so long."

He set it on his lap. "All good things in life only last so long."

The statement was morosely philosophical, both adjectives she rarely used to describe her husband in happier times. "How is Natalie?" he asked.

As Eleanor had hoped, Dorian managed to bring Gregory around to her side of the coin, By the time he returned to Eclatant, she'd already deposited Natalie at the Abbey, and they had no need to discuss it again. While his injury clearly lent extenuating circumstances to her new take on spousal diplomacy, the lack of argument boded well for the approach in the future.

"Natalie is well. I haven't seen her since I visited the Abbey ten days ago, but Rosemary's letters send only positives. She's still flummoxing her teachers with her talents."

"I miss her. I could use her sunshine in this room."

"You'll visit her when you're well." She didn't want to tell Gregory that even after only three months at the Abbey, Natalie wasn't the same bubbly, shiny child they'd known. Her growing maturity shocked Eleanor during every visit. Rosemary told her long ago that even as the witches' bodies resisted aging, their minds put childhood behind them before normal people. Natalie, with her prodigious power, was maturing unusually fast, even for a witch.

"There is something esoteric about her," Rosemary had told Eleanor. "Something beyond the norm, even for our kind."

She didn't want to worry him, so she decided she'd let him see Natalie's progress for himself. She didn't want to make Natalie seem unhappy. Far from it. The child grew like grass under a hot sun and seemed as serene as a spring-fed pond on a breezeless morning.

Eleanor bustled around the room for a while, tidying up and chattering about Ticia and Cyrus, trying to illicit a laugh out of him. Ticia came to show him her artwork, and he put on a happy face and gave her some friendly pointers. Pansy brought Cyrus to visit. The baby, chunky cherub that he was, sat on Gregory's lap and babbled. Gregory whispered to him and rubbed his hands over the baby's fuzzy head, while the child's weight gradually exacerbated the pain that constantly radiated from his belly to his feet. When it became unbearable, he said, "Take him, dear. I'm too tired."

How odd to hear Gregory address her as *dear*, or by any other endearment. He usually stuck to her given name, or, when he felt either friendly or condescending, *wife*.

"As you wish, Husband," she replied. She kissed Cy and handed him off to Pansy once more for his morning nap.

For many reasons, she felt a connection to Gregory unlike anything she'd felt for years. Compassion for his injuries; their shared love of Cyrus and sense of responsibility for the nation; his increasingly thoughtful demeanor. Still, she couldn't manage to replicate his affectionate nickname with a reciprocal *dear, darling,* or, HighGod forbid, *my love.*

"What if I die, Eleanor?" he suddenly asked.

She froze with a water pitcher in one hand and a cup in the other. "You won't."

"But I might."

"We all die eventually."

"But my chances are better than most these days." He faced her. "We both know my leg is not healing properly."

"It will just take time." She approached the bed and sat on the edge. "But… if you should die. You have Cyrus. He's your heir. If something should happen to him, HighGod forbid, you have Ticia." Eleanor still hadn't told Gregory that Ticia rejected the idea of being queen, not when she'd spend years trying to convince him their daughter should wear the crown. "But you will not die. You're too strong. And too stubborn."

"If anyone knows how stubborn I am, it's you." He chuckled.

"There's a sound I thought I'd forgotten."

"Oh, spitfire, Eleanor, how can I laugh? I know what is coming. Even I learned, in my history classes, of the carnage of the Ogre Wars. We only won through scheming, after thousands of people and unicorns died. The dragon population depleted. We won't be so lucky as to use the same trickery on them again. I fear this time, we will have to simply keep fighting and hope to finally beat them down."

"You got the best of one ogre in this battle."

"But there were only two of them, and we lost almost twenty men—over half of those who accompanied me. Three unicorns, dead. We don't even know that we killed it. We never found the body."

She searched for something mollifying to say but came up with nothing.

"Gammonreil sent word. More ogres have escaped," he continued. "There are now over twenty roaming the mountains between here and Svelya. Sporadic attacks on both sides of the border. From your vision in this fascinating little toy"—He held the kaleidoscope before his face—"we know Oliver is involved. We know he's moving the ogres, but still don't really know why, or who is helping him. For whatever reason, he seems to be keeping them somewhat in check. But we both know there's no reason for him to remove them from the camps if he doesn't plan to put them to work for him. When he does, they'll be hell bent on appeasing their god. I fear we'll be fighting them for years. Our men will do what they have to do to protect their women and children. The stallions will do what they must do to protect their herds. To the death, compounded a hundred thousand times. For what else can men and stallions do? Should I live, I shall oversee it all."

Something about Gregory's lament bothered her. She handed him a cup of water. "Drink. The witches will smite me if I let you get as parched as a thirsty dragon in a drying riverbed."

"May I keep this?" He held up the kaleidoscope. "It amuses me. I do feel better, seeing the dragons. Who knows. Perhaps I'll see something of value, like you did."

Despite hours of trying, Eleanor had not seen Ezra Oliver in the kaleidoscope again. She had a hunch he'd sensed someone spying on him and covered his tracks once more. "Take it, just promise me you'll think about Mr. Oliver," she said to Gregory. "You may have more luck than I've had." She stood. "I'm going to the Paladine. The mare called River has had her first foal. A filly."

"That's lovely." He took her hand and squeezed it. "I'm tired. Can you close the curtains? I think I'll sleep."

Eleanor contemplated Gregory's lugubrious pessimism as she fidgeted with the curtains. *What else can men and stallions do?* he had asked. His resigned melancholia irked her. It smacked of some gallant martyrdom, and they weren't even officially at war yet. Gregory saw one path: to fight nobly and futilely until the end of all ends. *It is what men have always done.*

She tiptoed out of the bedroom. *How would a woman wage a war?*

The answer came from everywhere and from nowhere. *She wouldn't if she could help it.*

Eleanor planned to meet Teardrop in the small, quiet courtyard on the eastern side of the palace for the mile ride to the Paladine. She was lost in thought as she changed into her riding clothes and made her way through the Great Hall. Chou landed on her shoulder. She told him that, by her estimation, Gregory saw no other option but to repeat his royal forebearers long dive into a prolonged massacre.

"If we fight them," said Chou, "we are indeed dooming a great portion of our male population—human and unicorn."

"Chou, I cannot stand to think about how many men have died in wars. They march off with some twisted idea that it's noble carnage because a king commands it. Why can't the other men who lead them come up with any other solution?"

"You yourself are realizing that the rooster's talons are often more effective than his crow."

"I don't just mean talk. What about novel, creative solutions? Hazelbeth devised the plan to trick the ogres into the camps. She finally ended a war the kings and generals and magicians would have continued fighting until the last man died."

"You seek something more effective than talking or killing."

Eleanor thought of Cyrus, sleeping snugly in his cradle. If this war continued as long as Gregory feared it would, it might still be going by the time he was old enough to join it. "Clearly we can't trap the ogres in the same way. They've found a way out, and really, having them sitting on our doorstep is probably not the ultimate solution. But neither is Gregory's way—an endless war we can't win. We need to get rid of them, *permanently*."

"That spell is easier spoken than cast, Eleanor."

She clipped down a little-used, narrow stairwell leading to the eastern exit. "I refuse to believe the only solution is to send a generation of husbands and fathers and brothers to be honorably mowed down like tender stalks of wheat before a scythe for a hopeless cause. I want to stop the war before it happens. A woman's way will solve the underlying problem, not create another one."

"What problem are you solving now?"

She turned at the sound of Dorian's voice. As always, it filled her with joy and spasms of paranoia. Since Cyrus's birth, they'd been even more careful in their interactions, lest Gregory have one iota of reason to suspect the little boy's true parentage. Ironically, their love for their unexpected child had forced them further apart. They hadn't so much as held hands since the irresponsible romp in the circus that gave them Cyrus.

Shadow partially shrouded him, for he came from a gloomy, intersecting passage that led to the dungeons. He leaned against the wall. Perhaps he was trying to pass for a decorative suit of armor.

She looked up and down the deserted hallway. Few people had reason to use leave the palace by the eastern exit, and even fewer visited the dungeons. Perhaps they might steal a moment. She took a deep breath and stepped into the welcoming spot of darkness beside him. They shuffled down the passageway and around the corner. Chou whistled a warning, but he lit on the antlers of a mounted deer's head and took up watch.

"Why are you coming from the dungeons?" she whispered.

"I visit the Dungeonmaster once a month. To make sure the facilities are ready, should we have any particularly notorious prisoners."

She touched his right hand. His whole hand— he'd lost the smallest finger on his left hand years ago, battling giant, carnivorous birds in her defense. Their pinkies intertwined. At the touch of his skin, she felt tingling in places she's forgotten existed. She tried to focus on something practical, sensible. Mulling over one of their looming national crises might snuff out her lust. She detached her hand from his and chose to speak of alliances with foreign nations. "It sounds as if you're expecting a notorious prisoner. You still suspect Agnes of wrongdoing?"

"These days, once I doubt someone, I keep distrusting until I'm proven wrong."

"I've spent time with her. She seems rather melancholy, but then again, she's hundreds of miles from Gammonreil and all she loves—and there are at least twenty ogres between her and home. It's enough to make anyone glum." Eleanor had learned enough over the years to know almost anyone could prove deceitful. She and Dorian had actively participated in one of the greatest deceits in history by simply loving each other. Still, she didn't want to believe Agnes, one of the few people she considered a friend, was a turncoat.

"We don't have much time to figure it out. If she's *not* a devious spy, she should return to Gammonreil soon. King Peter gets weaker every day. Samuel may be king sooner than we think, and if she's true, he'll need her counsel. We'll have two relative novices on the greatest thrones in the known nations. It's not particularly comforting when we may be at war any day."

"Why must war be a given?"

"You can hope for the best and an inspired, peaceful solution to our problem, Your Highness, but I have to prepare for the worst. I've been thinking—perhaps the Oracle can tell us something about Agnes."

"She might very well sense something, but honestly, sometimes I'm more confused when I leave her side than I was when I arrived. But Agnes has mentioned wanting to meet the Oracle. I'll visit Natalie next week, and we're to visit with Hazelbeth. She wants to meet Natalie, although she receives few visitors these days. Why meet with a five-year-old novice?" Eleanor put both hands on the side of her head and squeezed. "It's unnerving to have no control over your own children."

"I understand that feeling very well."

"I always think of you when I make decisions for him." She touched his bearded cheek. "If I take Agnes with us, and the Oracle senses nothing, perhaps that will ease your mind."

"The only thing that would truly ease my mind would be an hour in your arms."

Her heartbeat picked up. She backed up and peeked around the corner. Chou still stood sentry. He climbed from one branch of the dead deer's antlers to the next. His blue head bobbed and weaved on his impossibly long neck like a ripe berry on a wobbly stalk.

She returned to Dorian. Almost of its own fruition, her free hand slid from Dorian's waistband to his crotch. He was hard and hot, like the hilt of a sword not long removed from a smithy's fire. He groaned, grabbed her by the waist, and pulled her closer. He bit the side of her neck.

"Pssst!"

Eleanor glanced at her feet. Chou had hopped down the passageway. He shook his head violently. If it truly were a berry, it would have detached from his neck and splattered on the polished wooden floor.

"Just one kiss?"

Dorian didn't need to ask twice. She grabbed the back of his head and pressed her mouth to his. His tongue parted her lips. Whatever fire had lit his loins, he'd transferred it to hers, as sure as if her thin riding leggings had caught on fire.

A squawk of outrage broke the kiss. She stepped away, her heart pounding. Despite the sexual gymnastics she and Dorian had experimented over the years, that kiss left her feeling as titillated as a virgin playing spin the spoon.

Chou hissed at them. "Idiots!"

"He's right. We are idiots," she whispered.

"This idiot can live on that kiss for months. Go now, and hurry. But you'll take Agnes to the Oracle?"

"Dorian Finley, if you asked me to take Agnes to the Red-headed Hussy, I'd agree. That's how under your spell I am."

"I'm under yours, my queen." He kissed her hand, and she laughed when he tugged his tunic into place over the tent his arousal had raised in his leggings. "I suppose I'll head back to the dungeons. It's unlikely I'll pass anyone. Some cold, dank air and a few torture devices should deflate this."

She covered her mouth with her hand. She fought back hard peals of laughter as Dorian hobbled down the corridor, clearly weighed down by his still turgid member, and disappeared into the shadows.

Chou was not amused. "Eleanor, that was quite stupid."

"It was, Chou. But I feel happy for the first time in months."

"You won't be happy if you're dead."

"How do you know? They say the afterlife is pure bliss."

"I'm serious. Do *not* do that again."

"Yes, my feathered father figure." She stroked his head, and they resumed their walk to the eastern exit. "I'm sorry. I don't mean to scare you, but I have to find a little joy somewhere. It will wear off soon, and I'll be paralyzed by fear again."

"Good. That's the way I like it."

"Dorian's… ahem… manhood … so distracted me that I didn't get a chance to talk to him about my theories on stopping the war."

"So far you have a general hypothesis that men cannot solve great conundrums without resorting to butchery, but you have no specific notions or schemes to rectify the situation through any other means."

"What an eloquent summarization. Hurry. Teardrop is waiting for us."

Eleanor felt tentatively hopeful for the first time in weeks. She could work with a general hypothesis, as Chou put it. Every precise idea started with a vague one. She knew how to wrestle theoretical notions into specific ones. HighGod knew she'd done it before.

Eleanor loved Rosemary's office at the Abbey, as the space seemed to represent her old teacher perfectly: tidy, even a bit sparse, except for the tall, skinny stacks of books, arranged by color and size, that flanked the desk. Eleanor and Agnes arrived as Rosemary packed up her small satchel with a few apples, charcoal pencils and paper for taking notes, matches, and a pouch of dried lavender to burn in the Oracle's cavern. "You know how she loves the smell," she said.

Eleanor introduced the two witches. Rosemary offered a smiling welcome, and Agnes accepted it. Eleanor detected curiosity on the part of both women. While Rosemary tied her satchel to the woven loop at her waist, Agnes squinted at the stacks of books. As they walked into the courtyard, Rosemary watched Agnes out of the corner of one eye. The Svelyan witch inhaled deeply. "I've rarely smelled so many different colors of magic," Agnes said. "So many talented women in one place."

Eleanor knew nothing of the smells of magic, but it made sense that if each witch's magic had a unique color, and a tone, and left residue behind, an individual's magic also had its own scent. To other witches, anyway. As usual, Eleanor smelled hay, goats, and burning herbs.

Rosemary shielded her eyes with one hand. "Now, where are they? It's their playtime. They might be anywhere."

They wandered the Abbey's grounds, looking for Natalie and the rest of the girls from her alchemy class. They passed witches young and old, most of whom had heard of Agnes and wanted to say hello to the first Chief Sorceress. At first, Agnes's white skin glowed with the sunrise of pinkish red blush. By the time they found Natalie and her friends outside a shed full of old farming tools, the sun had risen fully on Agnes's face. She beamed at each witch, took her blessings, and asked after her personal work.

Ten other girls surrounded Natalie, all of whom looked to be three or four years older than her. She held both hands aloft, and a red halo circled her head like a rotating crown of rose petals. A sparkling silver bucket and a clear watering can floated in the air before her. She waved her arms, a mystical maestro crossed with an enchanted gardener. The can tipped and sprinkled water into the bucket. Natalie's pinky finger twitched, and long-stemmed daisies and daffodils exploded from the bucket. Water doused the closest girls. They laughed and clapped, and the wet ones wiped their faces and arms on their aprons. The can and the bucket vanished. The flowers drifted toward the ground but disappeared before they hit the bright green spring grass. Natalie examined her wiggling fingers, as if she were pondering ways to improve the spell.

"Hello there, girls!" shouted Rosemary.

The girls turned at the well-loved voice, and several of them skipped toward the Abbottess. "Did you see Natty's spell, Mum Rosemary?" asked a girl with chin-length black hair. "Quite good, don't you think?"

"It's just a parlor trick," said her chubby, curly-haired friend. "Nothing important."

Eleanor thought the little girl to be a younger, magical version of her old friend Anne Iris, who never met another woman with whom she didn't want to compete.

"I'd like to see you do it so neatly, and you're ten, not five."

"Clarys, Ruthie, that's enough now. You're fighting in front of your queen, about her own daughter's talents."

The girls peered around Rosemary's back, as if just realizing there were other visitors. Natalie finally noticed them and ran to Eleanor. She wrapped her arms around her mother's legs. "Hello, Mother."

The formality in her voice hurt Eleanor's feelings, but she counted her blessings. Only her friendship with Rosemary and her crown allowed her to have any continued contact with her daughter. If she didn't turn up every couple weeks, Natalie might have totally forgotten her family by now.

"Hello, darling." Eleanor knelt beside her small daughter. Natalie watched her with somber green eyes. *HighGod, she's so lovely.* Natalie had unknowingly saved dozens of young men at Court the heartbreak of falling in love with her by becoming a witch.

"How are you? How is Dasha?"

At every visit, Natalie asked after her health, perhaps out of politeness, and then immediately asked about the young unicorn. "He's well," Eleanor said. "He misses you. I'm hopeful you can see him soon." Really, Eleanor wasn't sure when that might happen, but Dasha and Natalie pined for each other. She didn't have the heart to tell either of them they were in for a wait.

"How is Ticia, Cyrus, Poppa, Chou, Uncle Dorian"—she counted them off on her fingers—"Teardrop, Pansy, Cricket, Grandfather— oh, he's dead. I always forget."

"Everyone is well, Natty. I'm happy to see you."

"It's nice to see you, too. I've been waiting for you to arrive, so I can have my visit with the Oracle." She cocked her head, like a kitten listening for a mouse's squeak. "Who have you brought with you?"

"Oh, yes. Natalie, this is Agnes." The other girls crept closer, their curiosity peaked by this woman who was clearly one of them, yet seemed so foreign. "She is the Chief Sorceress of Svelya."

The girls gasped over this news. "I have heard of you, Mum Agnes!" called out Ruthie, the chubby girl. "Can you teach us something?"

"Oh, yes, please! Please do!" The girls jumped up and down in place, all except Natalie, who watched Agnes with her appraising cat's eyes.

"Well...I suppose so." Agnes smiled at them. "What are you working on?"

"Before lunch, alchemy." Natalie took Agnes's hand. "After lunch, we shall have locomotion lessons."

This didn't pass Agnes's language filter. "Locomotion?"

Natalie raised her free hand, and a rusty shovel dislodged itself from the dirt and floated toward her. It stood at attention, as if awaiting her command. She flicked her wrist and the shovel spun wildly, a windmill without the mill, before shooting up through one of the open windows of the shed. Eleanor heard it clang against some other tools before it landed with a thud somewhere in the musty darkness.

"Ah, in Svelya we say *yannis-daya*. It means, hmmm... free moving."

"I like that. Free-moving. Can you show us some how you move things, freely?" Natalie asked.

Agnes looked over her shoulder at Eleanor and Rosemary. Rosemary nodded, so Agnes walked toward the shed. She sat on a stump, and the girls settled into a semi-circle around her. She picked two daisies from the grass beside her. "Lifting heavy objects is difficult, girls." She let go of the little flowers and they hung suspended in the arm before her. "But there is equal difficulty in the fine work." As she spoke, other daisies dislodged themselves from the ground, and began weaving their skinny stalks together into a tight chain. The girls smiled and laughed.

"I think that's harder than lifting big things!" said Clarys.

"There are plenty of daisies," said Agnes. "Why don't we all try? We can make crowns and bracelets. Be daisy maidens!"

The girls cheered and reached for the red and white flowers around their crisscrossed legs. Agnes adjusted little fingers, handed out flowers, and gave pointers. Puffs of multi-colored magic surrounded the girls' heads and hands. Pinks and blues and oranges, a chocolate brown, many shades of white and yellow. Agnes's dark green wove in and out, somehow a more mature, substantial, adult shade. Eleanor watched, her heart overflowing with love and pride. Natalie's bright red outshone them all.

Rosemary and Eleanor sat in the grass themselves while Agnes gave her impromptu lesson on free movement. They munched Rosemary's apples. "I'm rather glad we have a chance to talk in private," said Eleanor.

Rosemary shook out the bell sleeves of her robes, and two matching napkins fell into her hand. She handed one to Eleanor. "Use it quickly, it will disappear soon." She wiped her mouth. "What, pray tell, have you got up your own sleeve?"

"Not enchanted napkins." Eleanor told Rosemary her thoughts on the futility of Gregory's anticipated Second Ogre War. "I just know there must be some other solution. We came up with one once."

"The ogres won't be tricked again. Anything we do, they will regard with suspicion."

"I'm not talking about tricking them. I want to get rid of them. Once and for all. Without fighting them."

"It sounds like you just want them to vanish." Rosemary snapped her fingers.

Eleanor rested both elbows on her knees. "Yes. That's it, Rosemary. I want them to simply vanish."

Like they vanished right from under the noses of the Ogre Watch. She sat up straight. "Why can't they?"

"You mean, why can't they disappear, like they disappeared from the camps?"

"Yes! We can use magic, but not to trap them. To get rid of them!"

"First, there's the fact that no one but Oliver knows how to perform the magic we'd need to move them."

"Has anyone at Afar Creek or First Covey really tried?"

"No. We were consumed by the Burning, and the troubles around it, for years. It took us a long time to recover." Rosemary sounded rather defensive. "As for the Coveys, you'd have to ask Mr. Jones, but I haven't heard of any concerted effort to master his technique. We don't even *know* his technique."

"But if we did—we have the Oracle, for goodness sake. She's more powerful than Oliver."

"Eleanor, the Oracle is weak these days. I don't know if she ever fully recovered from the last battle with Oliver."

"Still… we could send them somewhere far cross the sea. They can't swim, so they'd never return." Eleanor babbled on before Rosemary turned naysayer. "I must do more research!"

"You're getting ahead of yourself, dear."

"But, Rosemary, don't you see how it might work?"

Rosemary shrugged, her face full of affectionate exasperation. "In theory, yes. If we get rid of them, then we wouldn't need to fight them."

"Exactly!" The new idea charged Eleanor's entire body, as if Natalie had infiltrated her veins with blood red magic. "Will you set some witches to work on it?"

"It certainly can't hurt."

"Mother. Mum Rosemary." Natalie ran toward them, dragging Agnes with her. They were bedecked in daisy chains, as if they were preparing for an old-fashioned village Awakening Fest. "Will the Oracle feel better soon?" Natalie let go of Agnes's hand. She rubbed a daisy chain between her fingers until the flowers fell off and pooled sadly at her feet.

"She's told me the Oracle is ill," Agnes whispered. "Just came out with it, out of nowhere."

Before Rosemary replied, someone called out to her from across the field. Two witches trudged toward them, their faces as dark as the dried mud coating their boots. The older woman was breathing hard by the time they reached the tool shed, so her younger companion spoke for her. Eleanor recognized her as a healer who had visited Eclatant to examine baby Cyrus. She'd declared him as healthy as a pampered, prized racehorse.

"We've just come from the Pool. The Oracle is not well," the young healer said. "I think it's time we move her into the hospital."

"I can't imagine she'll want to leave the Pool," Rosemary said. "She draws strength from it. Can't you post someone with her in her cavern?"

"She should be close to all the healing tools at our disposal. She agreed to come. She asked us to bring water from the pool for her to drink, and we also need to set up a basin, so she can watch."

Rosemary took Eleanor's arm. "I'm sorry, but clearly today isn't a good day for your visit."

Given this new turn of events, neither of Eleanor's dual purposes would come to fruition today. She would find no clarity about Hazelbeth's interest in Natalie, nor would the old witch magically assess Agnes. It was frustrating, but if the Oracle was ill, she shouldn't make a fuss. "Of course. I understand."

"No. Nooooo-wa!" Natalie stomped her foot. "I want to meet her! I've been waiting *so long*. Dragon's bloody teeth!"

"My goodness. Natalie Matilda," Eleanor said. "You can't speak that way."

"You can't tell me what to do, Mother. *You're* not in charge of me anymore."

Rosemary took Natalie by the arm. "Child, that is your mother. More so, she's your queen."

"It's all right, Rosemary," said Eleanor, her heart shrinking in her chest. She knelt. "It's true. I'm not in charge of you every day, but I want you to be the best person you can be. Stomping your foot and swearing isn't the best you."

Natalie's big green eyes filled with reddish tears. A little gruesome, honestly, but she was still Eleanor's baby. "I'm sorry, Mama." She threw her arms around Eleanor's neck. "Sometimes I don't know what to say or think or do."

Eleanor rubbed her back and whispered soothing words. Natalie wasn't the picture of serenity after all—even if she was better off here than she would be at Eclatant. Eleanor wished with all her heart that HighGod had chosen a simpler life for this lovely little girl. *At the very least, I need to bring Dasha to see her. Perhaps a visit with him will help.*

Rosemary leaned down and brusquely kissed Eleanor's cheek. She said goodbye to Agnes, her mind clearly on the tiny, wizened old woman who had guided the Abbey for a millennium. The healers collected the other young witches and marched them off to their alchemy class.

"Will you walk me to class?" asked Natalie. She looked up at Agnes. "And you?"

"Of course," said Eleanor.

Agnes smiled a sad smile. Her blue eyes were blossoms attached to greenish tears. They streaked her face like thin flower stems. *Witches' tears flow like red blood and grow like green grass*, thought Eleanor.

"Sometimes, Natalie," Agnes admitted, "I don't know what to do either."

CHAPTER 15

GRAVE, GRAVE DANGER

THE NEXT MORNING, AGNES flagged down Chou Chou as he fluttered around the castle listening for rumors and gossip among the early rising servants. Eleanor's feathery secretary returned to her chamber and reported that Agnes would arrive immediately after breakfast. She tried to push Agnes off until the afternoon. She was always anxious to check on Gregory as soon as she rose for the day herself.

"She insisted," said Chou.

"Horns and fire. Did she tell you what she wants to discuss?" Eleanor asked, as she braided her own hair and stuffed a piece of bread and jam into her mouth. She ran her hands over her plain cotton dress. She'd forewent formal grooming so as to visit Gregory earlier and carry on with the rest of her hectic schedule. Now, she'd be stuck here, listening to Agnes's assessment of Afar Creek Abbey, her homesick lamentations, or even her opinion on some new book. Normally, she'd be interested in or compassionate to any of the above, but first she wanted to make sure her king wasn't any closer to death, and hence, her infant son any closer to replacing him.

"No," said Chou. "She merely said she must speak to you as soon as possible."

"Fine, fine. I do hope she's not late—"

The Fire-iron knocker on the outside of her door struck wood, and Pansy bustled from the bathing room to open it. "Mistress Agnes to see you, Your Highness," said the maid.

"Hmmm," said Chou. "I told her half-past seven."

Eleanor looked at her clockworks. It was only a quarter-past.

"She's early, so she'll catch the worm." Chou did love his bird colloquialisms. "Should I leave?"

Eleanor started to nod, but given Dorian's suspicions, she thought better of it. Better to have Chou's discerning opinion of anything Agnes might say. "No, but stay in the background. She might not even notice you, if you can keep your beak shut."

"We both know that's unlikely," Chou said, but he settled onto the mantelpiece and stuck his head under his wing, an eavesdropping piece of décor.

Agnes sat on the armchair across from Eleanor's blue sofa. Eleanor offered her toast and jam, but she declined. "I will take a glass of water, if you have it, Your Majesty. I'm parched."

The witch's eyes were red. Eleanor always felt thirsty herself after a good cry. Given the state of her eyeballs and her premature arrival, something was bothering her.

As Eleanor handed her a glass of water, Agnes said, "Natalie is a lovely child."

"Thank you."

"My Carthean has improved these last few years, but I am still not having enough words to fully describe her."

"Your Carthean improves all the time, but you don't need an expansive vocabulary to describe her to me. She is a gift to us. Now, she's a gift to the world."

"Do you understand how exquisite her magic is?"

"I don't know as much about magic as you do, clearly, but from everything Rosemary says, she's blessed with unusual power."

"Those little girls are all wonderful. I remember when I was discovering magic. It was like every day was my birthday. New spells. Potions. I started to understand how the world works. It's like a creature. Thinking beings are its mind. The wind is its lungs. The sea is its blood, and the clouds are hair. The earth is like its flesh. All other creatures are the working parts. I doubt I'm saying it right in your tongue. I don't even know if other witches or magicians would describe it as I do. But that's how it's always felt to me."

"I bet Natalie would understand you."

"I think Natalie is well on her way to understanding more than I ever will. Such a beautiful Abbey, with Rosemary at its helm. All those girls will be her sisters, and she'll meet the Oracle, the greatest witch in history. HighGod, what a future she has. What a future they *all* have."

Eleanor shifted on the sofa. She fought the urge to stand up and ease Agnes toward the door. "This is all so nice to hear. I'm so glad you enjoyed visiting—"

"The Abbey is in danger. All of them—the children, the grown women. Rosemary and the Oracle. Natalie. She is in grave, grave danger."

Chou Chou raised his head. Eleanor felt as if Agnes had just poured her glass of cold water down her shirt. "What do you mean?"

"The ogres will come for them. All magical beings. Witches, magicians, unicorns, dragons. Even fairies, if they can find them."

"Why?" Eleanor asked, hear heart sinking. She felt she already knew the answer, but she asked anyway. "How do you know this?"

"Because Ezra Oliver told me."

For the next two hours, Agnes told Eleanor her tale. She rambled on, and Eleanor sipped her tea with few comments or questions. She merely handed Agnes a new handkerchief as her green tears soaked through cotton square after cotton square, until the pile beside her looked like a bouquet of summer leaves. The story started in the strangest of places—with King Peter Mangolin's lechery.

"When Peter elevated me, I thought I'd finally earned the respect I've always sought. Of course, I'd heard the stories about Peter's women, and how he brought them to the palace from the brothels of *Lir Yamanas*, the Island of Pleasure. I planned to look the other way, like the rest of the High Council. I didn't know he'd drag me into his perversions. I quickly learned that the old Chief Magician had procured them for him, and he expected me to do the same, but he figured that a witch could gain the trust of younger girls. The ones who hadn't yet fallen but teetered on the cusp in poverty on the streets. When I balked, he told me I had no choice. For months, I was doing his dirty work, and it was a kind of torture I've never known. When I met those young women, they were full of trust and still had hope. Within days in Peter's *service*, as he called it, he'd snuffed out their light. I delivered them to brothels, the only places that would take them after he tired of them. The few times I complained, he told me not to concern myself. He said witches didn't understand such urges, and I merely *imagined* the girls were traumatized. I started to hate him. I thought he wanted me to be his Chief Sorceress because of my talent. Of course, he made use of my powers, but he was just as interested in my being his… what are you calling it?"

"Pimp?" Eleanor suggested.

"Yes! That's it. He even took to making comments about *me*. He said I looked so lovely and sensual standing beside the throne. He sometimes touched me…my back or stroked my arm. Rubbed my shoulders." She shivered. "As if I, a *witch*, were some sort of parlor dancer. No one has ever talked to me that way, nor any other witch I've known."

Eleanor's skin crawled as she talked, as she remembered Peter's disgusting evaluation of her twelve-year-old daughter. Agnes was right—no normal man found witches to be remotely sexual beings. It was perversion of the highest order, akin to pedophilia. She made one of her few observations by saying, "Strange he has such a problem with his son's choice of lovers. At least Samuel's companions choose to be with him, and they're not children or magical beings."

"Exactly. How hypocritical, to judge his own son so harshly. Samuel is young, but he's a good, smart, kind man. I was thinking, *Peter is old and forgetful. He's outlived his usefulness.* As his mind clouded over with age, he pushed me harder to satiate his urges. The lower his hands crept on my waist. I knew four years ago; the sooner Samuel is on the throne, the better. So, I... encouraged Samuel's speedy ascent to the throne."

Understanding dawned on Eleanor. "You didn't."

Agnes nodded. "I poisoned the king. His illness is my doing. A long acting spell. It takes two, maybe three years to reach its ultimate conclusion. I spent months creating it. As far as any of the healers, or anyone else knows, the king is wasting away of old age."

Eleanor's mouth hung open in shock.

"You are thinking me horrible, but you must understand, I did it for the benefit of the poor girls of Nestra. I did it for Samuel himself, to rid him of the terrible burden of his father's disdain. But mostly, I had to act, for all of Svelya. If I hadn't intervened, Peter could have been holding on for ten years. Every day, he would be less a king and more a batty old ... what's the word... pervert."

"And no one knew—wait. Oliver found out?" Eleanor remembered Oliver's letter.

...my control over you has only reiterated what you know deep in your heart—that you're a criminal of the highest order...

Agnes nodded.

"He's blackmailing you?"

She nodded again. She covered her mouth as she sobbed. Eleanor rubbed her temples as Agnes continued. Oliver had come to Agnes while she slept. He'd asked her for her deepest secrets, and her dreaming mind had given them up. In a crowded, strange tearoom she'd never seen, with a green and white painting of a witch on the wall and strange people making fizzy drinks from metal machines, she told the magician she'd poisoned the king. She also told him Prince Samuel took male lovers. She woke up in a panic, thinking, *what a strange dream, but at least it was only that.* Then the letters started coming, delivered by a fairyman from seemingly nowhere, disappearing in a pile of ash as soon as she read them.

"He first came to me around the time you arrived in Nestra. At first, I wasn't sure exactly what he wanted, but I knew if he let it be known I'd poisoned the king, I'd be dead the next day. He also said he'd make sure the High Council knew about Samuel, which would cause untold chaos at Gammonreil and threaten the stability of the crown. I had to do as he asked. He had curiosity about your husband, and you, but I had nothing terribly important to tell him. Not until he asked about your route to Cartheigh."

"Vigor is *dead* because of you."

"I'm so sorry. I also told Oliver that King Gregory would be traveling between Peaksend and the Mines. He set the ogres upon his party."

"Our *king* may die because of you," said Eleanor, flabbergasted.

Agnes slid from the chair onto the floor before Eleanor and clutched her skirts. "That's why I'm telling you now. I realized I couldn't continue when I saw your husband laying before me with his leg torn apart. I tried to force myself to enable Oliver's goal of killing Gregory, but even as I waffled about unicorn hair— of course I know unicorn hair has healing properties— I just couldn't do it."

"But you told Dorian he should stay at Peaksend. You offered to try to cut off his leg."

"Only because I genuinely believed that to be the best course of action! I agree with the healers from Afar Creek. I *still* think he must lose the leg." She flopped backwards into the chair, overwrought. "Listen to me, Your Highness. Oliver is trying to tempt me into joining him, rather than simply do his bidding to cover my mistakes. But I won't.

I can't. I'll tell you everything he's told me. If you decide I must die, then so be it."

"Go on," said Eleanor.

"He's taken the ogres from the camps in the same way he took the dragons—as you have suspected. He approached them in their dreams, just like Hazelbeth did five hundred years ago, but not with a trick. With a bargain. If they will help him make magical space for his great plan, he'll remove them all from their captivity. Give them free reign to smote as much destruction on the known nations as they see fit. But they must destroy all the magical beings first. The witches, the magicians, the unicorns and dragons, and even the fairies that work for him. He'll destroy his own kind to reach his goal."

"What is his goal?"

"He wants to blow open a place between our world and the one beside it."

"It *is* all connected. I knew it. Oliver's plan. The ogres. Other worlds and the space In Between them." Her initial triumph and putting the pieces together fizzled as more questions arose. "But why does he want to open a door? I mean—I see how it would be interesting, from a magical perspective. But it seems like quite a lot of work to satisfy curiosity."

"In that world, there is no magic. But there is great power in other ways."

"Metal carriages that fly through the sky."

Agnes nodded. "Yes! Yes. Many strange things. I am not seeing any of it myself, but Oliver has. When he was in limbo, many years ago. He traveled between worlds for months. But while he could see these new realities, his *body* could not visit those places. He is wanting to open a true door, so he can move between the worlds. Bring their contraptions and machines and medicines here. He believes their powers—whatever they are—will combine with his magic and make him the most powerful person in existence. Allowing him to perform feats of magic unimaginable in this world alone."

"He wants you to help him?"

"The ogres will move on after they kill as many as possible, as they always do. When their god doesn't appear to deliver them to paradise, they'll seek other lands to ruin for his pleasure. The known nations will be left in shambles. The Desmarais and the Magolins and anyone else who would challenge Oliver will be gone, and he'll rebuild. He'll be a god, the savior of the world he destroyed."

"If he's targeting Gregory, Samuel will be next."

"And the Kells, and the Talessees. The Abbeys and Coveys in all nations, stripped of any power. He's already killed most of the martial magicians who joined him from the Covey. Yet even as he would kill off anyone who might lead, he does not was the daily responsibility of ruling. He seeks someone he can trust to keep things stable. He desires only to travel between worlds, and then he will sit in his ivory tower and experiment with whatever he finds in them. He thinks I'm the best person for that position."

Eleanor sipped her tea, trying to take it all in.

"He tries to convince me I'll do greater good for whoever is left than I ever could as the Chief Sorceress of Svelya. I've refused him, of course, but he persists in asking me. Don't you see? I can feed you all manner of information."

"I—I don't know. This is so much to comprehend." Eleanor's mind spun. "I always figured Oliver wanted to get rid of the Desmarais so he might rule Cartheigh himself."

"Perhaps he did, years ago, when he stole Caleb's Horn. He was bitter and angry. He believed King Casper never appreciated him and stunted his power by turning him into a bureaucrat. When you sent him into limbo, everything was changing for him. He glimpsed the workings of the universe. For years, he's been trying to create magical space and sow insecurity in Cartheigh. Hence his campaign against the witches and the Oracle and his plots to get rid of your husband and his family. With the ogres, he's thinks he's finally found a way to achieve all his goals through one means."

"Why haven't the ogres launched a full attack yet?"

"He's over two hundred years old. He's simply tired, although he hates to admit it. He claims moving ogres is more difficult than dragons, even if they are of similar size. Dragons are like Fire-iron. Ogres are like granite. He can only move one or two beasts with each visit and must take time to recover. He knows the combined armies of Cartheigh and Svelya might do damage to thirty attacking Ogres. He's waiting until his forces are stronger."

Eleanor pressed her fingers to her temples.

"I know what I deserve. But I couldn't let Natalie, and all those other girls, and that beautiful Abbey, just sit there like ducks in a pond, surrounded by bird dogs. Even if you kill me, you know more than you did before I confessed, and hopefully, it will help you. Now, I'll face whatever you give me."

"I must turn you over to Gregory," Eleanor said. "He may kill you himself, right there on the spot."

"I won't try to defend myself."

Eleanor looked into the witch's desperate eyes. "I'm sorry, my friend. I won't try to defend you either."

Agnes couldn't be held in the dungeon like other important prisoners. Oliver's fairymen could not suspect she'd confessed, lest she go the way of the late Brother Marcus, slain in his cell by Oliver before he provided the crown with any more useful information. Four guards stood outside the door, and Orvid placed three of his most powerful martial magicians inside the room. The martials posed as valets, but between them, they possessed enough firepower to blow the bedroom to smithereens if Agnes did anything remotely untoward, magically speaking.

Beyond confinement, Gregory could not decide what to do with her. He recognized only three reasonable options. Let her rot in her chamber, put her to death, or accept her offer to spy on Oliver. For the short term, he chose the first option. For two weeks, she remained in seclusion in her room, whispering spells to herself and casting greenish light. "She sits on the bed," reported Chou, after a week of daily visits to her window. "I never see her walk around or lie down, but I suppose she must sleep, and she must get up to use the chamber pot."

"Does she eat?"

"I've seen none of that, either, although there's always a tray on the desk. Just green light like shifting leaves and breezy whispering." He shivered. "That bedroom has become a jungle before a thunderstorm."

After a fortnight, Gregory finally reached two important decisions. First, he announced that the royal family would forego the Solsea summer holidays for the second year in a row. Leticia took the news like the death of a loved one. Eleanor gave her a stern speech about her father's health. Through tears, Ticia acknowledged that Gregory could not make the journey, and therefore, they must remain at his side. Although Eleanor didn't inform Gregory of her rather selfish reaction, upon reflection, Ticia felt terribly guilty for her dramatics. She knitted him several new pairs of socks, despite the oppressive summer heat.

Gregory came to a second important conclusion in a rather roundabout way. On a warm Tuesday evening, Eleanor met with Dorian and Orvid in Gregory's chamber, where he held all his important meetings of late. He still couldn't sit in on a throne long enough to revisit the High Council Chamber. He did make an attempt at kingliness, however, by sitting in a highbacked, squashy armchair in front of the fire with a robe draped across his injured leg. His wife and his two most important advisers sat on smaller, less squishy chairs around him.

"As you all know," Gregory began, "I called you here to discuss Agnes. There is, however, something else we must discuss first. I suppose the *other* something is also about her, but not wholly— I'm sorry, let me begin by saying..." He shook his head. "Orvid, help me here. I'm still no good at leading these meetings."

"We've had a letter from Samuel," said Orvid. "It's a week old and written on an evening when Samuel didn't think his father would see another morning."

"King Peter is surely dead by now. I expect we'll receive a rider from Gammonreil in the next day or two with the official announcement."

"So, Samuel rules Svelya," said Eleanor, her stomach dropping. As king, Samuel would need a wife sooner rather than later. She and Gregory had never addressed the issue of his marriage to Ticia with any finality. They'd protected Samuel from the truth about himself for long enough, but if Dorian didn't tell Gregory he was marrying off his daughter to a man who preferred other men, she would.

"How do we know Samuel wasn't party to Agnes's betrayal?" asked Gregory.

"She swears he wasn't," said Eleanor.

"As you can imagine, I'm not eager to take her word for it."

"Will you tell him—about why Oliver blackmailed Agnes?"

"I haven't decided." Gregory took a piece of parchment from the end table beside him. "He starts out with the sad news about his father, but then, it gets even more interesting." He unrolled it and started reading. *"It is with great sadness and utter shock that I read the letter from Mister Orvid Jones about the betrayal of our Chief Sorceress. I understand why you would question our loyalty to the friendship between Svelya and Cartheigh. To that end, I must address the proposed marriage between myself and your daughter, the Princess Leticia."*

HighGod, here it is, thought Eleanor. Samuel would propose an immediate marriage. She had to head him off, right now. "Gregory— you must know— Samuel, well, he's—"

Eleanor scooted to the edge of her chair. Such an uncomfortable topic! How dare her perfidious tongue, which usually flapped like a damp towel on a wash line in a high wind, suddenly tie itself in bulky knots. "They can't marry. They can't because—"

Gregory held up one hand, and Eleanor, ever mindful of her resolve to be tactful around her husband, bit down on that clumsy organ until she tasted blood.

"He writes, *I cannot marry your daughter.*"

"What?" Eleanor grabbed a purple napkin and held it to her mouth. Her bleeding tongue touched cool cotton. Blood darkened lavender to magenta.

"I give the Duke of Brandling permission to reveal my secret to you. By telling you this, in many ways, I am entrusting the peace and security of my people to you. I will not write of it."

Gregory set the parchment in his lap. Dorian's mouth hung open, a crooked crescent moon of confusion. "That's what it says?"

"It does indeed. So, Lord Brandling, it seems you have a story to tell."

Dorian began tentatively, for who knew how to discuss homosexuality with one's sovereign? It wasn't detailed in any etiquette book. He haltingly told Gregory of how he came upon Samuel and his friend, Louis, in the sculpture room at Gammonreil. How Samuel begged him to keep the secret, for fear of his father's wrath. He acknowledged Samuel had run away from Gammonreil because his father found out, and he only agreed to return because Peter allowed Louis to return to court. Finally, he told Gregory that Peter had grudgingly agreed they would never discuss Samuel's personal habits, as long as Samuel agreed to marry, produce an heir, and live a seemingly normal life.

Gregory listened in silence. When Dorian finished, he stared at the fire for a moment before picking up Samuel's letter again. "*Once Dorian has explained to you, you will be aware of my predicament. When I am king and can make my own decisions, I shall name my sister's children as my heirs. I am placing my trust in you, my fellow ruler, to keep this secret for me. I am being honest about why I cannot marry your daughter, and*

I believe giving you this information proves my fidelity. I ask that you do not share it with anyone else. I believe your wife and your Chief Magician are aware of the situation. He expresses undying fealty, reiterates the importance of our alliance given the extent of Oliver's plan, and closes by saying he will leave it up to me to decide the fate of Agnes."

"Greg," said Dorian. "I'm so sorry I didn't tell you. I made a promise to Samuel, and I wanted to keep it as long as possible. I feared for the boy's life if the news got out. I wanted to think of other reasons why Ticia shouldn't marry him."

"You assumed I'd allow it to get out? That I'd undermine a fellow king and ally?" He pointed at Eleanor and Orvid Jones. "You two also felt this way?"

The three of them sat in fidgety silence. Gregory exhaled, long and hard. "It's of no matter. I can see why you would have thought that, in the past. The idea of two men…" His lip curled in distaste. "I probably wouldn't have handled the news very well. I would have balked at the suggestion that I respect such a man and align myself with him. But I am a different person these days. Perhaps the crown has tightened around my brain and restrained my nature. Hearing you speak, Dorian, I think to myself, if Samuel is a good ruler who loves his people, and honors his alliances, why should I care what he does with his dick?"

"Why indeed?" asked Orvid Jones, his face aflame at his king's reference to another monarch's roaming phallus.

"So, wife, you should be pleased. Ticia has been saved from a marriage to a foreign king. It sounds like he won't marry at all, if he plans to name his nephews as his heirs. That's his business, I suppose."

"His revelation is enough to make you believe in his loyalty?" asked Dorian.

"Yes, verily. Any ruler who would give me information that could lead to a rebellion is to be trusted. Now that the cock has flown the coop, so to speak, and it seems we have another egg in our pot. We must crack it, before it explodes on its own. Give me your positions again."

"I believe we're all in agreement, Your Majesty," said Orvid. "Agnes has voluntarily provided us with vital information."

"If it's true."

"We've all spoken to her. I believe she's sincere," said Eleanor. "What might she gain from revealing her association? If Oliver finds out she betrayed him, she's as good as dead."

"Perhaps he put her up to it, to lead us into a trap."

"She admitted she gave away our location in the Catfish Fight. She caused Vigor's death. She knew that alone would be enough to get herself executed. I don't think she would have offered such specific information, if Oliver put her up to it." She rested her elbows on her knees. "Gregory, she said she'll spy for us. We've never had someone embedded in Oliver's schemes."

"How will we monitor her?" asked Gregory. "I don't fancy her wandering around Eclatant, unsupervised."

"I can track her," said Orvid. "If she cooperates, it's a simple spell. I will know where she is at all times."

Gregory flinched and shifted his injured leg. "If you're all in agreement, it's settled. The turncoat Svelyan sorceress shall serve as a turncoat spy for Cartheigh, against our own turncoat sorcerer. What a tangled web we weave."

Dorian cleared his throat. "If I may, Your Majesty, I'm surprised you're not angrier with Agnes. About Vigor, and about your leg."

"Does my reaction please or displease you?"

"More the former than the latter, for I believe firmly in her usefulness."

"You thought I'd order her hung from the belfry of Humility Chapel, eh?"

Dorian shrugged.

"You know me well, Your Grace. Of course, I'm angry with her. But what's done is done. The question now is can she be of value, and can she redeem herself?"

"I agree. Everyone deserves a chance at redemption."

"Well spoken, Your Grace."

Eleanor almost felt as if she were eavesdropping as she listened to them. Everything about the exchange relieved her, from Gregory's thoughtfulness and prudence to Dorian's honest offering of his opinion and Gregory's receiving of it.

Redemption, indeed, she thought. *After all these years, we're all in need of some.*

"Enough now, my friends," said Gregory. "I need to take a load off this leg."

Dorian and Orvid put an arm around Gregory's shoulders and helped him to the bed. Orvid excused himself, eager to speak to Agnes about the tracking spell. As Gregory settled into bed, he reached under his pillow. "Eleanor, I forgot. I want to return this to you." He held up the kaleidoscope.

Eleanor thanked him as she slipped it into the pocket of her simple afternoon gown. She wanted to look for Oliver again. Perhaps she'd get a chance to keep an eye on Agnes as well. She patted his Gregory's shoulder, kissed his forehead, and took her leave. Dorian stayed behind, waiting for the Chief Paladin to deliver his monthly report on the unicorns' health. In the past, she might have felt guilty for the chaste peck she laid on Gregory's forehead. She hated to remind Dorian that she was, and always would be, Gregory's wife. These days, however, both of them were so concerned over the king's health, and the tensions between the three of them were at their lowest point in years. She almost felt as if she and Dorian were Gregory's parents, and Orvid his doting uncle.

Now they would add Agnes to their quirky family, but not as a trusted blood relation. For now, she was like the young wife of a rich, widowed grandfather. She had to prove her noble intentions to the rest of the relations.

Eleanor sat on a wooden chair in one of the witches' sickrooms. Even through her petticoats, her tailbone dug painfully into the flat, unyielding seat. The chairback, covered in peeling red paint, scratched her shoulder blades. One leg was shorter than the other three. Every time she shifted, she nearly tipped over. Natalie and Rosemary shared a softer couch in the corner, given their respective age and youth, while Agnes sat in a replica of Eleanor's dismal chair as further penance for her sins.

The Oracle's health had improved, but not enough to return to the relative seclusion of her cavern. Instead, Hazelbeth received her few fortunate visitors in one of the Abbey's larger sickrooms. She lay in a four-poster bed, under crisp white sheets and a bright purple and green patchwork quilt. A fire crackled cheerfully in the hearth, and some thoughtful healer had brought in a sack of dried lavender. One of the healers tossed a few leaves and flowers into the flames. The soft scent complemented the gentle lighting.

At the foot of the bed, a Fire-iron basin of clear water from the Watching Pool bubbled gently, as if with its own current.

"She'll wake soon," said Rosemary.

"How can you tell, Mum?" asked Natalie.

"Watch her eyelids. When they flicker, she's in a dream. When one is in a dream, one is close to waking."

"I'm always in a dream, Rosemary, and I'm always close to waking." The Oracle pushed the covers away from her face and struggled to sit upright. Her squirming alarmed one of her caretakers. She swooped in like a motherly stork descending upon a baby bundle and adjusted the pillows behind Hazelbeth's head. The old witch wore a thick woolen sweater, despite the fire and the quilt. With little more than skin covering her ancient bones, surely even HighSummer at high noon would seem chilly.

Once she settled in a more dignified position, the Oracle peered around the room. "You've brought the child to me. This is Natalie Desmarais?"

"Yes," said Natalie. She stood and walked to the bed. Eleanor thought she might be afraid of the crone under the quilt, but nothing in her somber expression belied fear. "You're feeling better. I feared you might die."

"Not yet. Hold out your hands."

The firelight danced over Natalie's hair. Crimson light wafted around shoulders. She leaned over the bed like the sun rising in Hazelbeth's colorless eyes. Hazelbeth gently blew the child's red-gold tresses back from her face. "Show me your light, girl."

Natalie turned her palms to the ceiling, and magical power spilled like blood from her hands, as if she were being crucified. Her smile, however, portrayed bliss, not pain.

Hazelbeth sighed, as if in her eons of existence, she'd rarely seen anything so beautiful. She rested one hand on her thin chest and touched Natalie's outstretched fingers with her own.

"Oh, child," said Hazelbeth, as Natalie's magic retreated to wherever it went. "Thank you. I will rest better knowing you are in this world."

The statement raised the hackles on the back of Eleanor's neck. Why would Natalie, gifted as she was, be the source of comfort for the all-powerful Oracle?

Rosemary dragged another of the draconian chairs toward Hazelbeth's bed. The Oracle patted the quilt beside her, and Natalie perched her little bottom right there and crossed her ankles, as if she were waiting to hear a story from her grandma.

"You've brought someone else. Who is this?" Hazelbeth squinted into the darkness beyond the ring of firelight.

Agnes crept toward the bed. She knelt beside the Oracle. Her eyelashes quivered like melting snowflakes. "Agnes of Gammonreil, Wise One," she said.

"I have heard tell of you. Your position, your talents, and your recent unsavory associations."

Agnes sputtered out apologies, but the Oracle held up one hand. "It is not for me to forgive or pardon. That is for the king. I only ask that you tell me what you know about Mr. Oliver."

Eleanor touched Natalie's knee. "Darling, perhaps you should return to your room."

"No. I prefer to have her with me."

It didn't seem appropriate for a five-year-old child to be party to discussions about national security and lunatic magicians, but true to her recent resolve, Eleanor kept her mouth shut and listened. Haltingly, Agnes told Hazelbeth everything she'd told Eleanor. Her face flamed with humiliation. Twice, she had to stop and collect herself. Eleanor and Rosemary chimed in, clarifying their observations and the crown's decisions. Once she finished, the Oracle's chin sunk into her chest, a contemplative hermit crab retreating into its borrowed shell.

"It's all connected, Wise One," said Eleanor. "Just as you suspected."

"I suspected he was using the In Between to move the ogres. I didn't anticipate his cumulative purpose."

"Don't you know everything?" asked Natalie.

"I know more than everyone else, but less than HighGod. Tell me, Agnes, has Mr. Oliver said anything about the danger of tampering with the walls between worlds?"

Agnes shook her head. "Would it be dangerous to open such a door?"

The Oracle shrugged. "It's possible. Right now, there is a natural leak. What would happen if the leak became a flood? If the dam burst?" Her sparse brows came together, creating a canyon between her eyes. "I must meditate on this."

She closed her eyes, and as the seconds ticked by, Eleanor looked to Rosemary. *Do we go now?* she mouthed, silently. *Is she asleep?*

"Eleanor." Hazelbeth's eyes were open again. "Rosemary tells me you propose using Oliver's own magical discoveries against him.

Eleanor cleared her throat. "Uh, yes. Yes, Wise One. I feel we must get rid of the ogres. Not fight them. Not try to kill them. Send them away, where they can never bother us again. If Oliver figured out how to move them, I believe Afar Creek can do the same."

Agnes wiped her damp cheeks. "You want to *move* them? Where?"

"We haven't figured that out yet, but there's a bigger problem," said Rosemary. "We have no idea how the magic works."

Green light leaked from Agnes's nose. "I can help."

"My most powerful sorceresses are exploring spellwork. Our greatest scholars are combing our library and visiting the libraries at the Covey and Eclatant. They're researching ogres, of course, but also blood paths."

"Blood paths have nothing to do with—"

"But it may take time—"

"Rosemary," said Eleanor, gently but firmly. "I believe Agnes is trying to tell us something."

Agnes stood and walked to the basin at the foot of the bed. She stared at her own distorted reflection in the clear, shifting water. "Ezra Oliver promised me many things when he tried to tempt me to join him. He told me I'd be the most powerful magical being alive. After himself of course." The green light darkened around her. "What spell is his greatest magical accomplishment?"

Agnes closed her eyes. She snapped her fingers and disappeared.

For a moment, even though she knew such magic to be possible, Eleanor's brain couldn't process what had happened. One second Agnes stood before them, flint-eyed and solid, and the next she vanished. Unlike Oliver, who tended to fade away the few times she'd seen him disappear, Agnes blinked out of existence. Another click followed the snap of her fingers, as if the air around her had rushed to fill the space she'd occupied, a reverse bubble burst.

"HighGod," whispered Rosemary.

"She's coming back," said Natalie. "She's already on her way."

The sickroom door opened, and Agnes walked into the room. Natalie waved. "Hello, Agnes! Where have you been?"

Agnes walked to the Oracle's bed. She ran a hand over Natalie's hair. "Nowhere special, Natty. I just sent myself down into the courtyard and walked up the stairs. I reappeared behind a vegetable cart. I didn't want to startle anyone."

"How is it done?" The Oracle sounded like a chef asking after a cake recipe.

"It is difficult to explain," said Agnes. "There is no real spell."

"Not even an unspoken one?" asked Rosemary.

"No. That's part of the difficulty."

"I thought all magic required a spell at some point," said Eleanor.

"There are some spells that *aren't* spells," said the Oracle. "When I watch at the Pool, there's no actual spell, spoken or unspoken. The magic exists in my mind."

"Yes. That's exactly it," said Agnes. "When Oliver perfected the Blood Path, years ago, he did something no one thought possible. He used a spell to move an object from one place to another. But that kind of magic cannot move a living being. It wasn't until he spent those months *trapped* in the In Between—the space between worlds— that he began to see a way to use the In Between to *travel*. It's like a road that exists all around us, all the time, but we can't see it. Even non-magical beings dance on the edge of the road each night as they sleep. Through the magic inherent in his own mind, he found a way to step onto the path. Eventually, he learned how to drag others along with him. He calls it *interpolation*."

"That's a big word," said Natalie. "What does it mean?"

"It means to place something where it doesn't necessarily belong," said Eleanor.

"Ah," said Agnes. "I wasn't sure myself, but it makes sense. Physical beings certainly aren't meant to be using the In Between like a highway."

"He told you this?"

"He's trying to entice me to join him, but I think it's more than that. He's alone, almost all the time. He only speaks to the few martial magicians he left alive to help him and a herd of ogres. He craves admiration above all else. He's made the greatest magical discovery of our time, and he has no one to congratulate him."

"Witches and magicians have used dreams to communicate for eons. Even I have mastered such spells, and I'm no Agnes of Gammonreil," Rosemary said and blushed. "You taught me, Wise One, and I visited Eleanor in her dreams. Are you saying this is similar magic?"

"In some ways yes, but in more ways, no." Agnes thought for a moment. "Since we're speaking of dreams, have you ever understood a dream while you're dreaming, but when you try to explain it, the words won't come?"

"Yes," said Eleanor, remembering her last conversation in the Oracle's cavern. "Yet the dream still makes sense to me. Words feels insufficient to convey the experience, but the experience is still there."

"That's how it is for me with interpolation. I can perform it with difficulty, but I can only move myself. I can only travel a mile or so, to a place I've already seen." She sat on the edge of the bed beside Natalie. "Oliver travels over hundreds of miles, to places he's only imagined. But I'm sure *you* could do it, Wise One."

"Are you saying Hazelbeth should move the Ogres?" asked Rosemary, as Natalie slid off the bed and onto the wooden floor. She whispered to herself, and the laces on her black boots tied and untied themselves in complicated loops and swirls.

"I appreciate your faith in me, Agnes. The realm of my consciousness is a vast kingdom, one I'm still exploring, even after all these centuries. Sometimes it feels as if it keeps growing and expanding, just to keep me searching for its limits."

"If you learned the magic," said Eleanor. "Could you move the ogres from here? From your bed, or from the cavern? Oliver's blood path allowed him hide in his office and remove Caleb's Horn from its pedestal."

"This is different magic," said Agnes. "Oliver touches the living beings he moves with him. Dragons, ogres, people. Sometimes only for a second, but he touches them."

Rosemary scowled. "Wise One, I don't think it's—well, wise, for you to consider—"

"In this you're right, Abbottess. If it requires physical contact, I cannot move the ogres. I cannot even move from this bed. What my mind would allow me to do, my body would fail me."

"There are other sorceresses in the Abbey, powerful women," Rosemary said. "Would you be willing to teach them?"

Agnes nodded. "Do you have some witches in mind?"

"I have someone in mind," said the Oracle, quietly. "Natalie, do you understand what we're talking about?"

Natalie looked up at Hazelbeth. "Yes."

Eleanor chuckled nervously. "Come now, Natty. You don't mean that."

Natalie stood. "Yes, I do. I have dreams where I can move from place to place. Many places. Not just here, and there, but everywhere. You want me to do what I do, in my dreams, right now?" She placed a hand on one hip. Her eyebrows scrunched together.

"I don't think that's a good idea," said Eleanor. "Rosemary?"

Rosemary shrugged, clearly intent on seeing what Natalie meant to do. Eleanor's pulse quickened. Ridiculous, asking a young witch who had only been in the Abbey for a few months to perform magic the Oracle herself had never done.

"You snapped your fingers," said Natalie, "and poof!"

"Yes. That's how it worked for me. But someone else I know, he doesn't go *poof,* he rather… slides away."

"I don't like sliding. If I'm to go, I want to go. I'll step onto the road, like I do in my sleep. Just… like…" Natalie squared her shoulders and closed her eyes. She raised her hands and rubbed her index fingers against her thumbs. *Snap, click!*

She disappeared.

Eleanor gasped. "HighGod in a *ditch!* Agnes, where is she?"

Another pop, and Natalie reappeared on the other side of the bed. She giggled. "Fun!" She snapped again, and this time, she reappeared by the fire. "Wheee!" *Snap!*

A few long seconds ticked by, during which Eleanor's banging heartbeat threatened to vibrate all her other internal organs into her limbs. Pounding feet came down the hall, and the door swung open. *"Ta-da!"* Natalie yelled.

"Natalie!" Eleanor fairly leapt across the room. She wanted to grab the child before she vanished again. "Stop it!"

"But I thought you wanted me to, and it was fun. Can I do it again? Maybe I can turn up in my room and surprise the other girls!"

The Oracle's voice floated up from the bed in a gentle command. "Not now, child. But you have done well. I am not surprised, but I am impressed."

"Rosemary," said Eleanor. "Take Natalie out of here. Now, please. Your queen commands it."

"Of course, Your Highness," said Rosemary, clearly taken aback.

"Take her to her room. And, Natalie…"

"Yes, Mother?" The child's confusion shone on her face. She'd done as the Oracle asked and done it well. She'd learned new magic, yet she'd upset her mother.

"It was lovely magic, darling. But for now, you must keep it to yourself. Like you did at Eclatant."

"But Mum Rosemary said I can practice all my magic at the Abbey."

"Not always," said the Oracle. "There are times when we must keep our mouths shut, and our power under our robes—even here."

"Yes, Wise One," said Natalie. "Yes to you, too, Mother. I'm sorry."

Eleanor hugged Natalie. "Don't be."

I'm the one who is sorry, she thought, *for I'm the one who came up with this idea, to move the ogres.* Somehow, what had seemed like a way to insure as little loss of life as possible, had put the life of her beautiful child in danger.

Chapter 16

Changes in All of Us

The Oracle and Agnes wasted no time in fully embracing the plan to move the ogres. Hazelbeth sunk into deep meditation. Her healers trudged back and forth between the hospital and her cavern, lugging buckets of water from the Watching Pool to refresh her basin. Rosemary chose several witches to participate in Agnes's instruction on interpolation. To Eleanor's relief, while Natalie learned to interpolate between Maliana and Solsea after only ten days of lessons, she could not take anyone else with her. Eleanor prayed the other witches would catch up to her talent soon and surpass it, so the attention would be taken off Natalie. So far, however, only one other sorceress managed to transfer herself from one end of the training ring to another. As for Agnes, she could carry objects like books and loaves of bread with her, but when she tried to move another person, she burnt her own fingers.

After three weeks, with Eleanor still wishing Natalie would fail to interpolate so much as a mouse, Chou announced the arrival of a letter from Rosemary. Eleanor was in the library, staring into the kaleidoscope and hoping for another glimpse of Oliver. Instead, she got a vision of Matt Thromba and his foremen discussing an upcoming dragon transfer. Interesting, but not interesting enough. Chou chattered at her as she opened Rosemary's note. "What treasures does the glass rainbow have for us today? Whisper, stuck somewhere in a northern bog? Perhaps Samuel and his manly lover in the midst of—"

"Please, Chou. First, Whisper is still our ally, even if he's returned to the wild unicorns."

"Even if he's a prejudiced donkey's bottom."

"As for Samuel, I'm not interested in seeing him with any lover—manly or otherwise." She opened the letter.

Dearest Eleanor,

Agnes has received one letter from Mr. Oliver. It arrived via a fairyman. Apparently, he hides the letters in the hills somewhere, and the fairyman delivers them. Even the fairies don't know where he makes his hearth.

Agnes read it aloud to myself and the Oracle. As she has stated in the past, the letter disappeared as soon as it revealed its message. Interestingly, he gave Agnes advice about interpolation. I'll not bore you, and truth be told, so much of it is still beyond me! I'll only say he told her to picture a wet sheet, folded in two, and then in three, and then in four. Then snapped open again, once its dry. Walk along the folds, he writes.

I say, how?

Agnes says, I shall try it.

Your Natalie, however, she said, yes, that makes sense!

So now, look what amazing gifts HighGod has brought forth in her! She truly is a wonder. The Oracle made sure you'll see.

With love,
Rosemary

P.S. The fairyman returned that evening, and Agnes sent her reply back with him. She made sure to lament his cruelty in forcing her to spy on us. She told him she's been staying between the Abbey and Eclatant, observing the witches and the royal family. I believe it made her happy to deceive him, as he has deceived so many others.

Her fingers trembling, Eleanor picked up the kaleidoscope. For once, she already knew what it would show her.

She spun the scope and lined up the etchings. The image came into bright, perfect relief, as if she were standing inside the Abbey's oblong, fenced training ring, where, for the past few years, young sorceresses learned martial magic so as to defend the Abbey against future attacks. Rosemary and two other witches stood in a little huddle in the sawdust. Rosemary's arms were crossed firmly across her chest. Her eyebrows came together like crossed swords; her lips pursed. One of the other witches, short and stout, folded her hands before her in prayer.

In the center of the ring… Natalie and Agnes. Natalie took Agnes's hand. The apprehension on Agnes's face told Eleanor they'd tried this before and it hadn't gone well. She closed her eyes and gritted her teeth.

In contrast to the agitation around her, Natalie appeared harmoniously composed. She took three long, deep breaths. She alluded to folds in a wet sheet by drawing red squares in the air before her. Her fingers flashed beside her ear.

There was a snap, but then two subsequent pops this time, because Ages also disappeared.

Rosemary hopped in place and clapped, and the other two witches hugged. Eleanor turned in place. The vision swept across the training ring, and there they were. Natalie and Agnes walked across the ring, hand in hand. Agnes grinned, and Natalie skipped and chattered excitedly. She let go of Agnes and ran to Rosemary, who scooped her up and spun her around. The other witches patted her back. Agnes joined them and kissed her cheek.

The vision faded. Eleanor slumped onto the sofa. "She can do it, Chou. She can transfer people."

"That doesn't mean she can transfer ogres over thousands of miles."

"She's learned this much in a few weeks. Give her another month, and Gregory will be asking her to move the dragons between their caves. Who needs a formal transfer, when your daughter can perform interpolation?" She laughed, bitterly. "She's in terrible danger, and I can't protect her."

"She's in danger anyway, from Oliver. She's contributing to her own protection by fighting him."

"I can't help it. What she's sharing with Rosemary, and Agnes, and those other witches I don't even know. I can never be part of that. I believe I'm jealous."

"You cannot be part of their innermost circle. I can never be human, and you can't be a bird. Is our love for one another somehow less?"

"No. Of course not." She rested her head on the arm of the sofa and closed her eyes. Chou walked across her bare shoulders, his talons like the comforting fingernails of a good back scratch. "I think I'll go see Ticia. She's so happy she doesn't have to marry Samuel, it seems every young man she sees catches her fancy."

"You should call Anne Iris to court. She can teach Ticia how to flirt unabashedly."

"Even Anne Iris has nothing on Sylvia."

"There's a blessing. Since Cyrus's birth, we've seen nothing of her. Even since Gregory's injury."

"She'll turn up eventually. Now that Gregory has a male heir, once he's healed, he won't need to visit my bed anymore. He'll need to find a release."

"I don't know about that. You two seem close these days. Although, there is something decidedly sisterly in your affection for him. Do you suppose his own for you has become filial in nature?"

"I don't know if Gregory has ever looked at a female person to whom he wasn't related by blood with brotherly affection." Eleanor didn't have the energy to speculate with Chou about the nature of Gregory's love. Given the harshness of their last few years of unemotional, procreative copulation, the idea of Gregory crawling into her bed again turned her stomach. She shook her head at the image. She wanted to lose herself in Ticia's silly gossip and hold her fat baby boy close to her heart while he fell asleep. She asked Pansy to cancel her afternoon lunch with the Head Chef and the Royal Florist, both of whom had been clamoring for a meeting to discuss the upcoming Waxing Fest, the second consecutive summer holiday at Eclatant. She tied up her hair with a white ribbon. It was too hot to wear it down.

"Take a turn around the library before you visit the children," said Chou. "It always cheers you."

"Not today, Chou. Although, I do need to start my research on potential ogre habitats."

"I do think, given the circumstances, you should *go to the library*." He lit on her shoulder and nibbled on the dragon choker, nestled at the base of her neck. She glanced in the mirror. At the moment, it glowed a soft lavender. Chou tapped the stone. "This morning I flew past someone on his way there. Someone who can help with your research and ease your heart."

She kissed his feathery cheek. "What a wonderful bit of information and a fabulous idea."

"I have to make up for rousing the specter of your marital relations. But you must be careful, lest I never encourage such an encounter again."

"I will. I promise."

With a few flaps of his wings, he settled onto his roost for his late morning snooze. Eleanor wrapped her fingers around the choker as she left her chamber. She called up the old memory of a younger, less gray, clean-shaven Dorian, and another hot day. A broom closet and a passionate kiss. The smell of spilled punch.

The choker warmed her hand. She didn't have to look at it to know it glowed bright red.

Eleanor stood beside a bookcase of royal ledgers. When she rested her elbow on the top volume, dust puffed up from the old leather. She almost sneezed, but she pursed her lips and held it in. The library was quiet, almost pensive. So much brooding knowledge. Each book waited longingly for someone to peruse its obscure knowledge. Old proclamations, rolled into tight tubes, strained against the bonds of their tattered purple and green ribbons. The dusty ledgers held tight to embarrassing financial errors and oversights.

The books had competition, because nothing and no one could brood like Dorian. He sat at their favorite table by one of the wide windows. She always hated to disturb him when he was deep in a book. He leaned on one elbow and buried his hand in his thick salt and pepper hair. His brow scrunched, his lips moved, and he gazed out the window with his quill tapping his chin. He resembled a composer with a new tune in his head, or a great novelist searching for the perfect sentence. As she approached, she caught the title of one of the books in his stack. *The Mating Habits of the Northern Ogre.* The title almost ruined her romanticized picture of him. Almost, but not quite. Ogre procreation or not, he was still her beautiful wandering poet; her elegant, contemplative philosopher. The handsome price of her dreams, who wasn't a prince but had unwittingly fathered one.

She took a step forward, and the sneeze caught up with her. She tried to hold it in and the noise that escaped her was reminiscent of an angry, trapped mouse. Dorian's head jerked, and he dropped his quill. He smiled when he saw her. "HighGod bless you." He held out a handkerchief.

"You look so serious and regal, sitting there," she said as she wiped her nose. "And I descend upon you like a twisted bugle."

He looked around her and over his shoulder. "It's quiet. Can you sit?"

She nodded. "It won't be quiet anymore if I let loose anymore unbecoming snorts. It seems like sacrilege to sneeze in a library."

"I think HighGod will excuse your sniffling since you've come to unearth some wisdom that will save the lives of thousands."

She settled into the seat across from him and told him of Natalie's progress. "On one hand, we have someone who can move other living beings."

"On the other hand, it's a five-year-old girl and our beloved princess."

She pressed the handkerchief to her eyes. "What shall I do?"

"You don't have to answer that question today. We have to find a suitable destination before anyone moves anything anywhere." He slid a book across the table, *Observations from the Ogre Watchtower.* "They do have families, of a sort. They should go to the same place, so they're more likely to stay put. They can live in any climate. Wherever we send them, they're likely to thrive, so we need to make sure it's far away."

Eleanor pondered geography as she flipped through the book. "I don't fancy sending them south. There are islands across the Shallow Sea past Mendae. But they're close together. Even if they can't swim, they might come up with ways to build boats of some sort. Besides, tribes live on those islands. Even if we consider them primitive, we can't dump our monsters on others to save ourselves."

"Humans have a history of displacing one another through war. This is a kind of war, isn't it?"

"That's just the kind of manly philosophy I'm trying to avoid."

"Well, we can't send them east to run amuck in Kelland. Nor west, to destroy Talesse. North is Svelya. I think we may need to move beyond books." He stood. "Come."

They wandered narrows hallways between stacks of books and parchments. Dorian took lefts and rights seemingly willy-nilly, always angling toward the wall farthest from the entrance. "Are we going to the tapestry hall?" she asked.

"No," he said, as he stepped over a box filled with bottles of ink.

"Artifact cellar?"

"No. We don't need the Malian kings' shield collection or a box of ancient shark teeth."

They reached a dead end. A Fire-iron door stood before them. The inlaid pattern of polished wood displayed a sun, a moon, and a compass.

"The map room!" Eleanor said. "I've only been inside a few times. Once, Nathan asked me to show him the size of the world. We came here to find the biggest map." She braced herself for the habitual pain as she thought of her little red-headed son running his fingers along drawings of rivers, mountains, and cities spread out before him like a geopolitical quilt. To her surprise, however, a bit of joy also pervaded the memory. After all, Nathan had been so happy that day as he rustled around in the cool, dry darkness while Eleanor held a candle above his head.

"Such a curious lad," Dorian said tenderly. "Like his mother."

Dorian took one of the candles from the table beside the door. He lit two and handed the second to Eleanor. The map room had no windows, and the librarians kept it dry and dark at all times to prevent the oldest maps from moldering away. Without magical assistance, candles were a necessity.

They opened the door and stepped into the musty room. Some maps were rolled up, but more were laid flat in great piles, like bare mattresses. "It's arranged like a compass," Dorian said. He pointed to his left, then his right. "Lands to the west, like Talesse, and to the east, like Kelland. The southern lands are behind us, along that wall.

Cartheigh, right there in the middle." He walked past several stacks of maps in the center of the room, flanked by two purple and green Desmarais banners. "North, this way."

The maps of Svelya took up several bookshelves on the other side of the Carthean maps.

"Just more of the Quartic Ocean past Talesse," he said. "East of Kelland, endless plains, inhabited only by a few nomadic tribes. The flatlands hit the Impassable Mountains. Supposedly, they make the Scaled Mountains look like molehills."

"I wonder what is beyond them?"

"No one really knows. We know of no human civilizations in the Impassable Mountains. But they must end somewhere. Perhaps there are strange lands, full of wonders we can't imagine."

Other lands. Other worlds, thought Eleanor. *Our lives are so small.*

"Why not start in the north?" he asked.

For the next hour, they fished through the Svelyan maps. Eleanor found herself distracted by fascinating depictions of old Nestra, the logging city of Remley, quaint mountain towns, and fishing villages along the Quartic Ocean. They found a map of the last known natural dragon nesting grounds in the disputed lands between Svelya and Cartheigh. Eleanor sneezed several more times, and her stiff fingers were coated in dust. She swiped at her face with Dorian's handkerchief and doggedly kept at it.

She looked up at his gentle laughter. "What?" she asked.

"Your face."

Eleanor squinted at her reflection in the glass covering an ancient compass. Stripes of gray dust covered her cheeks and nose. Her eyes were puffy. She resembled a tired raccoon. "Oh dear. I'll certainly need a bath before visiting Cyrus. I shall scare him."

He gathered a few maps and rolled them into long cylinders, like paper trumpets. "That's enough for today. I'll take these to my chamber and study them."

"Why should you have all the fun?"

"Because you, my queen, don't have much in the way of free time."

"You aren't exactly a man of leisure. You're the king's most important adviser."

"You're one of his most trusted advisers as well. You're nursing the king, caring for two children, and visiting the Abbey every week. I'll study them at night. I don't sleep much these days. I have much on my mind—as we all do." He peered over her shoulder at the closed door. "I miss my family."

"Anne Clara?" she asked.

"I do miss my sister. But mostly, I miss my son and his mother."

His words wrapped around her heart like a sailor's knot. Her feet carried her closer of their own fruition. Only a foot or so of dusty air separated them. "We miss you."

"The door is closed, like the librarians insist."

"When did someone last visit this old room?"

He stepped closer. "No one comes here, except mothers with curious sons. Or at least, that's what my heart is telling me right now."

"Is it too dangerous?" she asked, but she traced a finger down his chest, her promise to Chou Chou forgotten.

"Probably." He took her hand and pulled her toward a corner of the map room. Somewhere, there had to be a far wall. An end to the rows of shelves and tables and piles of maps, but they could not see it. "The farther north we go, the darker it is."

Like he had in the old days, in the granary, Dorian knelt first. He set their candles on the floor and brushed dust from a low stack of huge atlases. Eleanor stood over him. She frantically searched the dimness, as if to reassure herself that no one prowled the piles of parchment. This was, as Chou would say, colossally stupid. Still, as had been the case in the tent at Gammonreil, and several other memorable occasions over the past fifteen years, she couldn't stop herself.

Dorian sat on the atlases and patted the massive leather-bound books below him. The bold letters across the cover spelled out *Atlas of the Known Nations*. "They're actually rather soft."

"This is where they keep the whole world," said Eleanor, as she sat on the corner of the atlas. She ran her fingers over the embossed designs: a tree, the sun, and a wave.

The two of them lay on their sides with their noses touching. He gripped her hands in his. "You're sure you want to risk it?"

"We're already lying beside each other on a bed of maps. The risk is taken."

"I'm going to make love to you from Svelya to the shores of the Shallow Sea."

She giggled. "Take me on a journey, Dorian Finley." In this moment, she somehow ignored the fact that their actions amounted to a hanging offense. The breadth of his shoulders blocked her fear.

He kissed her, long and deep, with his hands in her hair. He tugged her heavy skirts toward her knees, and his hand crept up the inside of her thigh. His fingers trailed sparks in their wake. She forgot about spies or nosy librarians or the executioner's block. He knew her body so well, it only took a few minutes for her back to arch like a tight bow and then release when he let loose a hot arrow of pleasure.

She clung to his neck, panting. Everything tingled from her waist down. Even through her skirts, she felt his excitement. He rolled her onto her belly, grabbed the layers of silk and taffeta, and pushed them aside. She gasped when he entered her. He placed one hand on her back and the other one her hip. He pulled away from her just before he climaxed and then collapsed onto his elbows.

He rested his forehead between her shoulder blades and mumbled about HighGod and perfection and how long it had been.

"Dorian," she said.

"Yes. Horns and Fire, Eleanor. What is it?"

"I love you."

He rolled her over and framed her face between his forearms. "I love you." Tears shone in his eyes.

"No—no, darling." She wiped at them. "We have so few happy moments. Let this be one of them."

He kissed her. "I'll try." He sat up and squinted into the darkness. As far as either of them knew, they were still alone. "Dragonshit. How are we going to clean up?"

"We have plenty of paper."

He gently poked her side. "I don't fancy wiping down my… my… you know. With scratchy five-hundred-year-old parchment."

She giggled as she handed him his dusty handkerchief from her pocket. "This will have to suffice for now."

He stood and pulled her to her to her feet. Her skirts obediently fell into place around her legs. Pansy and her iron had trained them well. She gripped Dorian's arm. "Now it's my turn to cry."

He kissed her forehead. "Don't fret, my love. We will leave this room together, and I will have a handful of maps. I'll carry them back to my room. You'll go check on our son. All will be well. We're safe."

"For now." As always, the fear returned quickly.

"*For now* is all we ever have," he said.

Eleanor didn't respond. She didn't want to acknowledge she couldn't guarantee Dorian's safety, that of her children, the magical beings Oliver intended to massacre, or the thousands of normal people who would be collateral damage to his schemes. As she fixed a bland, pleasant look on her face, she remembered that even as she feared him, she also wanted to protect Gregory. She wanted him to live, even though in the past, she'd wished for his death. In her younger days, when it seemed King Casper would live forever. Or when Nathan held the Bond secure in his small, pale hands.

I want Gregory to rule, and not just because the Bond is assured as long as he's on the throne, she thought as she walked toward the nursery. *Something has changed in him, and his evolution has wrought changes between us.*

The great king she'd glimpsed over the years had finally emerged, just when his country most needed a strong Desmarais ruler. While she'd never love him again the way a wife was meant to love a husband, she could work beside him. If he'd accept her presence, and Dorian's, the three of them might do great things together. She took a moment to ask HighGod to spare the man, and let the king live.

Dorian claimed to have time to study the maps, but that proved to be a wistful supposition. Gregory required Dorian or Orvid Jones, or both, to attend him through all his waking hours. They contributed to every decision he made. Dorian's brain was utterly addled by the time he retreated to his chamber each night. He barely had the wherewithal to write letters to his family in Harper's Crossing or catch up on casual reading—like his book on ogre mating. He tried to study the maps, with their minuscule, arcane writing, cumbersome size, and cracking parchment. His tired eyes strained in the candlelight, and he mixed up rivers and ancient roadways and forgot which town was which. *Perhaps I'm getting old,* he thought as he peered through a looking glass and tried to decipher the strange verb forms of Old Carthean.

To make any real progress, someone would need to sit in the library for hours, and neither Dorian nor Eleanor had time. She was still the unofficial hostess of the entire palace, and she continued to serve as the Desmarais' goodwill ambassador through her charitable work. Gregory often asked her to sit in on important discussions, in addition to the hours she spent attending to his erratic health. Despite her extra duties, she took little respite from mothering. She dipped in and out of the nursery multiple times a day to check on Cyrus and nurse. He was crawling and putting everything in his mouth. Pansy and his other attendants watched him like a flock of hungry lakegulls hovering over a single trout, but for her own peace of mind, Eleanor needed to lay eyes on him every few hours.

As for Ticia, with her young woman's fluctuating sensibilities, she required constant emotional support. "She's always on the verge of a cry or a rage," Chou told Dorian. "One day she's madly in love with this boy. The next day it's another, and she detests the last one for an arrogant fool or a simpering dolt. If she wakes with a blemish, she doesn't want to leave her room all day. She feels her hair is never right—"

"How can hair be wrong?" asked Dorian.

"I've spent enough time around ladies to know hair can be very, very wrong." Chou's tail wiggled irritability. "If Eleanor isn't there, I get all her mooning. I love that child, but I'm meant to fly, not bob along on the moods of a teenager like a duck in an overflowing pond. Eleanor herself was not so temperamental."

"We've always known Ticia favored Gregory over Eleanor, in manner as well as hair color. Besides, Eleanor didn't have the luxury of changeability with her stepmother breathing fire down her neck."

"Poor Eleanor. Unable to be appropriately sulky in her youth and now saddled with Ticia's dramatics."

Dorian suggested Chou encourage Eleanor to invite some young women to court to serve as ladies in waiting to Ticia, so they might share in each other's ups and downs. Chou flew with the idea, so to say. Within a week, Eliza's daughter Ursula arrived at Eclatant on a mission of feminine commiseration, and Eleanor and Chou's burden eased somewhat.

Even without Ticia constantly yammering for Eleanor's attention, Eleanor's plate also held a heaping serving of worry for Natalie. With every visit to the Abbey, she found Natalie's continued magical progress equally exciting and alarming. Natalie had interpolated Agnes to Harveston and back, and she would soon start practicing with larger creatures, like one of the Abbey's sedate cows. She traveled easily between Solsea and the Dragon Mines— farther than Mr. Oliver had ever gone, according to Agnes. Like Oliver, she visited places she'd never been. For the most part, if she had a detailed description or a proper name, HighGod guided her where she needed to go. Still, every time she interpolated to a new location, Eleanor feared she'd reappear somewhere dangerous, like a bear's den or the side of a high cliff.

Eleanor was still the gorgeous woman he'd met fifteen years before. She'd never rounded out, as mothers were supposed to do. Her hair remained lush and shiny. If she had any gray, it camouflaged itself well among the rest of the white blonde strands. Only the deep lines on her forehead gave away her age. He loved every one of them, because he knew they came from intense concentration and deep emotions. Sometimes, however, he longed to reach across the dining table and smooth them. There hadn't been a party or a tournament since Gregory's injury, and the Waxing Fest would soon be upon them. He vowed to ask Anne Iris and Eliza to handle the planning and make sure Eleanor danced and had a few glasses of wine. It had been too long since anyone at Eclatant experienced any manner of amusement.

Dorian would not add to her burden by admitting he didn't have time for the maps either. She'd only try to take on the challenge herself. The more he considered it, she might not be the best person for the job anyway. She was too close to it all, torn by her competing desires to get rid of the ogres and protect Natalie, but he could think of no one else he trusted with such an important task. No one was as organized and thorough and ravenous when it came to consuming knowledge.

I wish I knew someone who learned from Eleanor herself.

He grasped at the thought, as one will try to remember a lost word or the name associated with a familiar face. Many people had learned from Eleanor. After all, she'd been at the helm of a progressive girls' school for years.

Dorian sat at his desk and took up quill and paper. He knew exactly who he needed to recruit to be Eleanor's academic doppelganger, but someone else would require convincing.

Even though Dorian told her to expect them, Eleanor wasn't fully prepared for a visit from Pandra Tate, Maliana's most notorious madam, and Jan, Eleanor's former star pupil at Queen Camille's School for Girls. She hadn't seen Jan in several years, but she'd heard through the servant's gossip chain that she'd taken over the daily operations of Pandra's brothel, the Red-Headed Hussy. It still pained Eleanor too much to think about Queen Camille's itself, much less Jan, the girl she'd personally selected from the street urchins. She still felt the sting of King Casper's incredulousness when she begged him to allow Jan to work in Eclatant's library.

Pandra and Jan entered the palace through the discreet eastern entrance, and Pansy personally escorted them to Eleanor's chamber. Pandra, with her white skin, fiery hair, and penchant for equally fiery red dresses, would be easily recognized by the servants and most of the gentlemen at court. Eleanor did not want to incite gossip by openly entertaining two well-known whores.

Both ladies removed their hooded cloaks, and Pansy hung them on hooks by the door. Pandra wore a red gown with white pinstripes. Her long red hair had a single swoop of white in the front. She'd artfully looped the ivory streak into the pile of bright curls atop her head. Leave it to Pandra to somehow incorporate her own aging into her wardrobe, as if white stripes were all the rage on Pettibone Lane. Jan wore forest green, a complement to her olive skin and chocolatey brown hair. Long bell sleeves covered her arms. The right one ended in a stump, as it had since the unlucky day of her birth. She was well into her twenties by now, as slim and graceful as ever.

"Thank you for coming," Eleanor said. "Can I get you—"

"Pear juice," said Pandra. "If you have any whiskey, I usually take a shot at midday." She strolled across the room and plunked herself down on Eleanor's blue sofa. Jan followed her and sat gently on one of the armchairs. Pandra dared the sofa to break under the weight, while Jan seemed concerned about offending the chair below her.

Chou Chou flittered from his perch to Jan's shoulder. Jan gasped in happy surprise and stroked his head. He whistled fondly while Pansy served Pandra's spiked pear juice. Jan took a cup of tea and sipped politely.

"I understand, Jan," Eleanor began, "you're amenable to coming to Eclatant to assist me in my research."

"I am, Your Highness," said Jan, "but I hate to saddle Pandra with running the Hussy once again. She'd been like a mother to me these years, and she's earned her repose."

That stung some, as Eleanor herself once hoped to be a mother figure to Jan, whose own mother had abandoned her as a small child. "It won't be forever."

Eleanor handed Jan a ledger, and she took notes about various investigative topics. She asked remarkably interesting questions that made Eleanor herself think hard about her answers. Through it all, Pandra silently sipped her afternoon aperitif. Once Jan understood what Eleanor expected on her first day, she directed Pansy to take the girl to a guest room down the hall from the library. Jan gathered her two valises and kissed Pandra's cheek.

Once she left, Eleanor turned to Pandra. She expected to the madam to be halfway out the door, but she stood beside the mantle. Chou landed on a vase beside her. "Your cloak, mistress?" he said.

Eleanor glared at him for his rudeness. "Pandra, thank you for allowing her to come."

"I told you years ago, I don't hold girls against their will."

"But she loves you, and you have great influence on her."

"I love her. I never allowed myself to have a child. HighGod sent Jan to me, to make up for it. And Ruby, of course."

"How is Ruby?" Eleanor thought of the cheerful little orphan Jan had taken under her wing. She was a couple years older than Ticia.

"She's well, although she chose a life of servitude."

"Is she working in a great house?"

"No. She married a butcher's son. He fell in love with her and somehow convinced his kindly father to allow him to marry a girl raised in a whorehouse. Now she'll spend her life among dead animals, and hopefully, she'll survive childbirth a few times."

"If her husband loves her that much, I doubt it's servitude. Hard work isn't always such."

"You'll put my Jan to hard work."

"As much of it as she can stand. It's so important."

"So, the old magician has finally found a way to kill us all."

"I think most of us will die as innocent bystanders, but yes."

"Jan will do you proud." Pandra placed both hands on the back of a chair. "If she does, perhaps she can stay on."

"In the library? You mean not return to the Hussy?"

"You would do anything for your children, would you not? If it's a better life for them?" She crossed her arms over her chest. "I heard you sent your younger daughter to the Abbey."

"I did what I had to do for her. Even if it meant letting her go."

"I will do the same."

Eleanor crossed the small space between them. They were two women, separated by only a small patch of air, even if their everyday lives were worlds apart. Love for their children brought them together. "I will do everything I can to have her permanently placed in the library. Casper refused, but Gregory is a different king."

Pandra squeezed her hand. "Thank you." She gathered her cloak, and Chou scooped up her gloves in his beak. He fluttered before her, offering a red leather flag of truce after his rudeness. "I'll leave you now, before someone recognizes me."

As she walked to the doorway, Eleanor suddenly wanted to say more. "Pandra—"

The madam turned.

"As much as I abhor your way of life, a part of me respects it. You are freer than many of our sex. Always, women seek to placate men's desires and emotions. At least you take those cravings and feelings and turn them to your advantage."

"I've always said, at least when a man leaves my bed, I'm done with him," said Pandra. "I like your plan to avoid war, and I'm proud my girl will help you. Men have gotten us where we are now. It's time for a change, don't you think?"

She dropped a final curtsy and swept out of the room.

No matter what the witches did, the wounds on Gregory's leg refused to fully heal. The ogre's putridness spread through his flesh like a rat infestation in a dark cellar. On the good days, the wound crusted over. Gregory balanced his weight on his uninjured leg and hobbled around his room on a crutch. On the bad days, his bad leg swelled like an overstuffed sausage. He lay in bed and gasped for air while sweating profusely. The witches drained the fluid to give him a brief respite. To Gregory's credit, he never screamed. He passed out once, but he never screamed.

"I can't have anyone," he said, "not one of my subjects, hear their king scream in weakness."

Eleanor felt a growing despair. Gregory couldn't continue like this. She cried as she begged Dorian and Orvid to help her convince Gregory that the witches must remove his leg. Even Chou wept, in his birdie way, when he overheard them talking about it. As the closest witness to the enmity that had grown between husband and wife over the years, Chou had never felt any great affection for Gregory. Still, he grieved.

"Why now, when Gregory is finally ready to be king?" the parrot asked. "How cruel is HighGod, to take his might from him when he needs it most?"

She and Dorian decided to raise the issue on one of his good days. They didn't want Gregory to later resent them for taking advantage of his agony to press their position. Late one evening, they told the servants to clear the halls. Dorian eased Gregory into his wheeled chair and pushed him down the deserted passageway. Through sheer force of will, they helped Gregory hop, one-legged, down a back stairwell. Three pages lugged his chair down the steps. He resettled himself, and Eleanor lay a wolf skin dragon robe over his lap. She made sure to cover his bulky, bandaged leg. They left via the eastern exit and turned toward the main garden.

"The sunset will be lovely tonight," Eleanor said.

"No one will see me?" Gregory asked.

"Not many. But if they do, you look rather regal in that chair."

"Think of it as a portable throne," said Dorian.

"Like old King Peter's, eh? My grandfather also used such a chair in his old age. I remember running along beside it as a child."

"No one respected him less," said Eleanor.

Gregory chuckled. "He was near eighty and had decades of upright movement to earn the people's respect."

Eleanor squeezed his shoulder as they wheeled into the garden. Acres of manicured gravel paths spread out before them in intricate, crisscrossing rows of short shrubs. Gregory knew them all like his own handwriting. To their right, the hedgerow maze. The children loved to run through it looking for statues. They yelled their frustrations at dead ends and shrieked in triumphs when they found a Fire-iron throne, dragon, or sword. Eleanor wouldn't admit it, but the maze's claustrophobia-inducing twists and turns terrified her. She had dreams of turning a corner and finding a nameless monster instead of a cheerful sculpted unicorn. To her relief, Gregory waved Dorian toward his mother's flower garden. They took several rights and a left and rounded a circle. Queen Gemma's garden opened up before them—a hodge-podge of wild and cultivated blooms in an endless array of colors throughout every season. Gregory chose a spot beside the brown-eyed susans and cascading petunias.

"The flowers will match the sunset," he said. "Not just the orange, but pink and red and yellow." He pointed at some daisies and a flowering shrub whose name escaped her.

"You're like Ticia with your colors," said Eleanor.

"If I'd had more time, perhaps I would have painted more." He looked up at Dorian. "What would you do, if you had more time? No, wait. Of course, I know. Read."

Dorian shrugged. "You know me well, old friend."

"You'd do the same." Gregory smiled at Eleanor. "Funny, isn't it, how the two people I'm closest to can be so different from me? Yet so alike one another."

Eleanor wasn't sure she liked where he was going. Dorian clearly felt the same way. His jaw clenched, and he shifted his weight back on his heels.

"Do you ever wonder what would have happened if Dorian had been at the Second Sunday Ball?" Gregory asked. He could have been talking to either of them or addressing his musings to the flowers.

Every day of my life, Eleanor thought, but she said nothing. No innocuous answer existed. Dorian cleared his throat, as if he might have found a suitable response, but in the end, he said nothing.

"It's all right," Gregory said. "Eleanor, you've been trying to be more diplomatic with me these days."

She started to deny it, but he went on. "I've lived with you for almost sixteen years. All this measured thoughtfulness is quite unlike you. I never would have thought I'd do so, but I give you permission to be truthful. Even if your truth hurts me."

Dorian shook his head, but Eleanor decided that if Gregory wanted the truth, she'd give it to him. She'd never had the chance to do so, except in anger or fear. She might never again.

"I have ruminated on ways my life might have been different. But in the end, I have my children. I think I've done good things in this land by way of my station, and I plan to do more good. Despite the pain I've felt over the years, I would not change it. Everyone has trials. Mine are my own."

She felt relief in saying it out loud and recognizing it as the truth. No matter her fantasies, this was her life, in all its messy glory. She had made the most of it.

"I have caused much of your pain." Gregory looked to Dorian again. "And yours. You've both caused much of mine. But you've also brought me great joy. Laughter. Children. You've been of invaluable support and assistance. Even though there were days I wished you both dead."

A mutual death wish, Eleanor thought. *How we've loved each other and hated each other.*

"Bright rainbows and dark mud," she said. "Dorian once said that. The three of us, like bright rainbows and dark mud."

"That sounds about right," said Gregory. "As dark as the mud in that pig pit at the Godsmen's carnival."

"I've had the pleasure of laughing until I cried many times in my life. That, Your Majesty, was the best laugh of my life."

"And mine," said Gregory.

Eleanor took advantage of his contemplative mood. "Husband. You say I've been more measured in my dealings with you. I thank you for according me the same courtesy of late. Maybe we're both getting older and wiser." She knelt by Gregory's side. "I'm telling you this in the most reasonable way I can. We must remove your leg."

"I agree." Dorian joined Eleanor, on one knee beside him. "As does Orvid. Greg, you're afraid the people won't respect you, but Monument will still carry you. He'll be your legs."

"The truth is," said Eleanor, "your leg holds you back from being the king the people need. No man can be fully present and in command of himself when he's in constant agony. I'm afraid the infection will kill you if it spreads. Where would Cartheigh be then?"

"I understand what you're saying, and I appreciate your honesty. In all things. If it will appease you, I will consider it. Can you give me a few days?"

"Of course," said Dorian. "It's your decision, Your Majesty. You're the king."

Gregory pointed at the evening sky. The clouds were great pinkish orange stripes edged in gold. "If only I could capture that image in my mind and show it to Leticia. She'd make a pretty painting of it."

"You could share it if you painted it yourself," said Eleanor.

"Let's go back, shall we? I'm tired. But maybe I'll ask Ticia if I may borrow some of her paints. I may have to get used to hobbies I can do while sitting down."

Dorian pushed Gregory through the garden. Eleanor walked at their side as the red and orange sky turned to purple. Gregory pointed out bushes his mother or his sister had personally planted. Eleanor agreed with him and asked clarifying questions, but she scarcely heard his answers. The farther they got from the wildflower garden, the more surreal the conversation seemed.

Gregory had forgiven her and Dorian. He'd apologized for the ills he had done them.

Dorian once said the three of them were bright rainbows, and they were dark mud. Gregory agreed with him. In that moment, the dirt had been washed clean.

CHAPTER 17

MOTHER'S TRUCE

ELEANOR'S SENSE OF PEACE didn't last long. Within two days, Gregory took a significant turn for the worse. The witches battled day and night to keep his wound clean and drained and manage his fever and his pain. Orvid fretted over the king's befuddled state, the result of heavy doses of pain-killing herbs. He pestered the Chief Healer until she snapped at him. "It won't do very well for his brain to be sharp but his pain to be sharper!"

"It's true," Dorian whispered to Eleanor. "His brain will either be addled by herbs or by pain."

"How I wish we'd taken that damned leg weeks ago. Now he's too ill to even think about removing it. He has to be strong enough to survive the surgery."

To add to Eleanor's anxiety, Sylvia Fleetwood finally overcame the humiliation of her supposed bastard son's ousting from the line of succession and descended upon Eclatant. One might think she came out of concern for her longtime lover, but Eleanor struggled to believe in the veracity of their affection. She probably wanted to make sure Gregory didn't die without leaving her something.

Eleanor decided to head off their inevitable meeting, rather than wait for Sylvia to spring on her like a bejeweled, corseted jackrabbit.

Sylvia settled into the East Wing, where the Fleetwoods held their own lesser court. Before she had a chance to unpack, Chou informed the duchess's maid that the queen consort would visit her chamber within the hour. Eleanor chose a formal gown, the kind she wore to receive visiting diplomats or attend an important chapel service. The green skirt, purple bodice, and floral pattern of pearls and Fire-iron beads screamed Desmarais authority.

Chou sat on Eleanor's shoulder as she waked across the palace to Sylvia's domain. "I like this plan," he said. "Hopefully she'll still be in her traveling clothes. Sweaty and disheveled."

"When have you ever seen Sylvia look disheveled? I'm sure her hair, if messy, will fall in romantic waves around her face."

"You're right. The road dust would probably highlight her lovely cheekbones." Chou shook and nearly poked Eleanor in the eye with a pinfeather. "Still, it's better we go to her."

"She always has the upper hand when she's decked out in her full splendor with all eyes upon her. This will be a conversation between two people, not a performance for the whole court."

Sylvia's maid granted Eleanor entry to the chamber, but the woman demurely requested that Chou Chou remain on a Fire-iron perch outside the door. "Our duchess is allergic to feathers, so she is," the woman said.

Eleanor, who had fluffed Sylvia's goose pillows for years during her servitude in the Brice house, recognized the excuse as a load of dragonshit. Sylvia simply didn't like Chou, and he equally disliked her. Chou chortled his annoyance, but he flitted across the hall to the roost as Eleanor entered the duchess's ornately decorated bedroom.

Sylvia stood beside the fireplace with her hands before the fire. She turned, and as usual, her beauty clobbered Eleanor like a wet blanket whumped upside her head. Sylvia wore a simple pale gray gown with a delicately embroidered apron. She'd pulled her hair back with purple ribbon, and true to Eleanor's predictions, the pieces that escaped and framed her face were sensual, not messy. Not a hint of dirt on her alabaster skin.

Eleanor's own ostentatious gown suddenly seemed ridiculous—it was, after all, early morning on a nondescript Tuesday. Her crown sat heavy on her head, but she straightened her shoulders. Even from across the room, she towered over Sylvia. Her stepsister folded her hands before her waist. "Eleanor," she said. "How good of you to call. Shall we sit?"

All propriety demanded that Sylvia refer to Eleanor as *Your Highness*, but she covered her disrespect with her friendly tone. The two women sat on Sylvia's delicate gold and white furniture. The white queen stared down the black over a chessboard of tea and biscuits. They exchanged pleasantries, and Eleanor obliged the nervous maid by nibbling a chocolate macaroon.

"How are your children?" Sylvia asked Eleanor.

"Wonderful. Healthy and happy. How are yours?"

"Equally so. My oldest boy, Hector, is nearly fifteen. He'll attend the Waxing Fest as a grown man. Can you imagine? We have children old enough to attend balls."

"The princess is not quite old enough yet."

"What a pity. I'm sure Hector should like to meet her."

An angle, of course. As the next Duke of Harveston, and one of the richest men in Cartheigh, Hector Fleetwood would naturally be a suitor for Leticia's hand. Sylvia prattled on, all simpering smiles and veiled meanings. "I'm sure he'll have no lack of young women to keep his attention. He is the young Duke of Harveston. You never know who might turn up at a ball. The most unlikely people!"

A not so subtle illusion to the famed Second Sunday Ball, where Eleanor had unexpectedly appeared and captured the heart of the most eligible man in the room. At least temporarily.

"I'm sure Leticia would be happy to meet Hector someday. Although I wouldn't get your hopes up. We're in no hurry to see her married."

"Oh, horns and fire, they're too young for *that* still, aren't they?"

Sylvia acted as if Eleanor herself had raised the idea of Leticia and Hector. Years ago, such flippity-gibbiting would have made confused Eleanor. But no more. She wore this crown for a reason, heavy as it may be. She was the queen consort, and she would lay down some rules with the duchess.

"Sylvia, enough platitudes."

"Of course," Sylvia said. "Maisie, remove the refreshments."

For a moment Eleanor truly *was* confused, until the maid lifted the Fire-iron serving tray. "Not platters. Plati— never mind." She leaned around the servant as she picked up their dainty yellow china plates. "I mean there's no need to pretend I'm not here to remind you of your place. And your son's.

"Maisie, leave us please." The chubby maid curtsied, mumbled something about drawing Her Grace's bath, and disappeared into the adjoining room. Sylvia's pale cheeks reddened. Blood on the white flag of a false truce. "What do you know of my son, Eleanor?"

"You claim he's Gregory's child. Even if he looks nothing like Gregory, or any Desmarais baby."

"Many children favor one parent over the other."

"Gregory has never claimed him."

"That doesn't mean he won't."

"Gregory has a son. A legitimate son. Cyrus Desmarais." A half-truth, and a potentially dangerous one, but Eleanor didn't care. In that moment, she told the Question to go to dogs. The surety of the Bond would be less secure if it rested on the claim of a child with the name Fleetwood, with no way to prove parentage but the claim of his mother—a known philanderer. Even if her son carried Dorian's blood, he had Gregory's name, and his mother was a Desmarais queen. He was born in Eclatant and presented as the crown prince and heir in Humility Chapel before HighGod. A unicorn carried him down the aisle. If a rightful male heir existed, it was Cyrus.

"Your son doesn't exactly have red hair either, does he? I've heard he's quite blond."

"There is red in his hair. It's turning strawberry, like Natalie's." Another lie. Cy's hair was white as bleached-out straw. "I am Gregory's wife. Who lay with him thousands of times and bore him three other children."

"His wife who lay with another."

"I don't know what you mean."

Sylvia stood. "Oh please, Eleanor. You know I figured it out before Gregory did. I told you before Gregory sent him to Svelya. The only reason I have kept my tongue is because Gregory asked me to. Men and their pride."

"You make all the claims you want, about your son, and mine, and—"

"Who is being so loud? Sylvia?" It was a fragile voice, quivering, like the creak of the door that opened between Sylvia's chamber and the adjoining bedroom. A female form, wrapped in dragon robes, leaned around the doorframe.

For a moment, Eleanor didn't recognize Imogene Brice. She hadn't seen her stepmother since their last oddly congenial conversation during the ladies' luncheon, before Cyrus's birth. On that day, Eleanor had marveled at her timelessness. This frail woman with salt and pepper hair, could she possibly be that great beauty? Was she the evil monster who dominated Eleanor's nightmares for so many years?

"Mother," said Sylvia, "you should go back to bed. You might fall." She stood and crossed the room. The maid bustled around Imogene and Sylvia, full of apologies for allowing the latter to disturb the former.

Imogene squinted through her seeing glass. She pointed at Eleanor.

"Is that Eleanor? Eleanor, the queen?" She grabbed the back of a chair and wobbled. Eleanor stood with a vague instinct to prevent Imogene from falling. As she approached, Eleanor could not believe her eyes. Imogene had never seemed to age past a handsome, stately forty years. Now, she must be approaching sixty, but she looked closer to eighty.

"My other daughter!" Imogene said.

"It's Eleanor," Sylvia said as gripped Imogene's shoulder. "Not Margaret. Margaret passed on, remember?"

"Of course. How can I ever forget my *lost* daughter? But this is Eleanor. My *third* daughter. Girls—take me to the chaise."

Eleanor didn't know what to say, so she took her stepmother's other arm. She and Sylvia led Imogene to a long chair. She collapsed into it. "Might I have some water?" she asked.

As the maid scrambled for a glass, Eleanor elbowed Sylvia. Sylvia spoke under her breath, "She has a growth. Inside her skull. The witches say there is no cure. It came on suddenly, with headaches, about six months ago. Now she is…well, you see."

"Why did you bring her on such a long journey?"

"I told you. There's no cure. The witches have said she'll go any day. I had to see Gregory, and I couldn't leave her. If she's going to die, I'll be close by."

"Why is she—why is she being nice to me?" It sounded childish, but Imogene had always had a way of infantilizing Eleanor.

"She gets confused. She can't think straight with whatever is inside her head banging on her skull, and she's taking a lot of painkilling herbs."

"So is Gregory. It dulls the pain and your wits. If she's only being nice because she's confused, that makes sense."

"I can still hear you," said Imogene. Once she was prone, her voice strengthened. "I'm not as addled as you think, Sylvia. Eleanor, like it or not, you're my child. Aside from your witch, who had more influence over you than I? Now sit, both of you."

Eleanor wanted desperately to leave this room. To run away from this wretch that was once the bane of her existence. Even the oldest habits can refuse to die, however, and she did as she was told. She sat on the sofa beside the chaise, and Sylvia took the chair.

"It pains me to see you two still at odds." Once again… the same unexpected conciliatory sentiments she'd expressed when Eleanor last saw her.

Sylvia snorted and did Eleanor the favor of replying. "You put us at odds from the time we met."

"Our enmity is ultimately your creation." It felt odd to be on the same side as Sylvia.

"I suppose I should say I regret it, but alas, I don't. For His own reasons, HighGod placed two girls with limitless potential under my care. I acted based on my knowledge and emotions at the time, as we all do. You've both done exceedingly well for yourselves. The competition between you fueled your success. Perhaps neither would have risen so high if not for the wedge I placed between you. But the time comes when such endless circling of the gilded wagons becomes more harmful than beneficial."

"Forgive me if I find it difficult to believe you have my best interests at heart," said Eleanor. "I think Sylvia is correct. Your thinking is clouded by the witches' mushrooms and speckle-fern. The woman I knew would have our feud carry on to the next generation."

One dark brow crept up Imogene's sweaty forehead. "Am I the woman you knew, Eleanor? It's been fourteen years since last we spoke of anything substantive. Are you the same person you were then? Are your feelings the same?"

"No, but—"

"The most intense feelings—passion, hatred, hilarity, grief— by their nature, they are not meant to last for decades. Love, contentment, resentment, sadness, these are the emotions that endure, that incite thoughtfulness. Thoughtfulness leads to forgiveness, if given time—and properly addressed. Only fools and lunatics remain unchanging in their emotions. So I ask you, both of you, are we all the same women who lived together in the Brice House, in fear for our security? In fear of one another, in different ways?"

Neither Eleanor nor Sylvia replied. Sylvia chewed on the inside of her cheek. Eleanor wondered if she was trying not to cry.

"I say we are not those women. We're all comfortable now. Eleanor, here in the palace. Sylvia and I, with her sons and the Fleetwood fortune, in Harveston. Both of you, powerful in your own right, with the ear of the king of Cartheigh, for HighGod's sake. It didn't turn out how any of us thought it would, all those years ago, but it couldn't have turned out much better. Continued bickering between us will only bring problems. What do we have left to fight over?"

"That's easy for you to say," said Sylvia, her voice cracking.

"Why? Because I'm about to die?" Imogene chuckled. "Once your joys outweigh your sorrows and your fears, it's much easier to recognize blessings and be compassionate." She looked into Eleanor's eyes. "These days, I believe I would treat an orphaned child with benevolence. But the frightened, lonely, angry woman I was in my younger days saw only a threat."

Eleanor sucked in a hitching breath. Like Gregory, it seemed Imogene was, in her roundabout way, apologizing.

"Look to your joys, ladies," Imogene said, "even as you face continued trials, and see one another for who you are. As for me, I'm at peace with my life. If HighGod exists, I'll see Robin again soon."

Imogene's groom, the forbidden love of her life, long dead. For years, she unjustly blamed Eleanor for his loss, but from her little speech, Eleanor figured all was forgiven, even if the blame had been misplaced.

"I'm glad both of you loved deeply," Imogene said. "Even if it came about in strange ways."

She knows about Dorian? Eleanor thought, mildly panicked. *Who has Sylvia loved deeply? Gregory? If Imogene believes it, could it be true?*

Imogene winced and pressed her fist to her forehead for a moment. Eleanor remembered how she'd pushed her babies out from under her ribcage during the most uncomfortable months of late pregnancy. Perhaps Imogene sought to shift the alien presence in her own brain, to make more room for her thoughts. "I'll understand if you don't believe me genuine. Given how I've treated both of you in the past, it wouldn't surprise me if you tell me to stick my advice right up my backside. I'll give it anyway. Lay aside your quarrels. They are old, as I am suddenly old. Let them die with me." She coughed. "Oh, oh. Dragon's blood. My head. Sylvia, my head."

Sylvia stood and called for the maid. "The tonic. Maisie! Hurry."

Eleanor sat helplessly, unsure of what to do, while Sylvia and Maisie flickered around Imogene. They poured tonic down her throat as she whimpered and shuddered. She called out for Robin and then Margaret. "Sylvia, bring me my pearls! Tonight, the Waxing Ball— don't—don't hang on Gregory!"

"Yes, yes. I know."

"You mustn't be so obvious! She'll find out!"

"She knows, Mother. She's right here with us."

"What? Who?"

"Eleanor—Maisie, a wet cloth, please."

Eleanor stood and grabbed a damp rag. She lay it on Imogene's forehead. As the tonic infiltrated her veins, she quieted. Her incoherent musings softened to whispers, and she fell asleep.

"Should we move her, Your Grace?" the maid asked.

"No. Let her sleep here. But please, refill her tonic in the healers' dispensary on the first floor." The maid collected a basket and took her leave. Sylvia grabbed her clockworks. "Damnit. It's nearly ten o'clock. I told Melfin I'd be to Gregory before ten."

"Now wait," said Eleanor. "Did Orvid or Dorian give you permission to visit?"

To Eleanor's shock, Sylvia grabbed her arm, and despite her small size, she marched Eleanor toward the door like a tutor putting a troublesome child in the dunce's corner. "I don't need permission to visit Gregory. I haven't needed permission in years."

"He's ill, Sylvia. He's terribly ill. You have no idea what we've been through here the past few months."

"He's written to me, many times. He asked me to come, but I didn't, because I didn't want to be a distraction. Do you want to see his letters? To prove he wants me here?"

Eleanor felt the old, nonsensical, hypocritical rage over her step-sister's familiarity with Gregory. She'd tolerated years of humiliation, what with Gregory flaunting their relationship before the masses. Yes, she engaged an equally illicit love affair with Dorian the entire time. And yes, she and Gregory had finally reached a peaceful place that acknowledged and forgave the agony they'd put each other through over the years. But if Sylvia had been around, perhaps they'd still be at each other's throats. Perhaps she and Dorian would still be in danger. She shook off Sylvia's clutching hand and fairly snarled down into her face.

"You love my husband, do you? So you claim. Maybe you even fooled your own mother. Yet you come here talking of your son's illegal claim to his throne—"

"You brought up John-Caleb, not me—"

"Just remember two things. One— you'll play the part of calm, soothing friend, here to help nurse him. Two— not one word about the line of succession or Gregory acknowledging your son."

"You can't tell me what to do—"

"Yes, I can. I'm the queen. Your son's false claim to the throne is treason, Sylvia. Treason is punishable by death."

"Wouldn't you know. Since you whored with Finley and committed it yourself."

"Gregory has forgiven me. And Dorian. We, along with Orvid Jones, are his eyes and ears and his very beating heart. I'll not deny his fondness for you. If he's asked you to come, I'll allow it. Because I will do anything to help him heal and continue his reign."

Sylvia's chest rose and fell. Her dress might be demure and simple by her standards, but her cleavage still quivered fetchingly in her agitated state.

"My mother may have decided she wants us to be friends, Eleanor. Either from guilt, true tranquility, or just losing her mind. But I feel no such guilt, nor internal peace, and my mind is as sharp as ever. I'll do what you ask, because I love Gregory. I want him to live a hundred years and be the greatest king Cartheigh has ever seen. For him, I'll give you mother's truce. For now."

"For once, we're in agreement, Sister. Good day." Eleanor grabbed the door handle. She looked over her shoulder. "Oh, by the way, either Dorian or Orvid is with the king every hour of the day. I'll make sure they know of our arrangement." She slammed the door behind her, shutting out Sylvia's blotchy red and white face and her heaving bosom.

Chou woke and stretched his neck. "How did it go?"

To Eleanor's own surprise, she burst into tears. Chou squawked in alarm. "HighGod in a basket! Come here. We can't let the servants see you blathering." He fluttered down the hallway, and Eleanor followed him into an alcove between two servant's rooms. She leaned against one of the simple wooden doors.

"Dragonshit, Chou. To quote Matt Thromba, it was a botch up, and the princess nearly roasted."

"What do you mean? A fire?"

"No, no. My *heart* is burning." She gave Chou a blubbering summary of her conversations with Sylvia and Imogene. By the time she got to slamming Sylvia's door, she'd gotten ahold of herself. She sniffed, and since she didn't have a handkerchief, she wiped her face on her sleeve. The pearls scratched her face. How silly and vain, to meet Sylvia dressed like she was en route to her own coronation. She felt like they'd changed roles—Eleanor had gone from simple, elegant dignity to Sylvia's usual preening superiority. It didn't suit her.

"Chou, I'm afraid of her pressing John-Caleb's claim. Even given

Dorian's— well, you know— Cyrus is still the Desmarais heir. How can she prove John-Caleb is Gregory's son, unless Gregory claims him?" She paced as she switched topics. "Gregory does want her here. I have to honor his wishes, but I don't trust her. She'll keep scheming, and he can't tolerate any stress or excitement right now."

"Maybe Imogene is right about Sylvia's love for Gregory, even if you don't want to believe it."

"Even if she does love him, I don't think she can stop herself!"

"What of Imogene's advice? Can you take it to heart?"

Eleanor slumped against the wall. She slid to the cold floor in a lump of poufy silk skirts.

"Eleanor!" Chou landed on her head. "Now this is too much—you must stand up—"

"Who cares, Chou? I'm exhausted. Listening to Mother Imogene—who I've hated my whole life—speak of me as her child and talk about forgiveness... and counsel peace with Sylvia...I don't know what to think of it. Perhaps she and Sylvia planned it."

"It sounds like Sylvia shared your surprise, and I don't' think anyone can feign that kind of anger. Encroaching death can change people."

Neither of them wanted to mention Gregory in the same sentence as encroaching death, but Eleanor knew they were both thinking about the changes in him of late.

Eleanor wrapped her arms around her knees. "There's too much death in my life. My parents, my dearest Margaret, and my sweet Nathan. These days it feels like so many who have loomed over my life, for good or bad, are fading. Casper, dead. Peter Mangolin, dead. Vigor, dead. The Oracle is weakening every day. Gregory so ill. Now Imogene, one foot in the grave and the other in a greasy pan, when she might be teetering toward redemption. Yet somehow— Ezra Oliver lives on."

"Your Highness!" It was Maisie, Sylvia's chubby young maid. She clutched her basket of healing tonics. "Are you hurt or sick?"

"No, child." She stood and shook out her skirts. "Just tired."

"My mistress can be tiring, Your Highness." The maid blushed. "Forgive my impudence."

"No need to forgive." Eleanor patted the maid's arm.

"No need to mention you saw Her Highness in a state of repose, either," said Chou.

"Of course not. Might I—" She pointed at one of the bedroom doors.

"Go right ahead," said Eleanor. She said good-bye, and she and Chou set off for their own wing of the palace. There would be time to ponder Imogene's bizarrely insightful comments, but at the moment, she was intent on warning Dorian and Orvid of Sylvia's impending arrival before Sylvia herself had a chance to swoop in. If they were lucky, the sight and smell of his festering wounds would scare her away. Even if she truly loved Gregory, the Duchess of Harveston was no nursemaid.

The next day, when Eleanor arrived for her morning visit with Gregory, she found Sylvia already in his chamber. Dorian stood by bed, the picture of discomfort, while the duchess hovered over the restless king. Eleanor ignored Sylvia, as if she were a common chambermaid come to change the sheets. In return, Sylvia paid Eleanor no more mind than she would an apprentice healer delivering a tonic.

Despite everyone's strained tactfulness, Eleanor didn't want to leave Sylvia and Gregory unsupervised. Who knew what drivel she would drip into his mind? In an equally alarming scenario, she might suggest an intimate act to raise his spirits. His heart couldn't tolerate such exertions. She resolved to linger for a while, but Dorian promised he'd remain with the king until Orvid returned from his meeting at the Royal Mint. He was conferring with the Treasurer about a new coin in Gregory's honor—any mention of which made Gregory bemoan the absurdity of seeing one's own face on a penny. Secure in the knowledge that Sylvia would not inadvertently commit regicide via sexual escapades, Eleanor bid them all a pleasant morning and left for her next engagement.

The first time Eleanor skulked down this narrow passageway she feared her heart might give out from claustrophobic panic. Sixteen years later, she paid no mind to any creepy crawly creatures that might fall onto her head or scurry over her shoes. She followed flickering torches to a moss-covered oak door. She jammed an ancient metal key into a clunky lockbox, jiggled it until it clicked, and shoved the door with her shoulder. It creaked irritably before swinging on its rusty hinges.

Not much had changed in the Covey garden over the years, although whoever tended the plants these days had a fondness for boxwood birds over rabbits and foxes. A parrot-shaped hedgerow whistled and asked Eleanor for a cracker as she passed. *Chou Chou déjà vu*, she thought. The water in the fountains still flowed backward. The unicorn and dragon statues endlessly cavorted on their pedestals. Eleanor poked a glistening blue bubble with the old key. It exploded and showered her with light, exquisite perfume. She barely noticed the message carved in stone above the main entrance.

MEN OF GREAT POWER TO AID POWERFUL MEN

She'd read it many times. It described the best and worst of men, both magical and mundane.

The Covey's Great Hall smelled like burning incense and conflicting shaving tonics. Historical tapestries hung over her head. They stirred gently on a pleasant enchanted breeze. She accepted blessings from the magicians she passed.

"HighGod go with you, Your Highness." They all wore lumpy brown robes and clustered in milling groups like a herd of magical bison. "Best wishes for the king's quick recovery. Can we help you find something?

She smiled and told them she knew the way. She opened a set of intricately carved wooden doors painted with gold and white trim and peered into the library. Bulky wooden ladders lay against the floor-to-ceiling bookshelves. They creaked when the magicians climbed their worn steps. Like all such repositories, the room smelled of dusty paper.

Despite her simple russet-colored gown and her hair pulled back in a tight coil at the base of her neck, Jan stood out like a frosted cake among loaves of course bread. She sat alone at a rectangular table, the only woman in a sea of drably dressed men. The magicians leaned over their own work, whispered among themselves, and even pointed at her. They weren't sure what to make of this female person who wasn't even a witch. She was just… a woman. A beautiful woman with one arm, a pile of reading materials, and a charcoal pencil tucked behind her ear.

Jan looked up, as if she sensed a female compatriot. She beckoned to Eleanor. Eleanor removed four dusty books from the chair beside her and set them on the table. Jan hugged her and started chattering, as if they were equals and she'd never felt nervous a day in her life.

"Thank you so much for coming. I know it's hard for you to get away from the palace, what with the king so ill, but I've brought so much of my work here. The Chief Librarian has been kind enough to let me use this entire table." She beamed at a mustachioed old man who sat at the next table. "Thank you, Arthur!"

"Of course, child. What a delight you are." He pointed at Eleanor. "She's got the smarts of a whip-sting, that one! Make use of it, Your Highness."

Jan didn't give Eleanor a chance to reply to him. "I'm so excited," she said. "I believe I've found the perfect place to send the ogres!"

"Shhh." Eleanor didn't want anyone to hear they meant to send ogres all over the world like a flock of hideous migrating birds. Oliver might have spies among the magicians.

Jan bit her lip and nodded. Her gray eyes sparkled as if she'd just found a pot of gold or met the love of her life. She pointed her pencil a pile of maps and an ancient atlas. "I started in the map room at Eclatant, like you suggested. I agree with you and Dorian. It makes no sense to go south or west. I considered the Impassable Mountains to the far east of Kelland, but if the maps are correct, they truly are impassable. We cannot safely ask Princess Natalie to interpolate there. The entire mountain chain is composed of sharp cliffs, and from what I can tell, many volcanoes."

"That's completely out of the question." Come fair weather or fire, Eleanor would not agree to anything that added to Natalie's danger.

"Agreed. I said to myself, Svelya is the vastest of the known nations. But even Svelya comes to an end sometime."

"At the Quartic Ocean."

"Yes! But do oceans go on forever?"

"No one knows."

A hand landed on Eleanor's shoulder. She jumped.

"The Great Marauders knew," said Agnes.

"HighGod." Eleanor patted her chest. "You scared me."

Agnes sat across from Eleanor and Jan. "My apologies." Agnes waved at Arthur, who placed a finger over his lips and blew a *shhhhhhh* into his mustache.

"I thought the Great Marauders were a legend," said Eleanor.

"Most legends have some basis in truth. Jan simply had to dig deeper than anyone has gone in a thousand years to find it."

"The Marauders came to Svelya by boat three thousand years ago. They left their homeland and crossed the ocean after a blight killed their crops and animals." Jan held up an ancient book with a dull gray cover. The corners and spine had peeled and frayed. The pages were thin and crinkled, like the skin of an old woman's hands. The Oracle herself might have written it in her forgotten youth. Eleanor didn't recognize the writing.

"It's Early Svelyan," said Agnes. "Jan asked me to help her translate. This book confirms all the stories of my childhood. Tales of King Efram the Great and his queen, Mollya. The Great Blight and the journey over the ocean. Boats lost to storms and sharp rocks. The monsters they fought on the sea and in the mountains. The survivors finally reached the great falls of the Gammon River and founded Nestra."

"Where did they come from?"

Jan grinned, as if she'd found the last missing piece of a puzzle. She reached across the table and opened an atlas. "This atlas gave me my first clue. Look at this map of the Svelyan coast." She pointed her pencil at a tiny drawing in the far northern edge of the map. A puff of wind blew a boat southward, while an arrow behind it pointed back the way it came. Eleanor squinted at tiny text.

"In Middle Carthean it says *Lands of the Boatmen*," Jan said. "This told me someone once knew there were lands across the sea. I looked through all the maps in Eclatant's library, but I didn't find anything. Finally, in the Covey's map room, I found a box of small maps. Some were so old, they fell apart when I handled them. But this one survived." She unrolled another crispy, faded document.

Eleanor examined a rendering of three islands called Pan, Ello, and Rir. The artist had labeled the land mass to the north as simply *T'Farthyr Lands.*

Below the islands, an arrow pointed south, into an empty ocean. Two words huddled in the bottom right corner: *To Svlye.*

"The old name for Svelya." Eleanor pulled the map closer. There were several drawings of boats on the islands of Ello and Rir, but nothing on the smallest island, Pan. No city names. No labeled rivers or mountain chains. No landmarks of any kind. She ran her finger across the map's title. *Yar 27 o' Secynd Blite, First Age o' Efram.*

"The full expanse of the Quartic Ocean is between us and these islands," said Agnes. "If that's not far enough, nowhere is."

"Could Natalie go there?" Eleanor asked. "Even if we've never seen it?"

"We have the names of the islands," said Agnes. "We know people lived there once. There must be suitable terrain."

"We can't send her in blind," said Eleanor. "What if she lands on a volcano? Or in quicksand? What if it's covered in sheets of ice?"

"There is one specific place named in the book," said Jan. "It must be on solid ground.

The Marauders' temple, on the island of Ello. Alenestra."

"They named their new city Nestra. It makes sense."

"Here is a drawing." Jan showed Eleanor a page in her book. The sketch showed stone pillars in a circle, with a sacrificial altar in the center. Some macabre artist had carved a giant human skull into the altar's base.

"Ugh," said Eleanor. "Not exactly the kind of place I want to send my five-year-old child. Agnes, can you go to Ello instead of Natalie?"

"I would if I could, Your Highness. I swear. I can travel back and forth between the mines and Maliana. I've been taking Rosemary with me several times. But I have yet to understand how Natalie visits places she's never seen."

Eleanor rested her forehead on the table. "How can we keep her safe?"

"Have you thought of sending her with a unicorn?" asked Jan.

Eleanor stared at her yellow skirts, and the bit of polished wooden floor between her shoes. "I have, but I don't think Gregory will allow it. The unicorns are our greatest defense, and we've lost so many in the past year."

"We also have the loyalty of the wild herds," said Agnes.

"For now. Unless Whisper convinced Terin that the Bond is evil. If she's going to move an ogre, Natalie can't keep practicing with cows. She needs a larger creature. A unicorn can provide protection and practice. But the Bond will always be Gregory's primary concern."

"You can convince him, Your Highness," said Jan.

Eleanor promised to try, and within a few minutes, Jan and Agnes were ensconced in Old Svelyan. She left them to their work. Her mind spun as she walked through the Covey, down the passageway, and through Eclatant's Great Hall. It wouldn't be hard to convince Gregory that Natalie needed protection. He loved the child as much as she did, but he blamed himself for the recent unicorn deaths. Exactly one unicorn perished during his father's thirty-year reign. He'd lost seven already.

She could ask Terin to provide a guardian from the wild herds, but the chances of a wild unicorn agreeing to serve a human child in such a capacity seemed small. Besides, Terin was nothing if not prudent and contemplative. He may take months to decide whether to even ask for a volunteer. She needed a unicorn that wasn't beholden to Gregory or Terin.

She stopped in her tracks. Two kitchen boys ran up her backside with a cart full of root vegetables. Fortunately, her full skirts provided protection from the impact. The boys scurried around her, picking up carrots and turnips and apologizing profusely.

"Don't fret, boys." Eleanor took a carrot from their cart, bit off a hunk, and chewed thoughtfully. The solution was—to quote the old Godsmen's saying— above her muzzle and below her horn. "Not *all* the unicorns in the Paladine are bonded."

The boys glanced at one another, as if she'd asked them a riddle. "Ummm. And not all knights wear armor?" said the older boy.

She laughed. "Exactly. Heroes hide in unlikely uniforms." She patted the boy's cheek and set off for Gregory's chamber.

Eleanor caught Gregory at the opportune time. The witches had just refreshed his tonic. The medicine dulled his pain, but he was not yet so groggy that she questioned his ability to make a rational decision. To her relief, he agreed Natalie needed a unicorn for protection and practice, and Dasha was just the horned quadruped for the job.

He sat in his bed with a stack of reports and ledgers. After he made notes, he passed the documents to Orvid Jones to be marked with the royal seal. Sylvia sat in a chair beside him. She was knitting a scarf. She hummed pleasantly while Eleanor rattled on about her plans for Dasha and Natalie. A remarkably domestic scene. Gregory could have been a country squire. Sylvia, his devoted wife, nursing him back to health after a bad cold. He spoke of how happy it made him to see Eleanor and Sylvia at peace. Sylvia smiled down at her knitting as if the scarf were a babe in her arms. Since she was holding up her end of the bargain by not adding to Gregory's strife, Eleanor did the same. With a forced grin, she pronounced herself relieved that Sylvia had returned. As she talked, an idea came to her. "It's fortuitous that my dear sister came now, just before the Waxing Fest. I'm so busy these days. I hardly have the time for the planning." She beamed at Sylvia. "You're the best hostess in Cartheigh, Your Grace, while I still hardly know the difference between red wine glasses and white. Surely, you can take over this most important task?"

"Ah, I do have to look after Gregory. That's why I came. I also must see to my mother."

"We planned on a somewhat subdued celebration this year, given Gregory's health. But of course, if I'm asking too much..."

"Frankly, I think it's a fine idea," said Gregory. "Sylvia, you enjoy such trivialities, while Eleanor loathes them. She has so many other responsibilities. I have the witches, and Dorian and Orvid are always here. I appreciate your concern, sweetheart, but you'll be most helpful with the party planning. It's your true gift."

Eleanor bit the inside of her cheek. How galling, for Gregory to call Sylvia by the endearment he used for Eleanor in their happier days—and right in front of her. Notwithstanding her annoyance, she drew some pleasure from Gregory's little speech. The man Sylvia loved just told her, in front of her rival, that selecting hors d'oeuvres and arranging seating charts were her greatest talents.

"If that's where you need me, Your Majesty, that's exactly where I'll be," said Sylvia. She flashed her dimples at him.

"Splendid! Anne Iris and Eliza will be in town, and they can help you. I'm sure you'll come up with a lovely theme for the Waxing Ball." Eleanor stood. "Now I'm off to the Paladine to escort Dasha to the Abbey."

She kissed the top of Gregory's head. Orvid Jones followed Eleanor to the door. He dropped his voice to a whisper as he opened it for her to pass. "I'm sure Her Grace will thoroughly enjoy mulling over party themes in the supply closets while you endeavor to save known world." He winked and shut the door behind her.

Dasha followed Eleanor and Teardrop across Maliana to the Abbey. Four Unicorn Guards surrounded them like mobile points on a compass. At nearly two years old, he'd almost reached his full height, but his chest and neck still had some widening coming. Even mystical creatures must navigate adolescent clumsiness. He sometimes tripped over his own hooves. His dark eyes spun like parasols, and his nostrils couldn't seem to keep up with the parade of strange smells.

"I remember my first time in the city," said Teardrop. "So many sights and scents. If you are overwhelmed, close your eyes and follow me by sound."

Chou perched between Teardrop's ears. "Do you think that's wise?" he asked. "He's already having trouble keeping his feet in line with his eyes open."

Eleanor reached over to ruffle Dasha's forelock, as one might do to a disheveled little boy. "The Abbey is quieter," she said.

"But the smells are even stranger," said Chou.

They crossed under the Abbey's gate, and Eleanor asked the guards to wait for them by the chapel. Witches called out sing-song greetings, and chickens ran through the unicorns' feet. The young girls chased them and cast a rainbow of sweet-smelling spells to welcome and impress their guests. By the time they approached the training ring, a sheen of anxious sweat covered Dasha. Chou examined his own reflection on the unicorn's shiny neck and declared it a good feather day.

Eleanor dismounted and waved Chou away from the nervous colt. She brushed Dasha's long mane to one side. Teardrop bumped her muzzle against his belly to reassure him. Eleanor waved to Rosemary and Agnes in the far corner of the training ring. She opened the gate, and beckoned Dasha to follow her. He spooked at the sound of running feet. A red-headed blur blew past Eleanor. "Dash!" Natalie cried as she threw her arms around the unicorn's foreleg.

"Natalie, be careful," Eleanor said, but rather than stepping on her, Dasha quieted as soon as the little girl touched him. His ears pricked, and he nibbled on her dress.

"Natty." No hint of adolescence remained in his rumbling nicker. Terin himself couldn't have sounded fatherlier.

"You finally brought him, Mother! Shall he stay with me? Did Poppa say he can?"

"If Rosemary agrees, yes, he may. He's your unicorn now." She stepped out of the way of Dasha's razor-sharp horn. "As long as Dasha himself agrees, of course."

The unicorn raised his head. "Natalie is my best friend. I will stay with her, wherever she goes."

"Mother, can you lift me onto Dasha's back?" Natalie tried to crawl up Dasha's side. He stood serenely while she hung from his mane like a determined squirrel after a special nut. Her tongue stuck out, and she tugged with both arms, but the height defeated her.

"You haven't ridden much," said Eleanor, but Dasha knelt as if he were bowing to the little girl.

"She'll need to ride, if you want me to truly protect her," the unicorn said.

Eleanor lifted Natalie onto Dasha's back. He stood slowly but lurched at the end out of necessity. Natalie slid backward with panicked look on her face. She grabbed his mane. As soon as she had a good grip, she smiled again. Her legs stuck out from his sides as if she were doing the splits. "It's not hard, Mother, see?"

"He's not moving, darling," said Eleanor. Natalie looked so tiny, up there on Dasha's back.

"May I?" Agnes said over Eleanor's shoulder.

Eleanor stepped out of her way.

Agnes stood beside the unicorn and the child. "Natalie," she said. "It's true that riding such a great creature will not be easy, especially for a small person who hasn't even had much time to learn on a pony."

Natalie's usual eerie adult demeanor disappeared. "I am not *small.* I am *not.*" Her foot flopped against Dasha's side, in an attempt at a mounted, disgruntled stomp.

"There are ways your magic can help you," said Agnes. "Small or not. Can you think how?"

Natalie ran her hand over Dasha's neck in several long, thoughtful strokes. "When I'm walking on the fence posts or the roof, my magic helps me not to fall."

"What does that mean?" asked Eleanor. She'd raise concerns about Natalie walking on fence posts and roofs with Rosemary later.

Natalie looked down at her. "Magic is like a blanket, Mother. When it's thick. Like a bunch of pillows, all squashed around me. Holding me up."

"Is that true?" Eleanor asked Agnes.

"That's as good a way to explain it as any."

They watched as red light surrounded Natalie. Eleanor saw through it initially. Natalie whispered, and it thickened from her shoulders to her ankles. Eleanor could just make out the outline of her skinny body in her simple dark blue dress. She resembled a stuffed pastry.

"Is it heavy, Dash?" asked Natalie. She held his mane in her hands like reins.

"Not at all, little princess."

"Can we walk over to the archery targets?"

Dasha clopped gently across the ring. They reached the targets, and Natalie tapped Dasha's right shoulder. She clucked, and the unicorn broke into a trop. She bounced stiffly for a few strides, until she let her back relax and fell into the rhythm of his stride. Another cluck, and they were cantering around the ring, as surely as if they were about to compete in a dressage competition.

"Well, I'll be a dragon in bloomers," said Chou. Eleanor blessed him for coming up with a euphemism that adequately expressed the absurdity of her tiny daughter galumphing around the ring on a giant unicorn, as if she had come out of the womb and been strapped into a saddle.

"They've always been meant for one another," said Teardrop. "Dasha knew, from the first time he saw her. Just like I knew, with you."

Eleanor stroked Teardrop's muzzle. Rosemary came up behind her and squeezed her shoulder. "The Oracle agrees the colt can stay here. We'll make room for him and be honored."

"Not sure he's a colt anymore, with this responsibility," said Chou, with his usual quirky wisdom. "He's a stallion now."

CHAPTER 18

A MESSAGE

ELEANOR RETURNED TO THE Abbey the next day to observe Natalie's first attempts to interpolate with Dasha. Given his angsty reaction to the hullabaloo in Smithwick Square, she expected Dasha to be nervous. To the contrary, the young stallion was as serene as book of meditations.

"His responsibility for Natalie will help him keep his head," said Teardrop.

"I hope so." Eleanor rifled through her rucksack. She had a few extra pairs of gloves, a rabbit fur dragon robe, some sweet biscuits for Natalie, her change purse, and the kaleidoscope.

She found a little jar of soothing cream. She rubbed some on her hands and dabbed her lips. Anxiety drove her to chew on her lower lip, thus causing an unsightly line of red irritation below her mouth.

Rosemary sidled up beside Eleanor as Agnes approached Natalie and Dasha in the ring. "It should be fine," Rosemary said. "First, they'll travel from here to the south pastures, near Afar Creek and the Oracle's cavern. Then, from here to Rabbit's Rest Lodge."

"A few hour's carriage ride."

"Flat ground. Easy. Then to the lawn of Trill Castle in Solsea and back. Lastly, Agnes described the pass into Svelya, north of the Mines."

"Somewhere she's never been. Is it dangerous?"

"There are giant buzzards in the area, but they're harmless. Just smelly."

"What about ogres?"

"Unfortunately, we can't predict where the ogres will be."

"There will be ogres involved sooner or later," said Teardrop.

"I'd still rather she and Dasha didn't land in one's lap," Eleanor replied.

Agnes talked softly to Natalie, who watched her with intense, unafraid eyes. She had two handfuls of Dasha's mane. Her magic buffered her in an embrace. For all the witches' talk of comfort and reassurance, to Eleanor, the red cloud looked smothering, like a heavy sweater on a summer's day. Natalie asked Agnes a few quiet questions. Agnes squeezed her boot, patted Dasha's neck, and walked to Eleanor and Rosemary. Dasha tossed his head and scraped one foot through the wet dirt. His fidgeting reminded Eleanor of Teardrop's excited pre-journey squirminess.

"She seems perfectly comfortable," said Agnes. "I told her she can rest between trips if she wants to. She doesn't need to flitter off again."

"Doesn't she always rest?"

"Lately, no. I think it's a fun challenge for her. Like jumping around on a hopscotch board." Agnes's mouth twitched. "Mr. Oliver needs time to recover after these journeys. It pleases me that a five-year-old girl will best him at his own magic, I tell you."

Eleanor inhaled the hot MidSummer air. "She should give Dasha a chance to rest, even if she's not tired. We don't know how interpolation will affect him."

"Shhh, look," said Rosemary.

Natalie leaned up Dasha's neck. She spoke softly to him. His tail flicked left, right, left. Natalie adjusted her fur hat. Despite the heat, she wore warm clothes, as she'd face all manner of weather on her journey. She gripped his mane and squeezed her legs. The unicorn half-reared, took two strides forward, and they both disappeared.

The next thirty seconds felt like several days to Eleanor, but her clockworks told her otherwise. With a soft pop, Natalie and Dasha reappeared. The unicorn danced on his forelegs, and Natalie let out a happy whoop. They vanished again, and just as quickly, they were back. Another *pop, pop!* Gone once more. This time, they didn't return for nearly five minutes. Eleanor was near tears by the time they materialized again. "We're off to the north!" Natalie shouted. Once again, *pop, pop.* No child. No stallion.

Ten long minutes passed. Eleanor pressed her fingers to her eyes, as if to block out the image of an ogre carrying Natalie back to its stinking lair. She looked up when Agnes tugged her arm. "They're back."

Teardrop whinnied her relief. Eleanor and the two witches scooted between the fence rails and crossed the ring to meet them. Natalie slid to the ground, and Dasha pranced along behind her as she ran to the three women. She held both hands in front of her, like a chapelgoer with a special tithing. She offered Eleanor a willow branch from one of the ancient trees surrounding Willowswatch Cottage. In her other hand, a lump of quickly melting snow. She gave it to Agnes.

"From the mountain pass to Svelya," Agnes said. "Even in HighSummer, there is snow there."

Eleanor examined the branch. Its tiny leaves reminded her of elegant green lace. She remembered the soothing sound of a cliff breeze through the willow branches. Somehow, she held a piece of one of those arboreal behemoths; a misplaced seasonal memory. She tousled Natalie's hair. She suddenly felt afraid to hug this child whom she had brought into this world, yet in moments like these, seemed to not be of it. Natalie looked between Rosemary and Agnes. "Did I do well?" she asked.

"You know you did, child," said Rosemary.

Eleanor wasn't sure her opinion mattered, but she said, "We're very proud of you."

"Thank you, Mother," said Natalie. "Interpolating with Dasha was not hard at all. Shall we visit Ello now? I'm ready. *We're* ready, aren't we Dash?"

The unicorn nodded his head, up, down, up, down. His horn sliced through the red cloud that lingered around Natalie.

Eleanor laughed. "Today, Natty? No. You need to rest. Perhaps a few more trial runs to other places. How about Nestra itself, before Alenestra?"

Natalie didn't laugh or even return Eleanor's smile. "Mother, I am *not* tired. Nor is Dasha. We have work to do, and we're ready."

"Natalie," said Rosemary, the tone in her voice a warning. "I support you going, but not your rudeness."

Natalie sighed, and for a moment, their roles reversed. Natalie was the parent, placating a nonsensical child. "Truly, Mother, I'm *ready*. From what I understand, time is of the essence."

Eleanor crossed her arms over her chest. "Are you sure? Maybe, at least lunch first?"

"I ate six griddle cakes and a sausage for breakfast."

"I did tell her to make sure she eats up," said Agnes.

Eleanor felt Teardrop's warm breath on her neck. If it wasn't Chou's beak, it was Teardrop's muzzle. Always, some non-human creature whispering in her ear, calling her out. "If she's so galvanized, let her go."

Eleanor felt besieged. Who could argue with three witches and two unicorns? They're all maddeningly logical creatures. Still, she refused to be completely run over like a lone cornstalk standing before a plow. "At least a drink of water, and… and use the outhouse."

"But I don't have to go."

"Right now, young lady!"

Natalie jumped and ran toward the outhouse.

"I'm still her mother," Eleanor said.

"That you are," said Teardrop. "No mother lets her child go on a long journey without first using the outhouse."

"Someone else should go with her," said Teardrop.

Natalie had both consumed water and released it, as she'd been asked, and now she sat on Dasha's back once again, waiting for her final instructions. She wore a heavy winter cloak, thick woolen riding leggings, her fur hat, and the gloves Eleanor had brought for her.

"Someone besides Dasha?" asked Eleanor. "You think she needs more protection?"

"No," said Teardrop. "But while Natalie is brilliant, she's still a child, with a child's observations. We're sending her there to see if she can get there, but someone needs to make confirm the suitability of the destination."

"Hmm. I think Teardrop is right." Eleanor hoisted her rucksack over one arm and grabbed the spare dragon robe she'd thrown across Teardrop's saddle. She strode across the ring. "Natalie! I'm coming with you."

Rosemary followed Eleanor. "Would Agnes not be better suited?"

"Why do you say that?" asked Eleanor as she donned the thick wolfskin. She wiped her hands on her riding leggings. They weren't warm enough, but she had on sturdy boots and thick socks, and they wouldn't be gone long.

"Because she has magical ability," said Teardrop, in her maddeningly rational way.

"I don't care," said Eleanor. A silly reply, one Natalie herself probably would have dismissed as childish. She didn't care. She couldn't help with any of the magical mechanisms associated with this plan, but she wanted some say over the logistical ones. Besides, if her daughter would be dumped off on a strange island no human being had seen in thousands of years, she needed her mother to look after her. "Rosemary, do you have extra gloves?"

"Yes... but this is rather... that is to say..." Rosemary trailed off and held up both hands. She silently implored Agnes to intervene, while Eleanor's glare simultaneously warned her to do no such thing. The dainty witch was caught between a knife blade and an ax head. She straightened Natalie's booted feet and handed her a water flask. As the child attached the flask to a hook on her saddle, Agnes tucked her hair behind her ears and chose neutrality. "I'm happy to go, but I will leave it to the Abbottess and the queen to decide."

"You can both come," said Natalie.

"Child, I don't think that's wise. This is your longest journey yet."

"I can do it, Mum Rosemary. Agnes can ride with me. Mother and Teardrop can come, too."

"And Teardrop!" Rosemary shook her head. "No, Natalie."

"You're certain you can take us all?" Eleanor asked.

"Yes," the child said, unflinching.

"That settles it." Eleanor's heart banged in her chest like a tambourine during a spirited hymn, but she made up her mind. If Natalie believed she could take them all, then Eleanor would trust her.

Natalie spoke up. "Mum Rosemary, it's hard for you to imagine, because you cannot make the spells work."

Rosemary winced. "I've never claimed to be a powerful sorceress. But as the Abbottess, I am responsible for your safety."

"Keep in mind," said Teardrop, "two unicorns and two women aren't close to half the bulk of a grown male ogre, and you're expecting her to transport them."

"If you're all in agreement.... I suppose I'll find gloves."

Eleanor responded by giving Agnes a leg up behind Natalie. She wrapped her arms around Natalie's waist, so they looked like two children out for a playtime trot on a gigantic pony. Rosemary handed Agnes a spare bearskin dragon robe and gave Eleanor a pair of tick fur mittens. Agnes draped the robe over her shoulders. Eleanor mounted up and tied her rucksack to the horn of Teardrop's saddle.

"Come close, Teardrop," Natalie said. Teardrop scooted close enough to Dasha that Eleanor's leg touched Natalie's. Natalie, in turn, held one hand full of Dasha's mane, and reached across Eleanor's lap to take another handful of Teardrop's.

"Alenestra," said Agnes. "The cold island of Ello. The temple with the stone skull." Her voice shook. Teardrop trembled beneath Eleanor. The tempo had picked up, and the tambourine in Eleanor's chest fought to keep time.

"Be careful!" Rosemary called out. "Please hurry."

"We will," said Natalie. "Alenestra. The Stone Skull."

Eleanor expected a lurch. Maybe pain, or pressure, or nausea. Instead, everything went black, as if she'd simply closed her eyes. For the briefest of moments, she dreamed of a candle that didn't need fire. She just pulled a string, and it blazed with white light. Then she woke up.

She saw her own breath first, before the wind snatched it away. Her lashes fluttered protectively over her eyes. She wiped them, lest they freeze shut upon watering. She'd never felt cold like this, not even during her stay in Nestra. Socks be damned, her toes already ached.

Teardrop's belly expanded and contracted under the saddle. She blew her own cold respirations across a desolate landscape. Dasha bumped against the mare, as if a gust had blown him sideways. Agnes tightened her grip on Natalie. The child sank into her lap and blinked against the harsh sunlight. The damp, salty air told Eleanor they were close to the sea.

The unicorns stood on an uneven dune, where gnarled trees had given into the wind and grew sideways. They reminded Eleanor of capsized spiders. Bits of brownish grass cowered in the crevices between the lichen-covered boulders. Rocky hills formed an uneven horizon in front of them. Eleanor looked over her shoulder at tossing whitecaps. Gray water slammed against hard-packed black sand. The waves tossed white foam confetti at the circling sea gulls. The birds voiced their disapproval of their strange visitors – *keow-har-har-har-har*. Eleanor almost called out to them, before remembering that even if they could speak, like most large birds, they would only know the language of the Great Marauders.

Agnes pointed to a stand of tall rocks over the first rise. They were too tall and thin to have fixed themselves upright in such a manner.

"Alenestra." Eleanor half hoped someone else would suggest they'd gone far enough, and they should go home to Cartheigh, where MidSummer was appropriately hot. No wonder the Ancient Marauders had abandoned this brutal country.

Natalie and Dasha seemed overwhelmed by the strangeness of the terrain. Natalie tucked her face in her hood. Dasha looked to Teardrop in an unabashed plea for leadership.

"There's a path, of sorts, if we go through the rocks," Teardrop said. She picked her way through patches of sand and some puddles. "I believe this place will have great tides that move quickly."

"On Svelya's northernmost coast, there are drownings every year," said Agnes. "The tides rush in so quick and hard."

"Let's get away from here," said Eleanor. "Natalie will have to get closer to the temple when she returns. She can't land on the beach."

Agnes whispered in Natalie's ear as the two unicorns plodded toward the circle of stones. Eleanor marveled at the enormity of the rocks and their uniform arrangement. The Marauders must have used magic to position them. Eight structures formed a circle around the altar. Three roughly hewn stone pillars made up each edifice. The rocks leaned on each other, creating hollow pyramids. Eleanor felt as if she were inside a giant mouth, surrounded by jagged teeth.

Thousands of years of wind and rain had worn away the sculpture under the altar, leaving a lumpy rock with a vaguely human face, rather like the moon. Only the deep eye sockets remained.

"A quick drop off will be important, Natalie," said Teardrop as she appraised the temple grounds. "The ogres won't linger in a place that caters to strange gods."

"All gods are strange," said Natalie, her voice muffled by her robe. Her head poked from her hood. She squinted like a bear cub emerging after a long winter sleep and pointed at one of the stone pyramids. She'd acclimated to her surroundings, and her usual intense awareness returned. "There's something I need to see here. It's this way. That one, Dasha."

The unicorn walked toward the pyramid. Nothing special defined it as more significant than the others. If anything, it was one of the smallest and least impressive configurations, a boring molar flanked by two sharper canines.

Natalie clucked to Dasha, and he broke into a bouncy trot. Agnes wrapped one arm around Natalie and grabbed a handful of mane with her other hand. She slid to the right and took Natalie with her. Natalie's red magic enveloped them and pushed them upright before they toppled off. Natalie was nonplussed, as if falling from Dasha's back to the frozen, rocky ground would be of no consequence. A few broken bones didn't matter as much as that rock.

She asked Dasha to stop. "I'm getting down."

Before Eleanor or Agnes protested, Natalie swung one leg over the saddle and slid down Dasha's side. She clung to his mane as if she were escaping a burning building. She dangled for a moment, let go, and landed nimbly on both feet. She approached the rock.

Eleanor dismounted as Natalie ran her fingers over the weathered stone. She knelt at the base and pointed. "Here!" She tugged at the grass, but those hearty blades had found shelter from the wind and wouldn't release their hold on the soil. She yanked at the grass as if trying to pull up a heavy fishing net. Eleanor took a paring knife from her rucksack and hacked the grass away.

"It's a picture," said Agnes, from over Eleanor's shoulder. As Eleanor brushed the dirt away, a precisely etched carving appeared.

"HighGod. It's an ogre." Eleanor sat back on her heels. Her numb feet throbbed in her boots. The face was unmistakable. An oblong head, flat nose, and huge eyes that stared irritably out of the stone. There were two letters carved beside the picture. They vaguely resembled the Svelyan writing Eleanor had seen in Nestra. Agnes ran a finger over them. "These are ancient, but I can see the roots of our language. I think we would hear this as an *H*, and this a *B*."

"Initials?" Eleanor asked. "Wait. This makes no sense. The carving looks like someone made it yesterday. Are there people here? Why an ogre? The texts about the Ancient Marauders didn't mention ogres."

"It's a message," said Teardrop.

"For us," said Natalie. "From long ago. But this can't be all of it. There is more."

"Someone left us a message? How, or… why?" Eleanor asked.

"I'm trying to find out, Mother. I feel it. Oh, dear. I must hear all of the message. We cannot return until I do."

Eleanor and Agnes looked at each other with raised eyebrows. If Natalie didn't want to go back, none of them would be going. They'd been gone at least thirty minutes. Longer than Natalie had ever gone before. Rosemary was surely vexed already.

Natalie ran to the next rock, and the next, but she found no more carvings. Dasha nickered his concern as he followed her. By the time they returned to Eleanor, Agnes, and Teardrop, a sheen of sweat had beaded on Natalie's forehead. "Mother," she said. "I *must* hear the message."

"Perhaps we can return tomorrow and look again," said Agnes.

Eleanor rubbed her gloved hands together. They had to go home soon, lest they all freeze. She leaned against Teardrop to find warmth. Her head hit her rucksack, and the kaleidoscope poked her back.

She reached over her shoulder and felt the familiar cylinder through the pack. "Maybe we can see the message, instead of hearing it." She dug into the rucksack and handed the kaleidoscope to Natalie. Natalie took it and jumped up and down in place.

"Yes! This will do, Mother! Your kaleidoscope can show me!"

"I can't guarantee it, darling. I've never had much luck controlling what it shows me. But perhaps you will. The Oracle told me the right mind might have some control over its pictures."

Natalie put the scope to her eye, and Eleanor gently reminded her of the instructions for operating it. She trained the kaleidoscope on the ogre carving.

For the next ten minutes, the two women and the two unicorns followed Natalie as she crept around the temple grounds. She whispered to herself, and twice she cried out. Once, she even laughed.

When Natalie finally lowered the kaleidoscope, she had tears in her eyes. "I saw, Mother, but I don't know if I understand." She offered the toy to Eleanor. "Can you look?"

Eleanor took it. She started to give it to Agnes. As a witch, she seemed a better recipient of a magical message.

Natalie took Eleanor's hand and dragged her toward the carving. "No. Not Agnes. She wants you to see it."

"Who wants to me to see?"

"Someone."

Agnes shrugged, so Eleanor turned the kaleidoscope and put it to her eye. Right eye closed. Left eye, squinting. The colors shifted, and Alenestra appeared before her. This time, it was a spring day.

The light green grass and the little white and yellow flowers growing in bunches around the pyramids gave away the season. The tiny blossoms huddled beside the rocks as if seeking protection from the gods. No angel had heard their pleas, as someone had ripped up bunches of blooms and lay them on the altar. The skull no longer resembled a lumpy stone potato. It was a fierce, leering menace, with black pupils painted in its deep eye sockets, sharp white teeth, and blood dripping from its mouth.

A hundred odd people congregated in the temple's courtyard. Their shoes sunk ankle deep in viscous mud. Eleanor couldn't smell anything, but she imagined the air would reek of rotten vegetables. They clustered in family groups surrounded by bags and small hand carts. Some held wooden crates crammed with live chickens or ropes attached to the jingly collars of pigs and goats. Eleanor couldn't tell if their fur-draped bodies matched their gaunt faces. Nearly everyone, male and female, young and old, had braided, white blonde hair. An argumentative bunch of men stood beside the altar. To Eleanor's surprise, she understood their words. The undertones of their language were muffled, and her own voice seemed to translate in her head.

"The boat has already landed," said the tallest man. He had a long white beard, like a human Terin. "Efram wants to leave this place for good. Anyone who can't keep up will have to stay behind. We can't risk him leaving the rest of us here to face the blight. He's sworn this is his last voyage south."

"Lesel the Elder lost five sheep in one night," said another man. "If we stay much longer, our flocks will perish."

"The sooner the better..."

"Haybet!" A shrill female voice called out over the men's grumbling. The tone had a hint of command, but not enough to be a mother. A girl of maybe eleven or twelve years old, with one long braid down her back, shaded her eyes with her hand. "Haybet! Where are you?" The wind blasted past her. She gasped and pulled her hood over her head.

Eleanor could have chosen any of them, but something told her she should follow this girl. Eleanor tracked her across the temple grounds. She herself followed a younger child who darted through the crowd like a rabbit trying to lose a pursuing fox. The little one wore a white fur cloak. Ermine, or perhaps ice hare. The older girl stopped with her hands on her hips and looked around. Eleanor caught a flash of white in the shadow of one of the smaller pyramids.

The younger child crouched beside the stone as the older one stormed toward her. "Hello, Desi," said the little one, in a high, fey voice. Eleanor couldn't see her face, and her requisite long braids didn't indicate one sex or the other, but it sounded like a little girl.

"Haybet!" said the older girl. "Mother is looking for you! She's very angry."

A buzzing came from Haybet's lap. Bright blue light framed her hands, followed by smoke and a few sparks.

Desi pulled Haybet away from the rock. "What are you doing?"

"I made a picture!"

There it was. The ogre's face. Carved into stark relief on the stone. Haybet beamed up into her older sister's face. She was a pretty child, with round red cheeks and big blue eyes, pale lashes and a full, heart-shaped mouth. Her smile revealed missing front teeth.

"Oh, mercy," said Desi. "The elders will have you whipped. You can't draw monsters on the prayer stones!" She dragged the little girl backward. "We have to get out of here, before someone notices."

Haybet dug in her heels. "No! I have to sign my name. So they will know I left it for them!" Blue light shot from the child's hands. With five strokes, she carved the letters Agnes had described as H and B.

"You're not supposed to use that light! Not until we reach the other side of the sea. You know what will happen."

The little girl grimaced and tucked her hands inside her fur. "They'll send me back."

"If they let you come with us at all." Desi leaned toward her sister. Eleanor still hadn't gotten a good look at her face behind hood. "The Elder Witch is staying. They want the *youngest* witch to stay, too. To complete the circle and send us on our way."

"Poor Lana," said Haybet.

"Lana is a year older than you. If they know you're a witch, it's *you* that will be staying. So you *stop* it!"

"I'm sorry." Haybet hugged Desi. "But I felt I had to leave this picture, so when they come, they will know this is the right place."

"Who comes? For what?"

"I don't know, but they need to know this is where the monsters belong."

"The blight has already made this a monstrous place."

"Yes. It's the right place for them. We will all be gone. They can live here, in the blighted lands."

"I know the gods talk to you, little sister. I won't tell mother. But you have to hold it in. At least until we get across the sea. If other witches claim you then, at least you'll be safe."

"I'm afraid to cross the sea. So far from father."

"Father is with the gods. You know that. It's just a shell of him buried in the mound."

"Like a nutshell."

Desi stroked Haybet's hair. "That's what mother says."

"I'm afraid I'll forget him."

"It wouldn't be so bad though to forget this place. I'd like to forget being cold and hungry. I don't want to remember crying babies and animals and plants dying."

"I'd like to forget those things, too."

"The gods look kindly on you. I think you'll live so long, and you'll remember so much that you'll have to forget things just to make room for more."

Horns and fire, thought Eleanor. *Haybet. A magical child who talks to these gods of her youth, whoever they may be. Who will live so many lifetimes she forgets where she came from. She will forget even her true name, and she will take a new one, sometime in her long history. That name will be Hazelbeth.*

Haybet laughed. "You won't tell Mother about my picture?"

"No. But we can't tell anyone else, either. They'll think you've angered the gods by defacing the stones. A bad sign as we leave." The two girls walked toward the shouting people. The bearded man yelled for everyone to line up and be orderly or risk being left behind.

"If they think I did wrong then they don't know the gods very well." She drew a circle in the air before here. "The Elder Witch has her circle. The gods have told me Ello is part of mine. My picture made them happy."

Desi pushed her hood away from her face. Eleanor crept closer. The girl's profile was eerily familiar.

Eleanor walked behind Haybet, who stared up at Desi with adoring eyes. Desi put her hands on her knees and smiled. "You make me happy, little sister!"

She was a beautiful girl, this Desi. A long nose and slightly flared nostrils. Pale brows and long eyelashes. Her eyes were most arresting. One pale blue, like the washed-out sky behind them. The other, dark brown, like the dirt below their feet.

CHAPTER 19

MUCH

BY THE TIME THE reconnaissance party returned to the Abbey, Rosemary was lying across a hay bale with one arm draped across her face. When they reappeared, she sat up like someone had reached up through the hay and tickled her. She ran across the ring, reached up into the cloud of red magic encasing Natalie and Agnes, and pulled the child to the ground. She fussed over her cold hands and chapped cheeks. Natalie was unusually quiet—a magpie with a sore throat.

She mumbled as Rosemary wrapped another dragon robe around her shoulders. "The child and the old woman. They are one and the same."

Eleanor slid from Teardrop's back as Rosemary questioned Natalie and Agnes. Her eyes widened as they gave her the truncated version of their tale. Agnes dismounted and rubbed her bottom. "My body is already telling me I'm not accustomed to unicornback. Shall we meet in the reading room to discuss further? I need a soft chair and a warm fire."

"I'm exhausted, Agnes," said Eleanor, "and I need to return to Gregory. Can you tell Rosemary about the visit?"

"I can, but I didn't see what you saw, in the kaleidoscope."

"Natalie did. She's a child, but sometimes she sees more than we do."

"You believe this child, Haybet, she was truly our Hazelbeth?" asked Rosemary.

"I am certain of it. Once Natalie is fully recovered from her efforts, I think she'll agree with me. You heard her—the child and the old woman are one in the same."

Agnes agreed and promised to write with any updates, while Eleanor promised to return as soon as possible.

In the carriage, on the ride to Eclatant, Eleanor wondered if Natalie had noticed that little Haybet's big sister had strange eyes, like her own mother. She hadn't mentioned it, and unless she happened to catch the girls' conversation at just the right angle, she wouldn't have seen. The idea that Natalie had missed the similarity comforted Eleanor. She wasn't ready for the resulting speculation when the witches connected Hazelbeth with Eleanor, and therefore, Natalie. She needed time to think about all the potential ramifications of such a shocking consanguine association. If they'd merely had a glimpse into the Oracle's childhood, well, that would be an interesting and unexpected bit of lore. Something to add as a footnote to one of her history books. But the older girl... her face, and of course, her eyes. One blue, one brown.

Eleanor felt as if she'd stumbled upon her own childhood reflection staring out at her from one of Imogene's hand mirrors.

Was it just that the girl was blonde and thin, covered in smudgy dirt, as I always was?

She leaned against the carriage window. She had a headache, as if the cold wind of Ello had blown into her head through her nostrils and frozen into a block of ice. The ice threatened to crack her skull as it expanded.

No. It wasn't just dirt. The shape of her face. Her nose. And HighGod, her eyes. Eleanor always believed her own eyes were simply a fluke. A mistake—as if her creator added too much ink to the quill with which he drew her and dropped an extra blob of color where it shouldn't be.

Could she be related to Hazelbeth? As a witch, the Oracle wouldn't have had children, even in her youth. But Desi probably did.

Eleanor thought of her white blonde hair, so unusual in Cartheigh but commonplace in Svelya. She had seen one painting of her own mother. Imogene destroyed it after her father's death, but she remembered a woman of rare beauty—slender, blue-eyed, and fair-haired. Beyond her grandparents, her mother's family was an enigma. The mystery could very well have originated in Svelya.

Haybet spoke of circles. Had Haybet become Hazelbeth, the famed Oracle of Afar Creek Abbey, and Eleanor's great-aunt going back a hundred generations?

The carriage lurched to a stop, and Eleanor winced as her tender forehead bounced against the glass. She rubbed the spot and pulled back the curtain. She breathed a sigh of relief at the beloved face framed in the window. Dorian stood on the steps of Eclatant, waiting for her. The footman opened the door, and she stepped down the two Fire-iron stairs. She took Dorian's arm and squeezed. The hard muscle below his woolen cloak comforted her. She suddenly wanted to cry. Eleanor hated to feel helpless, or needy, but in that moment, she would have given up almost anything to drag Dorian to her room, lay with him on her bed in the crook of his arm, and have a good, long sob under his nonjudgmental protection.

"Your Highness," he said. "I know it's unusual for me to meet you here."

"Oh. I suppose it is." Her stomach twisted. The iceberg in her head had starting melting at the sight of her beloved, but it slid sideways and banged painfully against her temple. "Pray, is something wrong?"

"It's the king. He's getting worse."

"How much worse?"

"Much."

His words dominated Eleanor's thoughts over the next two days. She had no time to dwell on her potentially suspect lineage, or what it might mean for her daughter, as Gregory floated in and out of consciousness. Orvid and Dorian fretted about the extent to which the public should be made aware of their king's terrible plight. They no longer spoke of *when* the king recovered, but *if* the king recovered.

With the opening celebration of the Waxing Fest a mere three days away, Orvid, Eleanor, and Dorian met in Gregory's room. Sylvia wasn't personally invited to their discussion, but as she rarely left the king's side, she was party to it. Eleanor had assumed her undependable and squeamish, but she ministered to Gregory with the diligence and tough stomach of a seasoned healer. She didn't seem to care about her clothes, or taking a bath, or even eating. HighGod only knew when she got any sleep. She didn't flinch at the sight of blood or gore, and she held Gregory's hand when the witches drained his wound, despite the smell and his fingers bearing down on hers like lowering fortress gates. She tolerated Dorian and Orvid, and she sat quietly while the three men conferred on all manner of topics that must have bored her to tears. She seemed to know what Gregory wanted before he asked for it. Pear juice. Bread. A fresh pillow.

Only love incites such dedication, Eleanor grudgingly thought, as Orvid paced the room.

"We must cancel the Fest," said the Chief Magician. "We can't have thousands of people traipsing through Eclatant, wondering why the king is not present."

"No," said Sylvia. She wiped the sweat from Gregory's injured leg. He blinked, moaned, and rolled over.

"Dragonshit," he muttered and closed his eyes again.

Orvid bristled. "It's hardly your decision, Your Grace."

Eleanor put a hand on his arm. "Wait, Orvid. Let's hear what she has to say."

Sylvia paused for a moment, as if taken aback by Eleanor's

intervention. "Thank you… Your Highness," she said. Her voice firmed up, and she lifted her chin as she looked between Orvid and Dorian. "We can't cancel the Fest. It will raise more questions about his wellbeing."

"It's true," said a gruff voice. Gregory struggled to sit up. Eleanor grabbed an extra pillow and propped it behind his back. He leaned against it and grimaced as he pulled his uninjured knee toward his chest. "My ass is asleep. The ogre's rot in my leg is slowly killing me. Still, the Fest must go on."

"Your Majesty, are you sure?"

"Orvid, I know there's a strong chance I'm going to die."

The four of them were, collectively, everything to Gregory. Best friends, advisers, confidants, and in the case of the female contingent, lovers. Yet not one of them could bring themselves to correct him. Eleanor had lied to Gregory enough in her life. As much as she hated to admit it, he was right.

"I need to make sure that, at least one last time, the people know the Desmarais family is strong—even unto the death. They need to be reminded of the Bond that's kept them safe all these years. The Bond that will continue through my son."

Sylvia adjusted his pillow and offered him a glass of water. "There will only be one party at the palace," she said, "The Waxing Ball. I've lent out the rest of the hosting honors to the in-town aristocracy. The Smithwicks and the Harpers are likely to kill each other over who hosts the joust."

"We have plenty of Smithwicks and Harpers," said Dorian. "We can spare a few."

"The ball usually closes the Fest, but I think given the circumstances, we should *open* the Fest with a ball."

Get the appearance over with before he gets worse. Eleanor knew everyone else thought the same thing, but no one said so.

"But, Your Grace," said Orvid, wringing his hands. "Right now, His Majesty cannot even stand. How will be attend a ball?"

"Triumphantly." Dorian pointed at the doorway to Gregory's chamber. "It starts with you, Orvid, and a carpentry spell."

"I haven't performed carpentry in years, Your Grace."

"Either you need to remember how, or we need to get someone in here who can work that magic. We need a door big enough for a unicorn."

Two days later, on the day of the Waning Ball, Orvid successfully expanded the door to Gregory's chamber. It wasn't as easy as a typical carpentry spell, because the beams of Eclatant were made of Fire-iron. Still, the Chief Magician managed to stretch the doorway with minimal warping of the walls. He assured Melfin, Gregory's grumpy old manservant, that there would be no need to order new doors.

"Everything will be as it was by midnight tonight," said Orvid as he swept up Fire-iron shavings. Chou fluttered around the room, flapping his wings in an attempt to fan the dust away from Gregory.

"Midnight, again," Chou said as he zoomed past the magician's head. "Everything ends when the clock strikes twelve. Magical folk have something against late night carousing."

Eleanor sat on the edge of the bed, watching Gregory. The witches had given him something to make him sleep, so as to save his strength for what the night required of him. "I don't think the king will be much for late night carousing this evening." Ironically, it pained her to think of Gregory retiring early. Normally he was the last one standing at any party. Many nights she'd lay in bed, wishing he'd leave his whiskey and his friends and fall asleep by her side. Now, she'd wished he could spend all night happily tossing back drinks and singing tavern songs.

Dorian had thought to bring Monument to Gregory's chamber, in the hope the unicorn's presence would strengthen him enough to make an appearance at the Waxing Ball. Gregory himself liked the idea, but Orvid still had doubts. The magician had chewed his fingernails to bits worrying over how the evening would progress. Gregory's healer forced him to soak his fingers in a rejuvenating tonic to regrow them. Eleanor's mindset hung somewhere between Dorian and Gregory's positivity and Orvid's pensiveness.

That evening, Eleanor's anxiety accompanied her into the ballroom. She fidgeted as she waited with Anne Iris and Eliza. As the minutes ticked by, their presence helped her nerves. Anne Iris's chatter was bubbling champagne, while Eliza's gentle reassurance served as her after dinner aperitif. Eleanor wore a purple and gold silk dress. Although it was one of her lighter gowns, between the heat and her state of mind, sweat was inevitable. Chou sat on her shoulder. His red feathers clashed gloriously with Eleanor's attire.

Agnes remained at the Abbey, and Orvid had no time for magical decorating, so Sylvia improvised with copious freshly daisies and blooming crepe myrtle trees in giant pots. She also rounded up a few magicians for a touch of magical entertainment. Two apprentices led crackling lightning bolts across the floor. They were harmless, but when the dancers got too close, their hair still stood on end.

"Nice touch," said Eliza. "It's not Sylvia's Waxing Fest ballroom thunderstorm, but it's still rather summery. It will do."

"Better than all the freezing décor at the Waning Fest parties. I do so hate hiding my gowns under all that fur."

Eleanor started to reminisce about Svelyan fashion, in all its furry drabness, but Sylvia's appearance at the far end of the ballroom distracted her. She wore a dark purple silk gown with a modest boxy neckline. She she'd done up her hair in a simple chignon at the base of her skull.

"She's shockingly appropriate," said Chou.

"There's still time for the dragon to shed its scales," said Anne Iris.

Eleanor felt a warm hand cover her bare shoulder. She recognized him before she turned around. No one else had such large hands. "It's time," whispered Dorian.

As he spoke, Fire-iron trumpets blared, high and urgent. Four short long toots cascaded up the musical scale and four short blasts tumbled back down. Orvid Jones's magically amplified voice instructed the guests to make way for their king. His subjects dutifully pressed against the walls, reminding Eleanor of the Second Sunday Ball. She remembered how the crowd split like a broken seam before Gregory's advance, leaving her painfully exposed in the middle of the ballroom in her quickly disintegrating finery. She sighed as Monument stepped into the ballroom. Gregory's face was a regal mask, hiding his unbearable pain from the people who needed to believe in his might. The young man who had chased her though this hall had been handsome, whole, and full of youthful vitality. The grown king astride the unicorn stallion was far more majestic. The people fell to their knees as Monument passed. While the young unicorn was perfectly gorgeous and as composed as any battle-hardened knight, Eleanor wished Gregory's old friend Vigor could carry him on what might be his final ride.

As Monument's crossed the hushed ballroom, Eleanor noticed Gregory cradling something in his arms. The bundle took the shape of a chubby baby in a fur-trimmed green and purple cape, silk leggings, and tiny boots. She almost fainted.

Dorian squeezed her shoulder again. "It was a last-minute decision," he said. "We didn't want to worry you. Frankly, I didn't want you arguing with him. A good idea to bring the prince."

People called out blessings, and Gregory kept one arm firmly wrapped around Cyrus's waist. The baby watched the crowd with mild curiosity. He waved several times. The people laughed and waved back and praised him as the most blessed child that had ever walked the earth.

Gregory and Monument made it safely to the front of the ballroom. The unicorn turned and faced the crowd. He shifted his weight, right, left, right. He scraped the marble floor with one hoof. The whispering stopped, as if the maestro had struck a gong.

"My friends. My family. My allies. Many of you have forgone our traditional summer celebrations in Solsea to be here. I, too, miss the cliff breezes, so I thank you for sacrificing your holiday and braving this damnable heat." The courtiers laughed, and Gregory smiled and raised one hand to hush them. "I am so pleased you can join me, and my wife, Queen Eleanor, this evening in our home. Although Eclatant isn't just *our* home. It's the home place of our nation."

Gregory spoke about the glory of Cartheigh, the honor of serving its people, and the latent fear and uncertainty, but Eleanor wasn't really listening to his words. She'd heard him give many speeches, and he always rose to the occasion. Instead, she watched the people around her. Sylvia remained oddly appropriate. She hovered on the periphery. She whispered with magicians, directed servers, and watched Gregory with anxious eyes when she had a free moment. Hundreds of noblemen and women, knights, ministers, and important Godsmen hung on Gregory's words. Wives dabbed at their eyes with handkerchiefs. Their sentiments inspired husbands to offer the comfort of a gentle arm around the waist or a peck on the cheek.

Chou spun around on Eleanor's shoulder. His tail feathers tickled her chin. "It's going well," he said to Dorian. "The peerage is appropriately enthralled."

"... I want you to know I appreciate your fears. There is not one person among us who does not abhor the thought of ogres roaming unchecked. I ask you to trust in the crown, and in the Bond, as you have for the past three hundred years. Know the greatest minds in my kingdom are working day and night to ensure your protection. We will not cower in fear, and nor will we rush to sacrifice your sons in a senseless war. If we can resist the simple, easy temptation of violence, I have learned we can find a way around it. Remember, the unicorns stand strong with us. Our Bonded friends, *and* the wild herds. Our allegiances are strong. The dragons supply us with their iron, which has become our shield. I, as your king… as your… king…"

Gregory's eyes bulged, and he grunted. His injured leg spasmed. When he hunched over, a sheen of sweat appeared on his forehead.

"Oh no," whispered Eliza. "Eleanor—is Gregory all right?"

Dorian pushed past Eleanor and her friends. Gregory tried to stay upright, but his leg had locked. The flesh seemed to strain against his leggings.

"It's festering," said Chou.

"It's never come on that fast before." Eleanor handed her wine glass to Anne Iris, and followed Dorian.

Gregory wrapped his arm tighter around little Cyrus, and the child squirmed and cried out. Chou clung to the back of Eleanor's gown and peered over her shoulder. "He's going to drop the baby!"

Dorian shoved past the man in front of him. He stumbled and started to push back. When he realized he'd been accosted by the Duke of Brandling, he stepped aside and dragged his wife along with him.

Gregory took a deep breath and another. He seemed to be getting his wits about him. "I'm apologize. I still have some pain—"

Cyrus arched his back, as babies are wont to do when they want out of an uncomfortable situation. To Eleanor's horror, the child slid under Gregory's arm. His weight shifted and flopped onto Monument's neck. His boot snagged on Gregory's dress sword. Gregory grabbed for him, but his fur robe slipped through the king's gloved hand.

Eleanor started running. Her precious son, her baby boy, would soon tumble from the height of a unicorn's back and land on his head on the shining marble floor.

There was a flash of white, like a striking egret after a slippery fish. The startled baby prince stared at his mother with his mouth agog. The preciously packaged parcel of the Desmarais family's hopes and dreams dangled from the clenched teeth of a unicorn stallion.

Monument gently set the little boy on the ground and let go of his cape. As soon as the cold marble touched his bottom, Prince Cyrus started to wail. Monument snuffled his neck and whiffled in his ears. His silky muzzle absorbed baby tears. Cyrus stopped crying and looked up at his rescuer with huge eyes. He laughed and reached for Monument's horn. The stallion stood as still as a statute of his great ancestor, Eclatant. Cyrus used the horn to pull himself to his feet. He yelled with glee, clearly pleased with himself, and rocked in place.

The assembled courtiers went from gasping to laughing to applauding. Eleanor and Dorian cautiously approached their son. He reached for his mother, and she scooped him up.

"Thank you," she said to Monument. "You saved my baby."

"He's my future king," said Monument. "I will always protect him."

Eleanor wore dancing slippers, but she never had a chance to partake in a waltz or a jig. Too many people wanted to speak with her—to ask after her health, and the children's health, but mostly, Gregory's health. She responded with cheerful vagueness, as if the king hadn't almost dropped her little boy on his head. The repeated sentiments of the gathered nobility as to Prince Cyrus's clear affinity with the unicorns heartened her. Over and over again, she heard how Cyrus embodied the Bond, was a testament to its power, and would surely carry the Desmarais legacy into the next century.

Usually, she retired from such festivities as early as politeness allowed. Tonight, with Gregory making only his brief dramatic appearance, she felt she had to stay. As the guests finally disbursed, she noticed Sylvia in the corner beside one of the buffet tables. Her oldest son, Hector, stood beside her, flush with the excitement of his first formal fest party. He was a tall, comely young man, with his mother's black hair and eyes and the Fleetwood's olive skin. Many young women had noticed him throughout the night. While he had a handsome face, an old title, and a great fortune, those were not the only sources of his appeal.

When Eleanor met him, he smiled at her with genuine admiration. He asked thoughtful questions and listened with interest to her answers. He was quick to laugh and sweetly self-deprecating.

Eleanor said goodbye to the last few revelers. Eliza looked exhausted and Anne Iris looked tipsy, so she gave them leave to retire for the evening. She decided to ask Sylvia if she might assist in the complicated process of shutting down the ballroom. When she had to arrange such affairs herself, she was long in bed by the time the celebration ended. She relied on the staff to ensure the ballroom's restoration to pristine emptiness. She'd heard Sylvia preferred to keep her finger on the party's pulse.

Young Hector squeezed his mother's shoulder as Eleanor approached. "… you need a glass of water," he said, and he went to retrieve one.

"It was a lovely party, Your Grace," Eleanor said.

"It was. I'm glad Gregory made an appearance. It went as well as expected, given the circumstances."

Hector reappeared with a crystal water glass. He bowed as he handed it to his mother. "Your Highness, can I get you a glass of water?"

"No, Hector. But thank you. You're thoughtful. You should be proud of him, Sylvia."

"He is." Sylvia beamed up at her tall, handsome boy. "And I am. Go get some sleep, my love. It was quite a night for you."

"Yes, a jolly good time. Although, I do wish His Majesty could have stayed with us. Is he feeling better, Your Highness?"

"He's tired, as are we all."

"Goodnight, Hec," said Sylvia.

He kissed her cheek. "Sleep well, Mother. I love you. Goodnight, Your Highness." On the way out, he stopped to help a laundress who had spilled a basket of dirty napkins. The girl looked like she might faint when he lifted the basket and set it into her outstretched arms.

"He's a fine lad," said Eleanor.

"Thank you. He's always been a gentle soul. I hope being a rich man doesn't beat that out of him."

"If that's his true heart, it will stay that way—even under a Mendaen silk tunic or a suit of Fire-iron armor." Eleanor faced her stepsister. "Is there anything I can do to help before I retire?"

"No. I'll make sure Mrs. Perkins has the girls return Queen Gemma's wine glasses to the correct cabinet. Gregory won't want them getting mixed in with the everyday ones."

"I didn't know Gregory's mother had special wine glasses. Nor would I know what cabinet should contain them. I supposed that's my way of saying thank you for taking care of all this. I am a truly dismal hostess."

"Perhaps," said Sylvia. "But you're smart enough to let Eliza or Anne Iris take care of most of it. They were very helpful, by the way. Anne Iris only insulted my dress twice."

"I'm sorry. That was rude of her. She's never been one for holding her tongue."

"Nor are you or I. Eliza is the diplomatic one. Like Margaret was when we were small."

Eleanor felt a pang of sadness for her old sister-friend. "I miss her."

"I do too. Although I'm sure you don't believe it."

"I do. I've learned people can feel all sorts of emotions they never show or show emotions they don't feel."

"At these parties, most of the emotions we show aren't true."

"But you're very convincing."

"I have to be. Do you remember, the first party I attended at Eclatant? Right after you left the Brice house."

"The baby viewing for little Melissa Harper. She's all grown up and about to be married, if you can believe that. Time flies. I was jealous of you that day, because all the ladies loved you. I couldn't think of one thing to say to any of them."

"I asked you about Lady Pellerbee's draperies."

"I said I didn't give a damn about curtains, if I recall."

"You did! On one hand I thought you were very rude, and of course, at the time, I wanted nothing more than for those women to love me and detest you. But I also admired you, for speaking your mind."

"I've slowly learned to temper those urges. Ah, those women, how they wished I would drop dead and make room for their daughters."

"They didn't really like me, either." Sylvia paused for a moment, as if weighing whether she should continue. She took a deep breath and kept going. "I forced them to be nice to me by complimenting them and throwing lavish parties. But you remember how they talked behind my back. Called me a glorified prostitute. As if women haven't been marrying old men for money and power for all time, and as if men haven't been carrying on dalliances for longer."

Her vulnerable response surprised Eleanor, but her own equally heartfelt response surprised her more.

"You lived like a woman and a man. I suppose I did too, in my way, with my powerful husband, my books, and my interfering in national affairs." *Might as well be brutally honest, she knows anyway.* "And my infidelity."

The exchange simmered between them. Something was melting, like ice cubes meant to cool down hot soup.

Eleanor cleared her throat. "I hope Lady Pellerbee's draperies are still in her dining room—with the wrong beading."

"I visited her Maliana townhouse a couple years ago. She had the beads re-sewn, but the curtains are still as hideous as ever. She calls them gold, but I'd say they're more a shade of cat piss."

Eleanor laughed out loud. "She wears a wig these days, you know?"

Sylvia joined her. "Of course. Once, at dinner, she sat beside me, and I swear I saw a housefly land on her head and disappear into her wig. I kept watching, all night, to see if it flew out."

"Let me guess—it never did." Eleanor laughed harder.

"It didn't! It was so distracting! I feared it would fall out into my soup." Sylvia wiped her eyes. "Here. Laughing is thirsty work." She offered her water glass to Eleanor.

Eleanor took it. As she sipped, she realized Sylvia wasn't merely giving her a cool drink for a parched throat. It was a peace offering, at least for the moment.

"Thank you, Sylvia," she said as she returned the suddenly symbolic cup. "Your help was invaluable this evening."

"You're welcome, Eleanor." Sylvia gave the glass to a passing servant. "Now you go to bed too. You can take the early shift with Gregory. I plan to sleep until lunchtime."

Eleanor nodded and took her leave. As she walked away, she wondered if Sylvia was watching her, and what was going through her mind. After all these years, they had shared their first laugh together. She thought about Imogene, so frail and ill and oddly contemplative, and wondered if it would make her happy.

Eleanor checked on the children before walking to her own chamber in her stocking feet. She held her scuffed dancing shoes in one hand. The cold marble floor soothed her sore toes. She remembered her glass slippers, so long ago. Glass footwear should be hard and unyielding, but to the contrary, the slippers had spoiled her forever with their clandestine comfort. No shoe had ever molded so perfectly to her feet. She supposed none ever would.

Her chamber door waited for her at the end of a seemingly endless hallway. She picked up her pace, eager to be in bed. From a distance, the man standing beside the door appeared to be an unusually tall guard. As she got closer, torchlight revealed his dress leggings and dark green brocade tunic. She smiled when he stepped out of the shadows. "Oh, Dor. You're still awake. I must tell you; I had the strangest conversation with Sylvia tonight…" Her voice faded as she took measure of his somber, exhausted expression. "Is something wrong?"

"Gregory asked to speak to you before you retire," he said.

"All right." Exhausted as she was, she didn't hesitate. Gregory must be in great pain after tonight's exertions. He probably couldn't sleep. "Are you coming?"

"I'll walk with you and wait to walk you back. He wants to speak with you alone."

The old fear crept up the back of her neck—an ache in an old scar. *We're past all that,* she told herself, but Dorian insisted on accompanying her, so he was thinking the same thing.

She found Gregory alone in his chamber, except for Monument, who stood sentry beside the magically enlarged doorway. Orvid had renewed the spell and strung purple and green curtains across the wide opening. They threw strange shadows on the walls. Gregory lay on his back. He rolled toward her, a grown man tucked under the covers with his hand under his cheek, like a child waiting for a bedtime story. She sat in the chair beside the bed and ran her fingers across his forehead. He was too warm, but not as bad off as last week. When she touched him a few days ago, heat radiated out from under his thick read hair as if his head were a loaf of bread fresh from the oven. His dry, taunt skin was a hard shell covering his vulnerable interior. She'd ran to bathing room and retched into a chamber pot. She expected him to die right then and there, like Nathan had. Somehow, several endless nights and days later, he still held on.

"Hello, Wife," he said softly. He had lost so much weight. His brown eyes were huge in his face—a starved bear who had emerged from hibernation, yet found himself too tired to hunt for game.

"Hello, Husband. Is the pain bad tonight?"

"It is. Sometimes I wonder, is this pain as bad as the pain you endured to bring our children into the world?"

"It's a different kind of pain."

"Describe it for me."

"Well…" She thought back to her children's births. Leticia's was the worst, but the other three had been no stroll in the garden, either. "It feels as if a hot, sharp poker is grinding around in your insides, while someone is simultaneously constricting your guts in a hangman's noose. Oh, and toward the end, you're sure your pelvis will explode, like a split melon. Then there's the tearing—"

He chuckled. "That sounds terrible. Yet you keep doing it. All women do. Even though it might kill you."

"Some of us don't have a choice. But for those that do, in that moment, you think, *maybe I cannot do this*. But the baby and your body show you that you can. It's all worth it, when the child is in your arms."

"This pain is different. It feels sickly and disgusts me. It's not the agony that comes from expelling new life. It's the pain of slowly rotting on the inside. Constant, although it stabs me sometimes, as it did tonight. Thank HighGod for Monument's reflexes."

"You're welcome, sire, as is the prince, my future king," said Monument.

"I'm sorry I almost hurt your son," said Gregory. "I hope you know I would do anything to protect him and his legacy."

"Our son."

Gregory smiled. "Your son. And Dorian's."

Many times, over the years, Eleanor had felt terror in all its iterations. Never, however, had she felt as frightened as she did in that moment. It was the origin of all fear. The visceral fears of childhood combined with the logical rationale of adulthood and told her *yes, yes, you should be terrified, because this is real danger. This is immediate death for your son and your soul mate and, in a distant third place, yourself.*

The white terror induced by his simple statement must have shown in her face. He squeezed her hand. "Eleanor, sweetheart. I know. I have known for some time. I do not reject him or you. Or even Dorian."

"I don't understand." Nothing could have prepared her for this conversation.

"You and Dorian. Eleanor, if ever two people were meant to be together, it is you and him. For a long time, I tried to force myself to think otherwise. That you were both lecherous, ungrateful, terrible people. But in my heart, I knew. You said to me once, it could only have been him."

"I remember," she whispered.

"It should have been him, for you. Long ago. But HighGod had other plans for all of us."

Eleanor's voice left her. It flew away, borne on his words—a bit of dandelion fluff with no substance. Instead of trying to catch the potential responses floating above her head in nimbus clouds of inadequacy, she burst into tears.

She covered her face with both hands and sobbed. Monument tossed his head and snorted. His silky muzzle snuffled the side of her neck. She leaned against his hard cheek. Her tears rolled off his impervious coat and plunked into her lap, fat liquid blobs of relief encasing years of fear and guilt.

Finally, she shuddered, sucked in a breath or two, and lowered her hands. Gregory watched her. His eyes were reddish, as if his daughter had cast a weak spell over him. "I'm sorry I've made you so unhappy all these years."

Eleanor started crying again. "Gregory—no, please. I've done you wrong myself. Terribly. I allowed myself to fall in love with Dorian before we'd even been married a year. I never gave us a chance. I pushed you away when you wanted to make amends. I lied to you. Even when you didn't kill us the first time, we couldn't stop ourselves. Dorian is your best friend—"

"You couldn't stop yourselves. Do you hear what you're saying?"

"Well, I suppose we could have—"

"No. The two of you were flames burning toward one another on a single wick. I think this is how it was meant to be. I wish it had happened differently, but I don't see any other way the son of you and Dorian could end up being my heir."

"Stop saying that. What if someone heard you?"

"It's only you, and me, and Monument, and he already knows."

She pressed her fingers to her temples. "Please. I don't understand."

"Do you remember when I borrowed your kaleidoscope?"

She nodded.

"I thought, perhaps I could use it somehow, since you said it would show me important things. I asked Orvid to see what he could make of it. He allowed it to see into the past."

The vision on Alenestra made more sense. Natalie had directed it, but Orvid had given her the means to do so. "Only a magician as powerful as Orvid could alter the Oracle's spellwork."

"I'm blessed to have him in my service," Gregory said. "I asked the kaleidoscope to show me how to be a great king. I was afraid, especially after my injury. Of course, no one knew at the time how bad it truly was. Or no one wanted to tell me."

"We wanted you to remain hopeful."

"I know. The witches told me a calm mind would help me heal, but peace eluded me. I worried over the ogres and Oliver through the fog of their tonics. I worried about Natalie, and even though your plan to move the beasts and avoid war sounded promising, I worried about our armies. I wanted the kaleidoscope to give me a magical answer, so I might live up to the responsibility my father left me."

"What did you see?"

"All manner of random scenes. I saw the escaped ogres sitting outside of a cave, somewhere in the mountains. Villagers on the outskirts Navigation Ford. Some visions from the past. My father as a young man, at a joust. Myself and Dorian, soon after we met, drinking ale in a tavern when we snuck out of the palace. I saw you, Eleanor, sitting in the hayloft at your father's house, reading a book that looked to weigh more than you did. You were about fourteen. There was something of Ticia in you. Like a gangly filly."

"I wouldn't have turned many heads in those days, Rosemary's spell or not."

"We all have those awkward times in life."

"Not Sylvia. She was always lovely." She cleared her throat. "But I assume you eventually saw something of consequence."

"I saw you and Dorian, at the circus at Gammonreil. I watched you enter the tent. I saw you come together."

She felt her face, already red and puffy from crying, flame anew. She must surely resemble a squashed strawberry pie.

"It was painful, of course, but fortunately, you both had to keep your clothes on."

"Gregory, I'm sorry."

"At that time, wife, I myself was ravishing your eternally un-awkward stepsister. I didn't think of you, once, and I'm sure you didn't think of me. You don't need to apologize." He rubbed his stubble-covered jaw. "Then it showed me the two of you, in your chamber, with Cyrus. Just after he was born. I saw the way you looked at each other. The way Dorian held him. I know how a father holds his firstborn son." He closed his eyes and kept talking. "Of course, for a moment, I felt pain, and even some of the old rage. But then I realized—no. This is what the kaleidoscope is showing me. How to be a great king."

"What do you mean?"

"You're his mother. Dorian is his father. The two of you are the greatest minds in my realm. Dorian is the strongest, fastest, and the bravest. You are the kindest, the most compassionate, and the most dedicated to the people. Who else, but a child born of the two of you, should lead this kingdom?"

Eleanor's hands shook as she poured herself a cup of water. She heard what Gregory said. Still, she wanted to peek behind the chairs and curtains. Someone might be waiting to leap out, accuse her of treason, and lob off her head where she stood.

Who would it be? One of the Unicorn Guard? Orvid Jones? Perhaps Monument will skewer me with his horn. Or maybe it will be Sylvia. She bit back hysterical giggling. *She'll stab me with a steak knife. Or a crochet needle. Or a long hair pin.*

"It's probably unsettling to hear me say all this," said Gregory. "Do you want something stiffer to drink?"

"No." She turned around to face him. "But I am afraid, Gregory. What if you're trying to trick me?"

"I can see why you might think that. Come here. I'll explain to you how we came to be here, discussing your son's ascendancy to the throne."

She returned to her chair. She sat with her cup clasped on her lap, as if the two of them were about to engage in a tea party gossip session.

"After Nathan died, I wasn't sure I could carry on. The grief and guilt were terrible enough. But I also felt I'd failed my family. My father pressed me, day and night, to make sure you had another son. *Clearly, she's capable!* he'd say. In his eyes, the fault lay with me. And I agreed with him."

"Is such a lack really the fault of the man or the wife? The Godsmen would say children arrive when HighGod wills it."

"HighGod, yes. This is… it's very hard to talk about…"

"Then must you?"

"Yes. Yes. I must." He took a deep breath. "I should never have struck you, Eleanor. And I know there were times, in those years before Dorian left for Svelya, when I… *forced* you."

Eleanor's stomach dropped. This was indeed a difficult topic. "You're my husband, Gregory. You have your rights."

"So the Godsman say I do, but does that make it any better? Any different from a man who forces himself on a stranger?"

"I suppose not," she whispered.

"Forgive me," he said. "Forgive me for all of it, but mostly, for the receiving room."

The incident came back to her like a reminder of a nightmare.

Gregory taking her from behind beside his father's throne, just after he confronted her about the affair. "I… I don't know what to say."

"The months leading up to it were bad enough, what with our grief over Nathan and my suspicions, but I lost my mind when Abram Finley told me about you and Dorian. I honestly don't know how I didn't kill you both right then and there."

"I know it."

"It was a disgusting act, what I did to you that day. One of many. But I think that was the worst. When the rage faded, I was still angry, but I also felt great shame."

Eleanor bit her lip and thought of Imogene. "Someone recently told me that rage is an emotion that cannot last."

"I cursed us, Eleanor. HighGod wouldn't give me a son through you after how I acted. We both knew we'd have to keep trying, of course. But my heart told me it wouldn't happen. I thought maybe my guilt had redeemed me when Cyrus was born, but…." He shrugged. "Redemption came another way."

"I forgive you, Gregory," she said. "You're telling me Cyrus is safe, and I can forgive you anything."

"Thank you…. That lightens the load of my overburdened heart." He exhaled. "Can you get me a shot of whiskey? It sharpens my senses and dulls the pain." She obliged by retrieving a jug of whiskey from the cart outside his study. She poured hefty shot into a small Fire-iron cup and handed it to him. "But… where was I?"

"Explaining the Bond."

"Yes, right. So, as I came to believe I'd doomed our union, I wondered…. what would happen if I *didn't* have another son? Or a legitimate one, anyway."

"Sylvia's child."

"You can't blame me for wondering, Eleanor. The survival of the kingdom was at stake."

"I don't."

"I decided I needed to understand the Bond. Could it be passed through a female heir? Or an illegitimate male heir? In three hundred years, we've never faced this challenge. A male heir always existed. King Justin Desmarais, Caleb the First's grandson, had three sons. The Sage branch of the family, you know, but that line is dead now."

"I'm surprised there aren't more Desmarais then. Aren't we the only ones left?"

"In the early days, we tended to die in battle. Two of Justin's sons died in the Second Svelyan war. Sickness. Babies who don't see their first birthday. So it went, over three centuries. My father had only two sisters. My mother had two boys who died within a few days of birth, and me and Matilda."

"Did you go to the library to learn more about the Bond?"

He chuckled. "That's what you would have done or Dorian. But, in this case, you wouldn't have found much information. You know the unicorns rarely discuss the Bond, so it's all theory and speculation by magicians and scholars. Perhaps the kings themselves have never felt much need to understand it. It just exists—like my own heartbeat. No, I went to the source. I asked Vigor, the night I found out my father died. Before we left Svelya. He knew how desperate I was. He tried to explain it to me."

Despite her fear, Eleanor's intellectual curiosity won out. "You actually spoke to a unicorn about the Bond? What did he tell you?"

"We stayed up all night discussing it. But it comes down to this. There are three elements in the Bond. The royal family. The unicorns. The dragons. So, there are three requirements in the ones who hold it. First, and most simple, it must be someone with the Desmarais name. Second, the individual must be the king's intended heir."

"You mean the king must choose him?"

"In a way, yes. The king must see that person as the next ruler—or at least a capable ruler. The king must believe in the heir."

"What is the last?"

"The person must be worthy."

"How do you know if he's worthy?"

"Even Vigor had trouble explaining that part. It has to do with love and respect for the Bond. And ability. Or potential ability, if the intended heir is very young."

"So, if there were someone with the Desmarais name, that the king intended, the unicorns might find that person wanting? The Bond would cease to exist?"

"Perhaps. Although, if the king saw more than one member of my family as a potential ruler, perhaps the unicorns could reject one and accept the other." He winced and shifted his infected leg. "It's simply never happened, in three hundred years, that the king did not have a male heir the unicorns deemed worthy."

"You're saying Cyrus has your name, and you see him as the heir..."

"You've seen how the unicorns love him. From the first."

"It's true," said Monument. "Your Highness, your son is small, but the Bond is strong in him. I have always known it. I knew when he was still in your belly."

Eleanor thought she'd cried herself out, but she felt more tears. "So even if he is not your son by blood..."

"He's my heir, because of who he is, and because I want him to be, and so do the unicorns."

Eleanor covered her nose. She felt something bump her shoulders and turned to see Monument holding a silk handkerchief in his mouth. She took it and dabbed at her eyes. "Why did Vigor never explain it to anyone else? Why don't the unicorns speak of it?"

"The right person never asked the right questions," said Monument. "Not until His Majesty asked my father."

Eleanor faced the stallion beside her. "I didn't know Vigor was your father."

"Another unasked question," said Monument, with a hint of amusement.

"I loved his father like a brother," said Gregory. "Of course I chose his son as my next companion. Just as I chose your son as the next king. But Eleanor, if HighGod forbid, something ever happens to Cyrus, I want you to understand who lives today and is part of the Bond. Monument, tell her."

"You, Your Majesty. Leticia Desmarais. Natalie Desmarais. Either could rule."

Eleanor swelled with pride and the knowledge she had long sought—the heir did not have to be male.

"Cyrus Desmarais." Monument nuzzled Eleanor's cheek. "And Eleanor Desmarais."

"But I'm only a Desmarais by marriage, not blood."

"We've seen blood does not make a member of this family or seal the Bond."

She slumped in her chair.

"I have not decided exactly which direction the line of succession will follow. Clearly, Natalie being a witch raises some legitimate concerns. I know Leticia has no interest in ruling."

"She told you how she feels about being queen?" asked Eleanor.

"Yes. She's rather desperate to avoid the crown. But we both know the crown falls on one's head when HighGod wills it. I wanted you to know that you're of the Bond. As much as I am."

"What of Sylvia's son?"

"Before I understood the Bond, I wondered if that child might have a part to play—if he were my blood kin. But Monument does not see him as a part of the Bond. Whether he is my blood child or not, even if I gave him my name, he cannot rule."

"Is he your child, Gregory?"

"I suppose only Sylvia really knows. She's asked me to acknowledge him. I always told her I would not acknowledge him while there was still a chance I'd have an heir through my true wife."

"That must have been painful for her."

"Yes, but Sylvia is a pragmatic person. She knows I'll favor a legitimate heir over a bastard. Regardless, she will understand tonight that even if he is my son, he will not rule. There will be no challenging Cyrus's rule."

"Don't tell her about Cy, please. She might try to use it against him."

"I will not. No one but you, me, Monument, and Dorian will ever know his true parentage."

"And Chou Chou." Eleanor winced apologetically.

"That bird. I should have known he'd be party to the greatest secret Cartheigh has ever known. But I also know his loyalty to you. He may be unable to keep his beak closed about common gossip, but I trust he'll keep this to himself."

"He will. You could pluck out all his feathers and serve him on a platter, and he'd never tell."

"No one else can know. Not his sisters. Not even Rosemary."

"I agree."

He closed his eyes, and the color left his face.

"Gregory, this is too much. You must rest."

"Just pour me some purple tonic. The one made from mushrooms that tastes like mud."

She retrieved a small bottle from the apothecary closet and poured him a strong dose.

"Talk to Sylvia tomorrow," she said.

"No, it must be tonight." He opened his eyes, and the pain in them made her heart ache. "I don't know how much time I have."

"Don't say that."

"Eleanor, get Sylvia. I know you have no fondness for her—"

"I sense we've started to heal some old wounds while caring for you." She thought about her conversation with Sylvia that evening and her stepsister's attentive nursing of Gregory since she'd arrived from Harveston. "Not *your* wounds, unfortunately. Those between us."

"I don't know if I'm capable of loving someone the way you and

Dorian love one another. I don't spend enough time thinking about it. But she's smarter than she lets on—and more tender. She'll do anything for her children, just like you. She probably deserved more than I could give her, but I do love her. I owe her a final answer."

"If that's what you wish, I'll find her now. Will you speak to Dorian about all this?"

"You talk to him. I want our last conversations to be like our first. Laughter, boasting. Simple man-talk."

She wanted to tell him he had years of conversations with Dorian ahead of him, but in her heart, she knew it wasn't true.

"I love him, Eleanor. I still loved him, even when I hated him. He is the person I've held the dearest, for the longest, in my life. Perhaps I love him more than I loved my father. Now you will have a chance to make him happy. I believe you will do it."

She once again couldn't speak. She nodded, kissed Gregory's forehead, and fled. As expected, Dorian leaned against the wall outside the door. He stood up straight when he saw her. She closed the door behind her and collapsed into his arms.

"What...dear HighGod, Eleanor...is he angry?"

"He knows," she whispered. "About the child."

Before Dorian could panic, she shook her head. "No—no. It's not like that. I promise you. It's good."

"But you're crying." The anguish on his face pulled at her, but Gregory had just forgiven her for treason and declared her bastard son would be his heir, and she had to do as he'd commanded.

"I'll explain, I promise. But we must get Sylvia. Oh, Dorian," she said as she dragged him down the corridor. "Our boy is safe, and he will be king."

CHAPTER 20

A TRUE QUEEN

THE NEXT DAY MARKED the fifth morning since Eleanor's visit to the Island of Ello. Orvid Jones left the doorway expanded, because Gregory added Monument to his little group of attendants. Eleanor, Dorian, Orvid Jones, Sylvia, and the unicorn stallion kept constant watch over the king while witches and servants bustled in and out. Despite the width and breadth of the king's chamber, it felt claustrophobic in the room. Eleanor got the depressing impression that the witches had given up trying to heal him and were simply managing his pain.

Despite the Fest, and Gregory's condition, Eleanor decided she must take an afternoon to visit the Oracle and talk to her about what she'd seen in the kaleidoscope. It might have significance for their efforts to move the ogres, nuances she couldn't see. She had yet to decide if she wanted to discuss their possibly familial relations. If she were related, Natalie would be related.

Is that better for her or worse? More dangerous or less?

As she often did, she stared out the carriage window, lost in thought, as the sun crept toward its summer pinnacle. She desperately wanted *someone* to master the spellwork required to interpolate the ogres to Ello Island. Simultaneously, she fervently wished Natalie would fail in her effort. *That's the whole truth of it—I want it to happen, but I don't want Natalie involved.* How wholly unfair of HighGod, or the ancient marauder's gods, or whatever force or being controlled fate and magic, that she must wrestle with such juxtaposed desires.

She shared her musings with Chou Chou, who flittered in and out the open window. "Juxtaposed desires do seem to be a recurring theme in the sometimes-melodramatic saga of your life," he said.

Eleanor tugged one of his feet, and he tumbled onto the seat cushions. "That's the pot calling the cauldron black."

She left Chou flittering about the Abbey's main courtyard, much to the entertainment of the youngest witches. *Natalie should be with them,* she thought. *Not buzzing between Maliana and Nestra and a frozen, inhospitable island destined to provide a homeland for some of the foulest creatures on HighGod's earth.*

She found Rosemary outside the door to the Oracle's sickroom. The two women embraced. Rosemary offered Eleanor her favorite treat—a bag of chocolate-covered almonds.

"You got my note then," said Eleanor. "I'm sorry for the delay."

"No, did you write? The Oracle told me to be prepared for a royal visitor today. Since it wasn't going to be the king, HighGod help him, I knew it would be you." Rosemary took her arm. "I told her what you saw as best I could. Natalie visited her and also spoke of it. She's very ill. Prepare yourself. I believe her mind is still a new razor, but the rest of her is dull and rustier than ever."

Eleanor opened the door. "I lost my first son to the Burning, and I'm currently watching my husband die of an infected ogre wound. The sight of illness doesn't frighten me."

Indeed, she found the Oracle much diminished, even from her usual inhumanely depleted state. Eleanor saw every skinny vein under her translucent skin. Blood pumped weakly through those fragile vessels, thanks to the extraordinary effort of a heart that should have stopped beating long ago. She rested on her side in her huge bed. She looked up at Eleanor with watery eyes. Since her visit to Ello Island, those pale irises now reminded Eleanor of the washed-out sky above the stone altar.

Could this truly be the little girl she'd seen? That child had been so full of life. Her cheeks looked ready to burst with it, like perfectly ripe cherries. Did the same heart beat in this concave chest, encased in those brittle bones?

The Oracle's mouth twitched in recognition. "Sit, Eleanor," she said, in the scratchy voice of an unoiled hinge.

Eleanor sat in the rickety red chair beside the bed and inhaled the smell of lavender. Somehow, the witches covered any smell of decay or impending death with the Oracle's favorite scent. Eleanor would always associate lavender with the sound of the bubbling Watching Pool. The enchanted water lapped softly at the sieve's edges. Peaceful sounds and smells, to ease the fear of dying.

"I am not afraid of dying," the Oracle said.

"Oh. Can you read my mind?"

"No, but my current condition makes others think of their own deaths, so I try to reassure."

"Wise One, Rosemary told you of the vision I saw on Ello. There was a child—"

"I was that child."

"You remember?"

"When Rosemary first told me, I remembered only bits and pieces. But then your daughter called me by my true name. Haybet. I could hear *my* mother calling me." Her mouth twitched again in the hint of a smile. "I smelled the mud. There was *so much* mud. It sucked at our shoes as we walked across the dunes at low tide to the ships. The ships took us across the water to another land."

"Do you remember other things? Or just that day?"

"I forgot over many centuries. My early life is coming back to me faster than it left me, but there are still many things that feel just out of reach."

"Little Haybet...ah, you... left us a message. Do you know why?"

"I think it's just as I said back then. The gods want you to know you're doing the right thing by taking the ogres to Ello. My people left it because the land had soured to humans—as if the island itself detested us. It wasn't meant for our kind."

"What gods, Wise One?"

The Oracle lifted her frail shoulders in a tiny shrug. "Back then, I would have said the gods of Ello. We believed in the Grandmother and the Grandfather, and they had many powerful children. For the past thousand years or so, I would reference the HighGod you know. Even the ogres, they have their own god, vicious as they believe he is. Or perhaps the message came from someplace that has nothing to do with gods and is beyond our comprehension. Whatever it was, *something* wanted me to leave that message. I, for one, feel much better about your plan to move the ogres after getting a message from myself."

"It is good to know something bigger than all of us is blessing our endeavor."

"That doesn't mean it is guaranteed to be successful. Or it won't result in some death and destruction anyway. Even gods can be wrong."

"I worry about my daughter."

"You have good reason. She has an important role to play. Important roles don't imply happy endings."

"Can we not protect her? Agnes is close to being able to perform this magic."

"As are five other witches in the Abbey."

"So Natalie won't have to do it!"

"Eleanor, as of today, only Natalie has perfected the spell. Agnes cannot be overly involved in the ogre interpolation, lest Mr. Oliver find out. Even if we rid ourselves of the ogres, we have not necessarily rid ourselves of him. We need the information only she can give us. Natalie is brave and strong, and whether you believe it or not, she enjoys this work."

"She seemed strange on Ello. Distant. Tired."

"Magic can be tiring. Like a brisk walk makes one weary but also invigorates. If she's distant, perhaps you simply don't understand her much anymore."

A few fat tears plopped into Eleanor's lap. Whether she understood Natalie or not, she still adored her. She thought about Haybet and Desi's obvious love for one another.

No matter what I do, Natalie's power will make her special, even among the witches. If Natalie is the Oracle's blood kin, every precaution will be taken to protect her. The Oracle loved her sister. Maybe she—herself—will protect her sister's hundred times great-granddaughter.

The Oracle gently cleared her perpetually scratchy throat, as if uncomfortable with Eleanor's display of emotion. "I imagine it is difficult to hear me say that—"

"Do you remember Desi?" Eleanor asked. "Your sister."

The Oracle froze. Her mouth hung open, as if Eleanor had lit a blazing bonfire before her face, and the flames had hypnotized her.

Eleanor was reminded of the renegade catfishes' blank gaze, until Hazelbeth's eyes returned to sharp focus. They were palest blue and fiercely alive, not black and flat and soulless.

"My *sister.*" She squinted at Eleanor. The bonfire returned, and this time, the smoke confused her. "What trickery is this?" She pulled the blanket to her chin with her claw-like fingers. "You died so long ago. My heart hurt. It wasn't supposed to, but it did."

"How did she die?" asked Eleanor. It might have been cruel, but she did it anyway.

"She bled out, in Svelya, upon the birth of her second daughter. Oh, sweet Desi. Why have you come to me? Can you not rest?" The Oracle shook her head, as if trying to follow a confusing timeline.

"I am not Desi. I am still Eleanor Desmarais, Queen of Cartheigh. But if you look into my face, you will see something of your sister."

She leaned toward the old woman with her eyes wide. When she stared at someone, the person always noticed the oddity in her eyes. For the first time in her life, she wanted someone to recognize it. She scooted closer, until most of her bottom hung off the end of the chair. She braced both hands on the smooth, cool coverlet.

Hazelbeth flinched, as if Eleanor had smacked her. She mumbled to herself in a language Eleanor didn't understand. A tongue unspoken for several millennia. Her eyes rolled in her head. They rocked into place and settled on Eleanor. The awareness returned.

"You have my sister's nose, and the shape of her face. But most of all, you have her eyes."

"Is that a coincidence?"

"Child, you know it is not, or you would not have raised it to me. To think that Rosemary and I spent so much time wondering about you and your destiny. Were your eyes a magical sign? Did they signify good luck or ill? It seems they *are* a sign. A bright one. Right under my nose. I didn't see it."

"What do they signify?"

"That you're of my blood. Through my sister, and her daughters, and their daughters, and whatever daughters they had long after I left Svelya, who must have made their way to Cartheigh. I have forgotten how we all got here, but the child will have eons to understand our history."

"Natalie," said Eleanor. "If she's your heir, you must protect her."

"We always protect our own. No witch is disposable. But she's a child of my sister. Hmmm."

Eleanor didn't expect any declarations of love from the Oracle. She'd have to be content with a thoughtful sigh.

The Oracle closed her eyes. When she started snoring softly, Eleanor knew the visit had ended. Eleanor tentatively believed she'd bought her precious daughter the Oracle's special protection. A victory of sorts. Still, in her reverse contemplative carriage ride on the way home, Hazelbeth's words came back to her.

She will have eons to understand her own history.

Eleanor stroked Chou Chou. He perched on the door handle, worn out from entertaining the children. They'd fed him a handful of enchanted, extra sweet gumdrops. He proceeded to fly about in loops and circles for an hour. His stomach was tolerating none of it well. He stuck his red and blue head out the window, as if he needed the passing air to keep the gumdrops in his little round belly.

"Ugh. The green ones," he said and closed his eyes.

As the carriage rattled on, Eleanor realized she'd probably just sealed her daughter's fate by trying to protect her. Condemned her to a life that would last thousands of years. She'd outlive everyone she knew, even Dasha, and she would probably forget them all.

Once again, HighGod and his or her minions had vexed her with contrarian purposes. Eleanor told Chou Chou everything, and she would never wish a bellyache upon him, but she was glad he hadn't asked her any inquisitive questions. She didn't much feel like talking.

Two days later, Gregory Caleb Smithwick Leo Desmarais, Gregory the Second, King of Cartheigh and Keeper of the Great Bond, died in his sleep.

Praise HighGod, it was a peaceful passing, and his final hours gave his family and friends time to come together and see him on his way. When Eleanor returned to Eclatant after visiting the Oracle, she learned Dorian and Orvid Jones had moved Gregory to the Paladine, at his request.

With his final words, he recognized the Bond. "Let me die in the company of my brethren," he said.

He drifted in and out of consciousness as they lay him on a travois behind Monument. Dorian hooked the front corners to a girth around the stallion's broad belly. Dorian and Orvid each carried a rear corner. The unicorn and the two men, all beloved by the king, were early pallbearers. They delivered him to his death, as they'd soon escort him to his funeral.

The Paladins cleaned a roomy stall in a quiet corner of the brood mare barn. They settled him there, amidst the sweet smell of hay and oats. The unicorns watched over him. They peered over their stall doors and through the Paladine's wide windows. He rested silently, lulled by their gentle, compassionate nickering. His chest rose and fell softly, but otherwise he didn't stir. Not even when Leticia sobbed noisily or Orvid knocked over a rake.

Dorian sat cross-legged beside the travois. In a low voice, he reminded Gregory of the laughter and adventures of their youth. Orvid sniffled as he anxiously paced the aisle between the stalls. Rosemary and Natalie joined their vigil, but Eleanor didn't bring Cyrus to the barn. He wouldn't understand any of it, and he'd crawl through the hay and try to eat bits of tack. She wanted to quietly attend her daughters while their father left this world.

Leticia and Eleanor sat on a hay bale. Leticia leaned against Eleanor. She cried and dozed on and off. Natalie huddled on the ground. She rested against her mother's knees. Gregory's breathing grew softer and slower, the retreating tide of a dying hurricane. Dorian placed a hand on his chest.

"Greg?" he whispered.

Gregory drew one hitching breath and exhaled. His broad chest went still.

Dorian turned to Eleanor and her girls. He didn't say anything; his tears spoke for him.

Ticia let out a wail and buried her head in Eleanor's shoulder. Natalie's small, serious face crumbled. She turned away from her dead father and sobbed into Eleanor's skirts. She was not yet so much a witch that she'd forgotten her Poppa's love.

Tears coursed down Eleanor's face in a cleansing flow, like salty ocean water drying out a healing wound. Gregory the Second ruled for less than two years, but Eleanor would make sure the history books remembered him as a great king. Not because of his strength or his prowess with the sword, although she'd surely proclaim the story of how he singlehandedly crippled an ogre to save his men and his unicorns, which led to his own early death. She'd make sure Cartheigh remembered him as man who loved the Bond and put it before his own pride.

As she held her daughters while they mourned, she thanked HighGod for Gregory Desmarais. He had made her laugh and made her miserable. He had given her children and mourned their losses. Gregory, whom she had loved and hated; who saved her and trapped her. The husband she forgave, as he had forgiven her.

That evening, Eleanor sent the girls to stay with Anne Iris and her children at her townhouse on the outskirts of Maliana. Natalie wasn't ready to return to the Abbey, and Leticia couldn't stand to be alone in her bedroom at Eclatant. She sent Chou Chou for comfort and comic relief. Anne Irish promised to invite Eliza and her brood for the evening. They would play games, serve cake, and do everything possible to rouse the princesses' spirits. Eleanor wished she could sit with them all night, but the succession must be addressed. Eleanor, Dorian, and Orvid Jones met in the candlelit library around ten o'clock at night. A few scholarly magicians still poured over their books as if it were a bright Sunday morning. Eleanor passed Jan as she walked toward the quiet, windowless corner that housed dusty mathematics books.

"Your Highness," said Jan. "I'm terribly sorry about the king." She sat at a circular desk. Two candelabras cast light over her piles of books and old parchment. She'd placed feathers and strips of leather in the volumes as makeshift bookmarks. The books resembled boxy chapel bonnets.

"Thank you," said Eleanor. "It's good to see you here, even at this late hour."

"I want to be helpful. I will compile my notes on the ogres. We can discuss them whenever you can."

"Of course. It stands to be a difficult, busy time. The funeral… and Prince Cyrus's coronation. I have even less time to focus on the ogre interpolation, and now its commencement is imminent. Any relevant facts you find will be helpful."

"I also wanted to show you this, Your Highness." She held a book called *Sundry Existence Theorems* under the candlelight. There was a door in the cover. It looked at least a few hundred years old. "I found it in the basement while looking for more information on the ancient marauders, on the *Olde Magick* shelves. Since Mr. Oliver wants to break into other worlds, I picked it up."

"I didn't realize anyone wrote about such topics."

"It's the only such book I found. It seemed apropos, so I read through it."

"Does it vouch for the existence of these the other worlds?"

"I believe so. If I'm understanding correctly, ancient magicians may have known how to open such doors."

"Really? If that's true, the Oracle will surely want to know."

"I'm not certain, Your Highness. It's confusing. Heavy with magical theory and religious philosophy, and even natural philosophy."

Eleanor took the book. "Fascinating. I won't have much time to read anything myself, but I will send it to the Oracle and Rosemary."

"Eleanor!" Dorian's voice had the urgent tone people use in libraries and chapels and while babies are sleeping. A simultaneous shout and whisper. He leaned around a bookshelf and beckoned to her.

She held up one finger—*give me a moment*— and hugged Jan. She tucked the book into her roomy satchel, where she planned to deposit important documents about Gregory's death and Cyrus's coronation. She trotted past more bookshelves and tables. She sat beside Dorian and across from Orvid. "Forgive the delay. Jan wanted to offer her condolences—"

"Your Highness." Dorian put a hand over hers.

She glanced between the two men. They looked terrified, frankly. She glanced over her shoulder, as if a tradacta or an ogre stood behind her, ready to bite her head off. "Yes?" she asked.

"I don't know how to tell you this. Orvid, can you please?" Dorian's hand shook.

Her stomach cramped. "What is it? Cyrus? Oh, HighGod, the girls—"

"No." Orvid shook his head. "It's nothing like that. We must tell you..."

"We are as shocked as you will be. It's completely unexpected." Dorian ran his free hand over his head. Morbid *deja vu* made her contorting stomach twist into a sailor's knot. Had Gregory died and left Dorian not only a dukedom, a fortune, and a unicorn, but his penchant for harassing his hair?

Orvid leaned toward her. "We're not sure how to tell you—"

"By the Bond, one of you had better spit it out soon, or my head will explode like one of the Covey's enchanted soap bubbles!"

Dorian flopped backwards in his chair. His knee banged the table. He grunted and rubbed it. It was rather out of character, as he was usually a portrait of masculine elegance. Orvid took a rolled parchment from his own satchel and slid it across the table.

For a moment, Eleanor didn't want to open it. Perhaps Gregory had decided he didn't forgive her and had named another heir. Or written her son out of the line of succession entirely. Anxious curiosity overcame her, and she unrolled it with trembling fingers.

As she read, her eyebrows came together, as if Leticia had sewn them into one of her needlepoint pictures. Her heartbeat slammed against her chest.

Gregory hadn't written Cyrus out of the succession, but he had, in a way, chosen another heir.

"This says I am to be queen," she said.

"Yes," said Dorian.

"Queen in my own right. Not Cyrus's protector, or stewardess, but the true and lawful *queen.*"

Orvid nodded. "Until your own death, or you decide Cyrus is ready to rule. The choice is yours."

"This doesn't make sense. I'm not his heir. No king of Cartheigh has ever made his *wife* his heir."

"Gregory always did like to do things his way," said Dorian, "and stir the cauldron."

"This isn't funny, Dorian," said Eleanor. "Are you sure this is Gregory's true will?"

"I sat with him as he wrote it two nights ago, after he spoke with the Duchess of Harveston," said Orvid. "I saw him write it out with his own hand."

"Yes, it is his writing, but... was he of sound mind?"

"Did you think he was, when he talked to you that night?" asked Orvid.

"Yes. In pain, but perfectly lucid. But he spoke to me of *Cyrus* being his heir."

Dorian scooted closer to her. "But didn't he also tell you who *else* carries the Bond?"

"Monument told me. Gregory, but he's gone now. Leticia, Natalie, and Cyrus. He did say me— it's true. But I didn't imagine he'd make me *queen!* Not when there are three other potential rulers!" Panic set in. "What do we do about it?"

"Do about it? We follow the king's wishes," said Orvid.

"But...I don't know if I can... what will the High Council say?" She was near tears. It was all too much, to lose Gregory and be given this shocking news that all his responsibility would fall to her. "I'm afraid. I don't know how to be a true queen, not just a queen consort."

"No one knows, really, until he—she—is the ruler," said Orvid.

"I wanted this for Nathan, then Leticia, and now Cyrus. I never wanted it for myself."

Dorian took her hand again. "Look how Gregory rose to the occasion when he became king. We all knew he had greatness inside him, but there were legitimate questions as to whether it would ascend high enough to be let out." The tenderness in his eyes pulled at her. "Your greatness has been on display for years."

"It's true, Your Highness," said Orvid, softly. "You know how I've admired you since we met. There was a time when we were not friends—"

"You had your reasons," said Eleanor.

"It was difficult for me to comprehend… what is between you and the duke. It felt like betrayal of a promise and a duty larger than both of you. I still don't understand it. But I cannot deny the greatness in either of you. His Majesty, before he passed on, he forgave you. I know he's right in this choice."

"Cyrus is a baby," said Dorian. "It will be many years before he can rule. You're a historian, Eleanor. The old books are full of young rulers who lost their crowns before they reached maturity, what with those in power scrambling for influence. It's brilliant of Gregory, really. If you're queen in your own right, and not just lord protector, Cyrus's rule is more secure, not less. While he's growing up, the most capable person in the country will prepare the way for him."

"With our undying loyalty," said Orvid, "and support."

"Eleanor," said Dorian. "Think about all the good you can do. You'll be in full command of the crown's charitable endeavors."

"You're saying that to tempt me—"

"But it's true!"

Something stirred in her chest. "I can rebuild Queen Camille's..."

"You can build a Queen Camille's in every city in Cartheigh."

"But there is so much more that goes into ruling a country."

"You can manage all of it."

She clasped his hands between hers and leaned her head on his shoulder. Orvid looked away, but he didn't reprimand them.

"Dorian, is this really happening?"

"Do you remember when Leticia was born, what you said to me while you lay on that birthing bed?"

"I said, *I can't do this.*"

"What did I say?" he asked.

"You said, *you can, and you shall.*"

Dorian kissed her gently, and she knew what she would do. For her country, and for her son. Even if it was selfish, she'd do it for herself. For her mother, her daughters, Rosemary, and all the other women who were taught to doubt themselves.

"All right. Chief Magician. Your Grace. For the love I bear my country, and with love in my heart for my late husband and respect for his decision, I accept the crown."

Orvid exhaled and took the scroll from her. "HighGod bless the Bond," he said. "And HighGod bless Her Majesty."

Eleanor didn't sleep that night. The next morning she felt like a haggard new mother with a baby at her breast. The heavy bags under her bloodshot eyes were mushy rotten apples, weighing down her entire face. Chou had begged her to sit in a steamy bathing room with soothing compresses on her face, but she didn't have time for such luxuries. She must make sure she looked the part she was trying to play, so Pansy started her elaborate toilette before dawn.

She entered the High Council Chamber, resplendent in a purple, green, and gold silk gown with a three-foot train. Pansy had perched one of her most elaborate crowns atop thick coils of upswept hair. She took measure of the High Council. They exuded tension and anticipation, but not outright panic. Surely, they assumed she appeared solely in her capacity as the late king's widow and the new king's mother. Dorian already told her the High Council speculated that he, the Duke of Brandling, would be named Lord Protector. A predictable, comfortable outcome for most of the assembled lords.

Once Orvid Jones read Gregory's will out loud, all signs of contentment or resignation disappeared. Faces paled, lips locked, and arms crossed over elegant brocaded tunics. She stood before an agitated contingent of the most important men in the kingdom. They included two generals, the Royal Treasurer, some ministers and magicians, and the senior-most Godsman of Humility Chapel. Others were granted the privilege of membership based on the size of their fortunes (the twenty-five-year-old Barron of Solsea) or their breadth of their experience (ninety-year-old Sir Quincy Smithwick, Gregory's great uncle on his mother's side). Some were a mongrel mix of position, wealth, and experience, like the wildly wealthy Duke of Sage, Randall Porter. He was a distinguished, iron-haired nobleman who doubled as the Ambassador to Talesse. Not one of these distinguished fellows looked pleased to learn she'd be ruling over them all.

They were too dignified and savvy to announce their surprise and displeasure, but wary glances flitted across the Fire-iron High Council table like signal fires. It seemed silly to have worried about the bags under her eyes. They cared more about what was (or wasn't) between her legs.

Dorian and Orvid didn't give the High Council time to ask many questions. They hustled their new queen from the High Council Chamber with excuses of bereavement and funeral planning. The whispering started as Eleanor approached the door, as unsettling as the first bold buzzing of early evening cicadas. She tugged at her tight-capped sleeves on the walk to her room. A bead of sweat slipped over her collarbone. It tickled between her breasts before the thick satin absorbed it.

"Damn this summer heart," she said to Dorian. "I must remove these clothes. I can't breathe."

His objective response to the mention of clothing removal clarified his own unease. "We can wait for you outside your room."

She didn't mind Dorian waiting for her, but the idea of Orvid Jones hovering outside the door while she stripped naked was disconcerting. She said so as Pansy tugged at the long row of embroidered buttons that followed the line of her spine like baby dragon scales.

"The bit of privacy you've had in this life will be even less, Your Highness," said Pansy as she wrestled with the clasps.

Chou paced the back of the blue couch. "Less privacy. More responsibility. More people trying to unseat you, and some, quite literally, by sticking a sword in your back. Remind me why anyone wants to rule a country?"

"Thank you for the uplifting assessment of my new role." Eleanor stepped out of the gown and stretched. "I'd like my riding leggings, Pansy, please."

"Riding leggings, for a queen meeting her advisors?"

"It's just Dorian and Orvid," said Chou, as if they weren't arguably the two most powerful men in the country.

Eleanor changed into her leggings, one of Gregory's old cotton hunting shirts, and a pair of soft socks. She flopped onto the couch with a cup of tea in her hand and her father's ancient red horse blanket on her lap. She felt a pang of sadness for High Noon. The faithful old gelding finally died during Dorian's long exile in Svelya. She reached behind her head and grabbed Chou Chou. He squawked when she hugged him tight. "Don't you go dying on me anytime soon," she said.

"How morbid. I'm in the prime of life."

"I know, but I can't lose anyone else."

"You shall never be rid of me, dearest." Chou huddled in her lap and clucked like a broody hen.

Pansy opened the door for Dorian and Orvid. The duke sat on the sofa beside her and the Chief Magician took the armchair.

"The Council," said Orvid. He didn't need to elucidate.

"What do we do about it?" asked Eleanor.

"We need to prove your worthiness," said Dorian.

"The unicorns approve of her," said Chou. "What greater approval do they need?"

"I agree with you, parrot," said Orvid, "but most of these men are over forty years old. Their wives barely read. It will take something impressive to convince them to wholeheartedly support a woman."

"They'd rather Cyrus were crowned right now, despite his age," said Dorian

"Then they'll start jockeying to be his protector." Eleanor tucked one foot under her other leg.

"If we earn the High Council's enthusiastic support, the rest of the nobility will fall into line. The common people already love you, but even in their eyes, its best if your reign starts off with a bang."

"Fireworks?" asked Chou.

"Some literal. Some proverbial."

Pansy tapped Eleanor's shoulder. "Your Highness, there's a note. From the Duchess of Harveston."

"It must be about Gregory. Condolences. I'll read it later."

"Her valet asked that you read it right away."

Eleanor ripped the envelope, eager to read Sylvia's note and get on with their conversation. Given their recent interactions, she had reasonable hope of civil, gracious communication. She didn't need any extraneous family matters intruding upon her already cluttered mind.

She would not get her wish. While the tone was civil, Sylvia's words leapt off the page and gamboled before her eyes, the letters as graceful as the woman who wrote it.

"My stepmother has died," she said.

Chou hopped in her lap. "Oh, dear."

Eleanor set the paper beside her. She pressed her fingers against her temples, trying to make room for this new loss. But was it a loss? Not in the same vein as the many others she'd suffered, but it was still the negation of a life of great personal consequence.

"I can't think about it now. I can't." She tapped Chou's silky head. "Please go to her. Give her my deepest regrets and tell her I will call on her as soon as I am able."

Chou twittered an affirmative and took off from her lap.

"Now, gentleman, have either of you any ideas for grand, sovereignly spectacles?"

"Nothing yet." Dorian, a master strategist, looked embarrassed by his lack of inspiration.

"In the meantime," said Orvid, as he skimmed a letter, "Rosemary has written from the Abbey. They're ready to start the ogre interpolation. They've even solved the problem of maintaining physical contact. At least for smaller creatures like unicorns."

"Since when are unicorns considered small?" asked Dorian.

"Most beings are small compared to ogres." Orvid ran his fingers along Rosemary's neat writing. "It says here, *the ogres' bulk will require physical contact, but Natalie can interpolate several others as long as they're within reach of her cloud of magic.* Hmmm. That should give her a range of about ten paces in a pinch. More, if she has time to spread her light about. Then she says, *I request armed assistance, in the form of the Unicorn Guard, to travel with her.*"

"I'll go," said Dorian. "I'll take Senné."

Eleanor leaned into the sofa's squashy embrace. She almost told him it was too dangerous, but in the end, Natalie couldn't ask for better protection. "Agreed. You should go. But she'll need a unicorn to ride herself. Dasha served her well until now, but he's too young to face ogres. Monument?"

"He's the grandest stallion in the Paladine," said Orvid. "The strongest and the fastest, and we've seen his bravery."

Eleanor took a contemplative moment. "You're right. He is the strongest in the Paladine. But another stallion is even stronger, faster, and braver."

Dorian's brow wrinkled. "Terin?"

"He pledged himself to our cause. I believe he will come if I ask him. Imagine, a wild unicorn on the streets of Maliana." She sat up so fast, she dripped tea on High Noon's blanket. "That's it! We need a spectacle, don't we?"

"Brilliant." Dorian handed Eleanor his handkerchief. "We should ask him to bring a contingent of his fellows to aid in this endeavor. We'll shoot two fairies with one arrow. Further the universal cause of saving us from the ogres, *and* advance our personal purpose by showcasing the might of our new queen." Dorian rested his arm along the back of the sofa, behind Eleanor's head.

"Ahem. Your Grace, the king is only a few days gone," said Orvid. "We can't have people thinking you have untoward intentions or wield undue influence."

Dorian removed his arm, but Eleanor saw no reason to tiptoe around the topiary. "Orvid, Dorian and I have been discreet for sixteen years. We won't do anything to raise any concerns or besmirch Gregory's memory."

Orvid flushed. "Of course, I just… your best interest…"

She softened as he fidgeted and forced herself to remember this was all new to him, too. "I understand your fears, truly. Trust that we are aware of appearances." She handed him a glass of cold water. "I'll write to Rosemary, and we'll send four of the Unicorn Guard north to meet with Terin. Can a party be ready to leave tomorrow?"

Dorian nodded. As Eleanor talked, plans and tasks ordered themselves in her head. She felt her own voice steady. Orvid handed her parchment and a pen, and she spent the next thirty minutes writing a note to Rosemary and drafting orders for the Guard. She asked questions as they arose in her mind, and Dorian and Orvid answered them. She had almost forgotten about Chou's consolation mission, until he fluttered red in the windowpane, like a lost bit of Natalie's magic.

"How does the duchess fare, Chou?" Eleanor asked.

He flew across the room and landed on the table between Eleanor and her advisors. "She would not see me. Her valet said she's had no visitors since the king died. Not even her son, Hector. The boy himself stopped by her rooms twice while I perched on a dampened torch in the hallway. Neither of us were granted admission."

"Please try again tomorrow," Eleanor said.

"I will, Your Majesty."

Eleanor paused with her quill hovering above the parchment. It was the first time her parrot had referred to her by that weighty moniker of supreme authority. She waited for Chou to add a teasing addendum, but he tucked his wings and perched behind her, seemingly awaiting her next command.

Your Majesty. A weighty title, but she could get accustomed to it. More accustomed than she'd ever be to heavy velvet dresses. Gregory wanted her to bear it, and she planned to make him proud.

PART III

CHAPTER 21

A PARTICULARLY NOBLE CREATURE

THE WEEK OF GREGORY'S funeral and her coronation flew past, and Eleanor had little time to dwell on specifics. She clung to small memories—like the smell of the yellow roses that adorned his casket. She recalled the chill of cold Fire-iron against her bare shoulder blades as she sat on throne she still thought of as King Casper's, waiting for Orvid Jones to place the crown of the Desmarais kings on her head.

She slept with the crown beside her pillow on the night of the coronation. Orvid had shrunk it with a spell, so it wouldn't slip down over her ears. Caleb Desmarais himself had commissioned it, not long after he took control of the Dragon Mines. It was simpler than many of the crowns and tiaras she'd worn over the years—Fire-iron with a large center emerald flanked by two amethysts. Inside, an etching of a unicorn and a dragon, and the initials, CD. She rested her fingers on it all through that restless night. She asked for the blessings of Caleb, Casper, Gregory, and all the other Desmarais kings.

During all the hubbub, they learned Terin had accepted Eleanor's invitation and her request for his help. The stallion and his peers would arrive at Eclatant at noon on the first day of HighSummer. Three days after the coronation and two days after the final heartbreaking funeral service and Gregory's internment in the Desmarais burial vault on the Paladine grounds. Even as Eleanor mourned him, she knew he'd want her to focus on the tasks at hand, and the uproar over the unicorn's visit provided a functional distraction from her grief.

Orvid sent callers to proclaim the news throughout Maliana. Mounted messengers carried the tidings across the country to Harper's Crossing, Sage, Harveston, Solsea, and Point-of-Rocks. Orvid even sent a message via falcon to King Samuel in Svelya. Collective excitement grew, and shopkeepers decided to close their businesses. Magicians and witches cancelled tutoring sessions so children might watch the historic arrival. Wealthy Malianans set up elaborate picnics on their lawns and opened their gates to take in the view. Eleanor allowed the servants to congregate in the courtyard with the High Council and their families, Godsmen and magical folk, and royal visitors and ministers.

By half past eleven, Chou informed her the townspeople were lining the streets and cramming into Smithwick Square. Once he delivered his report, he took off again on another scouting mission. Eleanor stood in a portico off the Great Hall. She wore a relatively simple green silk gown. Her hair flowed loosely beneath the magically shrunken crown. She tapped her foot to keep from pacing. Dorian stood beside her, and he placed a steadying hand on the small of her back.

"We're certain they're coming?" she said.

She'd asked him that question several times, but he patiently replied, "Yes. Frog himself saw them on the Outcountry Road just an hour ago."

Eleanor didn't particularly like Dorian's grouchy raven, but even Chou Chou acknowledged his dependability and his keen eye. "Is my attire appropriate?"

"You look as if you welcome wild unicorns to the palace at least once a week."

"I do wish Chou were here, instead of flying around town. Even if he is a bird brain and sometimes his chattering drives me mad. There's something comforting about him just the same."

Dorian smiled. "My attempts to assuage you pale in comparison."

"If you took me in your arms it would surely improve my state of mind." She was slowly getting used to saying such things aloud without fear of imminent death.

"In my mind, you're always in my arms."

"Thank you, that helps."

"Not as much as a sarcastic comment and a feather in your eye."

"But a very close second."

Orvid poked his head around the door. "Our unicorns are assembled, Your Majesty. A regiment of the Guard, as well as Monument, Senné, Teardrop, and Fortune."

"It must be an important day if Fortune came out," said Dorian. King Casper's unicorn had settled into gentile retirement. He held his own court in the sunny paddock outside his stall and told stories to the foals.

"Not many want to miss this. The wild ones have passed through Smithwick Square and are approaching the Covey."

"Are the people pleased?" Eleanor asked.

"Apparently some are crying in the streets. The children are running ahead of them and laying flowers on the Hundred Heralds, so I'd say so." Orvid beckoned to her. "Come, it's time for you to make ready to greet them."

Dorian gently pushed her toward the open two-story doors. "I'll be just behind you," he said.

Eleanor nodded and walked toward the sunlight to welcome her visitors.

The Bonded unicorns sensed their wild brethren before Eleanor saw them. They tossed their heads and whinnied. For once, Eleanor couldn't clearly read their cues. She sensed excitement, and welcome, but possibly a hint of skepticism. Teardrop stood between Senné and Monument. She twitched and tossed her head. Eleanor wished she were close enough to touch her old friend and hear whatever words she whispered to the two stallions beside her.

The cries and cheers of the townsfolk permeated the thick palace walls. The crowd in the courtyard twittered and stood on tiptoe. A few gentlemen lifted their small children onto their shoulders. The Unicorn Guard had hustled everyone into a semicircle around Eleanor. She wasn't sure what to expect when the wild unicorns entered the palace gates. She imagined they'd rush in like a tumbling white sea foam.

Instead, Terin walked calmly and purposefully, as if he were simply directing his mares to a better patch of grazing. Eleanor marveled at his size and his air of effortless command. If he were a man, he would have simultaneously been a general, a judge, and a king. As he led his followers into the courtyard, the whispering and chattering built to calls of welcome and applause. The wild unicorns spread out behind Terin like the unusually long tail of a white peacock.

"How many are there?" Eleanor whispered to Dorian.

"At least thirty. More than we expected."

Eleanor met Terin beside the statute of Caleb Desmarais astride his stallion, Eclatant. Terin's fellows assembled around him. They didn't form precise lines like the Unicorn Guard, but they still exuded an intimidating militarism. Most were stallions, but a few large mares had made the journey south. Two black unicorns stood out in the snowy whiteness. One especially exotic spotted stallion looked as if HighGod had gotten bored of white unicorns but couldn't fully commit to black, either. Twigs and bits of grass stuck in their manes. They must have run hard to reach Maliana so quickly, but none appeared winded. They peered at the castle walls from beneath luxurious forelocks that partially obscured their faces. Their sharp horns were a battalion of raised lances, and their ears waved like the wings of a flock of settling doves.

The crowd hushed when she raised her hands. She tipped her head in a bow, and Terin did the same. His nostrils vibrated, and his breath warmed the space between them. To a nose accustomed to the smells of mud and grass and Fire-iron dust, each shallow inhale posed a question. He glanced up at the statue of Caleb and Eclatant before his dark eyes settled on Eleanor.

"Welcome, Terin," she said. "We are blessed by your presence, and that of your friends."

"Thank you, Your Majesty."

Orvid stationed Paladins throughout the crowd. They muttered translations for the gathered courtiers, as most of them couldn't understand the Bonded unicorn's language, much less the wild ones' speech.

"Your visit would be a rare honor at any time, but it is of particular consequence in this time of transition for our country, when we are simultaneously threatened by violent invaders. All beings of Cartheigh are in danger when ogres roam free. The thought that we are unified in our defenses is of great comfort to me. The crown is grateful for our alliance with the wild herds. I believe we will all be safer for it."

"With all respect, Your Majesty, we are here not because of the crown on your head, but because of the person who wears it."

The Paladins whispered frantically. Excited courtiers passed their messages to those around them.

"Whisper reported to me of the conditions of the unicorns here."

"Did he." Eleanor tried to keep her voice mild. She scanned the crowd and found Whisper, in the row behind Terin. She recognized him by the length of his mane and his longish ears. A derisive snort floated across the courtyard. Senné nipped a visibly irritated Teardrop. She stomped one hoof but took Senné's advice and said nothing else.

"He found the unicorns to be happy and beloved by your family. He reiterated the impression you made upon me when you stayed in our company. We agree, you are a particularly noble creature."

Eleanor breathed a sigh of relief. Apparently, even garrulous Whisper adhered to the unicorns' propensity for plainspoken honesty. He might not have wanted to like what he'd seen in the Paladine, but he didn't lie about it. She made a mental note to thank him for his positive appraisal of her unicorns and her person.

"Your late husband exceeded my expectations of a human king. I have found Lord Brandling to be decent as well. Even that strange man, Matt Thromba of the Dragon Mines, is not nearly as offensive as I thought he would be. But it's because of you, Your Majesty, that we are here. You are the one who convinced me we can work together once more, as we did five hundred years ago. Perhaps our alliance can go beyond this present conflict, with you as the leader of your people."

Eleanor gave the Paladins a moment to translate before she spoke. She paraphrased words she'd heard Gregory recite several years before, and as she often did, she hoped he somehow heard her. "Thank you for your kind words. I pray I am worthy of the trust placed in me by my people, the unicorns of the Bond, and those of the wild." She raised her arms and spoke to her subjects. "Now, all of Maliana… please join me in making our guests feel at home."

The people cheered, and the bonded unicorns whinnied their welcomes. Eleanor heard her own name tossed around the crowd. They shouted blessings and good wishes for a long and healthy reign.

Eleanor stepped closer to Terin. He snuffled at her neck, and she stroked his. Despite his size and the scent of grass and rain clinging to him, for a moment she almost felt as if he were one of her own. "We have made arrangements for your shelter in the Paladine, should you desire to rest."

His reply reminded her that he was not of the Bond and never would be. "I would feel trapped between your four walls, as would any of my herd. We will sleep under HighGod's stars, as we always do."

Dorian sat on a bale of high, in a meadow adjoining the Paladine's stud barn. As he watched the stallions graze in paddocks behind their stalls, it struck Dorian that the Bonded unicorns were not part of the High Council. Casper and Gregory regularly consulted with Fortune and Vigor. Later, Gregory turned to Monument. Dorian and Senné shared the same intimate, brotherly moments. Gregory and his father had valued their unicorns' counsel as much as they valued the insight of their human advisers. He wondered aloud why they'd never actually invited them into the High Council Chamber.

"Most of the Council wouldn't understand us," said Senné.

"We had translators in the courtyards yesterday."

"True," Senné's ears spun thoughtfully. "Our character doesn't lend itself to such human exercises. No one says as much, but the wild unicorns all recognize Terin as their leader. Still, he rarely calls upon the wild stallions. We stallions of the Bond work well together, but we have no deep affinity for one another. Our affections are for our mares and our children. The mares themselves are more communal, but even they don't confer on many decisions. It would be unnatural for a unicorn to sit in a chamber room and listen to men convince one another of the righteousness of their own opinions." He yawned. "There's no need for us to participate. The king informs his stallion of his decisions, and his stallion tells him if he agrees or not. It's simple."

"I suppose it is." Dorian picked at the hay beneath him. "This will be an interesting gathering, then. Eleanor, Orvid, and myself, with our communal philosophy. Four stallions who disdain such meetings of the minds."

"Four stallions and a mare," said Senné. His ears waved in the direction of the stud barn.

Teardrop ambled across the brownish late summer grass. Eleanor sat on her bare back in her riding leggings. Her long, strong legs dangled at the mare's sides. With one squeeze, Teardrop would take off, but Eleanor would not be unseated.

"I should have known," said Dorian.

"Did you think I'd be the loan female voice among all this manly energy?" Eleanor asked.

"Orvid Jones does not exude manly energy," said Teardrop as Eleanor lit on the ground.

Eleanor bopped her gently on the nose. "Hush now. Here he comes."

Orvid, Terin, Whisper, and Monument joined them. Eleanor and Dorian sat beside one another on one bale, and Orvid took the other. The five unicorns surrounded them. The humans, sitting on their piles of hay, were baby sparrows in a swan's nest.

"So, my friends," said Eleanor. "We are here to determine who shall accompany my daughter, and Dorian and Senné, on her missions to remove the ogres from Cartheigh."

"I'm willing and able," said Monument.

"I admire your bravery," said Terin, "but you're young and inexperienced."

"Pardon, my friend," said Senné. "You have no ogre interpolation experience either."

Terin regarded the black stallion with mild curiosity. "Nor do you, but somehow your presence is a given."

"I go where Lord Brandling goes."

"If I do this," said Whisper. "Would I be expected to carry a person on my back?"

"You would," said Eleanor. "You've seen my daughter. She's very small."

"The size of the child is of no consequence. The issue of magnitude is the servitude inherent in carrying a human being, like a pack mule."

"I resent the insinuations endemic to your statement," said Teardrop. She clearly hadn't forgiven Whisper for his snide skepticism of the Bond, but Dorian hoped she wouldn't antagonize him. Despite the competition between them, Terin seemed to value Whisper as a sort of second-in-command. He was as large as Monument, and a hair taller than Senné. His haunches were like two marble boulders, and his horn measured the length of Dorian's sword, plus half. He'd be a fine addition to their interpolation mission.

"You yourself stated that the unicorns here are well cared for and beloved," said Eleanor.

"I did what Terin asked of me and spoke true of what I saw. That doesn't mean I relish the idea of carrying a human child anywhere—in this world or any other."

Terin's restless hooves dislodged lumps of dead grass. "Peace, Whisper. I share your hesitance, but these unusual circumstances call for adaptability."

"The child's safety is of the utmost importance," said Eleanor. "She's the only person, witch or magician, who can perform this spell."

"She is small," said Terin. "I'll think of her as a butterfly, perched on my shoulder."

"Thank you." Eleanor waffled between terror at the thought of her tiny daughter sitting atop that white mountain of muscle and comfort that Terin willingly chose to protect her.

"If Terin is at peace with it, I will also carry her." Whisper rubbed his muzzle along his foreleg. "Butterfly," he muttered.

"But why should you both go while I stay here?" Monument sounded like Ticia, complaining that she was too young to attend the Waxing Ball.

"Here is what I propose," said Eleanor. "All three of you shall go."

"All at once?" asked Dorian.

"No. We shall rotate the party. Dorian and Senné, along with Terin and Natalie, will go first. Then she will take Dorian and Monument, and she'll ride Whisper. HighGod willing, other witches will soon learn to interpolate. It will go smoother if several of you are accustomed to the task."

"It's a fine plan," said Orvid. "Now, shall we discuss—"

"Perhaps I should go first, with Terin, rather than Senné," said Whisper.

Senné's ears pricked. "I told you, where Lord Brandling goes, I go."

"Whisper and I *do* already know one another," said Terin.

"But *I* know Princess Natalie," said Monument. "It only makes sense that Senné and I go first."

"Monument," said Teardrop, "Let us be honest. Princess Natalie has been at the Abbey for most of your close tenure with the royal family."

"Why is this mare here again?" asked Whisper, his ears laid back against his head.

Under different circumstances, Dorian would have laughed at Teardrop's outraged expression. She looked like the village prude accused of whoring. "I am here at the request of *the queen*, my most treasured companion—"

Terin snapped at Whisper. "I warned you against letting your teeth hang out."

"Terin, you must admit, a mare—"

"Silence!" Eleanor stood and glared at the huge creatures around her. The sparrow was clearly finished with these persnickety white waterfowl. Given their squabbling, the unicorns were less swanlike by the moment. They'd become a gaggle of grumpy geese. "Terin, no disrespect for your leadership, but I am the queen here. You four are without a doubt our greatest stallions, and a credit to your species. I plan to include all of you on this most important mission, with gratitude for your service. I will not be distracted, however, by the particularities of who accompanies whom and in what order. I want Dorian to go, and he and Senné are of one mind. Monument and Whisper, you are both great warriors, but on this first mission, I will defer to Terin's seniority. Are we all on the same page of the ledger?"

The unicorn's blasé postures belied their embarrassment. Whisper went back to rubbing his muzzle on his foreleg and grumbling about butterflies. Monument and Senné sniffed the air, as if testing the wind for an incoming storm. Teardrop's tail switched once, twice, and then went still.

"Yes, we are," said Terin. The great stallion peered almost sheepishly out from under his forelock. "It's true you're the queen, and your plan is logical."

Orvid jumped to his feet. Dark circles had appeared under the arms of his tunic. "Very well! What a productive meeting. I'll be heading to the palace now to write to the Abbottess. Good day, all!" He grabbed his rucksack and walked as fast as his skinny legs would carry him toward the Paladine gate and his awaiting carriage. He traded bickering unicorns and their deadly, swinging horns for the sanity of his dusty office back at Eclatant.

The wild unicorns bid their own goodbyes. They headed for the south meadow, where they'd set up an open-air campsite of sorts. Whisper said to Terin, "What is a ledger?"

Terin grumbled an unintelligible response. Monument retreated to the brood mare barn to visit one of his first children. Teardrop asked Eleanor to walk her to her stall and give her a rub down with a soft cloth.

"Perhaps soak it in cold water," said Dorian.

"That sounds like a good idea, don't you think, dearest?" Eleanor led Teardrop with a hand looped in the mare's mane. Dorian and Senné were left alone, standing beside the two hay bales.

"An historic meeting," said Senné.

"These bales should be bronzed." Dorian looked at Senné slyly out of the corner of his eye. "Hmmm. Now I understand why unicorns wouldn't want to join the High Council. Our insipid human habit of arguing with one another is very gauche."

Senné snorted a self-deprecating laugh. "I need a cool down as well."

Dorian laughed. He tugged Senné's forelock, and they headed to the stud barn in search of cool rags and cooler heads.

CHAPTER 22

Ogre Interpolation

AN HOUR AFTER SUNSET on a Saturday night, Dorian sat on Senné's back in the Abbey's training ring. A cloud of Natalie's red magic engulfed him. He thought of the red décor in Pandra Tate's brothel, the Red-Headed Hussy. The layers of squashy furniture in varying hues from scarlet to crimson to magenta always made him feel morbidly surrounded by organs—hearts, lungs, livers. In a doubly macabre analogy, today's adventure felt like being swept through an artery.

For the past two days, Dorian, Senné, Terin, and Natalie had blasted between various town and locals in Cartheigh. They'd visited a chapel on the outskirts of the Talessee capital, Talay. They'd gone to Ello and back twice. Dorian had spent an hour on each visit exploring the topography around Alenestra. He'd found little to alarm him, just a damp, surprisingly empty land. Ello seemed almost void of animal life, save for insects, rabbits, lumbering raccoon-ish creatures that hissed like housecats, and obnoxiously loud seagulls. If any other creatures lurked on the island, they lived far inland, or they were adept at hiding and had no interest in revealing their presence.

Dorian was not yet accustomed to taking breaths that were more magic than air. His nose tingled, and he pinched it to keep from sneezing. He wore an armored Fire-iron vest, a heavy cloak covered by a dragon robe, and thick leather gloves. He carried his sword, his bow and quiver, a Fire-iron shield, and the dagger he kept in his boot. Two water flasks hung from his saddle horn, along with a bag of dried meat. The unicorns didn't require armor, but Senné wore a saddle and the casual rein looped over his muzzle. Terin donned only the little fur-wrapped fluff ball of Natalie herself. She sat astride his bare back and gripped a handful of mane.

Despite their relative familiarity with interpolation and their destination, the addition of ogres to any endeavor significantly raised the stakes. Rosemary, Agnes, Eleanor, and Dasha would wait for them, anxious landlubbers praying for the speedy return of wandering sailors. He saw no precise lines or facial expressions through the haze of bloody mist, but the familiar shifting figures brought him comfort. "HighGod carry you!" called Rosemary.

He turned to Natalie. "Now, Natty. Tell me again where we're going."

With her big green eyes and gray rabbit fur hat, she resembled a curious kitten. "The northernmost ogre camp, outside of Nestra. Mr. Oliver has not yet interpolated any of the ogres from that camp. Agnes has visited there, and she explained it to me."

"Where will be land?"

"Inside the Restraints. Near their temple. It's made of rocks coated in black mud with a roof made of sticks. It is nighttime, so the ogres should be sleeping."

"When we arrive, what then?"

"We move fast and be quiet." She narrowed her eyes, as if she were already deciding which ogre to touch.

"Yes. Good girl. We're going now!" he called out.

"Please take care!" Eleanor's voice cracked. "Hurry back!"

"Are you ready to go, Lord Brandling?" Natalie asked, as if they were going into town to visit the market.

"Yes, Your Highness. I am at your service."

"Then hold tight to your mount." She whispered under her breath, and everything went black. A dream image rose in his mind. His son, Cyrus, sat on the edge of cliff. His baby legs dangled over the ledge. The image faded before Dorian panicked. He woke to the rumble of uneven snoring, like disgruntled thunderclaps.

Northern Svelya was not as cold as Ello, but that was not saying much. Dorian trusted Senné to guide their party over the rocky ground. The waxing moon was bright enough to light their path but also reveal their presence if any creature stirred in the camp. Natalie darkened her magic. She hid Terin's white effervescence behind an enchanted curtain the color of long dried blood. The wind whipped past the Restraints and chapped Dorian's cheeks. He pulled his fur hood tighter around his face. Just as Natalie had planned, they'd opened their eyes a few yards away from the ogre's hulking temple. The ogre's earsplitting snoring vibrated the mud-thatched huts, but otherwise, they were still. The ogres had piled rocks and sticks around their crude homes like farmers would stack baskets of winter grain. The layer of dirt beneath the unicorn's feet was like an old shoe leather, dry and weathered and cracked with wrinkly fissures.

"Only creatures who eat rocks could survive here," whispered Dorian.

"They also eat the occasional rat," said Senné. "The creation of the Restraints trapped a sizeable rodent population."

"Rats and rocks. No wonder they eat anything they can get their hands on when they escape. We're doing them a favor. Ello will be lush to them."

"Shhh," whispered Terin, as if anything could hear them over the grinding snores. "Princess, which shelter?"

Natalie squinted into the moonlight. The wind blew bits of

strawberry blond hair into her mouth, and she spat them out. "The one with the two round windows, closest to the temple."

They approached the hut. Terin was just tall enough to see inside. "There are four of them, asleep," he said. "Two adults and two young ones. Should you try the small one first?"

"No," whispered Natalie. "I'll move the adults first, so the small ones don't wake up alone in a strange place."

Her empathy for the ogres made little sense, given one of them had murdered her father via proxy in cold blood, but she was young. If it made her feel more comfortable to start with the larger ogres, so be it.

Natalie slid from Terin's back. She barely made a sound when she lit on the ground, but a puff of dust covered her black boots.

"Listen to me, Natalie," Dorian said. "We will be just outside the door. Well within reach of your magic. As soon as you touch the ogre, we'll be braced to go. If one of them wakes up, you run. Don't stop or try to touch anything. You're a jackrabbit, and the wolf is coming after you. We will distract them and return to the Abbey as quickly as we can."

"If you are trapped, scream," said Terin. "We will come in after you."

She swallowed and nodded.

The child and Terin went around one side of the hut, while Dorian and Senné took the other. The snores from inside were like a cheese grater scratching away on Dorian's nerves. Senné placed his hooves so softly that he might have walked across a carton of eggs and cracked not a one. It didn't much matter, however, as Dorian figured he could trot around the hut on metal horseshoes and the ogres would continue snoozing, as long as his hoofbeats matched the rhythm of their snoring.

Senné rounded the corner. Terin and Natalie peered around their side of the building like two puppets entering from side stage. She stepped around the remains of the ogres' last meal—crumbled rock filets and a salad of bramble branches. Terin clung to Natalie's heels like a shadow at sundown. She peered inside the hut. She flinched at whatever she saw inside and wrinkled her nose, but she pulled her hat down over her ears and tiptoed inside.

Senné crept forward, his hooves as light as a Kellish balletta dancer on pointed wooden shoes. Dorian dismounted and drew his sword. Both hands sweated in his leather gloves. If the ogres weren't snoring so loudly, perhaps they'd be able to hear his battering heartbeat.

He desperately wanted to peer inside the shelter, but it seemed too risky, so he tried to rely on his other senses. He listened for scampering feet during the momentary breaks in the ogres' out of tune symphony. Senné's ears waved as if a housefly buzzed them. Terin pressed his long face to the side of the building. His fluttering nostrils just reached past the doorway. All three flinched when an ogre passed gas in a long, trumpeting blast. Terin jerked his head as the noxious fumes rushed out the door like the putrid enchantment of a long dead magician.

How can something that subsists on dry rocks produce such a stench? Dorian wondered. *Unless they recently celebrated one of their god's foul holidays with a celebratory rat stew.*

As if summoned by his very thought, a monstrous gray rat, roughly the size of his late mother's pygmy Talessee spaniel, but with none of that animal's cuddly appeal, poked its long nose from underneath the pile of discarded brambles. Dorian's eyes widened as it crept toward Terin's hooves.

Senné bumped his nose against Dorian's shoulder. If the rat spooked Terin it would expose them. Even worse, HighGod only knew what kind of festering diseases the creature carried. Terin might end up in the same straights as Gregory, rotting away from the inside out. Dorian waved as the rat brazenly approached, but Terin stared down his own nose in disgust and tried to dispel the smell of ogre gas.

"Terin," Dorian whispered, trying to stay calm. "Terin, beside you—"

The rat nibbled at Terin's right front fetlock. He looked down, and it hissed at him as if his majestic presence offended its pestilent sensibilities. Terin struck it with one wide hoof, and it rolled away from him. It leapt to its feet, switched its scaly tale, and lunged at him. It took two bounding leaps, and in serpentine zip zags, it jumped from Terin's rear haunch to his shoulder. Dorian clutched his sword in a panicked moment of indecision. Should he try to intervene or leave Terin to it?

The rat had a mouthful of Terin's mane. He reared, and the creature squealed and lost its grip on the silky hair. It hit the ground and Terin speared it clean through with its horn. It let out a shrieking squeal, like the cry of an injured rabbit, and writhed on the end of Terin's horn. Without further thought, Dorian stepped across the doorway and sliced its head off with his sword.

He glanced to his left. Inside the gloomy ogre's hut, Natalie crouched only a few paces away from a sleeping ogre. A smaller one stirred and rolled over onto its side. Natalie froze and stared at Dorian framed in the doorway. He mouthed to her, *hurry, please*, and she took two more steps toward her intended target.

A fierce hissing to his right further raised the hairs on the back of his neck, and they were already soldiers at attention. He slowly turned his head. Their compatriot's death cries had summoned three more huge rats. They crouched on their haunches with tails whipping, like irritated cats.

"Damnit," Dorian whispered. He sensed Senné shifting behind him. Terin tossed his head, and the gory lump slid from his horn. He bared his teeth silently at the rodent interlopers. Dorian raised his sword. Rat blood dripped down the shaft toward his hands.

The largest rat's hiss morphed into a yowl. Dorian stepped toward it. He'd strike its spitting, whining head from its body before it bit them or slipped into the hut and attacked Natalie.

The air suddenly thickened, like cold molasses. Tendrils of red mist crept around Dorian's legs. The rat hid its face between its paws, as if the red magic were a flame and it had stepped too close. Once again, everything went black.

This time, Dorian momentarily dreamed of a huge bridge. Impossibly long metal ropes held it up. Even in the warped rationale of the In Between, the idea of walking across such a precarious monument terrified him. Fortunately, he woke before his dreaming feet stepped onto the smooth white rock leading up the incline to the bridge's precipice. When he opened his eyes, he was back at the temple of Alenestra. He shook his head to dispel the lingering fear of the dream bridge. The cold burned the inside of his throat and dried out his mouth quicker than a mouthful of sawdust.

Natalie crouched over a sleeping ogre. Miraculously, it had barely shifted position. One lanky arm remained draped across its forehead. It still snored. She let go of its stringy hair and sprinted to Dorian and the unicorns. They retreated to the edge of the dunes.

"We did it," she said. "Not we must return and get the rest."

"Natalie," said Dorian. "There were rats. Not normal rats. Smarter and bigger. Fiercer."

"Then you must keep them at bay while I get the others."

"We may need to regroup."

"We can't move one ogre at a time," said Terin. "It will take months. We'll return and stand guard outside the hut again. Little princess, can you go between here and the ogre camp without us, while we keep the rats away?"

"No! We're supposed to stay with her."

"Like Terin said at the Paladine, we must be adaptable," said Senné. "We didn't foresee an antagonist rat population, but we shall deal with them."

"But what if one of the ogres wakes up when Natalie is here by herself?"

"I can move fast, Uncle Dorian," she said. "I need you more there than here."

Dorian felt absurd, having this conversation on a strange island in the middle of nowhere, with a child, two unicorns, and a sleeping ogre. He'd promised Eleanor he'd keep Natalie as close as possible. Instead, he'd send her to the other side of the world with an unconscious ogre as her gruesome chaperone.

"I'm a child," said Natalie, "but I'm also the one who must achieve this task. I know what Rosemary and my mother and Mistress Agnes would say. But this is the best way. Nay, it's the only way."

Dorian stabbed his sword into the squidgy earth. It yielded to his blade in a way the dry, cracked ground of the ogre camp never would. The pressure to make a decision made him claustrophobic. He ripped his hat from his head and twisted it in his hands.

He tried to make an objective assessment. There were dozens of huts in the first camp alone, and two more camps after that. They wouldn't have time to reassess their every move or confer with the women who waited at the Abbey after each interpolation.

"You win, Your Highness," he said. "Let us seize the moment and interpolate more ogres."

Natalie grabbed Terin's mane and shimmied onto his back like a cliff lemur. "This time, we'll be ready for the rats," she said.

With that happy thought, Dorian made ready for the world to go black again. When it did, he dreamed of a lion-sized rodent. It bit his arm with rotting teeth. The dream didn't strike him as a vision from the In Between. It was a product of his own overwrought mind. As such, it was doubly traumatic, for no such creature should exist, in any world. The vision lasted only seconds, but he had time to see his own horrified face reflected in the fabricated monster's yellow eyes.

Eleanor had spent much of her life in long, desperate stints of waiting. Regardless, the wait for the first interpolation party was uniquely agonizing. They finally reappeared: triumphant Natalie, two self-satisfied unicorns, and the much-abused Duke of Brandling. That gentleman looked as if he'd aged a year or two from the stress of the whole affair. Natalie gave a detailed description of the ogre camp's sights, smells, and sounds. She noted that their skin felt like burlap under her fingers. To Eleanor's alarm, she finished with anecdotes about vicious giant rats stalking them from one ogre hut to the next.

"Uncle Dorian and the unicorns handled those stubborn creatures well, Mother," she said. "They kept coming and coming, even when we killed their friends!"

Eleanor started to ask for adult clarification, but Dorian waved his hands. "I need a bath," was all he said. Eleanor directed Agnes to take him to one of the dormitories to clean up. It would be highly abnormal for a naked man to take his repose in the witches' living space, but these were abnormal times. If Dorian needed a bath to remove the grime of ogre interpolation from his skin, he would have one, immediately.

Notwithstanding the savage rodent development, Rosemary declared the first interpolation a success. They had moved four ogres from the first hut, three from the second, and a single, huge male from the last. According to Agnes, that left twenty-nine huts in the northernmost camp. Natalie made another run the next day, and each day after it. Within two weeks, several other witches finally caught on to the magic. Agnes wished she could join them, but she accepted her role as secret liaison to Ezra Oliver. Olive's fairyman appeared in her room late at night every other week. From his correspondence, Oliver seemed unaware the ogres were disappearing from the northern camp. He remained focused on the smallest camp, near the Carthean border. As Agnes had surmised, his age did not serve him well. He may have used his two hundred years of magical experience to perfect interpolation, but he didn't have the stamina to interpolate ogres every day.

Natalie and the other young witches required no such repose or recovery time. As the Abbey's interpolators improved their skills, Rosemary whittled down the interpolation parties to partnerships. One witch and one unicorn. They emptied the northern camp by the beginning of MidAutumn and moved on the larger of the two remaining camps.

The rats proved to be a bigger obstacle than the ogres. The latter were always sleeping like the dead when the interpolators landed in the camps. None seemed inclined to remain awake to confirm the identity of their brethren's kidnappers, but after all, Oliver had promised he'd remove them from bondage. When they found themselves seemingly delivered to their long-awaited paradise, instead of the Scaled Mountains, they rejoiced. Early in the clearance of the second camp, a novice interpolator dropped one ogre on top of another on her first trip to Ello. She and Monument retreated into the dunes as the ogres woke up and explored the temple. Their huge feet dug trenches in the muddy earth as they conferred with one another. The male beast grunted and shoved his female companion. In turn, she kicked him and jumped in place. She squealed like an excited ape. Eventually, they must have settled on a positive deduction. They yelled and beat their chests as they galumphed away toward the low hills.

As further evidence of their happy adjustment to their new home, they took to pushing over the great stones of the temple at Alenestra. True to prediction, they would not tolerate any gods but their own. "There are dozens of decapitated rabbits on the altar," said Terin, as Eleanor rubbed down his legs after a particularly long day of magical traveling and rat defense.

"A gift to their god for delivering them," said Eleanor.

"I'd prefer a basket of cheese or a bouquet of flowers," said Chou, "but I'm not an ogre god.

On an early MidAutumn morning, the Oracle requested a meeting with Eleanor and Natalie before the day's work began. Natalie sat on the edge of the bed, and Eleanor sat in the wobbly red chair beside it.

The little woman remained in the state of living decomposition Eleanor had witnessed on her last visit, despite her healers' ministrations. She asked for the latest news.

"We've cleared the northernmost camps and moved on to the last one. The smaller one, near the border. I visited there two years ago," said Eleanor. "That camp has been that source of Oliver's harvest, so to say, and there aren't many beasts left."

"The interpolators may encounter him there."

"We're being cautious. Sending bigger parties again."

"Is Ophelia's rat bite healing?"

"She'll lose her arm. After what happened to Gregory, we can't risk any kind of ogre borne pestilence festering in the wound."

"It's sad, Wise One," said Natalie. "But she's proud of herself for helping us."

"Call me Auntie, Natalie. Please."

Natalie gave Eleanor a questioning look, as if to confirm she had permission to use such a casual term of endearment with one so important.

Eleanor nodded. "You may do as Auntie says, Natty." Rosemary had no interest in keeping Natalie's relationship to the Oracle a secret. The idea of a prophetic heir gave the Abbey a sense of security. Despite her lingering fears about what a consanguine association would mean for Natalie's future, there was no point trying to hide it.

"All right… Auntie. Ophelia is resting in a sickroom down the hall, but two more witches work will start working with us today—Ione and Penelope."

"I don't know them. In my younger days, I knew every witch, cow, sheep, goat, and chicken in this Abbey. I even knew the sparrows and a few crickets. But I am sure these young women are capable, if they've learned this spell." She asked for water, and Eleanor held a cup to her lips. "I have other reasons for calling you here today. My eyes aren't what they once were, so Rosemary and Agnes read your book to me."

"*Sundry Existence Theorems*?" asked Eleanor.

"Yes. I'm impressed your young scholar found it, hidden among all those tomes. All the books I've read over the centuries, in so many languages, and I've never read anything that definitively explored this topic. Anything I learned on my own, I gleaned from feeling the universe around me."

"How do you feel the universe, Auntie?" asked Natalie.

"By staying very still. Like a shy child, it will come to you if you wait long enough."

Natalie scrunched her eyes closed. Her nose wiggled like a hungry bunny's.

"Don't try too hard, child. Remember, stray cats often approach people who ignore them."

Natalie's face relaxed.

"Now, *Sundry Existence Theorems.* The book theorizes that while there are umpteen worlds, some are indeed closer than others. Agnes said that Mr. Oliver will try to break into the world *beside ours.* That makes sense. The In Between, as we've been calling it, is softest along the borders between closely connected worlds. It is a wide promenade, not a treacherous mountain pass."

Eleanor looked over her shoulder, as if she might see this other world beside her like a painting or a map. She thought of a well-trod path between worlds, firm enough to bear Oliver's proverbial weight, but soft enough to allow bits of reality to leach from one plane of existence to the next. She tried to wrap her mind around it all, but she kept picturing a creepy old magician skipping along a muddy road, looking for a safe place to leap into the ditches beside it.

"We must open the door," said Hazelbeth.

Her words pulled Eleanor back to the here and now. "Pardon?"

"Open the door. Push him through it. Close it behind him. He'll be trapped."

"Wait— I thought it could be dangerous."

"It could be dangerous, if left open too long. If I am reading this book correctly, ancient magicians did it once, briefly. The door became unstable." She shrugged. "I believe it caused some small earthquakes."

"Earthquakes! Even small earthquakes can do great harm, Wise One. Besides, wouldn't he just use magic to open it again?"

"When those ancient magicians crossed over, to their horror, they found very little magic in that place. So little, their own magic failed them. They made it back, but they barely saved themselves and their power."

"But I thought Oliver needed space to perform the spell—isn't that the heart of our problem with the ogres? He wants to destroy magical beings to make space. It seems like there would be endless space in such a place."

"That's what he thinks, but while too much magic weakens spells, too little magic is worse. Magic requires a balance. Our world is built on it. Even if Oliver killed most of the magical beings in the known nations, there would still be more magic here than in the word next door. It had some magic once, but its people beat all the enchantment out of their atmosphere. They persecuted magical beings. They hunted magical creatures until they died out. Unicorns and dragons and fairies became the stuff of legend."

Eleanor couldn't believe any decent, thinking beings would hunt unicorns. They were not deer or pheasants. They were defined by their own wisdom and kindness. Often their smarts and compassion superseded the human versions of those virtues.

"Some traces of magic remain," Hazelbeth continued. "There are those who can sense the future. Or use locomotion or see ghosts. They must hide their abilities, for their own people would question their sanity. But there is not enough to support power like Oliver's. His magic will die there."

Eleanor shook her head, as if trying to shimmy Hazelbeth's words around in her mind until they made sense. "If we can open the door and push him through, his magical power will fail him, and he'll be trapped?"

"Yes. It won't be like when you threw him into the water of the Watching Pool, or interpolating, where his physical being remains in the In Between and he can find a way back. Once the door is closed, it's closed. There will be no magic on the other side to reopen it."

Eleanor took a moment. "We've learned over the years that it's virtually impossible to kill him outright in battle. He always gets away." She looked up at Hazelbeth. "In a way, it's the same theory we used to get rid of the ogres."

The Oracle nodded. "Not fighting. Not talking. More effective than either."

"Where will we do it, and who will perform the spell?"

"Beside the Watching Pool," said Hazelbeth. "I don't know exactly how the ancients did it, but the *Sundry Existence Theorems* addresses rivers as conduits. The waters of the Pool started us down this path many years ago."

"Who will perform the spell?" Eleanor asked again. Her eyes narrowed, but before she voiced her concerns, the Oracle raised one hand.

"Do not fear. Your daughter will not be asked to do it. She's too precious. I will do it."

"How? Won't you need the magical space Oliver is always going on about? The Abbey oozes magical power, day and night. It's surely crowded here. I don't understand."

Natalie opened her eyes. "You don't need to understand, Mother. Auntie doesn't need to make special space. She can open the door herself, because the Pool will help her."

Eleanor looked to the Oracle in a silent plea for clarity, but the old witch shrugged. "Meh. That's about as well as I could explain it myself."

"You can open the door, Auntie," said Natalie. "I'm sure of it!"

Hazelbeth stroked Natalie's fingers. Their two hands, young and old—like the beginning of life touching the end. "I believe I can, child, although I need to consult the universe about it."

"Can I consult it, too?"

Eleanor interrupted their collegial chat. "We risk bringing Oliver here, to the Abbey, again? He's doubly bent on killing any witch he sees."

"It is a frightening prospect, so we must handle it delicately. Our plan must be ironclad. Let us all think about it. You, Rosemary, and Agnes. Your beloved Duke of Brandling. Mr. Jones—and oh, how about this young woman who found the book? Between us, we have many great minds."

"I will think on it too," said Natalie.

"Yes. Your mind is finer than all of ours. Shiny and new. Come closer." She beckoned to Natalie, who leaned toward her, still unafraid, despite the fact that the Oracle resembled an animated corpse.

Hazelbeth pressed her finger into the center of Natalie's forehead. She chanted under her breath. Natalie closed her eyes. The witch pressed harder and Natalie gasped. She pulled away. She rubbed the spot on her forehead. White light dissipated from it.

"Should you ever need my help—and I sense you will, soon— touch that spot."

"I will. But when will I need help?"

"You'll know. You've been fortunate in this adventure of moving ogres. But just because something starts out smoothly does not mean it will stay such. The road often gets bumpier the farther it gets from town."

"We've already been very far from town," said Natalie. "Oh! Do you mean the road in the In Between?"

"It's a turn of phrase, Natty," said Eleanor, gently. She exhaled her relief. The Oracle had offered Natalie her special protection as she'd hoped.

The Oracle closed her eyes, and Eleanor felt a gentle hand on her shoulder. Rosemary held a finger to her lips and beckoned Eleanor and Natalie toward the door. Natalie tiptoed across the floor, but as soon as she passed the doorway, she sprinted down the hallway, calling out for Dasha and Agnes. Rosemary and Eleanor stepped aside for a nurse to enter the room and check on Hazelbeth, and once she'd closed the door behind her, Eleanor rested her head on Rosemary's shoulder. "How much did you hear?" she asked.

"Enough to know we're to start thinking of another creative solution to a seemingly impossible problem—how to lure Oliver here to the Abbey and shove him through a magical doorway into another world before he kills us all." Rosemary wrapped an arm around Eleanor and squeezed her, as if she were not much older than Natalie. "Even if we can devise such a plan, will Hazelbeth have the strength to perform the spell?"

"She believes she does."

"She'll need to save every bit of strength he has left. Every visit and request for advice weakens her."

"If you think she needs to be secluded, I support that. I shan't request an audience with her, and I'll make sure Orvid and Agnes understand."

"Bless you, Your Majesty," said Rosemary. She kissed Eleanor's forehead. Eleanor and Rosemary were about the same height—a rarity for Eleanor, who usually towered over other women. Thankfully, she and Rosemary almost always saw eye to eye.

As Eleanor commanded, no one bothered the Oracle. On the other hand, everyone bothered Eleanor, day and night. She had thought herself harried as a princess, and then as a queen consort, but nay. Now she ruled over all her subjects and their lands and their squabbles. Every bit of tension was amplified, and she had to squeeze even more activity into each precious hour. Already, she looked back on the days before her coronation as leisurely. She lamented the same to Chou Chou as she got out of bed one morning as the sun rose.

"Should I wear a gown or my riding clothes?" she asked. "I'm to meet the High Council after breakfast, but I won't have time to change before the meeting with the Paladins at the brood mare barn."

Chou lit on the top of one of the bed posters. "Hmmm. A difficult choice. You may offend the Council with your scandalously visible two legs. Or, you may offend the laundresses. They'll have to clean your muddy dress after visiting the Paladine."

"Damnit, Gregory and Casper never had to think about these things. HighGod's fiddle, I'm wearing pants. Rulers have always worn pants in this palace." She fished through her bureau and selected a pair of dark purple cotton leggings with suede patches on the inner thighs, and a long white tunic. She wore a tightfitting cotton chemise underneath the shirt and a leather vest trimmed in wolfskin. If her nipples decided to stand up, she'd be covered. "I don't see how Casper kept this up for thirty years. Nor Gregory for two, honestly."

Chou gripped the blue silk curtains in his beak and slid down to the mattress. "You're still learning. Both Gregory and Casper were trained to rule from the time they were children. For one, they learned to lean on those they trusted. Come now, you, and Dorian, and Gregory—the three of you made amends. Love ultimately drove your reconciliation, but necessity surely hastened it. When Gregory became king and realized how much he needed the two of you. Think, Eleanor. Did Gregory attend every single meeting with every counselor?"

"No. He had Dorian. Or me. Or Orvid. Sometimes General Claiborne. Or… the senior Godsman… but Gregory always made the ultimate decision."

"Did he really?" Chou's head feathers went spiky, like raised eyebrows.

She thought for a moment. "Not always, I suppose. Often, I

would have already made a decision. He simply approved it or made adjustments."

"Sometimes he contradicted you, like when you met with the Kellish ambassador and wanted to honor his requests about the wool tariffs."

"Yes—he made the final decision. That reminds me—I didn't *like* his decision. I need to meet with Mr. Falintoss."

"Let Orvid meet with him and negotiate, if you want to reduce the tariffs. It's your prerogative. You're the queen. But let Orvid *speak* with him and report in his estimation."

"Should I? Tariffs are so important."

"Everything is important when you're the queen. But you cannot be everywhere at once. Do you trust Mr. Jones's judgment?"

"Yes, of course. You're right."

At that moment, Pansy announced Agnes's unanticipated arrival. She proclaimed the visit to be of the utmost importance. Eleanor sat at her dressing table and untwisted her hair from its messy overnight braid. "Send her in, Pansy," she said. "I'll manage my hair. Since I'm embracing masculine attire, I can dress myself, too. Can you make sure Cyrus eats all his porridge? He won't sit still, so the nursery nannies follow him around, spooning it into his mouth. It's not fitting for a young prince. He'll sit at a formal table in a few years."

Pansy grumbled about spoiled children and irresponsible nursemaids as she blew past Agnes. She looked as if she might sack the indulgent nannies on the spot if the little prince wasn't securely strapped in his high-feeding chair.

"I trust her, too," Eleanor said to Chou. "She's a hard-handed ambassador, and she'll handle the porridge affair without an international incident."

Agnes sat in the chair behind her. "Thank you for seeing me. I know how busy you are, Your Majesty.

Eleanor smiled at the witch over the shoulder of her own reflection.

"Just a bit of diplomacy between the queen's chamber and the royal nursery. Now, what can I do for you?"

Agnes didn't return Eleanor's expression or her banter. "I received a letter this morning. Oliver knows additional ogres have been removed from the camps."

Eleanor raked her brush over her hair. The ends snagged, but she pushed on through the tangle. "I see."

"He's never sent such haphazard correspondence. Flimflam sentences. Repetitive speculations. Poor grammar! He's flummoxed. He suspects some sort of trickery from the Oracle or maybe Orvid Jones."

"Have you replied yet?"

Agnes's hands shook, as if she'd lost her preternatural magical youth and age had caught up with her. "No. I wanted to speak to you first."

Eleanor turned around. "What else did he say?"

"He went to the smallest camp, and there were only two ogres left. He took them with him to the Scaled Mountains.

"Oliver did us the favor of removing the final residents of the camps. They're all empty now."

"Once he moved those two, he went to the larger camps. Both deserted. He doesn't understand how they're gone if the Restraints are still operating. I've had a letter from King Samuel. The Watchmen report that the Restraints continue good order, as we've wanted. It's a mystery to Mr. Oliver."

"You don't think the Watch has been compromised?"

"King Samuel promised all three camps will be turned into monastic coveys once this is all over. The magicians will live in ease and comfort, studying on the crown's dime. They won't lose that chance after years slaving away at the Watch. But I'm not concerned myself about the Watchmen, Your Majesty. At this moment, I'm not even worried so much about Mr. Oliver. I fear the ogres themselves."

"The beasts in the wild?"

"Yes. Apparently, the ogres hiding in the Scaled Mountains know the camps have been emptied. They're in a frenzy. They think their prophecy has been fulfilled, and they've been left behind. Oliver promised he'd help them escape in return for killing off the rest of the magical folk, but they have no loyalty to him—only to their god. If their fellows are removed from the camps, there's no need for them to wait on Oliver's timeline any longer. They're bent on catching up to their friends who've already been delivered."

"Oliver has no control over them anymore."

"He acknowledges as much. He has no idea when they'll launch a full-fledged attack, but its imminent. He said, *they'll do as they will to appease Cra, and I must make do with whatever magical space their violence gives me.*"

Chou whistled and landed on Eleanor's head. "There are scores of ogres roaming in between Cartheigh and Svelya."

"They'll attack settlements on both sides of the border," said Agnes. "I also fear for the wild unicorns, and even for the Dragon Mines."

Eleanor stood. Chou hopped from her right shoulder to her left as she turned in a circle. "Don't reply to him yet. We must make sure the message we send him is the right one."

"I understand," said Agnes. "I won't send a word until I hear more from you." She looked relieved, as if the hangman's noose had been removed from around her neck—at least, temporarily.

"You don't think he suspects anything of you, do you?"

She shook her head. "No, but he's desperate and flustered. I'm terrified he'll pay more attention to me." Her eyes widened. Green mist seeped from her skin in a protective cloud. "I should stay away from conversations between you and your other advisers. He may be finding some way to spy on me. He may be spying on me right now!"

"Calm yourself," said Eleanor. "We'll provide you with as much protection as possible. Your help has been invaluable to us. My late husband would not have forgotten that. I won't. I'm sure your king,

Samuel, will also be grateful. But now you must hold fast. Only come to me if you have news. Otherwise, stay in your room."

She nodded and stood. "Thank you, Your Majesty, and thank you for forgiving me my previous mistakes."

"Your mistakes are what ultimately led to you being so useful in this matter. Without them, you wouldn't have the magician's ear."

Agnes curtsied and left the room.

"You believe we can trust her?" asked Chou.

"Yes, I do."

"So do I. Still, I noticed you didn't tell her exactly about the Oracle's suggestion that Oliver open the door beside the Watching Pool."

"Even if I trust Agnes, that doesn't mean I want her to know our entire plan at this juncture. Especially when I haven't figured it all out myself yet."

"I feel so important, being in the know! Who would have thought it? Once upon a time, a wee chick arrived at Brice House as a birthday gift for little Ellie. Now he's a royal adviser."

She stroked him. "Funny. I don't even remember that birthday. It's like you've always been with me."

"You were four years old. I was only four *months* old."

"How is it you remember, and I don't?"

"The superior memory of my kind," he said simply. "But you were so lonely before I arrived; you probably shut out those sad recollections. Even before your father's death, you were a solitary little thing."

"Not by choice. Thank goodness my father had the wherewithal to bring you home. Where would I be without you?"

"You'd be trying to attend far too many meetings on your own, instead of leaving it to Orvid and Dorian."

"I could not ask for wiser, more loyal advisers—feathered or otherwise. Truly, I am blessed among sovereigns." She tugged on her riding boots and tried to remember the agenda for today's High Council meeting, but Agnes's revelation elbowed its way to the forefront of her mind.

How could she focus on the day-to-day running of the kingdom when Oliver's meddling threatened the kingdom's very existence?

The sooner they came up with a way to trap Oliver behind a magical doorway, the sooner she'd be able to concentrate on taxes and budgets again.

CHAPTER 23

A SMALL CRIMSON CYCLONE

INITIALLY, DORIAN REJOICED WHEN he realized less than sixty ogres remained in the known nations. The camps were empty. Sixty odd beasts remained scattered about the mountains. Little more than a week's work for Natalie and her friends. He considered himself a realist, but for once, he fell victim to the naivety of one who is thoroughly exhausted by his work. A tired man might underestimate the distance to the finish line in a long race. If he only has a few miles to go, it's easier to keep running. Likewise, Dorian's optimism was a form of self-protection.

Reality came for him quickly, on his first renegade ogre search party. He and Senné joined the other members of the interpolation teams as they followed the ogres' southward trail of destruction. The creatures destroyed two farmsteads, a tiny village hamlet on the northern Clarity River, and a magician's trading outpost, before attacking a herd of wild unicorns in the Great Marshes. Several dozen people died in less than a fortnight, including four magicians, a nomadic hermit witch, and five wild unicorns. The carnage was fast and brutal and complete. In retrospect, whisking serenely snoozing, snoring ogres from the camps and carrying them across the sea was a simple task, almost trite. In the second iteration, they were tracking the marauding beasts through the mountains and forests and marshes, stumbling upon their kill sights, and approaching them while they dozed sporadically under the stars. Double the discomfort, double the disgust, and double the danger.

They relied on wild unicorns and the Unicorn Guard to send word of their exploits and position to Afar Creek and Eclatant. With each new bit of information, the interpolation parties vanished from the Abbey grounds as soon as darkness fell. They reappeared as close to the ogres' crude campsites as possible, struck like unexpected lightning in a cloudless sky, and removed the offending ogres to Ello. On one ill-fated mission, Senné and Penelope interpolated two ogres, but when they returned with a third beast, they found the others already awake. The beasts panicked when their compatriot appeared beside them. Their yells woke the latest delivery. He stumbled to his feet, fists swinging, and struck Penelope before she remounted. Her head struck the unyielding rock of the skull altar. She collapsed into a coma when they returned to the Abbey and died two days later. Senné mourned as if she were his own sister.

For over a month, the team gained new members as more witches learned the spells. Despite Penelope's death and Ophelia's missing arm, witches and unicorns continued to volunteer. Somehow, Natalie remained unharmed and eternally positive. Dorian would never say so to Eleanor, who continued to obsessively worry over her, but he believed Natalie truly enjoyed ogre hunting. Her stories were so high-spirited that young Dasha begged to be included on an interpolation mission, but Natalie, in her wisdom and with great love for him, refused.

"You are too young, Dasha," she said.

"Your Highness is not much older than me," said the unicorn in a pique.

Natalie kissed his nose. "It is true, but I plan to live a very long life. I cannot lose you before that life really begins."

For almost two months, they chased the ogres across the countryside.

As LowWinter ended, there were only three ogres left in the wilderness. Nearly two-hundred humans, magical and mundane, and fourteen unicorns had died in ogre attacks, but the interpolation parties could finally see a waxing moon. Dorian wanted to keep Natalie home for the last mission. There seemed to be no reason to tempt fate. As he readied Senné for what he hoped would be their final trip, a small voice over his shoulder demanded otherwise.

"I mean to come," she said.

"Do you now."

"Don't patronize me, Lord Brandling."

Dorian should have been surprised by a six-year-old using such a highly conceptualized turn of phrase, but nothing Natalie did surprised him anymore. Not her use of large words, her giggling and skipping, her fearlessness in the face of murderous beasts, or her stubborn refusal to eat her vegetables.

He turned to her, such a small person with such a significant life ahead of her. He knelt before her. "I would not think to patronize you, Your Highness. I'm sorry if it sounded such. It's just that your mother is the queen, and she would rather you stay here and be safe."

"I am the next Oracle. I know what will be safe for me, and what will not."

"Will this journey be safe?"

"No. But I will survive. That is enough."

He took a deep breath. Eleanor was meeting with Rosemary, Orvid, and Jan in the Covey library and wasn't due at the Abbey until after lunch. They were hammering nails into the wobbly, mismatched planks of their plot to lure Oliver to the Watching Pool. So far, the plot was a flimsy structure, one that a competent architect of schemes and intrigue would surely condemn. He wouldn't distract her by asking permission, and he wouldn't burden her with additional fear while she worked on such an important, stressful project. Nor could he, however, deny the determined girl in front of him. Natalie reminded him of both Gregory and Eleanor in that moment. A stubborn, redhaired, waifish child who would not be deterred from her duty to Cartheigh.

Senné whispered in his ear. "She's our most accomplished ogre snatcher. These are the wiliest beasts yet. It only makes sense that she'd go."

Dorian took Natalie's hands. "Listen, Your Highness. You may come. We will bring Ione as well." Natalie started to protest, but Dorian shook his head. "You, me, and Ione. Two witches and a warrior. Senné, Whisper, and Terin. This is my bargain."

"Yes, Uncle." Natalie was too smart to argue with that compromise.

"You come home at the first hint of real danger. If you have to leave the rest of us. Your mother would want me to make you promise."

"I promise."

"Then go ready yourself. The ogres will be asleep soon."

She ran off, her steps light. For a moment, she could have been any little girl. Running to collect a doll, tell on her big sister, or get the first helping of cake. Then she turned a cartwheel and spun in a gleeful circle. Red light whirled around her, simultaneously chaotic and controlled.

She was not a normal little girl. She was a small crimson cyclone, bursting with excitement over an ogre hunt. She was the next Oracle of Afar Creek Abbey.

The last interpolation party finally located the remaining ogres in a sheltered copse of trees fifty miles northeast of Maliana, a mere day's walk from Dorian's hometown, Harper's Crossing. His beloved sister lived in the Crossing with her family, and he even worried about his estranged brother, fool that he may be. Abram's wife was a sweet, patient woman, and they had three sons. They lived in his ancestral home, Floodgate Manor. All his childhood friends lived in the Crossing. His beloved home, Laralee, the seat of his dukedom, watched over the lesser estates on Lake Brandling like a spinster aunt supervising her upstart nieces and nephews. Abram managed the servants, some of whom had worked at the estate long before Dorian was born. The Crossing was a happy, peaceful place, where life was slow and predicable. Of all the picturesque cities in Cartheigh, only Solsea was smaller and more secluded. There were few fortifications beyond the antique Fire-iron cannons in the Artisan's Museum at Cedarbough Covey. Any soldiers the region produced were on active duty at Eclatant or Peaksend. The idea of three ogres rampaging along the shores of Lake Brandling terrified him. The town of Harper's Crossing was a fat black rabbit in a snowbank, about to be picked off by a pack of winter-starved wolves.

Dorian dismounted behind a dense blackberry thicket. He and Senné crept around the perimeter of the ogre's campsite, trying to find the best point of attack. "A female. Two young males," said Dorian. "All asleep, thankfully."

"Not for long. It's almost dawn," whispered Senné. "Should we return tonight?"

"They'll move on when they wake. They'll be in the Crossing by this evening."

"We must move quickly then. Look, they're already stirring."

The young male ogres still snored away, prostrate on their backs. The larger female rolled onto her side and then her back. She moaned and mumbled in the grunting ogre language. She raised one clunky arm, dropped it onto her belly, and started snoring again.

"Let's return to the others." Dorian mounted, and Senné picked his way through the darkness. Natalie sat on Terin's back, while Whisper carried the teenage witch called Ione. Ione had jet black hair and dark skin, curtesy of her Mendaen mother. She was quiet, serious, and fierce with her bright orange fireballs. She and Whisper made a surprisingly effective team, as she rarely spoke, and he rarely shut up—in an inversion of the usual unicorn-human relationship. While Whisper had yet to admit it, Dorian suspected he was very fond of her. She sat on his back as if she were born there, with one hand woven through his lush mane.

Whisper and Terin were draped in dark magic—deep crimson and a rusty orange that bordered on brown— but the points of their ears and their muzzles gave off an eerie luminescence, like little pieces of the stars hovering too close to earth. Dorian saw the outline of his hand when he held it before his face. The early rising songbirds had started their sunrise serenade.

"We must hurry," he said. He explained the ogres' family dynamics.

Terin exhaled in two short blasts. His withers twitched. "A mother and her sons, if I had to guess. Sow bears are always most vicious when defending their cubs."

Natalie would take the largest ogre first, and Ione would immediately follow with one of the younger beasts. Dorian and Senné would stay behind and keep an eye on the smallest one. With the plan fully in place, they approached the sleeping ogres.

To their collective dismay, one was an unusually early riser.

Mama ogre sat on a log with her elbows on her knees. She blinked into the pre-dawn gloom. Her sons still snored away beside her, as blissfully catatonic as any growing teenage boys after a long night of rabble-rousing.

"Damnit," said Dorian. "What now?"

"We can't attack," said Senné. "Not with the mother ogre fully awake."

"We can't wait, either. They'll be in the Crossing in time to destroy the evening market."

"We can distract her," said Whisper. "Draw her away from the other two, so we can move them."

"What then?" asked Ione.

"Then there's only one ogre attacking Lord Brandling's home."

"If we move her children," said Natalie, "I think she will stay here and look for them."

The rest of the party paused to consider it. Terin nodded his great head, up and down, up and down. "It's true. Mothers are mothers. They won't leave their children without at least looking for them. If she stays here, we can move her tonight."

"Or maybe she'll head straight for the Crossing, eager to appease her god by murdering a few dozen villagers," said Ione.

They all looked to Dorian. He would have the final say. He chewed the inside of his cheek. If they waited, all three ogres would be in the Crossing soon. If they managed to move the younger ones, at worst case, there would be one angry mama. Best case, she'd remain here, befuddled, and they could interpolate her that evening.

Dorian chose the best case and prayed to his own HighGod that motherhood manifested itself the same way across all species. Even the most repugnant ones.

Dorian and Senné stood outside the ogre's campsite. Natalie cast a spell that mottled Senné's dark hide to a mix of green and brown and gray, so he blended in with the surrounding trees and brambles. Dorian blew a few notes on his woolybuck call. He kept it in his saddle bag when he traveled across the country, in case he ever needed to hunt for his supper. The long, mellow lowing of the buck call replicated the sound of a baby woolybuck calling for its mother. He hoped Mama Ogre would be enticed by an easy meal.

The creature's head swung languidly in his direction. When she stood, her knees popped like the grand finally of a Waxing Fest fireworks display. She stretched her arms over her head, smacked her lips, and looked down at her sleeping sons. She nudged one of them with her foot. The boy-monster didn't move. She scratched her backside before lumbering toward the woods.

Dorian and Senné retreated. For the next thirty minutes, they played a warped game of cat and mouse with the increasingly annoyed ogre. Twice, she started to give up and turn back. Dorian blasted the buck call, as if the imaginary baby woolybuck needed Mama Ogre to put it out of its misery. Each time, the prospect of fresh meat lured her back into the woods. As she bumbled around, Dorian and Senné maneuvered closer to the campsite. Dorian peered through the blackberry thickets. The clearing was blissfully free of lazy ogre youths. Dorian patted Senné's neck. It was time for Mama Ogre to return to her campsite and the shock of her missing children. He slid the buck call into his saddle bag. A few minutes later, Mama Ogre roared her exasperation at the indifferent forest. She stormed toward the clearing.

Dorian hunkered low on Senné's back as the unicorn skirted the campsite. Daylight was upon them, in all its revealing glory, and he caught flashes of red amidst the dark green pine needles. In nature, only parrots, blood, and Natalie's magic took on that particular shade. Chou remained in Maliana, and HighGod willing, no one was bleeding. That left one only answer. Odd, given Natalie's self-control. She knew they must stay concealed. He glanced over his shoulder.

Mama Ogre had noted her children's absence. She turned in a circle and called out to them. "*Urghhhh—Marurgh!*"

She stood freakishly still and waited for a reply. She called out again. She got no response beyond the chirping of the birds. They seemed to be laughing at her, as if she were a confused hunk of poorly carved limestone. She fumed at the insolent starlings and kicked up crumpled boulder and sticks. She flung bones and antlers at the trees, as if to impale the avian naysayers with the remains of her family's last kill.

The birds fled in a great vibrating flock. They continued taunting her as they flew off to more peaceful perches. Unlike landlocked creatures, they could afford to be rude to irate ogres. She watched them go and dropped the dismembered animal leg she'd been gripping like a battle ax. "Urgh? Marurgh?" she asked, as if questioning herself. Her arms hung at her sides like skinned, trussed-up pigs. For the first time,

Dorian saw the ogres as beings with some manner of feelings. It didn't rouse much sympathy, but it was an interesting perspective.

Any time for compassionate contemplation drifted into the sky after the birds, borne on a cloud of leaking magic. The Ogre's eyes narrowed. Even her sludgy brain recognized that the forest should be green and brown, not bright red. With a shout, she blundered toward the crimson aberration. Natalie must have tried to reabsorb the magical mist, but it was too late. The ink had already left the quill, and the color had already stained the ogre's memory.

Senné forewent any attempt at clandestine tiptoeing. He plowed through the shrubs and leaves toward their compatriots. Whipping branches left welts like bee stings on Dorian's face. Terin and Whisper's coats returned to their usual blinding white as Natalie and Ione retreated on foot. Ione fired spells at the two unicorns while simultaneously trying to hold Natalie upright. Natalie joined her, but their haphazard attempts to hide their protectors only made them stand out more. Terin and Whisper were coated in splashes of orange and red and greenish brown forest camouflage, as if they'd just rolled around on one of Ticia's landscape paintings.

"Your Highness, stop conjuring! Save your strength," Ione said. She lifted Natalie and ran for the sheltering branches of an ancient oak tree. Natalie tucked her left hand against her chest. Real blood— not mystic scarlet air or a cascade of red parrot feathers— dripped down her arm.

Dorian dismounted before Senné stopped. He hit the ground running with his sword drawn. Senné joined Terin and Whisper in a stockade wall fortified with horns and sharp hooves. Their disguises faded, taking the hodgepodge of color with them. The three stallions faced the ogre, two white eagles and a dark osprey staring down a giant buzzard. The ogre screamed nonsense, interspersed with a few *Urghs* and *Mururghs.* She demanded to know what they'd done to her children. In her rage, she turned on a cedar tree. She ripped it clean out of the ground, roots and all, and threw it at the unicorns. They jumped in coordinated surprise but held their ground.

The ogre charged them. They dodged and whirled, as graceful as their winged likenesses. They stabbed her with their horns and slashed with their hooves. When one stallion lunged for her vulnerable belly, the other two distracted her by going for her eyes. The ogre spun and struck blindly, narrowly missing her flighty targets. Dorian hoped she'd get dizzy enough to collapse.

The ogre hadn't paid him much mind so far, so he crouch-ran to the tree where Ione huddled over Natalie. Ione stood and spun around at the sound of his footsteps. One of her bright orange magical orbs narrowly missed his right arm. Her face paled to gray under her dark skin. "Scales and fire, Lord Brandling, I almost hit you."

He knelt beside Natalie. "I'm sorry. I snuck up on you. But I'm glad you missed, or I might not be much help in this sword fight."

He tried to touch Natalie, but she moaned and pulled away.

"One of those young ogres," said Ione. "When we dropped them off, it woke up. It grabbed Natalie's little hand, and it wouldn't let go. I'm surprised it didn't rip her arm right from her socket or kill her right there. It almost seemed afraid."

"How did she escape?"

Ione's dark eyes were two wide wagon wheels of wonderment. "She tugged and tugged and it wouldn't let go. She cast fireballs at it, and still, it held on. But then she started crying, and it looked at her as if… it felt sorry for her. It let her go."

Dorian pulled Natalie's hand away from her chest. "But not before it ripped her hand apart." Her index finger and middle finger were crushed and bloody, and her thumb was bent at an unnatural angle. "It probably infected her with the pestilence that killed the king."

Natalie looked him with green eyes made brighter by tears and fear. "Will the healers take off my hand? Like Penelope?"

"We'll let them decide that," said Dorian.

"Should I take Natalie back to the Abbey?" Ione asked.

Natalie grabbed Dorian's arm and shook her head. "I have to stay."

"Natalie, you promised me—"

"Ione can't take *all* of you to the Abbey by herself. She's not strong enough to interpolate three other people and three unicorns at once."

Ione grimaced. "She's right. But you're injured, little princess. You need a healer."

"I will not leave you all here!"

The ogre screamed, Senné whinnied, and Dorian flinched. He had to help his horned comrades and keep the ogre from storming off in the direction of the Crossing. "I don't have time to argue," he said to Ione. "Stay here; try to keep out of sight."

Ione nodded and huddled beside Natalie again, as if trying to blend in with the tree trunk. She watched Dorian slink toward the battle. He felt her gaze upon him, the heavy load of her dependency on his protection, until the tree's bulk blocked them from view.

For the better part of an hour, through what felt like a race with no end, Dorian fought alongside the three stallions against Mama Ogre. Her strength and her wrath seemed limitless. Twice, Dorian got close enough to make substantial cuts on her belly, and Terin's horn found its mark in the soft spot under her chin. None of those blows, however, matched the near lethal strike Gregory had made on the one-eyed ogre during the Battle of Peaksend Road. Despite her injuries, Mama Ogre would not give in. Her stomping feet kicked up years' worth of decaying leaves. Her fists were a rockslide; her irate lamentations the grind of locked carriage wheels on a mountain road.

The unicorns were nimble enough to avoid physical contact with her, but they were exhausted. Their sides heaved like waves on a stormy sea. Dorian, on his two legs, wasn't as quick. He got in another slash on her belly, but he didn't duck fast enough to avoid her retaliatory strike. The edge of her fist caught his shoulder and sent him flailing across the clearing. A sturdy cedar stopped his forward momentum. His head hit unyielding bark. He blinked and the world spun and wobbled. *Have my eyes detached from my skull?* he thought. For a moment, he hovered in the dream space. He saw himself looking down at his own two eyes, still attached by long strands of flesh but dangling against his chest. He hitched up his breath to scream.

Blackness eclipsed the vision, but it wasn't a welcome magical escape from this nightmare. Senné stood before him and prevented the ogre from smashing in his skull. He grabbed the stallion' mane, and Senné dragged him away as he scrambled astride. Somehow, his muscles knew how to pull him onto the stallion's back, even if his brain couldn't communicate correctly with his limbs.

Dorian hugged Senné's neck. Despair washed over him. "We can't beat that creature. Get Terin and Whisper. We must be close enough for Natalie's magic to reach us, quickly."

Senné cantered toward the two witches, who still huddled beside the tree. Dorian slid from his back.

"Natalie—we must get to the Crossing. Warn them the ogre is coming. We must go, now."

Natalie's eyes were a little clearer, as if she'd grown accustomed to her injury. Dorian's own mind felt clouded over with pain and fear. He'd never felt so hopeless in a battle. No matter what he did, innocent people would surely die today because he hadn't been able to beat this monster.

"Uncle," said Natalie. "Let me go to her."

"What?" Maybe her thoughts were not as clear as her green eyes looked. "No. All we can do is go to the Crossing and warn people to hide."

"She's angry because we took her children. Angry mothers are very strong." She struggled to her feet. "But I have a strength, too. Special strength. My Auntie gave it to me."

"Hazelbeth?" Dorian grabbed the child to keep her from falling. He turned to the other witch. "Ione. Please. Before this monster kills all of us. Let's do *something* right here."

"I think Natalie knows what is right," Ione said. "She will be my Oracle someday. I trust her."

"She's not the Oracle yet!"

Natalie smiled at him. "But I am. I always have been. She's part of me, and I'm part of her." She took a few stumbling steps toward the three stallions and the rampaging ogre. She tucked her injured hand inside her fur cloak. Blood crusted on the soft hair along the sleeve.

"No. Natalie. Your mother—"

"My mother loves me. All mothers love their children."

Mine didn't, Dorian wanted to say, but the words wouldn't come, and they wouldn't matter anyway. Clearly, this ogre cared more about her offspring than Dorian's own mother had for him. Eleanor did love Natalie, however, if love was a strong enough verb. Dorian must protect her.

He reached for her, but he met a wall of bright orange light that felt like slick glass, and he could reach no further. Ione's power kept him in his place. His head swam, and he vomited against the tree trunk.

"You have a concussion, Your Grace," the witch said as he retched and fell to his knees. He clung to the leaves and dirt below him as if they would keep him from floating away. He raised his head and watched Natalie approach the ogre.

For a moment, the ogre didn't notice the tiny person who walked toward her as if she were ten feet tall and her hand wasn't destroyed. Once Natalie released her magic, however, the ogre turned to her, a bull drawn to a red flag. She screamed down at the child, her breath a southbound, rotten wind.

"I'll send you to your children. Complete your prophecy. Isn't that what you want? To go to the land promised to your people?" Natalie pointed at the ogre with her whole hand. "But you *must* stop this. You must calm yourself."

The ogre pounded her first against her thighs.

"*Stop it.* Or I will have to make you stop."

Now the ogre took a few rushing steps toward her, but Terin stepped between them.

"My friends are angry," Natalie said. "They'd like to kill you, and perhaps you deserve it, as repayment for whatever lives you've recently took. But I don't want *anyone* to die. Not them or you. Not me, either."

The ogre paused for a moment. Dorian doubted she'd understood one word, but she seemed to sense something different about this small human. She narrowed her eyes in suspicion. Whatever the difference, she didn't approve. She charged.

Natalie brought her injured index finger to the center of her forehead. White light exploded from her face.

The blast lifted the ogre off her feet, and she crashed into a tree. It bent backwards with her weight, and then whipped forward, slamming her into the ground like a flyswatter smashing a bug.

She lifted her head once and mumbled *mugurgh.* He eyes rolled. With a gasp, she slumped facedown into the leaves.

"Now we'll take her to Ello," Natalie announced.

Dorian scrambled to his feet and hobbled toward her. He crumpled beside her, so they were roughly the same height. The three unicorns clustered around them, and Ione put a hand on his back. "Are you sure you can do it, Your Highness?"

Natalie collapsed into his arms. "Perhaps Ione should do it."

Ione beckoned to Whisper. "We will go. The rest of you stay here. It won't take long."

"Don't kill her," said Natalie. "Just take her to her children."

Dorian sat in the grass, his head pounding, with the injured child in his lap. Senné and Terin stood watch over them, although once Ione and Whisper disappeared with the unconscious ogre, there were no more monsters left to fear in their world. At least not the ogre kind.

"You see, Uncle," Natalie whispered. "Auntie said I'd know when

I needed her help, and I did." A bruise marked her forehead. Drying blood dripped down her face.

"You told me you knew you'd survive," said Dorian. "Did you know because you are the next Oracle?"

"I didn't really know," she said. "I only knew that's what I wanted. Mother used to tell me if I believed something with my whole heart, it could come true. I tried to believe Poppa hadn't died, but it didn't work."

Dorian's heart hurt. "I wish it had worked, Natalie. I miss your Poppa every day. He'd be so proud of you. You risked yourself to save all of us. He did the same thing, several times."

"Will you tell me those stories?"

"Yes." He kissed the top of her head. "Every Desmarais child should know the glory of her forefathers."

"You can tell me as I lay in the sickroom, after they take my hand."

Before Dorian replied, Ione and Terin reappeared silently, ten paces away from them. "We left her there. The young ones were already awake. I didn't see them, but I'm sure she'll find them. HighGod knows she's louder than my own mother was, calling to me as a child, and she was a Mendaen opera singer."

"I'm sorry, Your Highness," said Dorian, choking back tears. "I'm so sorry about your hand."

She smiled through her pain. "It's all right. I don't need hands to perform magic. One can live a long life with one hand. That's what I plan to do."

CHAPTER 24

BLUE WATER

AND SO, AFTER OVER five hundred years, the last ogres left the known nations. A small girl removed the majority of them, and for her efforts, she lost her hand. After their experience with Gregory, the witches acted quickly, before any pestilence infiltrated the rest of the limb. They doused her with a strong tonic, and she fell deeply asleep. They finished the surgery before Eleanor arrived at the Abbey. The senior healers anticipated a complete recovery, but they kept the child in a magically induced slumber to give her extra time to heal.

Eleanor had little time to rejoice over the first great achievement of her reign or mourn her small daughter's loss. She had only an hour at Natalie's bedside before her other duties called her back to Eclatant. Eleanor, Dorian, Rosemary, and Chou Chou spent four hours in deep discussion of the proper response to Ezra Oliver's letter. Over several pots of tea and a basket of cookies—and with multiple trips to the water closet for all humans involved—they analyzed their precarious position from every possible angle. The meeting left Eleanor's brain feeling quite mushy, but she knew they'd left no thought *un*thought. They called Agnes to Eleanor's chamber.

"Don't you think it's time we use the king's receiving room for such meetings?" whispered Chou. "Or the High Council Chamber? What about Gregory's old study? You could always—"

"No," said Eleanor. "I've told you, Chou, I don't want to move to Gregory's old chamber, or, HighGod forbid, Casper's. Turn them into museums or save them for Cyrus. This room has been my home for almost two decades. Besides, this is an intimate gathering. I like the privacy and the informality."

Eleanor had told everyone to wear comfortable clothes. She herself wore her riding leggings and had High Noon's blanket on her lap. Dorian wore an old pair of leggings and some battered boots he'd had since she met him, and Rosemary and Orvid were in varying states of magical repose with their frumpy winter cloaks. Rosemary even wore a pink woolen cap over her white hair. The fire crackled cheerfully in the hearth, and the room smelled like mint tea. Agnes entered the chamber and settled before them, anxious and tense on a backless stool. The gathering was like a literary society meeting crossed with an inquisition.

Eleanor thanked Agnes for coming, and Rosemary handed her a quill and set a small bottle of ink on the round table between them. "I shall dictate the letter," said Eleanor. "You write it down, word for word. Except—well, you should add your own accent to it."

Chou chirped in from his perch on the back of the couch beside Dorian's head. "You must also write the opening yourself, so it follows your usual line of communication."

Agnes bent over the letter and scratched out a few lines. Chou flew across the room and landed on her shoulder. He peered into her lap, where she balanced the parchment on a copy of the Carthean-Svelyan dictionary. He whistled his approval. "Just your general salutations and wishes for good health. She also includes condolences on misplacing a herd of ogres. Carry on, Your Majesty."

Eleanor nodded and began.

"I have earned the trust of the Abbottess, Rosemary. She speaks to me often of the Oracle's poor health and her declining power. The Oracle is so

weak the witches have removed her from the Watching Pool. I myself have been sent to the Pool, as part of the rotating cast of sorceresses that stand guard over the water. When I sit beside it for hours, with nothing to do but think, I get the smallest inkling of what the Oracle has observed these many centuries. There is great power in the Watching Pool. Remember, water from the Pool first revealed the other worlds to you. There is a connection between the Pool and the dream road you seek to tread, and the Pool is without its true Guardian. You claim the greatest magical power in our world. You seek to be the most powerful being in all existence. Why not try to work your spell beside the Pool? If there is a place in our world where it can be done, it is there.

By whatever means, the ogres have left the known nations. I have seen no evidence the witches of Afar Creek were involved, especially given the depleted state of their leader. It is possible that Orvid Jones and the magicians of First Covey are responsible, but if they are, Queen Eleanor has kept their maneuvering secret. If you can harness the power of the Pool, however, maybe you don't need ogres. You won't need to create space by destroying magical people and mystical creatures. I don't know what will come of your finagling with the most intimate workings of the universe, but I feel this is the lesser of the evils you have forced upon me.

If you are so inclined to try, write to me soon, as I will have watch duty at the Pool for the next four days. I will make sure you were not disturbed. Please don't forget your promises to me. Once you have achieved your goal, you will desist in your abuse of me. I am sick of living in fear of your retribution. I am tired of keeping your foul secrets. As I have for months, I refuse your offer to join you.

Agnes of Gammonreil."

Agnes's quill scratched away on the parchment, and her tongue poked out from the side of her mouth like a meticulous schoolgirl. When she finished, she sat up straight and stretched. Chou Chou fluttered above her head to make room for her outstretched arms and then landed on her shoulder. He muttered to himself as he reread the letter. He shook himself and whistled an affirmative to Eleanor.

"We're all in agreement that it appeals to his vanity enough, but not too much?" Chou asked.

"I believe so," said Eleanor. "Agnes?"

"His vanity is his greatest downfall."

"It's the downfall of many," said Rosemary. "But none so much as Oliver. I believe it protects you as well, Agnes."

"It's congruent with my usual communication with him."

"Fearful and frustrated, yet defiant," said Chou. "It also points him away from the witches, if he cares to search for the ogres."

"I'm sorry you and your magicians must be the decoys, Mr. Jones," said Eleanor.

"Psst…the witches bore the burden of interpolation," said Orvid. "It's the least we could do."

"Thank you all for your insight." Eleanor twirled one finger toward the ceiling in a universal signal of conclusion. She'd seen Casper use the gesture a thousand times, and without any conscious thought, she'd adopted it. It felt decidedly sovereignly.

Orvid and Agnes stood, as her rotating royal finger commanded. Chou landed on Orvid's shoulder. They would retire to Agnes's chamber, and she'd call the fairyman to collect her letter. While Eleanor trusted Agnes, she was taking no chances. Orvid would stand outside her door and monitor the magic she performed within. Chou would hide in the rafters to observe the fairyman's letter retrieval.

"I wish a swarm of bees could deliver this letter," said Chou. "Delivery by fairyman seems too pleasant and dignified."

"Fairies are hardly pleasant or dignified," said Dorian. "They're crude, foul little bounty hunters."

"They still work for him, even though he planned to let the ogres kill them all."

"Who knows what he has promised them, or what lies he tells," said Agnes. "Even fairies, as crafty as they are, aren't safe from his exploitation." Dark memories skittered behind her eyes like a cockroach infestation.

"You're doing a good thing, Agnes," Eleanor said. "I believe you'll be free of him soon."

Agnes snapped her fingers, and two misty green dragons flew out of her hair. They spat chartreuse fire before disappearing. She called over her shoulder. "No one will be free of him until we send him through that door, Your Majesty." She stalked to the door with her shoulders set and her chin jutting, like a rebellious child intent on finally proving the injustice of her parents' rules.

You must be at the cavern when it happens. She insists. Bring the kaleidoscope.

When Eleanor read the opening of Rosemary's note to Dorian, she feared his head might explode. He stormed around her chamber, making extremely valid points.

You're the queen. We can't risk you.

Why you? What will you bring to this situation?

It will be only you, an enfeebled old woman, and a sorceress posing as a spy and therefore of limited use in protecting you?

And Orvid Jones? Well… that's a little better, but it's still not enough protection.

We just lost one ruler. Now we place another in mortal danger?

Casper would never allow Gregory to participate in such folly!

This is ridiculous.

I'm coming with you.

What do you mean, she doesn't want me there? Absurd!

You're the queen. You're the queen. You're the queen!

Eleanor told him she didn't know why the Oracle wanted her there when she pushed Oliver into another world, only that she insisted. They would have to trust Hazelbeth's wisdom, or her intuition—or whatever combination thereof inspired her strange, dangerous request.

That is how Eleanor ended up spending two nights in a hidden alcove in the Oracle's cavern. She slept on a pile of dragon robes, with the Oracle huddled in a ball on the next pile of fur. Orvid Jones took the far corner. He sat upright, even when he dozed. A jug of water and a basket of dried fruit and beef sustained Eleanor and Orvid. Hazelbeth ate nothing, but she did sip from a flask containing water from the Watching Pool. She slept most of the time. During her waking moments, she silently stared at the blue effervescence wobbling along the dirt floor. The Pool's light reached around the corner and into their little hiding place, as if the water longed to touch its old companion. The Watching Pool never slept.

Eleanor didn't dare light a candle, so she couldn't read. She couldn't risk talking to Orvid. They were meant to be as silent as moss on an old grave. She passed the time napping and thinking. During one afternoon, she relived her entire life in her mind, just to have something to do, as if she were writing her autobiography. She smiled at times and stifled laughs, and when she thought of Nathan, a few silent tears tracked down her cheeks. *The Oracle has lived far longer than I ever will, but I've certainly crammed a lot of living into my thirty-four years.*

Rosemary stationed Agnes beside the Watching Pool with her own pile of warm robes and simple sustenance. She purposely avoided looking in the direction of Eleanor, Orvid, and the Oracle. She maintained the appearance of a solitary, monotonous watch over Hazelbeth's abandoned domain.

The task was nothing if not mind-numbing. By the morning of what seemed like the third day, Eleanor understood how prisoners in solitary confinement lost their wits. Nothing ever changed in the cavern. Only Rosemary's routine morning and evening visits gave her some indication as to when she should try to sleep. The sound of her teacher's voice broke up the monotonous burbling of the Watching Pool. She had always found the Pool's aquatic chatter soothing, but after three days, it was like the ping of hail against a glass window.

I wonder, she thought, as she flexed her ankles and wrists to keep the blood moving, *if one can die of boredom the same way one can die at the hand of a maniac magician. At least the latter would be quick.*

"Someone is coming," whispered the Oracle. Her voice scraped the dimness like an iron rasp on a dragon's claw.

"Rosemary?" Eleanor's own words chafed her throat.

"No." Hazelbeth's eyes were bright blue fireflies flickering in her face. "It is the *other*."

Eleanor's pulse beat its bloody fists against her temple. No one could tell in the dim, bluish light, but she was surely as pale as a banshee in winter. Suddenly, boredom didn't seem so bad.

"HighGod." Orvid shuffled closer. "He's truly come?"

"He has. Mr. Jones, please lift me. I must get closer. Eleanor, you have your *mar'menon*?"

For a moment, Eleanor had no idea what she meant. She was terrified, as if someone had just told her she left Cyrus unattended in the bathtub. Then she remembered Agnes's definition, back at Gammonreil. *Mar'menon*. The Svelyan word for kaleidoscope. The glass rainbow.

"Yes," she whispered. "I have it."

"When the door opens, you must look through it."

"How will I know it's open?"

"When is a door not a door? When it is ajar."

"I'm sorry?"

"You have seen many open doors in your life. You'll know."

Eleanor pressed against the thick tree roots that formed the cavern walls. She held her hand in front of her face. In the Pool's bluish light, it glowed like the limb of a frozen corpse. The water's reflection created creepy wiggling shadows on thick clusters of woody entrails, turning roots into bluish octopus tentacles. The fishy smell of mud dominated the remaining traces of old lavender.

A shadow slowly overcame the lumpy outline of Agnes on the cavern wall. Darkness swallowed darkness, and the vampire bat closed in on the terrified mouse. Eleanor couldn't see him, but she recognized his nasally voice.

"Agnes of Gammonreil," said Oliver. "How goes your watch?"

"Well enough. I'd started to doubt you'd come, so your presence is a relief. Will you finish what you started and take your strangling hand off my throat?" Agnes sounded bitter and angry. She revealed no hint of hopefulness.

Oliver offered his own question instead of answering hers. "Is the old witch dead yet?"

"She's nearly so."

"What will they do without their seer?"

"Not all Abbeys have seers."

"But Afar Creek does. It always has. Tell me, has the seer said anything about where the Ogre Watch has hidden the ogres?"

"Ogre Watch? Um. Ah. Hmm." Oliver had thrown an unexpected plot twist into the story Agnes had carefully memorized, but she recovered quickly by espousing ignorance. "Did the Ogre Watch move the ogres? How?"

"It's the only plausible solution. Who else has access to the beasts? There's no one else who can move them the way I do, not even my old apprentice, Mr. Jones. The Watch must have somehow convinced the creatures to move camps, to hide them from me. Probably somewhere in the Scaled Mountains."

"There are indeed many areas of the Scaled Mountains that even my people have not explored."

"I don't know how much faith I have in your little idea, but it's worth a try. If I can open this door now, then I can be finished with ogres. If not, I'll visit the old camps and get the information I need out of the Watch. Hopefully, that won't be necessary. Torture is a messy, unpleasant business. I don't fancy removing anyone's fingernails. Nor do I relish the thought of scouring the mountains for disgusting beasts."

"What if you can't find the ogres?" Agnes asked.

Eleanor wished she'd just say the proverbial password. *Blue water.* It would indicate Oliver had entered the pool, and he was focusing on his spell.

Agnes's shadow stood and walked closer to the pool.

"Eh," said Oliver. "I'll slay that dragon when it appears. But with your knowledge of Svelyan geography, you'll still have your uses."

Her shadow covered its gray face with a gray hand.

"Don't weep, child. You cast your spell, so to speak, and now you must face the consequences."

"For how long?"

"As long as it takes. But come now, let's be positive. You can go home. Back to your cold mountains and your terrible rabbit stew. Although, I'm sure you've come to enjoy our Carthean hospitality during the short-lived reign of Gregory the Second, moron that he was."

"The late king was kind to me. As is the queen."

"Ah, the queen. If there's one magical talent I've never mastered, its prophecy. I never would have predicted that odd young woman with the cracked shoe would one day rule this country." He cracked his knuckles. "In all honesty, if I'd come through the ranks as her vassal, things may have turned out differently. She has more gumption than any of the Desmarais kings. They grew up too fat and happy."

"Queen Eleanor wouldn't want someone like you in her service."

"You didn't know me in my younger days! I was such a patriot. Determined to protect Cartheigh from your frozen countrymen! Until Casper's disrespect and ineptitude pushed me right into King Peter's arms. Then Eleanor..." Oliver laughed and slapped his hands against his thighs. "She pushed me— quite literally— into this enchanted water! She set me upon my destined path, in all its figurative, theoretical glory.

She shaped my life's trajectory, and she showed me the In Between. The dream road that connects one world to another. I'm here because of her, and she is where she is because of me."

"How so?"

"I proved to be a challenging rival all these years, of course. I helped her prove herself and reach her full potential."

Eleanor fidgeted. Oliver's words struck home in an annoying way.

"You should hurry," said Agnes. "Rosemary will return in the evening. You may need to try multiple times, since you don't even know if you can do it."

"If it can be done through magic, I can do it." His shadow moved along the wall, closer to the Pool. He leaned down. Perhaps he was removing his boots. "If it doesn't work, it's because your theory failed."

"What is that?" asked Agnes.

Oliver straightened and held up something too small to cast much of a shadow. "A key, of course," he said. "If I open the door, I will hardly want to come back here and use it. With this, I'll be able to open it wherever I choose." He leaned down again. Two clumping sounds meant he'd tossed his boots aside. He removed his outer cloak and set it aside. Eleanor imagined a rock or a crooked root, away from the wet. He stretched his arms over his head, an aged grappler preparing to wrestle the fabric of the universe.

Eleanor leaned around the tree roots. She saw Oliver's hand and the Fire-iron key he clutched. He walked forward, out of her sight again. His shadow slid along beside him like a pet snake. He hopped in place. The shadow also hopped along, as obedient shadows do.

"That blue water is colder than it looks," said Agnes.

Eleanor nodded to Orvid Jones. He hitched the Oracle up in his arms and slunk toward the pool. Hazelbeth's sunken eyes seemed to absorb the energy of her old home. They shone from her face like they'd filled with cerulean water. As if she were holding back tears made from the Pool itself. Eleanor followed a few feet behind him with the kaleidoscope in her right hand. She'd already spun the scope so the bird met the leaf. She'd only have to lift it to her eye to see what the Oracle wanted her to see.

Agnes watched Oliver intently. She gave no indication she'd noticed Orvid or Eleanor. Oliver stood ankle deep in the pool with his back to them and his arms outstretched. Orvid set Hazelbeth on the ground beside a boulder. The old witch's lips moved silently. Her liquid eyes rolled in her head. Orvid backed away as if she were a lit firework.

His heel hit a root and he stumbled. He caught himself, but not before the sound of scraping gravel cut through Oliver's magical trance. He spun around.

His eyes narrowed as he recognized the Oracle and Orvid Jones, with Eleanor crouched behind them. His head jerked in Agnes's direction, as if he were looking to her for help. She conjured three green fireballs. They hovered beside her face. Before he commanded her to strike, one of them shot at Oliver's arm. His key flew from his hands, plunked into the pool, and disappeared with a hiss.

"HighGoddamn you, Agnes of Gammonreil," he snarled. "The punishment for treason is death—but the punishment for regicide? You'll burn, you know. The world will know you killed your king, and *you'll burn!*"

"Oliver!" Eleanor cried. "Here we are again!"

"I won't be distracted this time by you, Eleanor Desmarais." Creamy light solidified into five menacing fireballs. They rotated around his head like moons in orbit. "If I have to kill you all, you've brought it on yourselves. Especially you, you old wretch. I would have allowed you to die in your bed—"

Hazelbeth's eyes were spinning wheels. They ground against her skull and threw blue sparks. She mumbled to herself without acknowledging Oliver. He covered his face as the water around him whipped into a frenzy. Hazelbeth's remaining hair stood on end.

To Eleanor's astonishment, a waterspout formed around Oliver, like the ones she'd sometimes seen on the Solsea horizon. It stretched and contracted—cylinder, triangle, square, rectangle. A great groaning came from the air itself, as if the atmosphere were giving birth.

Light pierced the darkness, but it wasn't magical. It was common sunlight, in a place where the sun never shone. Oliver looked over his shoulder, his expression a mixture of terror and elation.

"I *did* it! I opened the door!"

"You did nothing." Hazelbeth's voice came from everywhere and nowhere. Her signature magical blue energy shot from her face. On the edges, blue transmuted from purple to bright red, like a truncated rainbow.

The Oracle's projectile struck Oliver's chest. He flew backward, into the sunlight.

"Eleanor!" Agnes screamed.

Eleanor ran across the cavern, past Hazelbeth. The old witch kept firing magic into the hole between worlds. She held the kaleidoscope to her dark eye.

Later, she tried to explain what she had seen to Dorian, but she found she could not do it justice. Once again, she thought of dreams. Remembered but nonsensical; recalled but never in the right words.

Some elements of the vision were simple. Some were impossible. Some were simply impossible. The iron birds of Gregory's dreams whizzed past her, growling with the lung capacity of a thousand ogres. She witnessed other strange modes of transportation. Some resembled carriages with no horses. Others were long metal caterpillars creeping along metal roads. Some were like mutated insects. Whirling circular wings grew from their backs. They hovered over huge square buildings where healers in green pants and white coats ferried the injured to and fro on wheeled beds.

Flat boxes attached to walls displayed moving paintings. People carried small black rectangles in their hands. They spoke to them and stared at them and poked them with their fingers. The women dressed like men. Some men dressed like women. There were an inordinate number of dogs, but she didn't see birds on anyone's shoulders. She saw no horses.

All this flashed by her in a few oddly endless moments. Time stopped, yet it rushed on, faster than Gregory's grumbling metal birds.

Short narratives appeared amidst the overlapping, flashing images. As one simply knows things in dreams, she recognized that some of these short stories were part of this world's now, while some came from its past. Soldiers in heavy green uniforms blasted each other with weapons she didn't understand. People huddled in groups while fiery thunder rained down on them and destroyed their homes and chapels. She took a few steps on a beach that should have been beautiful, but instead, strange multicolored rubbish covered the sand. She cried as she watched an otter covered in sticky black tar trying to swim through dismally fouled water. When a man in a gray uniform ripped a small child wearing a yellow star from her mother, Eleanor knew both of them would die soon, far away from each other. She screamed in her own head and tried to pull away from the kaleidoscope.

Hazelbeth's voice sounded in between her ears. *Not yet. Not yet.*

She saw women who wore long dresses with full sleeves— dresses Eleanor herself might wear. They carried signs and chanted. People lined the streets around them. Some cheered them on, but more jeered and taunted them. It was an older memory of this world. Older than the vision of dark-skinned people who marched in lines with their arms linked.

She turned around and saw countless women bent over desks with piles of books before them. Women sang and danced before millions of people in risqué clothing. Their short pants and tiny tops would be enough to get one hauled off to prison for obscenity in Cartheigh, unless one was in the employ of Pandra Tate or her colleagues. Women strolled beaches in equally scantily attire. Their hair flowed down their backs, and they laughed and rolled their eyes at men who called out to them.

They ran, just for the sake of running. They looked into their own giant kaleidoscopes at the far-off stars, and they fought beside male soldiers. They stood before groups of men, dressed in short skirts and men's shirts. The men listened to them—even if Eleanor could tell some of their attention was begrudging. They cuddled their children and read to them; they sat beside their sickbeds and cheered their games. Some clearly had husbands, but some were alone. Some were with other women.

A solitary woman stood on a podium, and once again, Eleanor *knew* what she *knew*. She wasn't sure if it had already happened, or if it would happen soon, but this woman was a ruler. A leader of a great nation, chosen by her people. She exuded power and command and passion for the citizens of her country. She stood inside a chapel or a great hall the likes of which Eleanor had never seen. Huge boxes hung from the vaulted ceiling. They displayed her moving portrait. The people cheered for her as confetti rained down on them all. They celebrated her ascension —just like Eleanor's people had celebrated hers.

She struggled to get where she is, Eleanor thought. *All the women who had come before her cleared her path.* The violence she'd seen was the way of men, and slowly, the people of this strange world finally decided to try something different.

Good, said the Oracle, in her head. *You see the time for change is coming, in our world and others. But look here... there is one more vision I'd show you of this place...*

Eleanor looked over her shoulder. A pastel palace with round turrets loomed before her like a giant Waning Fest gingerbread cabin. It seemed out of place in this world of square corners and dark windows. People milled around it, smiling into their little black boxes. They gathered around a pretty woman in an ostentatious gown with unwieldy hoop skirts. She had blonde hair and wore a sparkly tiara. She embraced myriad little girls.

They wore replicas of her fantastical costume, complete with their own bedazzled tiaras.

They wore glass shoes.

Eleanor squinted into the kaleidoscope. They weren't glass, no—but some other clear material made to look like it.

She swung her head right, and there were armies of little girls, all dressed in the same poufy skirts and clear shoes. They read books filled with pictures of a pretty, sad looking young woman in rags. As they flipped the pages, she went to a ball dressed in finery, lost her glass shoe, and by the end, her rags had become a lovely wedding gown. She hung on the arm of a handsome prince.

Every book ended the same way, with a message spelled out in looping letters.

She lived happily ever after.

No, Eleanor thought. *No, she didn't. That's a lot of dragonshit!* She wished she could place herself in their stories, with all her years of struggle and heartbreak on illustrated display. She'd show them they would have to fight. Life would be beautiful, and it would be tragic, full of laughter and tears and many carriage-loads of hard work. It would all be worth it, but there was no such thing as happily ever after.

There are lessons to be learned from both worlds, and in both worlds, Hazelbeth said. *Teach them, and be taught. Be the tutor and the student.*

Eleanor lowered the kaleidoscope. She looked through the enchanted doorway, into the word next door. This was no dream—it was another existence, as it was happening in a moment of shared time. The clear blue sky hugged the razor-sharp outline of monolithic silver buildings. Closer to the ground, shrubs grew in clumps beside cracked stone pathways strewn with cast off bags and boxes and bottles. A metal caterpillar streaked past on its raised road, far above Ezra Oliver's head. The magician stood alone, his face a mask of terror and wonder. He held up one hand, but no magical light came from his fingers. He shook his fist. His eyes widened in shock.

He turned and looked Eleanor squarely in the eye. As she watched, he aged from a spritely man who looked to be about seventy, to an ancient wretch who had surely surpassed a century. He took two wobbly steps toward her. He reached for her. "Don't leave me here! I promise… I promise—"

With that, in a puff of blue and purple and bright bloody red, the Oracle slammed the door.

Eleanor dropped to her knees. The Oracle lay across Orvid's lap with her eyes closed. Her mouth hung open, and a line of bluish spittle ran down her chin. "HighGod," Eleanor said. "Is she dead?"

"No," said Orvid. "Not yet. Agnes ran to find Rosemary."

"Did you see anything?"

"Not much. It was too bright, like walking out of a dungeon into a sunny afternoon. I think I saw some buildings. It looked like Oliver tried to come back."

"But Hazelbeth shut the door. Is he gone? Truly gone?"

Hazelbeth's head rolled in Eleanor's direction. Her eyelids twitched. "He cannot return. He has no magic." She panted out the words. "He'll age like a dying leaf during the first cold spell."

"He did look terribly old. He looked older than—" Eleanor stopped, embarrassed.

"Older than me?" A trace of smile graced the Oracle's cracked lips. She wiped her mouth with one skinny arm. "I'd dissolve into a pile of dust if I crossed that threshold. But he will die. Human beings cannot live two hundred years without magic to keep them alive." She coughed, and a bit of blood seeped from the corner of her mouth. Red blood and blue spittle became a purple smudge.

When she closed the door, her magic had the same hue. Blue and red makes purple. Natalie?

"Horns and Fire," whispered Orvid. "Where is Agnes?"

"Wise one," Eleanor whispered. "The red magic—"

Hazelbeth coughed again.

"She's too weak to talk," said Orvid.

"But did you see it? Her magic was red. Red like—"

"Agnes! Abbottess!" Orvid looked past Eleanor. Greenish light lit the cavern, as if the trees had turned themselves upside down, and their leaves were growing through the ceiling instead of their roots. Agnes appeared, followed by Rosemary. A travois floated behind them.

Rosemary and the healers huddled around Hazelbeth. They cast white and pink and yellow light over the old witch and whispered about herbs and strengthening spells. Agnes stepped into the Pool. She fished around in the bright blue water, straightened, and waded toward Eleanor with a sparkly something in her hand.

Orvid lay Hazelbeth on the healer's travois. The first witch snapped her fingers and spoke a quiet spell, and the little cot levitated. Two healers took positions at the front and rear of the travois. Their fingers grazed it to keep it steady. Their compatriot scooped water from the pool into a clay cup. She held it to the Oracle's parched lips. Most of it dribbled down her chin, but they managed to get some moisture into her. A good thing, as she resembled a dried-out sponge.

Agnes handed Oliver's key to Orvid. "Would this have worked?" she asked.

"I don't know," he said. "But no one else will ever know, either."

Orvid closed his fist over the key. Creamy light seeped around his closed fingers. He squeezed, and a sharp *crack* made Eleanor jump. He opened his palm. Nothing remained of the key but a little Fire-iron dust.

"Your secrets are safe now, Agnes," said Orvid.

"Yes. I am being very happy. I'm wishing… wanting thanks… How are you saying it?" Agnes couldn't find the right word in Carthean, so she burst into tears. She babbled in Svelyan and threw her arms around Orvid, who stood there like a wobbly nail in a loose hole. His eyes widened, and he gingerly patted her back. She turned to Eleanor and hugged her just the same. "Thank you—both of you. For forgiving me, and for keeping my secrets. I can go home now."

The healers gingerly escorted the Oracle, on her levitating bed, toward the Abbey proper. Rosemary joined Eleanor, Orvid, and Agnes. She accepted one of Agnes's blubbering embraces. "Is it true?" the Abbottess asked. "He's finally gone?"

"As Hazelbeth says," said Eleanor. Despite the old witch's assurance, Eleanor wished she'd seen Oliver die, as morbid as that was. He'd slipped past them so many times before.

"Praise HighGod!" Rosemary raised her arms. Orvid stepped out of hugging range, so she hugged Eleanor instead.

Eleanor turned to follow the healers. "She showed me things. I have so many questions."

"Not now, Eleanor."

"But she insisted I be here. She wanted me to see something important."

"You know she's too weak. Go back to the palace and rest. You look exhausted yourself.

"I don't even know what day it is."

"It's Thursday, and you have a kingdom to run. If she seems well enough to speak to you, I will call you."

Eleanor almost argued with Rosemary. She did indeed have many questions about the things she'd seen in the other world, but she also she wanted to ask about Hazelbeth's use of red magic— Natalie's magic. If the Oracle was nearing the close of her heretofore endless tenure, that could mean monumental changes for her little girl. Natalie had done significant world-saving of late, yet it seemed there would be no rest for the interpolation weary. Eleanor never stopped thinking about her daughter, despite all her competing responsibilities.

As if she'd called out to them, those other concerns shoved their way toward the front row of her thoughts. An excitable crowd of problems, trying to get closer to a charismatic preacher. In the end, she had to let the topic of Natalie's future sit beside the pulpit while she addressed the whole congregation. She called for her carriage and returned to Eclatant.

CHAPTER 25

A SOMEWHAT NORMAL COUPLE

TWO DAYS LATER, AS the clockworks ticked toward midnight, Eleanor and Dorian sat on opposite ends of the blue couch in her chamber. She'd dismissed Pansy for the evening, and the children were long asleep. Chou had decided to stay with Ticia for the night. Orvid Jones had retired an hour earlier. His sleepless stint in the Oracle's cavern had so exhausted him, he didn't take note of Eleanor and Dorian's scandalous privacy. Or perhaps he no longer cared.

Eleanor herself felt painfully aware of Dorian's presence. He'd trimmed his beard. It was showing more gray all the time, and she found the silver terribly distinguished and dashing. He'd draped one leg languidly over the other. He wore the same old leggings he'd donned for their inquisition of Agnes, but he'd removed his old boots and set them on the floor, so he wore simple green wool socks. He picked at his pale-yellow tunic and the tiny black unicorn hairs that always imbedded themselves in his clothes. He bought his shaving tonic from a merchant in Harper's Crossing. Whenever he moved, her nose caught a hint of pine. She wanted to bury her face in the crook of his neck and inhale his intensely masculine smell until her lungs burst.

She returned to her work in the hope of distracting herself. A heavy farmer's almanac lay across her lap. Hardly full of exciting topics, but she tried to make them so.

"In the year Desmarais two hundred eighty-four, a plague of Mendaen cotton beetles decimated the wheat crop in Harveston." She looked up from taking notes in her ledger. "If they eat wheat, I wonder why they're called cotton beetles?"

"Perhaps they don't eat cotton. Perhaps they sew little tunics and socks for their six feet."

"Speaking of socks." She fished one of Cyrus's baby booties from between the sofa cushions and threw it at him. He caught it before it bounced off his nose.

"How dare you toss the footwear of the crown prince," he said, but he held the little sock in his huge hand as if it were a china figurine. A beloved family heirloom. "You hate insects. Yet here you sit, voluntarily reading about plagues of them. Such dedication."

"Hush, silly. I need to understand weather patterns and insect infestations. If the harvest looks poor, I'll be better prepared when flour prices shoot up and beggars pour into Maliana from the countryside."

He slid a little closer. His hand brushed her knee.

"Dorian," she said. "I'm trying to concentrate on beetles."

"Pretend my finger is a beetle crawling… up… your leg!" He squeezed her kneecap. She squealed and jumped in her seat as he tickled her thigh. Her book spilled onto the floor, and she grabbed his wrists. "Stop, stop," she begged, laughing. "Please."

He stopped tickling her, but he didn't take his hands off her leg. His fingers rubbed her dark blue leggings. "Cotton," he said. "No beetle holes at all."

"Dor. What are we doing?" She looked over her shoulder.

"Nothing punishable by death. Not any longer."

"Is it too soon though?"

He looked up at her with a sad smile. "Gregory wanted us to be happy. Do you remember?"

"I do."

"I miss him, Eleanor. Every day. The fact that he gave us his blessing is a gift comparable to my dukedom or Senné or Laralee. He allowed me to love you without disrespecting him."

She touched his cheek. "I'm grateful to him, and I miss him, too. Five years ago, I never could have imagined I'd feel this way. He truly did set us free. Still, I'm afraid of what the living might say if they find out we're lovers."

He scooted closer and took her face in his hand. "No one needs to find out. But no one can kill us for it, either. Eleanor—we've never been alone like this. Where we weren't risking our lives by touching one another." His hand slid down her neck to her shoulder blade. "Since that is the case, let me. Let me touch you everywhere."

She could not refuse him when he said it so softly, so plainly, his voice full of hunger and tenderness. She prayed one of her ministers wouldn't wake in the middle of the night with a burning need to discuss Fire-iron yields or the uneven cobblestones in Smithwick Square. She placed Dorian's hand on the waistband of her leggings and lay back against the cushions. She closed her eyes as he began unbuttoning.

She watched the subtle tremble of the blue curtains between the bedposts over his shoulder while he made quiet love to her. For the first time in years—maybe the first time ever— there was little need to rush. They quietly explored each other, rediscovering long-neglected curves and muscles and tender, hidden places. When he climaxed, he held his breath and stared down at her with the old intensity. In the candlelight, the curtains became the rocky roof of the cave on the cliffs above Solsea, or the rafters of the granary on the edge of the Abbey's rolling pastures. She pulled him close, and he exhaled in two harsh breaths.

They lay there for a while, his chest expanding while hers contracted, and vice versa. He finally propped himself on one elbow and looked down at her. "You spoiled me at the circus," he said, in a veiled reference to their informal contraception.

She touched the edge of his nose. "I'm getting a bit older, as much as I don't like to admit it, but we still must take care. It would be rather obvious we're lovers if I came up pregnant, as Mr. Jones is the only other male in whose company I spend significant time."

"We will be careful. HighGod knows we know how." He pulled her close, into the crook of his arm. "This is amazing. We just made love in a bed, and now we're lying here, together."

"Like a somewhat normal couple."

"Like a husband and wife."

"I spent comparably little time in bed with my husband. Gregory slept in this bed approximately three times."

"We haven't slept in the same bed since the night Ticia was born."

"If I recall, neither of us slept much that night."

"No. I was in awe of you. What you'd been through, and what it felt like to be beside you. I didn't want to waste time sleeping."

She rested her chin on his chest. "I love you, Lord Brandling," she said.

"I love you, Your Majesty."

"Dorian."

"Eleanor." He stroked her hair. "We should use our true names. I want my love for you to be personal. I'm competing with so many."

"You've never had any competition."

"Tell that to the people clamoring for a glimpse of you at the palace gate. I'm sure there are a few out there right now."

"Hmmm," she said.

"It's not just the common folk. They've always loved you."

"Save those years Oliver's scheming encouraged them to burn me at the stake."

"A mere hiccup in nearly twenty years of heroine worship. Now it's the nobles, and the High Council, and"—his eyes widened in mock shock—"even their high society wives."

"Let's see how long that lasts. They'll sure surely remember how insufferably unfeminine I am before long."

He squeezed her. "You rid us of the ogres, Eleanor. Without war. You finally rid us of Oliver."

"Did I though?" She snuggled closer to him, as if she might hide from reality in his arms. "He's slipped past us before. I'm afraid we put out word too soon."

She'd asked Orvid Jones to hold off issuing a royal proclamation announcing total victory over Oliver and his horde of renegade ogres. The magician had insisted, and Dorian backed him up, so Eleanor acquiesced. The news had flooded Maliana like a MidWinter high tide, and then it spread nearly as quickly across the rest of the country, soaking the populace in relief and gratitude.

"The Oracle says he's dead or soon will be. From what Rosemary said, she's adamant."

"I wish we knew for sure."

"We may never know for sure. But I trust Hazelbeth."

"And I trust you." *But I'm still worried. HighGod, please let him be gone for good this time.*

He rolled onto his side and held her hands between his. "Eleanor," he said, his voice painfully earnest. "Will you marry me?"

She was unprepared for the abrupt change of topic, and for a moment, she stared back at him with no reply. She said nothing, despite fantasizing about Dorian asking her that question for years.

He rolled onto his back. "I'm sorry. That was a stupid question."

"No," she said, recovering her wits. "Dorian, I want to marry you. I always have. Gregory's blessing is the miracle that makes it seem meant to be. Even though I think he'd want it for both of us, I just don't know if I can. With my current responsibilities, I don't know if I can marry anyone. It's different for a woman, ruling in her own right. Cartheigh has never had a king consort. Does such thing even exist?"

"I understand."

"I'm not saying no. I'm just saying not now. It hasn't been long enough since Gregory's passing, anyway." She climbed on top of him.

"You're right. It's not the time." He stared past her at the curtains, but he wrapped his arms around her.

She rested her face against the light smattering of hair on his chest. She remembered the women she'd seen in Hazelbeth's vision. They went out in their world and made changes and earned their own gold, and they still took care of their children. Some had husbands, but those men did not seem to own or rule over them. She sensed they encouraged their wives. They were proud of them, and not just for providing sons. "I want to be your wife. But I cannot not be the kind of wife your mother was. Or Anne Clara is."

"I don't want that kind of wife. I love my sister." He chuckled, a bit sadly. "I loved my mother in some ways, even if she could never love me. I wouldn't want a wife like Anne Clara, and I certainly wouldn't want to be married to someone like my mother. I want you."

"What of your role? Would it be strange, having a wife who is technically more powerful than you are?"

"I'll still beat you in a swordfight."

"I'm serious."

He took a moment to reply. "I admit, from the time I first arrived at Eclatant when I was eighteen, I wanted to be part of the action, so to speak. I was no one special, just the second son of a reasonably wealthy family from Harper's Crossing, and I knew I'd have to prove myself. I don't know where I got the gumption to be so ambitious—the arrogance of youth, I suppose— but I wanted to be on the High Council. I wanted to make decisions that mattered. I wanted King Casper and Gregory to count on me. For years, I felt as if my friendship with Gregory put me where I wanted to be, but it also compromised my ability to make decisions about my own life, even as I influenced crown policy."

"I remember. I always hated feeling like you were kowtowing to Gregory. I can't imagine what it felt like from your end."

"When I fully embraced our love, the frustration eased some. I'd taken control of something in my life. Of course, in relieving one source of tension, I created something arguably worse. Years of guilt and fear and confusion. And guilt. Did I mention the *guilt?*"

She pinched his arm. "I felt guilty too, but yours was worse."

"You could hate him. He did terrible things to you. He never did anything but trust me and bestow wealth on me."

"It's not that simple, Dor. Lest I remind you, he wasn't always the kindest person, or the easiest to manage—even for you."

"I'm not saying that. He was an ass much of the time."

"He was. I do know what you mean, though. It was different between you and him."

"Once he sent me away, I realized I was still fulfilling my purpose. I was helping the crown by repairing relations with Svelya. My letters to King Casper still made a difference. In many ways, my role didn't change. Only my location shifted. While I missed home every second, I was grateful to Gregory for letting me keep doing what I'm meant to do. He said he'd let me live so I would suffer, and I know his pride factored into his mercy. But he could have had me killed. An accident or a sickening spell. Orvid would have performed it for him."

"He loved you. He couldn't have killed you."

"He didn't just let me live, though. He let me keep being *me.* During my time in exile, I learned so much about myself. When I was younger, I probably would have said I wanted power. In Svelya, I learned I didn't need it. I'd clearly proven my worth, just by remaining alive after what I'd done. I had no one left to convince, and I didn't particularly care about being *powerful.* More, respected… useful. What I'm trying to say in my longwinded way… is that I'd be perfectly happy being your husband while you rule. I want to help you. It's what I'm best at, and where I'm most comfortable. I'll stand beside you while you change the world." He chuckled. "Even on the days you're not changing the world. I want those simple days, too."

"You'll stand beside me when Leticia is driving me mad? Or when I have a cold? When I just want to sit in this room and read a book of poetry?"

"I shall join you in sitting on the latter occasions, but yes. I shall dance with you when you want to dance, and nap with you when you want to nap. Would you do the same for me?"

"Of course, although I refuse to eat beets with you. Disgusting."

"No beets."

"I'd like to show my children that kind of marriage."

"I'd like to show your children… and our child."

"Or our children."

He paused a moment before replying. "If HighGod blessed us."

"Let me think about it, please."

"I want you to think about it for a long while," he said. "In fact, I will never bring it up again. Not until you do. I want you to absolutely sure."

"As long as you know that no matter my decision, I am absolutely sure I will love you until the day I die. If there is a life beyond this one, I'll love you in that life as well. In all lives, in all worlds."

"And I you, my queen. And I you."

The next day, Eleanor was terribly sore all over. Dorian woke her before as the sun rose with his pressing needs—said needs quite literally pressed into the small of her back. She responded by mounting him and riding him enthusiastically, like a huntress out after the first fox of the season. Her passionate abandon resulted in embarrassingly chafed nether regions, so out of practice was she. In addition, she slept harder than she had in years during the hours in between sessions and had a crick in her neck. He teased her as she wrapped herself in a bearskin dragon robe and walked gingerly from the bed toward the bathing room.

"I need to get dressed and get to the Abbey," she said. "Natalie wants to move back into the dormitory. The healers say she's healing quickly, as witches do, but I want to see for myself that she's ready."

"Of course you do, Mama Bear," he said. He tilted his head like an inquisitive puppy. "Speaking of getting dressed for the day, if that braid is a corset, then your hair is bursting the seams."

She grabbed her hand mirror from atop her bureau. She squinted into it in the dim pre-dawn light. Long blonde strands stuck out all over her head, like escaped convicts dangling from the prison windows. "Ha. It's your fault. You were the one thrusting about, squashing my head into the pillows."

He put both bare feet on the floor and walked toward her, naked as a happy child on a warm beach. She opened the robe, and he stepped into her arms. She wrapped the fur around both of them and looked up at him.

"You are stunning in the morning, tousled hair and all." He kissed her forehead. "I'm proud of myself, for mussing it up so."

"You should be getting back to your own room, my love. It's getting light." She scowled as an anxiety inducing thought dawned on her. "The guard will know you've been here all night."

"If there's one thing I learned from being friends with Gregory, it's that the guards are silent as dead trees. I think they pride themselves on being blind to what they've not supposed to see."

She remembered the nights the guards had stood stonily beside Gregory's door, knowing full well he was inside, carousing with Sylvia or some anonymous hired company. She'd never heard a word about it. "True. But still...."

"Let me remind you. What we're doing is no longer a death sentence.

Worry is relative." He squeezed her. Their naked bodies pressed together, as if the warmth of the dragon robe were melting them. She felt him stir against her hip.

"Again?" She kissed his chest. Her hands started wandering of their own fruition.

"You said I needed to go." He traced gentle circles on her back.

"I did, didn't I."

"You said you were worried."

She answered by wrapping her meandering fingers around that which poked her midsection. He picked her up, and she wrapped her legs around him.

As he lay her on the bed and the robe fell away from them, she had a fleeting thought. She would never give up Dorian again. She'd simply have to keep worrying. After all these years, she was quite good at it.

"She's emerged." Chou landed on Eleanor's shoulder as she left the nursery after her morning visit with little Cyrus. He was over a year old and eating mashed fruits and vegetables and bits of bread like a champion, but she still visited with him several times a day to nurse.

"Who?"

"Sylvia. She's in Queen Gemma's garden."

Eleanor nodded. She didn't ask Chou how he knew this. Not unlike the Oracle, Chou just knew what he knew—albeit through non-magical, gossipy means. No one had seen hide nor horn of Sylvia since her brief, subdued appearance at Gregory's funeral. Eleanor had missed Imogene's hastily planned grand finale. Sylvia scheduled it on the morning of Eleanor's coronation, out of necessity. Chou attended in her stead and reported it to be a small affair. Sylvia's other sons were in Harveston, so only Hector attended his grandmother's internment in the graveyard behind Humility Chapel. Despite Imogene's poor treatment of him in the past, Raoul Delano graciously attended with his daughter, Maddy—the child of Eleanor's dear deceased friend, Margaret, and Imogene's only granddaughter. A few courtiers from Harveston rounded out the small crowd. According to Chou, those social leeches attended with the sole intent of earning invitations to the duchess's famous soirees. Eleanor wondered if Imogene would be disappointed at not having a grander send off. After all, she spent decades dragging herself up society's ladder.

"How much time do I have before I have to meet Orvid and Dorian?"

"An hour," said Chou. "Dorian wants to read Mr. Thromba's reports thoroughly himself before he briefs you."

"It's good news as far as you know?"

"Yes. The witches have been able to clear the water of any remaining ogre filth. Thromba reports the dragons are as content as ever they can be, finicky creatures that they are."

"I have time for a morning stroll. Still, the gardens are expansive. Can you flutter in that direction and help me locate my sister?"

Chou whistled. She detected a hint of disdain at Eleanor's use of *sister* with no pejorative prefix, but as always, he did as she asked. He took off from her shoulder and flew out the window. She paused to watch him hovering over the garden like a weightless rose. She sent a prayer of thanks to Cyril Brice. No father had ever given his little girl a more beloved birthday present.

Eleanor found Sylvia deep in Queen Gemma's garden, past the spot where she and Dorian and Gregory watched the sunset just days before Gregory died. The duchess wore a pretty blue and gold striped gown. She wore her hair loose and tucked behind her ear. Eleanor admired her profile—her full lips, delicately pointed chin, and long eyelashes that seemed to reach past her straight nose. She sat on the edge of a fountain. Eleanor had only seen it a couple times, on her long walks with Ticia and Nathan when they were small, and she wanted desperately to tire them out. The statue in the center of the fountain wasn't a unicorn, a dragon, or one of Gregory's ancestors. It was a cat, wearing a broad farmer's hat and a pair of tall boots.

Sylvia looked up as Eleanor approached. "Eleanor. Good morning."

"Good morning, Sylvia. It's good to see you out and about. I'm so sorry I couldn't attend your mother's funeral."

"I appreciate that, but I know you're probably not terribly disappointed you missed it."

Eleanor sat on the fountain wall beside her. Clumps of early spring daffodils sidled up against both women's skirts like shy toddlers. "I suppose that's not exactly the right word," said Eleanor. "But I feel guilty, so I'm apologizing anyway."

"You had a good excuse. You were being crowned queen and handling Gregory's funeral. I wish I'd had my own reason to stay away, but that would have been impossible. It's strange how I spent so many years being annoyed with Mother, resenting her, or trying to impress her. I thought about *her*, but I didn't think much about *us*. Me and her, and what we were to each other. I had to think about it during the funeral."

"Perhaps that's why I didn't want to attend. I mean—I would have attended, if I could have, but..."

Sylvia held up one hand. "It's done. We'll both find ourselves thinking about Imogene and what she wrought for the rest of our lives."

"She certainly gave us an earful the last time the three of us spoke."

"That she did. No need to talk about it anymore."

The silence stretched on, but surprisingly, it wasn't terribly uncomfortable, probably because Eleanor and Sylvia had both taken Imogene's earful of advice to heart. "What a silly fountain," Eleanor said. "I remember thinking that when I walked past here once with Leticia."

"Gemma had it made for Gregory. The Boots Cat was his favorite nursery rhyme as a child."

"I didn't know that. Not about the Boots Cat or the fountain. I guess there are many things about Gregory I didn't know. Things you do know."

"He liked to paint in the garden when he was young. He always knew which flowers would be in bloom. When he wanted to talk, we came here. No one bothered us."

"I'm sorry, Sylvia. You should have been his wife."

"You should have been Dorian's. I'm sorry I made Gregory suspicious about the two of you." She ran her fingers over the water. "In another life, maybe the four of us would have been friends. We could have had dinner together and played cards."

"They could have tried to teach us to play strike stick. I'm terrible at it."

"Me too." She drew a heart on the cement with her wet finger. "Gregory told me, before he died, about John-Caleb, and how he is not of the Bond."

"I see," Eleanor said, treading lightly.

"For years, I hoped you'd never have another son. I thought even if John-Caleb wasn't Gregory's child, maybe he'd acknowledge him anyway. To have a male heir. I didn't figure on the unicorns having much say in it."

"We know now they have more say in it than the royal family, really." Eleanor cleared her throat. "You're saying… do you mean…"

"John-Caleb isn't Gregory's child. There's no reason to pretend anymore, at least not to you. Not if he'll never be king."

"Whose is he?"

"I took a lover, after my husband died. A groom, in Harveston." She smiled. "Like mother, like daughter. But I didn't love him the way my mother loved Robin. He was a handsome man and a warm body. He died in the Great Burning."

"If you promise John-Caleb will never challenge Cyrus, I won't have any reason to tell anyone of his true parentage. Let them wonder."

"Thank you. A possible royal bastard might be entitled to his own title someday. Nothing too fancy. An earl, perhaps."

"I'll leave that up to Cyrus, who will, of course, know his true ancestry. Kings must know everything about their subjects."

"As must queens." Sylvia stood. "I'm returning to Harveston in a few days. I've been too long from Buckhill and my other boys."

"Will Hector go with you?"

"I haven't decided. He's old enough to be at court on his own—if he had rooms and supervision."

"I'd be happy to watch over him, as my own nephew. Gregory would have done the same."

Sylvia exhaled, and then she covered her face with her hands. When Eleanor stood, she towered over Sylvia, an oak over a weeping willow, as she had their entire lives. She rested one hand on Sylvia's trembling shoulder, and her stepsister went still.

"Leticia will be coming out in society soon. I think Hector would be a fine gentleman to ask for her first dance."

Sylvia wiped her eyes and cleared her throat. "That's very kind of you, Your Majesty."

"I have to return to the High Council Chamber now." Eleanor curtsied, and Sylvia returned the gesture. Eleanor felt a knot in her own throat as she turned. She'd only made it a few steps before Sylvia called out her name. She turned around.

"What is it like?" Sylvia asked. "Having all those men listen to you, like you're one of them."

"They don't listen to me like I'm one of them. They listen to me like I'm a woman they must listen to. I assume it will always be that way for me."

"It's not so different, even with a crown."

Eleanor thought for a minute. About how guilty she felt, leaving Cyrus with nannies for most of the day. How she scurried around the castle, trying to fit in a midday visit, and how she rushed to spend the evening hours with him, to tuck him into bed, and how she tried to be there when he woke up each morning. Ticia didn't need her as much anymore, but she still demanded attention at times, and as a teenager, she did it in a way that sometimes made an exhausted Eleanor want to flee the room. Then she'd shift back into girlish glee and silliness, and Eleanor would feel remorseful that she'd been annoyed with her. Of course, she also had to fit in visits to Natalie at the Abbey, even if Natalie herself usually expressed only absent happiness upon her arrival, and polite fondness when she left.

It was perhaps her biggest source of contrition—she loved her children more than anything in the world, but she never considered giving up her other responsibilities. Not even for them.

"Being a mother with a life outside of motherhood is a challenge for anyone. Crown or no crown. But I aim to make it easier for my daughters—and everyone else's daughters—if I can."

"I thank you in advance for my own granddaughters." Sylvia straightened up to her full height—diminutive, yet larger than life. "Now I have to return to my own responsibilities. I always sent Casper, and Gregory after him, thrice yearly reports from Harveston's Grain Master. One is due in MidSpring."

"Really? I didn't know that."

"After old Hector died, someone had to manage things in Harveston."

"I shall look forward to receiving it. I'll call on you to help with the Awakening Fest, if you're so inclined."

"Of course. I'll have my magicians start thinking of new entertainment ideas."

"No flowers, please. My hay fever."

"As you wish, Eleanor."

"Safe travels, Sylvia."

CHAPTER 26

SOMETHING OUT OF A DREAM

NEARLY TWO WEEKS AFTER Oliver's disappearance, Rosemary gave in to Eleanor's prodding and allowed her to see the Oracle. To her surprise, when she told Ticia where she was going, she asked to come along and visit her sister. So, Eleanor and her oldest daughter, along with eight of the Unicorn Guard, rode Teardrop and Cricket across Maliana toward the Abbey. The townsfolk ran out of their homes and shops to wave and cheer.

"Maybe we should have taken the carriage!" Ticia shouted over the din.

"It's good for the people to see us and the unicorns. You grandfather knew that, and so did your father."

Ticia waved, but Eleanor sensed her anxiety in the face of the boisterous, smelly crowd. She finally relaxed when the Abbey gate shut behind them and hid their admirers behind stone walls. She lit on the ground in her black riding leggings and black boots; a tall, slender beauty, with brown doe eyes and long hair the color of a vixen's tail. At almost fifteen, she was only three years younger than Eleanor had been when she married Gregory. Cricket nuzzled her friend's shoulder, and Ticia leaned against her comforting bulk.

"I don't know how you do that, Mother. It's exhausting."

"You hate those crowds so much, darling, yet you're dying to attend a Fest Ball."

"I'll be safe at the Fest Ball. I can chat and laugh with people we know. Not have a thousand strange eyes boring into me, expecting me to make a speech. I won't like feeling like a human altar or an ambulatory statue." She shivered.

"I understand," said Eleanor, who in truth would rather be gawked at by the cheering commoners than make small talk with flippant courtiers.

As Ticia and Cricket walked toward the sick house, Teardrop whispered in Eleanor's ear. "You and your daughter are very different creatures. It's a good thing she does not have to be queen."

Eleanor patted Teardrop's silky neck. "It is, isn't it?"

Eleanor and Leticia left Teardrop and Cricket outside the hospital. A bevy of young witches surrounded them. They *oohed* and *aahed* over the great creatures, offering them carrots and apples. A few minutes later, Eleanor joined Rosemary, Agnes, and Natalie beside the old witch's bedside. Once again, she was left with the creaky red chair. Natalie's arm was still wrapped in a clean white bandage. The limb abruptly ended in a thick hunk of tightly encased cotton.

I should bring Jan to visit, Eleanor thought. *Between them, they only have two hands, but they suddenly have something significant in common.*

After a few minutes of shyness, Natalie climbed into her big sister's lap. Ticia divided Natalie's strawberry blonde hair into sections and braided it, just as she had when they shared a nursery. The visitors waited quietly for Hazelbeth to wake from her nap.

"How is your packing?" Eleanor whispered to Agnes.

"It's going well. I will be leaving for Svelya in a few days."

"Terin and Whisper will accompany you to the Dragon Mines?"

"Yes. Then Samuel is having a retinue waiting to escort me to Gammonreil." She smiled.

"I cannot wait to feel the cold mountain air on my face and eat a *mensucca*."

"What is that?"

"Sheep liver pie," said Hazelbeth. She opened her eyes and stared at the ceiling. "I remember the first time I tasted one, after we crossed the sea from Ello. The first village we found… a village of the Old *Osy'v* people… they welcomed us. A widow took pity on my mother, struggling along with two small girls whose father lay dead in the ground across the sea. She took us in for a few days. After weeks of eating dried venison and nuts, that *mensucca* was a gift from heaven itself. The crust had a sweetness. A touch of honey. The carrots were just soft enough. The liver—"

"Yuck, Auntie," said Natalie.

"Natty!" Ticia gently flicked her sister's ear. "Don't be rude."

The Oracle laughed, but it dissolved into a fit of coughing. Rosemary held a cup to her lips. "From the Pool. Drink."

Bluish light turned Hazelbeth's gray lips black, but whatever healing power the water possessed soothed her throat. "Do not chastise the little one, Princess Leticia. I was near starving. Only a famished child could reminisce so fondly over sheep liver."

"She'll fall asleep soon," Rosemary whispered as Agnes adjusted the Oracle's pillows. "Do not waste what time you have on pleasantries."

Eleanor nodded. "Wise One. You gave Natalie the gift of your power. Dorian told me how she used it to save the last interpolation party from an angry ogre. I thank you—"

"I thank you, too, Auntie!" said Natalie. "Your magic is very warm, even though it is blue. Ione's was cold. Orange seems like it should be hot. Since it's the color of fire."

Eleanor continued, before the witches wandered into a discussion of the relative temperatures of magic. "But in the garden, when you opened the door between here and… wherever it was, there was red. And purple. As if blue and red had come together."

"I gave Natalie some of my essence. In giving, I also received." She gazed fondly at the little girl. "I don't know if I could have opened the door without her."

"Ticia," Eleanor said. "Take Natalie out into the hallway for a few minutes, will you?"

Ticia nodded and set Natty on her feet. "Come. Will you show me your favorite spell?"

Natalie's brow furrowed. "My favorite one? Horns and fire. There are so many!"

"One that doesn't require much space. The hallway is narrow."

"Be careful!" Eleanor smiled at them. "Natalie, mind your arm. Don't frighten your big sister with enchanted snakes or spiders!"

The door closed behind the girls. The grin left Eleanor's face as if Natalie's favorite spell was a scowling charm.

"Wise One, everyone thinks…" Eleanor struggled to say it, as if the words themselves might seal Natalie's fate. "Everyone at the Abbey believes… including Natalie herself…"

"Everyone at the Abbey believes Natalie is the next Oracle. Everyone *knows* it."

Eleanor exhaled. There was some relief in hearing it stated so definitively from the source of all prophetic magic herself. "All right. Everyone *knows* it." She slid her chair closer to Hazelbeth's bed. She took her hand, and it was like holding a pile of leaves. If Eleanor closed her fist, the old witch's fingers might crumble into a mound of dust and twigs. "You have lived this life. There will be much joy and wonder in it, but you know what she faces. She's already lost a hand, but I mostly fear for her heart. I don't want her to be lonely. I don't want her to forget how to love."

"Eleanor," said Rosemary. "I have told you before. Witches do love. Just not in the way you know love to operate."

"That's true, Abbottess," said the Oracle. "But the queen has legitimate concerns, for my existence differs from even yours. For centuries, I felt fondness and compassion. I felt responsibility and fear for the pain and suffering of others. Until Eleanor reminded me of my sister and my mother, however, love had left my emotional vocabulary. My repertoire of feeling expanded further upon the realization that I have living relations, and one of them is that supremely special child." She squeezed Eleanor's hand. For the moment, the leaves remained attached to the tree. "I thank HighGod that the queen and her daughter reminded me. It is the great reward of my last days."

"Don't say that, Wise One," said Agnes. "I want to return to Cartheigh next summer. There is much more I can do for our two countries. I should be a bridge between Gammonreil and Eclatant. When I am here, I hope to visit you beside the Pool."

"You are a good woman, Agnes of Gammonreil. You have earned our forgiveness, and I hope you have forgiven yourself. But you will visit with the young Oracle, not me. I am grateful I lived to see Svelya and Cartheigh reclining in the shade of friendship, but the final expulsion of Ezra Oliver was my last act for my two adopted countries."

Eleanor jumped at the chance to discuss Oliver. "Is he truly gone? When he first disappeared into the Pool, all those years ago, we thought him gone. I hope you understand why I fear he'll find his way back."

"You would be naïve if you did not have those fears—and a poor ruler to boot. You are neither." She pointed at Eleanor's rucksack. "I can reassure you. Do you have the glass rainbow?"

"Always," said Eleanor. She fished around in her satchel and removed the kaleidoscope. She handed it to Hazelbeth, who peered into it with one cloudy eye. She muttered a few words, spun the cylinder until the bird met the leaf, and handed it back to Eleanor. "Go on, child. Look."

Eleanor held the scope to her dark eye. She looked into a strange white world, full of beeps, whistles, and blinking lights. Like something out of a dream.

"Where did he come from?" asked a dark-skinned woman in a white coat. She wore her black and gray hair in long twisted braids. She'd pulled most of it away from her face, but one braid kept slipping loose. She tucked it behind her ear. She held a flat rectangular object that looked to be made of glass. As she ran her finger along it, words appeared and disappeared. "Calvin, you said the police brought him in?"

Eleanor realized she understood them perfectly, as if they spoke her language. *As foreign as this place seems,* she thought, *it must be very close to Cartheigh.*

A younger man and woman stood beside her. They also wore white coats. The young man had brown skin, while young woman was blonde and fair. "Yeah," said the man, Calvin. "Last night. Found him under a bridge. Thought he was dead until he started ranting. Apparently, he was screaming about evils witches and casting spells. Told Officer Hernandez he came through a magic door from another world. When Jose told him they were taking him to the hospital, he threatened to…." Calvin's finger traced the words on his own glass rectangle. "…Look, Dr. Jackson. Here it is. *Smote him into a thousand pieces and feed him to the dragons.*"

"Does he know his name? Anything useful?"

"Ezra Oliver. Said he's from a place called *Car… Car-thay.*"

With her heart hammering in her chest, Eleanor swung the scope to the right. There, in a strange white metal bed with strings in his nose and blinking, beeping ropes attached his body, lay the man who had harassed her for over sixteen years. He looked as old as Hazelbeth, for sure. His left eye was black and blue, and his upper lip was swollen.

"Carthay? You mean the neighborhood in Central LA?" asked Doctor Jackson.

"I'm from Chicago," said Calvin. "Just here for residency. The only part of Cali I know is the Bay Area."

"And Napa," said the other woman. She tapped his arm with a metal pencil. "You'll venture out of the Bay Area for a good Cabernet."

Calvin laughed. "I like my wine. Just like *you* like your spiked seltzer, Erin." Eleanor didn't really understand what they were talking about, but she recognized flirting when she saw it. "At least I have good taste in alcohol."

"Okay, Doctors," said Doctor Jackson. "You're both residents, and this is an emergency room, not a happy hour. Let's get back to our patient. Mister Oliver. No ID. Could be from La La Land. Any idea of his age?"

"Ten days older than dirt," said Erin.

"That's your medical opinion?"

"No. But seriously, Doctor J. He's got to be over a hundred. Really, I don't know how he's alive."

Doctor Jackson leaned over Oliver. She opened one eyelid and took his pulse and did a few other healer-ish things Eleanor had seen witches do. "Looks like someone beat him up. Poor guy. He's clearly demented. I'm guessing late stage Alzheimer's. Has psychiatry been in to see him yet?"

"Doctor Scott is supposed to be by soon."

"Good. If he wakes up, and he's still agitated, we'll need Doctor Scott to admit him. Get him out of the ER and over to the dementia ward on the psych unit. Let them figure out what to do with him."

Suddenly, the soft beeping from the machine beside Oliver's bed sped up. Doctor Jackson and her two assistants gathered around the bed. "Uh, oh," said Doctor Jackson. "His heartrate is through the roof. He—"

Oliver's eyes shot open. "HighGod damn them! All of them!" His arms flailed. The string hanging from his nose dislodged, and blood dripped onto his white blanket. "Eleanor Brice and the Oracle! That blasted Svelyan *bitch!* Curse them!"

"Sir— sir! Calm down." The woman called Erin leaned over him. "We're here to help you."

"Get away from me!" He held his hands before his face and wiggled his fingers. He was trying to conjure fireballs, but nothing happened. "My magic. They took it!" He started sobbing. "Where is it? What happened? I must get out of here and go home."

"Mister Oliver, correct? Mister Oliver? That's your name?" Doctor Jackson spoke loudly, as if Oliver were deaf as well as confused.

"The Desmarais—they won. They beat me. How? Not with unicorns. Not with Fire-iron. Just with one goddamn *woman* and her pack of minions." As Eleanor listened, Oliver fired off an increasingly hysterical and nonsensical litany. She caught Dorian's name, and Gregory's. King Casper. Something about ogres and the Oracle and Rosemary. "Goddamn *witches!* Curse them!"

"Cal. Get Dr. Scott in here. I think he's having a psychotic break."

Calvin ran out of the room; Oliver continued to thrash.

"How is he so strong?" Erin tried to take Oliver's arms. "He's too old—"

"My magic! My magic is gone!" Oliver floundered on the bed. He screamed a long wail of mourning.

"Jesus," said Doctor Jackson. "Where is Scott?" she called over her shoulder. "We need an orderly in four!"

Oliver chuffed and gasped. His screaming switched off, as if his vocal cords were sprung fiddle strings. He took one gasping breath, his eyes bugged from his head, and he collapsed backward. The machine by the bed went from frazzled beeping to one long blast. It took up where his screaming had left off.

"He's flatlining!" said Dr. Jackson.

For the next few minutes, Eleanor watched as people rushed in and out of the room—the three people called *doctors*, as well as women and men in long, loose greenish pants and shirts that seemed to be assisting them, called *nurses*.

Finally, they gave up trying to wake Oliver. He lay still, his arms akimbo, as if he'd tried desperately to cast one last spell before he died.

"That's it," said Doctor Jackson. "He's gone."

"Wow," said Erin. "That was intense."

"Given how far gone he was, and how old, maybe it's a blessing. Clearly no one cared enough to make sure he was in a safe place." Doctor Jackson rubbed her eyes. "Let's try to figure out who he was, anyway. Maybe we can find a relative to claim the body."

Eleanor stopped listening to their chattering. It didn't matter anymore. These healers in this strange place had confirmed what she wanted to know. Ezra Oliver was dead. She leaned into the vision just a bit. Enough to see his face one last time. Destroyed by age and whoever he'd met under the unnamed bridge who saw fit to punch an old man in the face. A defenseless old man, who just days before, had been the most dangerous person in Eleanor's world.

That's how Ezra Oliver died. Pitiful and unknown. With no one there to praise him or recognize his accomplishments. With the bitter knowledge that a door had opened, but he hadn't opened it himself. His plan had been his undoing. He died without magic—surely the saddest thing that could befall a witch or magician.

He was just an old man, who died alone. Eleanor felt sorry for him.

"Are you satisfied?" asked the Oracle as Eleanor lowered the kaleidoscope.

"I am," she said. "He is dead." The kaleidoscope vibrated in her hand. She looked down, and as she watched, the toy collapsed in on itself. She dropped it on the bed beside Hazelbeth. Fire-iron smoke wafted toward the rafters. With a faint hiss, the kaleidoscope disappeared.

"A fitting end?" asked Hazelbeth.

"For Oliver or the glass rainbow?"

"Both. But the kaleidoscope was never meant to last. It fulfilled its usefulness. More than even I predicted when I created it."

"Did you create it to help us defeat Oliver?"

"No. I created it for the reason I said I did. I wanted you to see your children while you were in Svelya. But I've grown accustomed to my activities revealing greater purposes over time." Her mouth twitched, as if she wanted to smile, but after being awake for a while, it was too much effort. "Like my interest in you. Do you think Mr. Oliver had a fitting end?"

Eleanor shrugged. "Right now, I feel relief but also sadness. What a waste of power."

"I am glad you see it that way. It is important for those with power, like yourself, to recognize a waste of it. You've learned a good deal about power over the years, have you not?"

"I have," said Eleanor. "But there's always more to understand. I'll learn as I live it, I suppose. Power reveals itself through strange means. Sometimes it's not obvious."

"Tell me, Queen Eleanor, of those strange means."

Eleanor thought for a moment. "Everyone thinks it comes from through battles and armies and wealth. Sometimes it does. Afterall, Caleb Desmarais secured his power by defeating the Svelyans and taking control of the Dragon Mines. I haven't been queen long, but I've found that I gained more strength through thinking and learning. And… forgiveness. Giving it and receiving it."

"Those things are great sources of power," said the Oracle. She patted Eleanor's hand. "Still, keep your armies well-trained and your coffers full. Find balance between might and knowledge and compassion."

"I will, Wise One. I promise."

She coughed again, and Rosemary once again offered her water. Once her throat had cleared, the Oracle said, "Bring the princesses. I would speak with young Natalie."

Rosemary called Natalie and Ticia into the room. Natalie chattered happily about the spells she'd shown her big sister. Ticia's hair had hints of blue at the edges, and Natalie's dragged on the ground behind her like a sheepdog's tail. Clearly, Natalie had no problems conjuring with one hand.

"Don't worry, Mother," Natalie said as she sat on Ticia's lap again with her hair draped over one shoulder. "The spells will wear off. Ticia won't attend her first Awakening Ball with blue hair. Mine will shrink."

"I'm glad, Natty," said Eleanor. "But let's be serious now. I think Auntie has something to tell you." *Something about how to be an Oracle and still be a human being, hopefully.*

Natalie turned to the Oracle with a gap-toothed grin. Eleanor was struck again by the resemblance between her pretty daughter and the little blonde girl from the island of Ello. It wasn't so much in the curve of her cheeks or the shape of her nose. It was in the rare, joyful confidence of one who knows her purpose from a very young age.

Hazelbeth called Natalie closer, and Ticia set her on her feet. She climbed onto the bed beside the old woman. She was as unafraid as the first day the two witches met—one far too wise for her young years, and one with more years and more wisdom than anyone had a right to have.

"Are you comfortable, Natalie?" asked the Oracle.

The child nodded.

"Good." Hazelbeth waved one hand, and Eleanor's mind returned to autumn metaphors. This time, instead of dead leaves, she thought of bare, spindly branches bending to a chilly wind. "The rest of you may go."

"Must we leave?" Eleanor asked, disappointed. She had hoped to hear whatever Hazelbeth said to Natalie. The witch had reassured her about Oliver's death. Now she wanted to be at peace about her daughter's life.

"Yes. Go please. My words are for the child alone."

Rosemary stood, as if she knew she needed to remove Eleanor from the room quickly, before she started arguing with an old, dying woman. "Let us take our leave."

Eleanor started to prove her right. "But—"

"Come, Your Majesty. You've been asked to give the Oracle and her heir privacy. Since you've been intent on exercising prudence of late, I *know* you'll heed the request."

Eleanor could not refuse a direct appeal to her own professed resolution toward diplomacy, lest she appear hypocritical or capricious. She stood and beckoned to Ticia and Agnes. They each kissed Natalie's cheek, and Eleanor stroked her silky hair. It was already retreating to a reasonable length. As Eleanor started to turn toward the door, the Oracle grabbed her arm with a surprising strong grip. Life lingered in the tree, even if the foliage had succumbed to winter.

"I have heard your concerns, and I will make sure the child understands," Hazelbeth said. She squinted up at Eleanor from the bed, her ancient face framed by the pillows, as if she were already resting in the clouds of heaven. "Goodbye, niece. Your eyes are a blessing, for they revealed the truth to me."

The two-toned orbs in questions stung with tears, and Eleanor wiped them. "Thank you, Auntie."

"Do not let anyone ever make you think they are any less than a miracle. As is the rest of your life."

Eleanor nodded, and the Oracle let go. She turned to Natalie. "Now, dear girl. Let us talk of things that only you and I can know."

Eleanor and Leticia mounted Teardrop and Cricket. It was nearly four o'clock, and the streets would be teeming with townsfolk on their way home for the evening meal. The merchants in Smithwick Square would pack up their wares and shout at passersby, trying to drum up a few late sales. Eleanor looked at her daughter's tense face. She noted her tight grip on Cricket's reins.

"Would you like to take a ride over the Abbey grounds, Tish? By the time we're finished, the townsfolk will be at home having their supper. The streets will be quieter."

Ticia smiled her thanks and nodded. Teardrop and Cricket turned toward the Abbey's chapel and the path leading out of the stockade walls and onto the rolling fields of wheat, vegetables, and apple trees surrounding the Abbey proper. They took the path along Afar Creek, toward the Oracle's cavern. They met several witches along the way. Some carried baskets of fruit, and others had rucksacks full of books slung over their shoulders. They met Ione as she returned to her room after guard duty at the Watching Pool. If Eleanor's instincts were correct, there wouldn't be much need for such sentries soon. The old Oracle would soon pass on, and the new Oracle would take her place. Eleanor sighed. It was a heavy release, but not as burdensome as it might have been the day before. She trusted that Hazelbeth, with her latently rediscovered appreciation for human closeness, would not allow Natalie to completely lose herself beside the pool.

"...Hector Fleetwood."

"I'm sorry, darling, what were you saying?"

"Ursula told me Hector Fleetwood will be staying on at Eclatant."

"Did she now." Ursula Harper, Eliza's daughter, was shaping up to be the Anne Iris of Leticia's life: a loyal lady-in-waiting and excellent source of gossip. "I told his mother I'd keep an eye on him if he decided to stay at court."

"That's nice of you," Ticia said. Her fair cheeks pinkened under her freckles.

"Would you like to meet him?"

She blushed harder. "I.... yes, of course. He's to be an important man. A duke, like Uncle Dorian, as soon as he's invested in his title. A princess should know him."

"He's a duke, yes. And he's handsome—"

"I suppose he is rather nice looking."

"But he's also a good man. Kind and smart and respectful of women. He's used to strong-willed ladies, given his mother." She winked. "But what about Patrick-Michael Harper?"

Ticia grinned back at her. "You told me yourself I shouldn't cast all my spells in one direction. I'm not even fifteen!"

"You'll be casting spells, my love, even if you're not a witch. The young men will swoon over you like overheated grandmothers at a summer picnic."

Mother and daughter giggled, and their unicorns laughed with them. "Patrick-Michael is handsome," said Cricket. "But Hector… well, he is a stallion of a different color."

Teardrop shook her head. "Like that painted steed from the marshes? Don't think I didn't see the two of your eyeing each other. You'll entice him to the Bond after all, daughter."

Cricket waved her ears. "Dasha took it up. I can always try!"

The four of them plodded on in happy silence for a while. The unicorn's hooves fell in and out of rhythm, sometimes matching up perfectly and sometimes going off beat, like the songs of all mothers and daughters. The air smelled of spring rain, and Eleanor was happy to put thoughts of autumn behind her. She remembered the first time she came to the Abbey, when she was only ten years old, with Rosemary. They'd walked these same paths on the way to visit the Oracle. How strange, on that day, the girlchild Eleanor and the mysterious old woman each had no idea she sat beside her only living blood relative. She wondered if Hazelbeth and Natalie were still talking. They must have endless topics to discuss—things Eleanor would never understand. For once, she didn't feel jealous. She just hoped HighGod gave the two seers time to explore their common talents before calling Hazelbeth home for a well-deserved rest.

"Are you still afraid for Natalie, Mother?" asked Ticia.

"I am always afraid for my children, darling. Being a mother teaches you the deepest love, but also the deepest fear. There is no fear like a mother's fear, but you learn to coexist with it. Just like you learn to live with love that makes your heart feel as if it might explode, like one of your sister's red fireballs."

"That kind of love makes a mother let her children follow their own paths. Like Natalie being a witch. Or me *not* being a queen."

"I am queen now, darling, and your brother is thriving. You don't have to worry about that anymore." Eleanor shifted in the saddle, so she faced Ticia. "But if those things had not come to pass, I would have tried to take this burden from you."

"I know you would have." Ticia patted Cricket's neck. "When I was younger, I would have done anything to avoid being queen. Perhaps in my silliness—my dramatic sensibilities—I would even have tried to run away. I mentioned it to Cricket, once. I said we could run away together. What did you say, dear?"

"I told you that while I love you beyond any other creature, I will not abandon the Bond for you."

"I'm sure Teardrop has shared wisdom with you when you said something equally ridiculous."

Teardrop snorted a laugh. "You know your mother well."

"I watched how Poppa put the country ahead of his own pain. I have seen you do the same. How hard you've worked and sacrificed your own happiness. For our people, and for your children. I know I am of the Bond. If HighGod forbid, something happened to you, or to my darling little brother, I would not shirk my duty as queen. As much as I would not choose it, and I am glad the mantle has passed me by, if it comes around again, I won't run from it."

As she talked, Eleanor's throat constricted. When Ticia stopped talking, she clearly expected an answer, but Eleanor couldn't provide one at first. Instead, she patted Teardrop's neck, subtly twirling her finger toward the early spring sky the way she'd seen King Casper do a million times.

"I think your mother is trying to say she hears you, and she appreciates your sentiment," said Teardrop.

"Yes." Eleanor choked it out. "Yes, darling. I hear you. Your Poppa would be proud of you."

"I hope so." Ticia smiled. "We always hear each other eventually, Mother." She clucked to Cricket, and the mare picked up a trot. "You told me the first time you and Uncle Dorian raced across this field, Teardrop nearly beat Senné. Can the two of you outrun us today?"

Just as she had years ago, when Dorian first challenged her to a race, Eleanor didn't let the black unicorn in front of her get a head start. She gave Teardrop her head, and Teardrop knew exactly what to do. Within moments, the queen and her old friend were racing their daughters across the Abbey grounds. Eleanor and Teardrop won, but just barely. Although she was no Oracle, that's exactly how she would have predicted it.

CHAPTER 27

WILL YOU BE MY WIFE?

Three Years Later

"TISH! DON'T DAWDLE NOW."

Eleanor called out to her oldest daughter, eighteen and giddy with young love and the sweet LowSummer breeze drifting over the grounds of Trill Castle. Eleanor sat on a Fire-iron bench beside a line of carriages. She watched the servants rush about with their early season enthusiasm on full display. They managed the royal family and their belongings with precise industriousness.

She happily left them to it. The two-day carriage ride included an overnight at the Egg Camp—one of the Desmarais' rustic hunting lodges. The coach's rocking turned her stomach, and she'd barely slept in the lumpy bed. She stretched to ease the pain in her lower back. They arrived three hours ago, and her nausea wasn't letting up. She sipped a glass of cold pear juice, but it didn't help her spinning stomach.

Chou paced the back of the bench. "If you still feel ill, you need to talk to Dorian."

"It's early. I don't want to disappoint him."

"If there's disappointment, you don't need to protect him from it. You should share in it. That's what he'd want."

"I haven't had the luxury of that mentality on the previous occasions I found myself in this state."

"You're in quite a different position. You have a supportive potential father who will soon be your husband."

"I said I'll talk to him, Chou. Do stop harassing me." She stroked his head, so he knew she wasn't cross with him. He was right, of course. As usual.

She stood. Her breasts hurt when she raised her arm and waived to Tish. "Leticia! You have enough luggage to weigh down a Giant Buzzard. The footmen need to know where to put it all."

At least six servants were wrestling with Leticia's trunks and garment bags and shoe boxes. She had moved into Eleanor's former chamber in the south tower of Willowswatch Cottage, as Eleanor now occupied King Casper's old chamber, front and center. It had initially felt strange to take over her late father-in-law's living space. By the end of the first summer, however, she peeked out the windows and watched everyone come and go, just as the old king had. It was a fine vantage point, and just like she'd told Sylvia several years ago, a ruler needed to know as much as possible about her subjects.

"Coming!" Ticia ran down the path between the willow trees toward Willowswatch Cottage, the largest and most imposing of Trill's hodgepodge of buildings. "Natalie, hurry up!"

Nine-year-old Natalie walked demurely behind her. Her head twisted this way and that, as if she were taking in every flower, butterfly, and bird. Several bitterbits, the tiny birds whose charming screeching gave the castle its name, landed on her shoulder. She smiled at them and whispered greetings in a strange language. With a pang in her heart, Eleanor wondered if Hazelbeth had taught Natalie any old Svelyan before she passed away.

"HighGod," said Ticia. "If you can see the future, you should be more excited for the duchess's party this evening! The first party of the season at the Falls. Could you just *die?* I have no idea what's going to happen. I'm in a tizzy about it!"

"I've told you, Tish," said Natalie. "I cannot simply *see* the future. Besides, I'm too young to attend parties."

"But if you're going to look like a child for years anyway, who would know?"

Natalie held her arms akimbo, and a few more bitterbits landed on her limbs. One arm ended in a narrow stump, but she didn't seem the least bit self-consciousness, and the birds didn't mind. She looked like a walking scarecrow, albeit one who attracted little yellow birds instead of frightening away large black ones. "I've *also* told you I'll grown normally until my menses. Only then will my aging slow down."

"It's unfair, isn't it, Mother?" Ticia said with a wink. "That Natalie shall have a lovely youthful face for decades and have no care for attracting a man!"

"There are more important things in life than attracting a man," said Eleanor.

"Of course there are!" Ticia spun around in a circle. Despite being almost ten years younger, Natalie watched her sister like a doting aunt.

"There's painting and unicorns and parties and chocolate cake," Ticia said. "Of course— I'm so looking forward to tutoring this summer. When will the Solsea Queen Camille's begin teaching classes?"

"The opening ceremony is in three days," said Eleanor.

"I'll wear my light green down with the lavender lace trim. The one I wore when the Meggett Fringe Camille's reopened. It will be a *stylish* yet *educational* tradition."

"That will be lovely," said Eleanor. It pleased her that Ticia enjoyed her charitable work—especially her time with the students at Eleanor's girls' school. Eleanor rebuilt Queen Camille's in Meggett Fringe two years ago, and her oldest child had proven endearingly committed to the school. Still, only Ticia could turn tutoring into a fashion parade.

"Don't give me that look. I know you think I'm being flippant. It *is* exciting to have a school here in Solsea, Mother. That doesn't mean I'm not equally excited about a party full of handsome men!"

"If you're really expecting Hector to propose this summer, I suggest you keep it down," Eleanor said, with a chuckle. "Your fiancé might not appreciate your enthusiasm for male attention."

"Hector loves me as I am, just like you said he should. He knows I'm a flirt. I think he enjoys watching me make the rounds. He knows where my true heart lies."

Eleanor thought of Gregory, and how he used to admire Sylvia as she floated around the ballroom with everyone's eyes upon her. How proud he was of her beauty and her sparkling charm. He knew everyone wanted her, but she only really wanted him. "Each couple has their own way, I suppose."

Ticia's gregarious embrace of courtly life never failed to remind Eleanor of Gregory. Natalie, on the other hand, had lost those early traces of her father's boisterousness long ago. As her power grew, so did her seriousness. Still, Eleanor found she understood Natty more than she understood her older sister. She'd long found it funny, how a mother could love her children equally, but relate to one so much more than the other. Eleanor never knew exactly what Hazelbeth said to Natalie the day before the old witch died. Whatever the message, however, it must have included reference to the importance of family. Even as the new Oracle, Natalie left the Abbey regularly and visited Eclatant. At first, Rosemary resisted, but as Natalie's responsibilities grew, she acknowledged the benefits of the child spending time with mundane people. If she was to hobnob with the non-magical on a regular basis, her family were as good a crowd as any. Hazelbeth had been several hundred years old, give or take a century, before she settled into permanent watch by the Pool. Natalie still had a lot to learn about life, despite being the most powerful witch in the world. Her family, and her unicorn, Dasha, helped her find balance.

"Yes, each couple has their own way." Ticia gave Eleanor a lovingly sly look. "Just like you and Uncle Dorian are the most boring couple of all time. What with your"—she wiggled her fingers in front of her face—"*simple ceremony.*"

"Silly girl," said Eleanor. "Grand wedding ceremonies are for first marriages and young people. Uncle Dorian and I don't need anything extravagant, nor does the crown need to pay for it. If we have you children and our close friends here with us, overlooking the cliffs of Solsea, that's plenty of romance."

If Tish knew that Eleanor and Dorian had spent the first sixteen years of their acquaintance in a state of intense romantic fervor, maybe she'd appreciate their desire for a bit of peace. As it was, Eleanor hadn't seen Dorian in nearly two weeks. He'd arrived at Solsea early to meet with the Orvid Jones, some animal husbandry witches, and the Fisherman's Guild about a disease afflicting the local lobster population.

"But it seems so humdrum. You discussed it like all your other meetings about the army and the Dragon Mines—*yes, we'll be married. I'll see you on the cliff on Saturday afternoon.*"

"It *is* rather sterile, Mother," said Natalie.

Chou whistled a chirping laugh.

"Thank you for your advice, my darlings, but now you two run along and help those footmen before one of them injures his back."

Leticia grabbed Natalie's hand and dragged her into Willowswatch. She gabbled on about her dress for Sylvia's opening party. Rosemary passed them on her way out of the cottage.

"Poor Natalie," said Chou. "She'll have to sit through Leticia trying on at least five gowns, only to decide she'll wear the first one."

"Once we leave for the party, she'll have all night to read those books she brought with her," Eleanor said. "It's so kind of Jan to find special volumes for her—especially when she's so busy as Chief Librarian."

"I think Tish amuses Natalie," said Rosemary. "If she wants a more risqué neckline, Natty can adjust it for her."

"Rosemary, how scandalous you are in your old age."

"You forget. I conjured your neckline for the Second Sunday ball, and it wasn't exactly demure."

"The girls are teasing me because we're not having a fancy wedding. Dorian and I decided it would be better this way." Just as Dorian had promised, he didn't bring up marriage again until Eleanor did, six months ago. Enough time had passed since Gregory's death, and she finally felt secure enough in her position. It made sense that the queen form an alliance with her closest advisor—the second most powerful person in the country. A perfectly rational union. Nothing scandalous about it. Still, Eleanor suddenly felt oddly defensive, as if she weren't doing justice to their love.

"It's up to the two of you," said Chou. "It's the most important wedding of the decade, regardless of the size of the party."

Eleanor suddenly needed to see Dorian. "Where is he? We've been here three hours and he hasn't come to say hello."

"He's been in the unicorn barn," said Rosemary. "Getting Teardrop and Cricket and Dasha settled in with Senné and the guard. Oh, and Monument, too."

"I'm surprised Monument is staying in the barn and not underneath the nursery window," said Chou.

"He's very attached to the little prince, that's for sure. But they're to be partners, so it makes sense," said Eleanor. "Is Dorian still at the barn?"

"No," said Rosemary. "He's in Walnut Cottage, getting it ready for Brian and Raoul and their families. Then he needs to set up Speck Cottage for Anne Iris and hers, and he's decided on the whole of Neckbreak Cottage for Eliza's brood. He asked me to send you down there. He has a question about the linens—"

Eleanor didn't wait for Rosemary to finish. She burned with the need to see her beloved. She handed her notebook to the witch and walked toward Walnut Cottage, across the rolling lawn where she'd picnicked with her children and read to them. She'd played umpteen games of lawn bolls and sipped many glasses of strawberry wine on this grassy field, and one afternoon, Anne Iris had broken a punchbowl and doused Eleanor in wet, sticky sweetness. The air smelled like it had on that day, when she found Dorian in Walnut Cottage. Her heart warmed at the memory, and she put her hands around her dragon choker. These days, they rarely used the spell that connected the necklace to Dorian's blue ring, but the memory still did the trick. She felt the spectite dragon warm her neck, as it always did when it glowed red.

She walked up the stairs of Walnut Cottage. Dorian had propped open the door. "Hello? Dor?" she called. Nostalgia washed over her. How young they'd been, when they finally gave in to emotions that had vibrated between them for months, their feelings like the wings of baby dragonflies.

He sat on the steps, his hands between his knees, spinning the blue ring on his finger. He looked up at her and smiled.

"Hello, darling," she said. "Rosemary said you needed help with the linens—"

Just like he had on that long-ago day, he strode across the little foyer. For a moment, she thought he was going to push her into the broom closet and ravish her, and she would have been just fine with that. What he did instead, however, was even sweeter.

"What are you doing?" she said, as he knelt before her.

"No questions yet, my love." He fished around in his pocket and retrieved a gold bag. He slid something into his hand. It sparkled.

It was a glass slipper.

"Dorian—where did you—"

"Shhh." He lifted her skirt and removed her leather traveling shoes. He lifted her foot and then slid the glass shoe over her toes. It fit perfectly, just as it had when she was eighteen.

To her surprise, he removed the other shoe. This time, she recognized the purple bag, because she'd kept it in her mother's music box for years. This slipper was damaged. Cracked, long ago, when she fell down the stairs as she fled the ball. It was the shoe she'd used to identify herself to Gregory. The shoe that made her a princess.

When she stepped into it, warmth spread through her tired, aching legs.

He looked up at her. "Natalie fixed the cracked slipper. You can still see the damage—the lines are still there—but it will hold now. Gregory kept the other shoe in his desk in his study. I found it there when I was sorting through his things."

She touched his hair. "Thank you. No shoes have ever felt more right on my feet."

He took her hands. "I wish I had been the one to see you first, dancing in these shoes. I wish I could have picked up the one you left on the staircase and seen you present me with the cracked one. Although, I would never have needed a shoe to recognize you. I've known you since the first time we danced together." He stood up and put both hands on the side of her face. "Eleanor, my love, my life, will you be my wife?"

"Yes. Yes. Yes." She threw her arms around his neck and kissed him.

Even though they were much older, and they had children and responsibilities, this kiss exceeded the passion of the broom closet. It was the kiss of half a lifetime of waiting and longing and dedication. The passion of the young is fleeting. Eleanor and Dorian had earned this kiss, and they made the most of it.

"Leticia teased me about our lack of romance," Eleanor said as they walked hand in hand toward Willowswatch.

"I admit, I did want to propose to you in a way that felt a little more passionate than our conversation across your desk in your chamber."

She bumped him with her hip. "You succeeded. My heart is so light, I feel as if I'm floating."

"It could be your glass slippers."

She pointed out a pretty spot along the cliffs, between two old oak trees, at the top of the long Fire-iron staircase leading to the beach. "There's a lovely spot for a small wedding ceremony, don't you think?"

"It looks very romantic. Ticia can't complain."

At that moment, a small brown-haired boy came racing toward them over the grass. Rosemary walked behind him, with Chou on her shoulder. "They knew, didn't they?" Eleanor asked. "Rosemary and Chou. About your plan and these slippers."

"Of course." Dorian knelt down as little Prince Cyrus bolted into his arms. He stood with his son on his hip. "There's a good lad. Did you grow this month?"

Cyrus hugged Dorian. "I've missed you, Uncle!"

"I've missed you. Would you like to play lawn bolls before your mother and I go to Mistress Sylvia's party?"

"Yes, please," he said. He leaned back and placed both hands on Dorian's cheeks. He stared at Dorian. Impossibly long eyelashes framed his greenish hazel eyes. "Uncle."

"Yes, lad."

"I want to ask you something."

"Of course."

"If you are to be married to my mother, can I call you Poppa?"

Eleanor's breath caught in her throat. Dorian hugged Cyrus close to him and looked to Eleanor for guidance over his shoulder. Eleanor knew Dorian would know how to respond, so she just nodded.

Dorian looked at their son. "You are Cyrus Desmarais. You're the son of Gregory, and the grandson on Casper and the great-grandson of Michael, going all the way back to Caleb Desmarais. You'll be king, and you're the keeper of the Great Bond."

"Yes. But I would like to have a Poppa, like other boys."

"As long as you remember who you are, you may call me Poppa, and I'd be the happiest Poppa in the whole world to hear you say it."

"That's good," the child said. He kissed Dorian's cheek and squirmed to be let down. "I'm going to see Monument now."

"Chou," Eleanor said, choking back tears, "will you go to the unicorn barn with the prince?"

"Yes, yes, of course, Your Majesty." Chou wiped his head with his wing. Of course, birds don't cry, but if he could have shed tears of happiness, he would have.

"I'll go too," said Rosemary as she blew her nose. "You two deserve a little time alone. HighGod knows it's hard to come by."

"Chou—Rosemary," Eleanor said. Her voice caught in her throat. "Thank you. Both of you. For everything."

The bird whistled, and the witch nodded, and they followed the little prince as he ran to visit his unicorn.

"So," said Dorian. "Someone will call me Poppa, after all."

She faced him. "Maybe more than one someone." She placed his hand on her stomach.

His eyes widened. "Do you mean—"

"Yes. It seems HighGod has indeed blessed us. But this child will be a Finley."

Dorian wrapped his arms around Eleanor and held her tight. She listened to the sounds of Trill Castle around her. The bitterbits. Some servants teasing one another as they hung sheets to dry. The high whinny of a unicorn just down the hillside. Beside her cheek, Dorian's strong, constant heartbeat.

She wiggled her toes in her glass slippers. "I think I shall dance tonight," she said.

"As long as you're not too tired."

"If I am, will you bring me home and take me to bed?"

"I am at your service, Your Majesty. I always have been."

So, Eleanor Desmarais, Queen of Cartheigh, returned to Willowswatch with her lover, who was soon to be her husband. She held her head high and rested her hand on her growing belly. She walked with purpose, in her blissfully comfortable, perfectly repaired, wholly unbroken glass slippers.

Now perhaps, dear reader, you are hoping we will leave her with *happily ever after*, but that is not how she would want it. She has many years ahead of her, and in those seasons, she'll face good times and bad, sorrow and joy, laughter and tears. On rare occasions, she'll have idle time, and she'll think back on the adventures and trials of her first four decades of life. She'll make the most of all of it, as she always has. Eleanor knows that no story ever really ends.

EPILOGUE

The Oracle sat beside the Watching Pool, like Hazelbeth had for centuries before her. She watched and listened to the universe. As her Auntie had told her, with quiet patience, what she sought found its way to her, just as a wary doe might gather her courage and step into the sunlight in a quiet glade. Beside the Pool, she discovered all manner of interesting things. She learned secrets about her own world, and the other worlds that sat along the In Between's dream road like landmarks on a detailed map.

Hazelbeth had also wanted her to pay attention to the people and places closest to her. As she began her watch on this fine HighSpring morning, Natalie Desmarais focused on little things, rather than the grand workings of time and space. The past and the present and the future swirled together like a creamy dessert, honey and molasses and spun sugar treasured memories and vague premonitions, until she could not tell today from yesterday from tomorrow. She knew her little brother Cyrus was, or would be, a great king, and her sister Leticia was, or would be, the next Duchess of Harveston, married to a man who adored her. She saw her two beloved half siblings—Margaret and Andrew Finley—the children of her mother and her stepfather, and she watched their lives play out with their own adventures. She recognized her many nieces and nephews, and she saw herself emerging from her cavern to spend fests and birthdays with all of them. She relished the role of eccentric but beloved Auntie. Her mother and the man she knew as

Uncle Dorian, but her younger siblings knew as Poppa, would continue to make history long after their simple wedding on the Solsea cliffside.

With the comfort of her family's love and pride in their collective legacy, she turned back to the In Between, and the old Oracle's final message. Oh, yes, Hazelbeth had insisted Natalie remember her loved ones and cherish the ties that bound her to them and their descendants long after they passed on and she remained living. But she also gave Natalie other instructions. She must use her mystical mind to seek out those places where her mother's life had been warped and reduced. She must find a way to tell the truth.

What has meaning and consequence become soft and harmless.

No, Auntie. Mother's life will be known, with all its joy and sadness and everything in between. Villains who are also heroes, and saviors who sin. Life does not arrive at a perfect state of happiness and stop there. It is full of bright rainbows and dark mud, and sometimes the view through the glass goes dark, at least temporarily. It is a pair of perfect glass slippers, cracked by a terrible fall, but still beautiful.

Natalie Desmarais, Oracle of Afar Creek Abbey, reached out into the In Between with all that she was, and all that Hazelbeth had given her. She searched for a way to tell her mother's story.

ALSO BY STEPHANIE ALEXANDER

The Cracked Slipper Series

The Cracked Slipper
The Dragon Choker
The Glass Rainbow

Charleston Green: A Novel

Author's Acknowledgment

The Cracked Slipper Series has been a ten-year labor of love. Since I began the first book in 2009, my life has changed immeasurably. I've been through the hardest times in my life, and come out the other side with an outcome that is beautiful beyond anything I thought it could be. Too many people have been a part of this process to name them all, but a few require special recognition. First, to my sister-cousin, Haley Telling, thank you for always cheering me on, and coming up with wonderful ideas for ways to get my work out into the world, and helping me keep my chin up when the process beat me down. This is a hard business, and your eternal optimism helped me remember that the stories are the heart of it.

Thank you to my mother, Dianne Wicklein, who I admire above all other women, and who is a testament to the redemptive power of tenacity and faith. Thank you to my three wonderful children, who have gone from babies to teenagers while I labored on this project and rebuilt my life. They are my reason for pushing myself on good days, and my reason for getting out of bed on bad ones.

Lastly, thank you to my husband, Jeffrey Cluver. I would call you my Prince Charming, but as this book has tried to illustrate, Prince Charming is overrated. Instead, I will call you my best friend, my closest confidante, the rock I cling to when I'm floundering in a sea of writer-ly self doubt. You read my first drafts; you give me feedback I didn't know I needed; you spark my imagination when it's feeling about as combustible as a wet match. Thank you for being you.

There are so many others, but I will have to thank them all in person, lest I risk running on for another hundred thousand words. But lastly, thank you to my readers, who fell in love with Eleanor, her journey, and the enchanted universe she inhabits. I hope I've done justice to her story, and your imaginations.

—Stephanie

ABOUT THE AUTHOR

Stephanie Alexander grew up in the suburbs of Washington, DC. Drawing, writing stories, and harassing her parents for a pony consumed much of her childhood. After graduating from high school in 1995 she earned a Bachelor of Arts in Communications from the College of Charleston, South Carolina. She returned to Washington, DC, where she followed a long-time fascination with sociopolitical structures and women's issues to a Master of Arts in Sociology from the American University. She spent several years as a Policy Associate at the International Center for Research on Women (ICRW), a think-tank focused on women's health and economic advancement.

Stephanie embraced full-time motherhood after the birth of the first of her three children in 2003. Her family put down permanent southern roots in Charleston in 2011. She published her first novel, *The Cracked Slipper*, in February 2012. Along with two sequels (*The Red Choker* and *A Ring in Blue*), the series has sold over 40,000 copies. *The Cracked Slipper* has made multiple appearances on Amazon's fantasy bestseller lists, and peaked at #11 in all genres. Stephanie has appeared on local and national media, been a contributor on many writing blogs and in writing magazines, and regularly joins with book clubs for discussions of her work.

In addition to her personal writing, Stephanie returned to the College of Charleston as an Adjunct Professor of Sociology and Women's Studies, and launched her freelance ghostwriting and editing business, Wordarcher, LLC. She has ghostwritten dozens of books, from novels to memoirs to academic theses. Beginning in the Fall of 2015, as a single working mother, she attended law school on a full academic scholarship, earning her juris doctor with honors from the Charleston School of Law in December, 2017.

She currently practices family law in Mount Pleasant, South Carolina, the Charleston suburb that is the setting of her latest novel, *Charleston Green*. Her personal experience rebuilding her life after divorce inspires both her legal work and her fiction.